A WIFE IN WATERCOLOR

B.B. SHAMP

SECANT
PUBLISHING

A WIFE IN WATERCOLOR

Copyright © 2021 by B.B. Shamp

All Rights Reserved

ISBN: 978-1-944962-97-5 (hardcover)
ISBN: 978-1-944962-98-2 (paperback)
ISBN: 978-1-944962-99-9 (epub)

Secant Publishing, LLC
P.O. Box 4059
Salisbury MD 21803

www.secantpublishing.com

This book is a work of fiction. Names, characters, places, events, and incidents are either the product of the author's imagination or are used fictitiously.

Cover design by Avalon Graphics

For Beck

CONTENTS

PART I
SARAH

Better to remain silent, better not even to think if you are not prepared to act.
- Annie Besant

CHAPTER 1

*I*n the wee hours of that steamy morning, he woke me with a roar, "Sarah Wise! I have a letter for you to scribe." I flung on a cloak and bumbled below stairs to his chamber in the darkness.

"Address it to Jonas Green at the *Maryland Gazette*," he said, pointing to his desk. "Announce the arrival of the prisoners."

I rubbed sleep from my eyes and sat, waiting for his words as he paced in his nightgown. My hand was steady, the letters smooth and arched across the parchment. I listened carefully and wrote while he bragged of his service to our king, of shipping the detritus of George's last war on his own people to our shore. They would be sold as indentures in harbor. In Robert's harbor.

My concentration slipped and from the corner of my eye I watched Master Morris play schoolboy, warming sealing wax, dripping it across a scrap of parchment. He heated the Cunliffe seal in the flame and pressed it over and over in the line of creamy red stain as he dictated. Drunk, yet obsessed with work, he leaned over my shoulder, his breath hot and yeasty.

He brushed me aside, the quill still in my hand. I stood, he sat. I thought he would read the finished letter when, in a wink, his hand slipped under my dressing gown and he laid the hot seal on my backside, searing skin. Stupefied, I yelped, and jumped away as he snickered.

"Marked by your master." He giggled, his head waggling. "We share the weight of Cunliffe."

Turnabout, fair play, I wanted to shout and glanced at the candle flame. In revulsion, I thought he might pull up his nightgown and bare his arse for me to brand. So, I wrapped myself tight and cursed my decision to become his housekeeper. I had not bargained for his macabre humor and odd hours. To be his vassal.

"You demean yourself, sir," I said, sniveling and lily-livered. "You should not treat me so, or I swear I will leave." I brushed wetness from my eyes. "You already whipped Jackson for not blacking your boots. Did that not satisfy enough that you have to move from slave to servant in your punishment?"

My words hit their target. In mocking despair, his hand over his heart, he said, "Sarah, come now. I tease. Do not be so hard on me. You are not my slave." He looked away. "The demand of dealing in human flesh ruins my judgement. So. Will it please you if I post banns come November as shipping season ends?"

This was the way he proposed. Words long awaited. A promise of security and of station, if not love. Certainly not the naive promise of my dead Edward so many years ago. After three years in his employ, Robert caved to my wishes. Then I caught myself with one thought, *shipping season never ends*.

I let my cloak fall open to test his sincerity. In my thin summer nightgown, I lay my hand on the back of his chair as if to steady myself and said, "You ask my hand in marriage? A winter wedding in front of God and Oxford?"

"Yes, yes. And a blue organdy gown with ermine trim for you. Does that make you happy? Will you promise to stay?"

Tempting, but it was not the promise I wanted. "M'lord. An arrangement of my hard work for your promise of loyalty?" I dared not smile. "Perhaps love will come of it."

"It's love you want, of course, and you have that, Sarah. I have grown very fond of you," he said, taking me in his arms. I held my breath and immediately thought of Edward's tentative touch. This would not be the same.

I turned my cheek to his breath and patted his chest. I was exhausted. "And I of you, sir. It's time we retired. Dawn comes soon."

"Stay with me. Let us comfort each other."

"Robert, I remind you. I'll sleep in my bed till our wedding night."

His disappointment was palpable, his hands fell from me and he hung his head. I took fast to the stairs. In the safety of my garret chamber, I lifted my linen shift, twisting my chin over my shoulder. The smart of his branding stung my honor more than my buttocks, but in the candlelight, I gleaned the purpled C of the Cunliffe seal. A present from Robert Morris and a new low, even for him. I fell face first on my bed too dispirited to form another thought.

Before long the cock crowed, interrupting an unfettered sleep. The four walls of my small garret chamber closed in, erasing a dream of my mother's kind eyes. I sat up, ready to look out my window where mosquito netting billowed like loose sails. Before I retired, I had set saucers on the windowsills and in my dead slumber hadn't heard them shatter in the wind, splattering clods of clabber milk across the floor. Black flies were captured in sour Scottish pudding, a remedy against their incessant biting in the night. Even on the third floor they found their way into my sheets.

Tilting my head to listen, I heard Robert call to Yearie for a sack of vittles as he left for the wharf. Steps creaked on the lower stair and the front door shut. Shirking his meanness of the night, I stretched, trying to remember his graciousness.

Widowhood brought me here, losing my parent's cottage. Evicted by the sheriff because I couldn't pay the rack rent.

"Suffer she does, a young woman of middling status, an ignominious consequence," said the Reverend Bacon to Robert, though he produced no succor when his church had provided shelter to others. Trudging the lanes of Oxford with Yearie in search of food. Sleeping in corn cribs and barns. Dragging my Phebe's cradle till Robert offered to store it in his stable.

5

"Where is the child?" he had asked.

"Kidnapped by the Indians, the sheriff says," I answered, clouded with confusion. Robert had looked at me differently after that.

The good folk of the village are my friends, but they could not afford to keep Yearie and me. Loyal and true, Yearie had held my hand through five years of meted tragedy that ended in three weeks of homelessness. Papa had sold her mother, and it seemed overnight my entire family was gone, and then the cottage, too. He said he'd had enough of her witchery.

I stood and glanced about my chamber. A bed and a chair, a mule chest and looking glass in return for work under the baleful eye of the Merchant of Oxford in Maryland Province. He factored for Foster Cunliffe and Sons of Liverpool, England, his taxes paid to his sovereign, George II, son of that German turnip hoer who stole the crown. The rope that tethered us stretched across the Atlantic. With his offer of housekeeper, I escaped marriage to three others in Oxford. Robert slyly couched his words as a *consideration* of his hand *if it was to my liking*. He said, "I need an educated, organized woman to help me in my business."

Carts clattered beneath my window. I drew my ruined shift off and knelt to sop up the clabber, throwing it and broken crockery in the ash can. Hearing a shout, I peeked over the sill and stared out at a glorious sight.

In the pink glow of dawn, the ship *Johnson* advanced through the white capped waters of the Chesapeake. Wind carried her at full sail, a wedge of geese swirling off the prow. Glistening with dew in the rising sun, her pearly canvasses seemed blessed by God. Redemptioners were her only cargo.

I sometimes kept the records of ships' cargo and four were at port awaiting loads of tobacco and lumber. Merchant ships and a slaver had arrived by way of the West Indies, their journeys uneventful. Our town breathed a sigh of relief when ships anchored safely as the threat of privateers was ever-present. Today was unusual. A shipload of our brethren, war convicts who brought needed skills. And some villagers were secretly sympathetic to their Papist cause, including me.

I hurried as all of Oxford would come from far and wide. And I had an act, a performance to play for Robert. But first, some pilfering. The floor wiped, I tied my cloak around me and slipped downstairs to his room, house keys in hand. Tiptoeing inside, I peered about in the blushing light and was delighted to see his money bag by his desk.

The irony was he trusted me but not his slaves, fearing the weakest in his employ. Each day at mid-morn, before he returned from the wharf with his accounts, Yearie and I plotted our doings in his chamber. Rummaging his tobacco notes, a cache of Spanish reales fell in my palm. I took only four. Putting the money bag back, I locked his door and raced up the garret stairs. A mouse hole behind the mule chest hid my insurance against calamity. I pulled out a leather sack, deposited the coins alongside the cross from my mother's rosary beads, and tucked it away with a prayer on my lips for self-reliance. If Robert's promise was a lie, I could stay or go.

Time to make haste. He expected I wear a cotton day dress to advertise his India fabric, ordering, "Keep it clean. We can sell it to a plantation daughter. Shop amongst the other gentlewomen and make business," he said.

"Robert, it's impossible to keep a dress like that clean on the wharf whilst they unload."

"Make it possible. The more a dress like that is seen, the more business for me and the tailor. The hand that feeds you, Mrs. Wise."

I succumbed as I always did, but to make the trip work for me, I had a list. Lemons, candles, and a stop at the Cunliffe warehouse for embroidered Irish table linen. Quick transactions. No taxes. Then, home to help Yearie and Hestia with dinner preparations.

"Sary—hurry, the ship be dockin," called Yearie from the stairs.

I jumped up on hearing her outside my door "I found reales just now," I whispered with excitement. "Time moves despite me. Has Jackson laid Hestia's fire? The meat from the smokehouse brought in?"

"He work hard afore he left for harbor. Master's whippin be nearly forgotten."

Jackson had slunk off last night, his face full of resignation, and my silent tears in front of Robert did nothing. In the clear light of morn, Robert's proposal seemed more exasperation than guilt—a worry he would need a new housekeeper if I left. Trapped by his own words.

"He wants me in the pink and gray," I said.

"Of course he do! Showin you off to the old plantation biddies."

Her laughter was low, a quiet rumble. In private, we were ourselves. Three years of minding our conversations around Robert as if we were Quaker women in church. I threw my cloak over the chair.

She tossed a fresh chemise over my head, dragging my hair upward. "Fine line between lookin the tart and lookin the lady." Her eyes dropped and she noticed the burn. "Sary, did he have you last night?"

"No, no. I didn't give in. He wished to punish is all. For crying over Jackson." Glancing over my shoulder, I saw her chin rumpled in doubt.

"I have a promise from him. Come November he will make good with a betrothal. We'll have station again."

The frown grew deeper. "Not me," she said. "I'll be *his* property with your vow."

"I won't let him separate us. I promise."

She muttered some incantation, a relic of her mother's island sorcery that I always felt was harmless and quaint. "Sary," she said, pursing her lips, her voice full of shame. "You forget my manumission."

"I do not. Help me manage his expectations. I'll keep my virtue and you'll have your freedom."

She pulled my purse strings and tied them round my waist over the chemise. She passed stockings and garters, pannier and petticoats, corset and, finally, the rose cotton dress. I had grown warm.

"Wait, Sary. You can't sweat like a common pig in heat," she said, handing me the fan.

"More like a trussed turkey."

"Makin business for Master with your body."

8

"Stop. I've sold many a dress this way and will today if farmer's wives don't spit on me first."

"They don't have consequence to buy his cloth. Not your customer."

Beads of sweat had formed on her upper lip. We struggled, working round the cooking hearth, in the kitchen garden before the midday sun, scrubbing the floors come night. Every job perfectly timed. I wiped her face with the cloth, and she pinned my hair off my neck. I slipped my feet into satin heels, she bent and buckled them and handed me pattens to carry down the steps, for it would do no good to fall in them.

She clasped her hands. "A straw hat?"

"No, the parasol."

"Well, stop wastin time."

I kissed her damp cheek. "When I return I'll set the dinner table."

The front door ground open and, in alarm, I heard Robert yell, " Sarah Wise. I have only a second!"

Yearie grabbed my shoulders. "Cheerful, now." She muttered in her mother's tongue that I had never bothered to learn.

"Take my keys," I said. "Finish his bag. Read and remember."

Lucky we were, one a slave, one a servant, yet we could read and write. Papa had tutored children of a rich province family and we went along to watch the little ones and learn. After he died, I kept up under Mama's instruction, reading the classics, keeping accounts and writing my own missives. Yearie could get by in a pinch. Together, we had become adept at forging Robert's signature, especially on Yearie's slave passes. As long as his life wasn't disrupted, he didn't care.

I powdered my glistening breast and sailed to the landing. Stopping to rest my hand on the carved bannister, I was aware of the picture I painted. The grand oak staircase, paid for by Cunliffe to impress our clients, was easy to traverse with its low-rise steps as long as I behaved like a lady.

"Sir. What need have you?" I asked, looking down at him. "I will take care of it immediately."

His hat shielded his face, his mood unreadable as he stood across from the harpsichord. He removed it to wipe his forehead. Florid-cheeked, he threw himself on the striped satin bench, breathing heavily. Horrified he would stain the cloth with the sweat of the wharf, I bounded down the stairs and took his hand to my bosom, drawing him to his feet.

"I hope that you are pleased with me," I said, standing back with a twirl.

"My lovely," he whispered and bent to nuzzle my neck.

He smelled like a fishmonger. Alarmed, I pushed him away.

Righting himself against the wall, he began, "Reverend Bacon will dine with us. James Tilghman and his wife have brought their child. They want an indenture and will stay overnight with us as he has other business. Prepare the guest chamber. Flowers, rose water in the pitcher, an orange. Captains Gildart and Matthews make seven plus the brat who eats in the kitchen. Get the tailor's boy, Jeremiah. Yearie can serve while he watches the child."

"Sir, you must not concern yourself. I am aware. We will set table in the gathering room since the party is so large," I said.

He rested his hand on the harpsichord and searched my eyes. "You wish to play, don't you?"

"As you desire." I curtsied.

"Reverend Bacon will bring his violin. We'll accompany you."

My fingers tapped his stained waistcoat. Sweat ran down his cheek from under his day wig. "Robert, you must wear an apron. All your vests are marked. Let me check the warehouse for a brocade and take it to the tailor. He will sew one if I arrive early." I gave him encouraging eyes. "James Tilghman is respected in Annapolis. He'll have connections on the western shore."

"I will not wear an apron on my wharf. Look like a yeoman." He brushed at the stain. "Tilghman says he is taking his law practice to Philadelphia." He grunted at the splotch and gave up. "You're right. There will never be anything but bridle paths, Indians and swamps above East Town. I'll have to move my stores west to compete."

"Mr. Morris, there is no one from Williamsburg to Philadelphia with your skill."

"Mrs. Wise, there is no one in the Middle Colonies as beautiful and desired as you."

"You flatter me, sir." We both lied. I curtsied again. "I am your servant."

He kissed me, rubbing my breast roughly and left—unable to rise to the level of a true gentleman. Mother warned me never to be a servant to anyone, not even a priest. She and Papa had wished an aristocrat for me and so I ended up with Edward, educated, and helpless.

I pulled my lace tucker across my breast. Hair tidied, I called to Yearie of the evening's changes. She stopped at the foot of the stair, nodding without complaint. She is my constancy. I gathered my parasol and gloves, shoved my feet in the pattens and clattered outside.

CHAPTER 2

A short walk to the wharf, I tippy-tapped along Front Street two inches taller, nodding at townspeople and farmers. Their furtive glances and whispers made my cheeks grow hot. I looked a peacock prancing in heels betwixt and between gray geese, so I took a breath, held the parasol high and smiled broadly at everyone. They knew me well and were glad at my good fortune to find a home, if not perplexed at my appearance. Change is for the better as we grow prosperous.

Warehouse men counted bales of wheat and pounds of salt pork. Wharf men directed plantation boats to the short pier while from the long pier slaves loaded barrels of tobacco onto barges for the *Liverpool Merchant*. The purest harvest ever collected at one time in Oxford, the bitter smell filled the air. I spotted Robert on a wherry. He doffed his cock hat to Captain Gildart who stood at the *Johnson's* gunnel. In tribute to Robert's welcome, his sailors lit their cannon. Wadding blew in successive percussion. The prisoners would be unloaded soon.

I skirted a wagon and slowed on hearing snippets of conversation. Four impoverished farmers were locked in bitter complaint.

"Aye, Morris filling his pocket whilst limiting our gain," said one.

"I were gettin paid on half-filled hogshead afore. He plays king with his Terbaccer Act."

"Half-filled? Well at least ye got paid, man. His inspector dumped the lot of my mine this day. Said it were trash orinoco, not up to standard."

They grunted. One spit. The last took his pipe from his mouth and said, "Virginie terbaccer be damned. If England don't have a taste for Maryland's weed, the Frenchies do. Morris ain't the only trader in these parts."

"Ain't that treason, trading with the French? Morris be the only one in the pocket of them gentry. He be bringing sterling to the Province, just not to us."

Words of agitation. If we weren't afraid of trading with the French, it was the Tobacco Act Robert sponsored and the legislature enacted.

The sun seared. I moved along thinking there were deeper dangers. The sheriff constantly warned of savages on the outskirts of town and a slave revolt from within. When I looked over the bustling heads of County Talbot's residents, there were almost as many bonded blacks as there were of us. Robert's harbor slaves were slick with sweat, bare-chested, and dressed in tattered sailor pantaloons. Worked like animals, they didn't have the wherewithal to revolt. Maybe those in satin livery who accompanied their gentlefolk for the indenture sale did.

I passed a stack of *Maryland Gazettes* that carried pages of rewards offered for runaways. Some escaped north to Philadelphia. Those who could swim stowed on boats sailing west over the Chesapeake. Those who couldn't ran for a maroon camp in the east swamp. They say a darker place was never seen. A snake pit of castoffs.

Squeezing through the crowd, I felt a touch on my elbow. I hesitated seeing everyone and no one in particular, then heard a familiar voice, "Meestress Vise, I haff need."

I felt an immediate revulsion in my being. The boorish Jacoba Vanderkoop, huddled beneath the shade of the apothecary shop, dirty and bedraggled, clasping a toddler, another holding her skirt. She grabbed my arm in a vice, and I couldn't pull away without someone seeing.

"Sarah, you must belief me." Her voice raspy, dry, her nails dug into my skin.

"Jacoba, I haven't seen you in a—"

"I vere sorry, Sarah. Forgiff me. So little, our girls."

"Jacoba!" I said, twisting my arm from her grip. "I do not have time to go over it all again."

"Dey vere sisters. You know dey're in das swamp." She glanced from side to side, a hunted look and said, "Dey're aliffe vith Pieter."

"You don't know that. Do not make it more painful." My heart was twisting, a kitchen rag wrung. "Phebe was stolen from her bed months before Pieter and Griet disappeared." I pushed my face into hers. "The sheriff cannot find them."

"He lies, Sarah. He lies."

The confusion in her eyes had been mine. The desperation. Running from door to door, I screamed for Phebe until the sheriff appeared, watching me as if I were an animal trapped. "I'll search," he said.

Jacoba's lips were crusted. Her boys whimpered and grumbled, and I moved back from their filthy fingers. Phebe, my five-year-old princess gone. Pffft, as in a witch's spell.

"There's nothing we can do," I said. "We have memories, Jacoba. Of our girls playing together. Learning to speak, and run, chasing the geese. Phebe and I were there when you buried your boy. Maybe they were little sisters, but they're gone now."

Jacoba was from the Dutch town of Lewes. Pieter was a shipwright building Maryland schooners in Skillington's shipyard. Another dream lost and a wife and children alone. She would not consume me today. Steps. Facts. That's how I got past my loss.

Like Phebe, Sheriff Goldsboro blamed the Vanderkoops' disappearance on marauding Indians. I was skeptical at first. Two abductions so close in time. Indians were naught but bobtailed stragglers, looking for a home, any land of their own. Phebe was taken in her sleep, leaving the cross from Mama's rosary beads buried in her bed. Indians love beads and use them as money. Then, after the Vanderkoops' disappearance, I believed.

Jacoba's face was grave, her eyes pleading. The sheriff allowed her to keep her cottage and Reverend Bacon had supplied money from the vestry, so why was she in this state?

I relented. "Jacoba, how are you?"

"De allowance of me from de church is gone, Sarah. Hungry ve are," she said, her voice low so others couldn't hear. "I tink ve perish before long."

"Go to my kitchen and tell Hestia to give you some stores. I'll speak to Reverend Bacon." Beneath my skirts my fingers wrapped around a conjure bag. Yearie's warning of Mama's house, of virtue and bargaining echoed in my ears. I plucked out a coin and dropped it in Jacoba's hand.

"Good lady, God bless," she answered.

"The Lord provides, not me," I said, surprised at my own terseness.

She patted my hand and wiggled her faded calico through the crowd toward my home, children at her heels. I could have been her. I *was* her not long ago. Never given an allowance from Bacon's church, I was forced to choose an offer so as not to starve. A niggle of anger crept round my brow. I was forced to beg and church council gave Jacoba handouts. She wasn't even from Oxford—but she was an Anglican. I wasn't.

Sailors swarmed the harbor. I passed a Chinamen tugging his mustache tendril as he haggled a price for his daggers. A turbaned Arab traded spices for gunshot. Cockney accents floated above the province twang of middling farmers, their brusque wives in tow. From far and wide, everyone wanted something from someone.

Before I took Robert's offer, I spurned a farmer's promise and gave short shrift to our hated sheriff, and even that of Quinn, the tavern keeper. A life of hard labor in a tobacco field, or with a cruel and loveless authority was not for me, nor was wiping tables and pouring ale. Yet, as I wove through the crowd, I began to think

Jacoba's troubles the sadder for she was driven to madness over the past years wondering if her husband was dead or alive. The thought that Phebe lived came to me and quickly I pushed it away.

I heard the crack of a whip as Robert's overseer yelled. Dipping my parasol against the sun, I saw Jackson fall as he heaved a barrel of tobacco. Our stable slave was a huge man but not equal to the weight a packed hogshead. The overseer was ready to strike again. I called out.

"Mr. Murray! Where is Mr. Morris?"

His whip hand fell to his side. "He brings a table, Mistress. To register the convicts." Jackson jumped up and pushed the hogshead, stacking it upright against others on the wharf.

"Ah, certainly. I didn't mean to interrupt, sir."

I hurried to the only shady spot under the eave of the tavern, passing two Indian braves wearing red militia coats and breech-clouts. An uneasy presence, they held muskrat skins to trade.

They riled me. No doubt they heard white men were selling white men if only for a term. They watched a gaggle of children chasing each other. A girl of nine or ten scurried past me and I called out to her, "Child, where is your mother?" A hand shot out, pulling her away and a voice scolded, a mother's face frowning at the braves.

On the edge of the crowd, wealthy plantation owners had lined their carriages, leaving their wives to market. Nothing bad could happen under the patricians' eyes. I needed to mingle and drum up interest in my dress, but curiosity claimed me. I dallied.

Murray shouted. The first Scot appeared on the pier. A year's confinement across the pond had done the work of any slave ship. Shackled ankles were chained to one hand. He shuffled barefoot, in rags that barely covered his nakedness. The dregs of the hold emerged behind him, squinting against the light of day. A filthy lot with open sores, some diseased and hoary, clutching a tricorn, a Bible, a drum. A passing vestige of youth or glimpse of virility. Hauling themselves along, one buzzing hive of stink and vermin, they wore an air of tragedy, of lost cause and tenuous hold, similar to the Caribbean slaves. I looked about at my neighbors and thought for all our pretensions at civility, Oxford had a unique ability to capitalize on the misery of others. Except for a cough or a snivel, the prisoners were silent. Their state of existence was so stark, I worried no one would indenture them.

They filed along the pier into the harbor and folks clamored for a look, pointing. I was sorry to see them act so. I hoped Robert found this descent of pitiable manhood into the colony a most unchristian act. But, a more naive thought was never had, for he knew only his business.

"Mrs. Wise, I be surprised seeing ya here. What brings a lady to such a display of man's inhumanity to man?" The tavern keeper taunted me.

"Same as you, Mr. Quinn. Are you wanting to see what the King has wrought?"

"No, Madam," he said bowing. "Mostly I'm wanting to see how many gawkers have a thirst. Tis better'n seeing em leave for another revival of river baptisms, though both religion and liquor be a balm to the soul." He pointed to a broadside—the latest evangelical preacher from Virginia ready to convert the poor and unwashed.

"Baptism and ale, Mr. Quinn? Always an eye to business."

"Shivering and shaking with the Lord," he said, revealing yellowed teeth, two hollowed in a perfect crescent by his pipe stem. I had never been fond of Quinn—he was a man who held a conceit that he was better than those who wrestled goods in harbor. Women were tools of his trade, their wiles purchased by any with enough coin.

Hearing another shout, I held onto a post and climbed a chair to get a better view of the registration table where heated voices rose. A redemptioner pressed in the face of Robert's under-factor, Henry Callister.

"Ye will spell it m'way or ahl have yer tongue on me plate!"

"It's on the manifest. Move along."

"Give me tha quill," he said, reaching.

Mr. Callister stood quickly, jarred his table and the inkwell spilled, making a streak across his record. Two burly yeoman grabbed the prisoner and held him back. Robert eased in, saying, "What seems to be the problem, Henry? Is this transport unhappy?"

"He objects to the way I wrote his name, sir."

"Well, we must accommodate him. Bring him here." He set the chair aright and took the seat, pulling his breeches up and stretching one stockinged leg. His spaniel, Tray, nestled under the table, watching the back and forth. The laborers dragged the man before Robert.

"And what, pray, sir, may I call you?" he asked.

"Yer an Englishman so call me yer enemy until the day I cut yer throat," said he as he struggled against the arms men.

"That would be difficult seeing as I hold your indenture and can make it your lifetime," said Robert, flint-eyed.

My heart beat faster. I knew the prisoner had nary a chance at freedom—or murder. No one would take him after such a display. He had doomed himself to shackles and hard labor in my Robert's employ.

"I see you are Alexander McIntosh," said Robert. "A lowly regular of the Highland army, late of Inverness. You shall be listed as such."

"Ye will list me as MAC-Intosh," he shouted. He rested his knuckles upon the table. As if speaking to a naughty child, he said, "Or ahl send yer dog barking tonight. The faeries will knock to mark yer death."

M'lord leaned back and gazed at the giant who threatened him. Resting his hands on the arms of the chair, his look complacent, he said, "I will call you what I will. An Irish Mick."

Robert wrote his name across the paper and tossed the quill aside. "Take him to the warehouse stocks. Let him go hungry till he shows some respect."

I know Robert well, have played on his weaknesses, but never had I seen his face so masked. The Scot hovered, an army of one, and although he was emaciated, I could see at one time he had been vigorous. His length was covered in torn breeches, a nobleman's jacket over a filthy linen shirt, his cravat and wrist laces gone. A young man's thew filled the shoulders of his coat. This said, his covering didn't make the impression, but the fierceness in his eye. His hate flowed out between them, storm water through a dike. His nostrils pulsed as a blowfish does. Beneath a ridged brow, his eyes were the cavernous holes of a deadman's stare that locked on Robert, sprawled in his desk chair.

I knew that Robert was threatened, but others were duped by his reasonable voice. He had earned the respect of Oxford and if they weren't indebted to him, they gawked at his power. Craning my neck, I saw his heel tap under the table, a bad sign that his coarser side would surface later.

Robert's wharf men wrestled the MacIntosh, dragging him by his shoulders. He struggled mightily as more workers laid upon him, slamming him to the dirt. He yelled what could only be called a war cry that hushed the crowd.

A drumbeat rose within the hundred men, pounding in four by four common time. The pace built, feet stamped in unison and voices joined, like field animals snorting, "Hoof, hoof." A lone prisoner sang, pure and true.

Now the prince has raised his banner
Now triumphant is our cause
Now the Scottish lion rallies
Let us strike for Prince and Laws.

The drumbeat pummeled in the morning air as the townsfolk stirred about, wondering what to do. I tottered on my pattens, pushing my way in. The MacIntosh shook loose of his captors and thrust his fist upward as he walked toward the warehouse.

A shot cracked and a ribbon of white smoke rose in the air. Arriving atop his huge sorrel, Sheriff Goldsboro held his flintlock. The man was a malevolent sea pushing the throng in waves. I followed his black cockhat, a white ostrich feather cresting its point, bouncing over the crowd. The masses parted revealing his big-headed dogs, Cane and Corso who ranged beside him, their brass helmets glinting in the sun. They were majestic animals, made ridiculous by their insufferable armor. Yearie's love, an Ashanti prince followed on a dappled gray, his ragged straw hat in contrast to the satin livery of a Goldsboro house slave. Tiberius' carriage was more deeply noble than his master's and the sheriff used this to his glory. They made an awful team, three in slavish servitude to one.

Goldsboro pursued the weak and defenseless. After Phebe disappeared, he brought his dogs to my parent's cottage. They eyed me from my stoop as he said, "You are ill-equipped, Mrs. Wise, to live on your own," as if it were my negligence that stole her away, not Indian aggression. He gave me a week to pay my back rent. My last face to face with him was as he laid the eviction notice in my outstretched palm. "Be sane and take the offer of my hand in marriage."

Yearie and I packed Phebe's cradle and, carrying it between us, walked out the door.

His entry on the harbor gave the assembled permission to draw their pistols and swords, pointing them at the helpless Scots. The air around us stilled except for the lone drumbeat hidden by tattered men. Its thrumming slowed…and trailed. With their guns drawn, I sensed a pitched slaughter might ensue at the hands of Oxford's men.

Goldsboro kicked his horse and rode into the swell of prisoners, knocking them down like so many sticks, entangling them in a pile of rotted cloth and human flesh. Cane and Corso herded those on their feet with graceful derision, their massive heads rolling back and forth, drooling and snarling. Drawing rein, the sheriff raised a cat o' nine and in his singular thin bark, hollered, "To your feet! Line up! Obey me or I will gibbet you like Guinea runaways. Look here!"

He pointed to the embarrassment of Oxford, the remains of two slaves inside ribbed cages that hung side by side from the gallows. Their skulls, picked clean by seabirds and whitened in the sun were encased in metal orbs, their skeletons clothed in rags slumped in iron ribbed cocoons. 'Twas a warning from the provincial legislature that approved their punishment and now, three months later, Goldsboro refused to remove them.

In that second of quiet, my impulsiveness flowered. Not being able to tolerate more of the sheriff, I fluttered my parasol and strutted out of the crowd in my pretty walk, swaying my skirts to Robert. He froze next to his desk chair, one hand on its back, his spaniel between his feet. His eyebrows arched in hillocks; he looked at me expectantly and not without amusement. "Madam?" he asked.

I pointed a toe beneath my skirt and curtsied. "M'lord, it appears we have a Scottish musician in the lot," I said, "Perhaps he could drum that we might dance a tambourin. Or call some couples for a poussette?"

Robert roared with laughter. He threw his arm about my waist and tossed me aside, calling, "Come, come, Goldsboro. We have business to complete today. Let us not be diverted by criminals...or coquettes."

Laughter erupted. The sheriff cast his whip about the redemptioners while we grumbled for him to stop. Robert was again in charge, and I could see in the flicker of eyes that everyone wanted our lawman gone. He was hated not just because he collected the governor's quit rents. The older farmers remember me warmly, accompanying my mother to the Anglican church, our step toward comity between the religions. There was a time before the sheriff when the village depended on goodwill and kindly humor.

Goldsboro bellowed one last warning and steered his horse across the harbor, his dogs and Tiberius behind. Mr. Callister righted the table while Murray drove the Scots to the same waiting pen he used for the Dominican slaves.

A new waistcoat for Robert was waiting to be made. I pushed through a cluster of my neighbors onto Front Street.

"Mistress Wise," said Mr. Landry, the cooper. "Do you need assistance?"

His blue eyes peered out from under curly white eyebrows. Marked by the pox and hard years in the sun, his face was tender as the grandfather I didn't have. I must've looked amiss.

"Do not worry, Mr. Landry."

I set my shoulders with as much dignity as I could muster. The force of Robert manhandling me wrapped about my neck in a spasm.

I stumbled through a pocket of sailor's doxies calling me to join them. Minding my dress, and clutching my shoulder, I dropped my parasol in donkey muck. Pattens were my enemy, for I had no arm to lean on, no man's support. I swayed, realizing my neck was frozen. I couldn't turn my head even a lick.

CHAPTER 3

Someone snatched my parasol from the stink. I raised my eyes to see the MacIntosh standing before me, his free hand outstretched. In his other, shackled and crusted with dirt, was the parasol. He wiped it carefully on his shredded breeches. I wasn't sure which was worse—the trousers, or the donkey's leavings. Perhaps it was the man's hand proferred.

My eyes roved past him wondering where his watchers had gone. I spied a fair-faced Derby boy—hardly whiskered, the ring of warehouse keys looped over his shoulder, a musket at his side. Straining to push the warehouse door aside, he had left the MacIntosh unguarded. And there the Scot stood, facing me with no malice of heart.

"Sir, it's no favor to offer my parasol. Dispense with it to the dung heap."

"Mistress, your humble servant," he said, bowing. "'Tis like ones from Paris. Ye would be wise to have its cloth replaced."

I was stunned at his audacity. And his knowledge. "That may be, sir, but the tailor has no time for such work. My husband will have another." I dismissed him with a flick of my hand.

He eyed with me intense evaluation. If I took this one home

23

Robert would scold me before throwing it to Yearie. Better to say it was stolen in the crowd.

"Very well. Ahl save it for the next lady who might appreciate its workmanship."

Airs. The man put on airs. The yeoman approached. Snatching the parasol from his hand, I held it away from my dress and sputtered, "Y-you do not know your place, sir."

"That of a beast?" he asked with a sardonic smile. "Au contraire. I be well aware of what ye thrust on me and, shortly, Oxford will find it changed." He gestured like a gentleman. "*Je suis désolé*, mademoiselle." Bowing deeply, his rags fell about him like the pauper king's robe and he left without my permission.

The yeoman followed him into the darkness of the warehouse, and I stood dumbfounded. Sure that the laborer wanted to lock up the Scotsman and return for the sale, I had to ask for brocade and tablecloths quickly. Had the heathen really spoken French? Mine was rusty but I thought he apologized as if he were leaving for a salon.

My curiosity was piqued.

The waterside warehouse doors were open, the loading pier beyond. Robert had ordered the street side locked against thievery. Cavernous and dark, the rafters were lined with swallows tweeting and fluttering in the dank air. In a corner, a white-faced owl slowly turned his heart-shaped face to me. I blinked, my eyes searched for light and rested on a family of black swans swimming in sunlight beyond the pier. Outside, stacks of dried tobacco leaves wafted their scent indoors, their dust leaving an acrid grit in my throat. I coughed.

"Mistress, what do you need? Does Mr. Morris know you come?"

I did not know his name. Robert had taken his most trusted to the harbor and left me with this pimpled rube, fresh off the boat. It was not my duty to explain our system of graft. Robert claimed his dibstones by setting the prices high for our fledgling guilds and craftsmen. We took Cunliffe goods without paying.

The boy seemed agitated; one hand hovered over a knife that

hung from his belt. The other stretched out against the MacIntosh's chest. I was a distraction.

"I can wait until you are finished with him," I said with some authority.

"Missus, ain't it best if you return when Mr. Morris is here?"

"I can't wait that long, young man. I need a bolt of brocade and the lace tablecloths."

I laid the parasol on the dry goods counter as the Scot shuffled away from the yeoman, rubbing his forehead with his free hand. "Help madam with her task, boy. I canna go anywhere shackled as I am."

The young man grunted and contemplated his charge. In the gray light, all the energy appeared drained from his prisoner. The warehouse must have felt like the hold of the ship save for the stink of tobacco. His massive shoulders slumped, his head bowed, and he leaned against the counter ready to be chained to the wall. Yet the yeoman did not take kindly to his stance so near the goods. He grabbed the Scot's manacles with one hand and shoved him with the other to the wood floor. The Scotsman sprawled like a newborn colt upon its first step.

Slapping the warehouse keys near the parasol, the yeoman reached under the counter for the bolts of cloth. Wrapped in gauze, a hefty lot spilled across the wooden surface. I hated opening them amidst so much dust and leaned over each end to pull a tuck loose, inspecting the colors and quality. The plantation wives would wear these materials for the fall cotillions.

"Missus, may I help?" asked the worker, his caked fingers tearing the wrapping.

Waving my hand, I said, "Please! Do not dirty the cloth."

I glanced at his disgruntled face in time to see the MacIntosh's arm raised over the boy's head, wielding a wooden mallet the cooper used. The yeoman followed my gaze too late as it crashed against his skull with the force of God's might. He disintegrated to the floor, the side of his head a mess of gristle and blood. I hopped away, afraid I was next. My ears pounded. My mouth agape, I couldn't speak.

Dead men dropped like flies in Oxford, but while I slurped air, I refused to give in to hysterics.

"And what, pray, sir, are you about?" I yelled. "Have you not caused enough trouble?"

"Aye, right. I'm not the one standing here blethering away. Ye might skedaddle aff, madam, if ye ken what's good for ye."

Well, that wasn't a threat of life and limb. Thinking fast, I said, "Sir, you kill Mr. Morris' man and give *me* advice? I will alert the authorities." I turned to run and remembering my pattens, stopped. His voice had given me pause. The Scot was not concerned with me.

He grabbed the warehouse keys. In the wink of a pickpocket's eye, he was rid of his shackles. Slinging a saddlebag on the counter, he scanned the shelves and tossed in packages of salt pork and corn, a pewter cup, the yeoman's knife and hatchet, and for extra measure, a flintlock and gunpowder. I tottered for the door.

"Doona think it, lady," he said, and I glanced over my shoulder to see the yeoman's musket pointed at me. Discovering a pair of boots, late of the missing Master Vanderkoop, he held the sole to the bottom of his foot and threw them over his shoulder. He spied a long sword and red campaign coat hanging on the wall and whooped, "Ah ma lucky man!"

The yeoman's blood pooled near the counter. My mind raced. There was so much in the warehouse, the cloth, the uniform, and even the yeoman might not be missed.

But the MacIntosh would hang from the gallows. If not, he was just another sorry beggar to occupy Robert's precious time, to divert him from his promise to me. I frowned. I didn't really want him to be found. A refugee of Culloden aligned with my very Papist sentiments.

"I'm not fond of assisting our sheriff. You cannot leave his body here for anyone to find," I said, pointing. "They will come for you thick and fast."

"Doona watch me dispose of him. If questioned, ye wouldna have to lie."

"Allow me to take my leave, sir. A word—head to the cypress swamp and the maroons across the Nanticoke River. Stay in the wood. There's an Indian trail past a village called Vienna. The patrollers will be looking for you so make scarce. A dank smell comes from the interior, maybe two days' walk. It's a drowned land riddled with mosquitoes and forgotten people."

I threw the keys in his sack. Finding the yeoman and his keys gone, perhaps Robert would think his worker another runaway.

"What mean ye, 'forgotten'?" he asked.

"Convicts like you. Vestiges of the Assateague and Nanticoke tribes, runaway slaves and indentures. They steal to live. Do not return here. They will hang you." I pushed the sack toward him. "When I arrived, the door was open. If I am asked further, I will feign ignorance. Go before I have a change of heart."

"Brave and resourceful, ye be."

"No, I wish to save face for my master. You will bring us nothing but trouble." I was stern, but had no effect.

Grinning, he bowed, a gentleman at court sweeping his hand to his side. He grabbed the yeoman's leg. I snatched my cloth, turned on my heel and strode to the street side doors.

"Madam. Ahl not lose sight of ye," he said.

He dragged the dead boy leaving a trail of blood. I was sorry for the yeoman's undoing, an innocent only beginning a new life in a new place. The MacIntosh would make fish bait of him and I didn't wish to see the swans' paddling disturbed by the body's splash. Questions would erupt in the tavern—talk of an investigation, but the planters wouldn't demand a hearing. Only Robert was worse the wear. The cost of transporting the prisoner and losing the yeoman. They would bemoan Robert's luck and be glad it was him that suffered. Their worn-out, gray, marbled dirt that was unable to produce decent tobacco was their greatest concern.

CHAPTER 4

*A*t the doors, the heat beat upon my head and breast and I realized I should not have relied solely on a parasol. Spreading my lace tucker across my chest against the sun's burn, I attempted to look the part of a modest woman. My appearance was incomplete, yet I felt a secret excitement. The spasm in my neck had disappeared.

The streets were packed. Poor freemen clothed in stained leather breeches and dirty linen sat on their plow horses. Plank-wheeled carts clogged the strand by the river, and I recognized the black coats of Quakers sitting atop wagons, uttering thee and thou to anyone who would listen. They had hitched rides from East Town near the headwaters of the Tred Avon River where they had a meeting house. I uttered an audible "Puh" at their hypocrisy for they claimed all men equal, except in the apparent service of a Scot, or a slave. They weren't alone. Even debtor-convicts who had earned their freedom and a headright of fifty acres lazed about hoping to purchase the dregs of Scottish labor.

"Good Mrs. Wise, you aren't at home readying your table for tonight?"

Mistress Handy, wife of one of the largest plantation owners, fluttered a fan against her glistening face. They had scores of slaves and a terrible reputation for their treatment. Her liveried footman, an enormous black of the West Indies, stood by her side. She had everything. Why did she need a redemptioner, too? She stared at my décolleté.

"Mistress?" I asked. My table was not of her concern.

"Vulgar," she said under her breath. "Prancing about like johnny cake in Belgian lace."

"Good Mrs. Handy, with all the excitement, Father Time has clear forgotten me." I grinned as if I had won a game of whist in her parlor. "I must be going if I'm to have guests."

"And save an hour for your kitchen garden," said she who had never bent in the earth a day in her life.

I bounced a short curtsy and tucked my fan in my bodice, tilting my head. "Oh, lady, it seems you are stifling in this sun," I said, looking pointedly at her gleaming cheeks and neck. "Have your man carry you to my front parlor and I will bring you a cool tea." Her manservant was unmoved save for a startled blink.

Letting it fly, she said, "Impudent tart."

I nodded and curtsied, holding on to my grin with hard eyes as I bid good day. I headed farther down the strand to make for Merchants Row. Stepping shakily across the oyster shells to the bakery, I gained a spot on the porch where I could see the progress of Robert's sale. The redemptioners were nearly gone. Robert stood by, tapping his whip handle against his leg, watching as a wizened farmer inspected an old Scot's teeth. Gripping the man's thighs and buttocks, he pronounced him good enough. He tied him to the back of his plow horse and dragged him through the crowd.

Robert brought Cunliffe's slaves in the same manner. A slave for life, indentures just five to seven years. I did not remember Papa purchasing Yearie and her mother when I was a little girl, but I liked to believe it wasn't as cruel before Robert came. Reverend White-head and his evangelicals were right, we needed to quit all human trade. For all their religiosity, Reverend Bacon and the Anglicans had no such sentiment.

My parents and their teachings, my husband and Phebe, even

Mama's rosary were becoming a distant memory. Oxford's trade goods blinded me and, despite my better self, I had a hunger for the things Robert purveyed, though no desire to own a slave. Yearie was not a slave to me. I could free her anytime. We were sisters.

I was ready to step from the bakery when, hearing seagulls caw overhead, I watched as they dove for carrion on the dock. The Union Jack unfurled over the harbor, then hung dead in the stillness. Captain Gildart clambered onto the dock from the *Johnson*'s pinnace, its oars pointing upward in salute. A lad climbed up and followed Gildart down the wharf. The child was dark-haired and slight, clothed in a frock coat of lime green, an unlucky color. I stopped and pressed against the porch post, charged with a vague worry.

"Mr. Morris, I bring you a present from Liverpool!" shouted Gildart.

My master laid the whip on the registrar's table and sauntered across the shells. His arms stretched to the child, who hesitated momentarily. Tightness fell from the boy's cheeks, and he ran into m'lord's waiting arms.

"Father?" asked the boy.

For the second time that morn, my mouth fell agape.

A child—his son? Was this a secret kept from me? I strained to hear his voice. He stepped backward, bowed and said, "Robert Morris, Jr., sir. Son of the late Elizabeth Murphey, I am arrived to the shores of your town."

CHAPTER 5

*W*hat to do? The day was hardly half-gone but as complicated as tracking an Indian in the rain. The western sun streamed high through my garret window, a hot breeze barely ruffling my sticky shift. Rebel sympathies for the MacIntosh, the yeoman's skull, my mother's voice— "God knows your thoughts, Sarah."

Robert was sitting at the tavern with his cronies drinking and slapping backs, introducing his son while I toiled. Suddenly, his reason for a betrothal became clear. Mama used to sing, "Sarah-Sahara, cook and clean and kneel in prayer, only then God provides an heir." And it was to be someone else's child?

"Hail Mary," those red-letter Papist words rang in my ears. I made the sign of the cross and put my dress away. With a glance in the looking glass, my future was clear. A brow puckered in anger, a mouth pressed tight wrinkling my chin. Leaning in, I spread my fingers across my forehead and placed my palms against my cheeks trying to squeeze the emotion from my face. This was no way to become a cherished wife, riddling my being in scorn. I changed into plain bodice and short skirt, tied a cap round my chin and tramped to the kitchen in clodhoppers trying to keep my face serene.

Steaming from a slow fire that Jackson lazed near, the kitchen was busy save for him. I shook my head in disgust watching him sweat. Hogsheads had broken him for the afternoon, and he was not allowed in the kitchen. He rolled fevered eyes at me, but I gave him no ken. Hestia shucked oysters and Yearie stood at the table squeezing lemons, her face bunched in thought.

I stormed through the back door to the garden, plucked a row of strawberries and dug a bowl of turnips. That pompous Handy woman. Grabbing my hoe, I plunged it into the dirt, throwing great clumps this way and that. Alone at last, I gave myself over to acting the brute. "Gad dem me, Mama. I'm cursed."

"Sary."

Yearie. A voice to shame. I attacked a molehill. "Strawberries and cream for the lemon cake. Some for you and Hestia. Jackson can eat cornbread and sausage."

"He be in a bad way."

"Who? Jackson? He's malingering. Hardly done a lick of work since he came to us." This wasn't true, but I felt mean. I leaned on my hoe and wiped my apron across my brow. "I will send him back to Handy." I told Robert not to take a field slave into our home, especially one from that plantation. Handy ruined good service for the rest of us with his cruelty. Besides, Handy could pay for his missus' finery from his smokehouse sales. It was not a fair trade.

"His back putrefied, Sary. It run with pus."

"Not from the beating Robert gave him."

"It weren't Master Robert. Findley drag Jackson from the stable a fortnight hence and made him a horrible lashin. I thought Jackson stronger, but he been hidin when he come home from the dock last few days."

"Findley came on our property? By God, I'll have him fired. He breaks an agreement."

Faced with my curse, Yearie cast her eyes to the ground. I knew how this would go. Handy was indebted to Findley for his strong hand over their slaves and couldn't risk looking for another overseer in the middle of harvest. My complaint would fall on deaf ears. I propped the hoe against a fence rail, picked up the basket of berries and turnips and followed Yearie inside. Jackson was sprawled by the fire in a delirium.

Pushing him from the hearth, he rolled face down on the brick floor. I caught my breath seeing his muslin shirt adhered in a criss-crossing of putrid yellow and brown trails on his back. Hestia snorted, her oyster knife waving in the air. "He'll not be getting in my way. I got a stew to make. A wharf man can get him out my kitchen."

"And have him thrown in a pile of sawdust?" I asked. "No. I'll not send for the barber, either. The man smells of gin."

"Just blow terbaccer up his nose," said Yearie.

"Or call it the smallpox," said Cook, turning thoughtful.

I shook my head, "We've seen the pox. This is a whipping."

"We got to remove his shirt," said Yearie.

"I'll get the basin. You get the rags."

Jackson groaned, the brick floor cooling his fever and waking him. His eyes were bloodshot, his pupils fixed. I poured hot water and said, "The jar of knitbone. Under the stairs."

I soaked a rag and knelt to lay it over his back. Yearie began dabbing at the crust until we slowly parted the shirt from his skin. Purple welts seeped. A dead animal smell rose to my nostrils.

Set up in a sticky paste, I laid knitbone linen over his wounds. He mumbled in surges. Such a severe whipping, I had never seen. Suffering for days, he was afraid of being returned to Findley. We helped him crawl to the dog's straw. Robert would decide. It was his household and I hoped he would make this public.

Hestia was angry. "All this work and we healing a slave. Just putting more load on my shoulder."

"Good Hestia," I said, "Try hard. We'll have lemon cake tonight. I'll plate it here, so the guests won't ask for seconds."

"You can't fool me, Sarah. You were going to eat it wit us after you got out them stays." Her eyes smiled even if her lips didn't.

"Well then, stop grumbling. Listen here, the master's son has arrived from Liverpool." I looked around. "He'll sleep in here tonight. We'll need the pallet from the stable and bedclothes from the attic."

"A son?" asked Yearie with a grunt. "Where he gonna sleep after the guests leave?"

I searched her eyes and came to it. "The gathering room." It was hot in summer and cold in winter having neither insulation nor a fireplace. Four walls, an oak floor and matching six over six windows. A tavern-sized room with no bawdy women to serve, only wooden benches for discussion and decision.

In May, it resounded with the hot words of lowly farmers over the Tobacco Act. Talbot's small farms were spent from the weed. So, Robert suggested loans to pay their quit rents, allowing their land to lay fallow. In a year, he said all would rebound. But Mr. Burnham, their sober representative warned, "I will not contract debts greater than may be paid over the course of my own existence, gentlemen. My family will leave Oxford under its present hierarchy and find a place of our own on the frontier. You, sirs, have yoked us as the King would, like oxen to your land."

No one likes that word—yoke. Robert's meeting room was now only for the gentry to gather in. Young Robert could sleep in a corner until frost laced the windows and the kitchen was a warm welcome. He would not take the guest chamber. I was firm on this.

"Is the table set?" I asked.

"No one to bring the boards from storage," said Yearie as she pointed to Jackson's destruction.

We hurried to the stable and lifted the cherry dining boards from their canvas. Covered in spider webs, they would take some hard polish. I lifted one and beneath was Phebe's cradle, her embroidered linens piled inside. I heard a sharp cry and when Yearie's touch brought my eyes to hers, I realized it was me who made the sound.

"Leave it, Sary," she said. "We can't dawdle, nor can you give in."

I nodded and we carried the dining boards inside, ran to the front parlor and removed the top from the round table and set it against the fireplace. Lifting the base, we duck walked it through the wide front hall and situated it in the middle of the gathering room. In unison, we each bent and pulled out the gate legs before placing the dining boards atop. A minuet of laying table.

"Lock them, Yearie. I'll check the yeast bread, get the polish and the tablecloth."

When I returned, Yearie had opened the side door and dragged the benches to the flower garden. Our new Philadelphia dining chairs lined the wall and she stood barefoot on one tacking Dutch lace to the top of the window frame. It was beautiful.

"Where on earth did you find the lace?" I asked.

"I trade Miss Vanderkoop— her scarves for a store of ham and beans. Her boys like to starve."

"I saw her today. I heard she kept her goat but sold the cow. She has family in Lewes. Perhaps Robert will pay her passage on one of our ships."

"Be there not a swain in the hinterlands in need of a wife?" asked Yearie.

"Reverend Bacon would never marry her off again. What if Vanderkoop isn't dead?"

"He's gone with the wind, Sary."

"Sad. She'll be dead in a few years; she looks so deranged."

Yearie climbed down from the chair. "We had many a bad night walkin the streets. That woman still sleeps in her own cottage," she said, shaking her head. "I be forever thankful you not sell me like she sell her cow."

I clasped her to my breast. "Oh, my sweet Yearie. We wore pudding caps together. We will never part. I swear." I looked in her eyes, so direct and honest. "We are sisters, aren't we?"

There was a clatter at the front door and furtive whispers. I caught a glimpse of Robert and, pushing Yearie away, I shook my head in warning. She busied herself with the silver on the table lining it up as my mother had taught us.

I grabbed the new candles and, holding them above, said loudly, "M'lord, you will be delighted to know I am in receipt of the last bayberry candles. The dinner will be to your satisfaction. An evening of taste, wine, music, and song."

My master pushed his son to me, a waif of about thirteen. His head came past my shoulder, had the roundness of his father's, but a street urchin's countenance. I smiled and approached. His face was clean and cushioned in a filthy cravat, recklessly tied. I could smell him ten feet away. He shifted feet and, glancing to the floor, bowed and swept his tricorn out from his heart. At least he had manners.

"M'lady," he said. "I am Robert Morris, Jr."

At that very moment I realized what a picture I presented. A farmer's wife in workaday togs. "Young sir," I said. "Welcome to your father's home. I hope it will be to your satisfaction."

He waited for his father to speak. Robert took him by the elbow.

"Mistress Wise, this is my son, late of Liverpool and his maternal grandmother's care. Wouldst my good woman secure him a bath and provide him with sustenance until dinner is served? 'Twas no grub at Quinn's."

It was late. I could see the sun on the last half of its journey in the western sky. Guests would arrive in a few hours.

"Jeremiah be in the kitchen," whispered Yearie curtseying, her eyes on the floor. "I'll have him bring the washtub."

"What's no-good Jackson doing?" asked Robert. "Clean the boy up for Master Tilghman who will help with his future plans." He paused and pointed to the table. "And straighten the linen."

With a wave of his hand he moved us aside and raised a goblet to the window, twirling it in his fingers as the cut glass spun its shimmer across his face. "You'd think my house was full of fingerless lepers. Polish the crystal. Hold it thus to the light and make sure each one is in no way smudged, or it will fall on you tomorrow."

"Yes, Master," we said as one, bouncing in obedience.

"My lord," I began, so soft as to not wake a church mouse, "you must come to the back porch where I will treat you to a wave of the fan. 'Tis hot enough to make one's blood boil."

He grumbled and began unwinding his cravat. "Make this dinner perfect, woman."

"Always, sir," I said, smiling. "Come with me, young Rob. I'll take you to the kitchen to meet Jeremiah."

"Do something about his dress!" shouted Robert as he stalked off. "He doesn't have clean breeches and he cannot wear sailor's petticoats to dinner."

I scanned the child up and down. His father expected too much. I couldn't wash and dry a shirt and breeches in the two hours left. Jeremiah would help him bathe and I would figure it. I led him to the kitchen where Jackson lay moaning in fevered throes. Young Robert's eyes widened with fear.

"Do not be bothered," I said. "Just an unruly servant."

Jeremiah dragged the washtub to the fire and trundled buckets of water from the well. 'Twas cold and brackish, but short of a swim in the river our water was the only way to clean months of grime from the child's body. I was sure there was milk and cream under his swarthy complexion. The air was sultry and a cold bath could be refreshing. Young Robert stood like an oak next to the tub.

"For what do you wait, young sir?" I asked, tapping my foot. "Get in. I have much to do."

"I can't."

"Of course you can. Your father has demanded it. You will not sit at table in your present state."

He turned his shoulder and jerked his head in Jackson's direction, a grimace on his face. Jeremiah froze from his task, utterly shocked at the boy's recalcitrance.

"The Devil, mistress," said young Robert, "He shan't see me as I came into the world. It's an abomination. Remove the witch's consort."

I gave the boy a stern eye. Evangelical or Papist superstition? "You, child, will, listen," I said, each word a petal, plucked from a flower. "I cannot move the slave, nor can I move you, but you can move the washtub. Drag it to the porch where you will have your privacy. There will be no further accommodations of your insolence, or you'll face your father's wrath."

For the first time, he looked at me to take stock of my importance. From my pinned cotton apron and gingham skirt to my grimy leather shoes, I looked a kitchen maid. Here was a child who had been raised by a grandmother and as I stared back, I realized that having him in my household would be no easy task. He was used to having his way exactly as his father was accustomed, without any of his humor or occasional elegance.

"Mistress, move the tub with the help of the slave," he ordered, his cheek turned. "I am my father's son and will not be asked to labor unless at his command."

I couldn't help it. I cuffed him across the ear—hard. He grabbed his face and swore, "God's breath, you bitch. Strike me again and, and…"

"And what?"

It was his father. He leaned against the doorjamb wearing only a loose linen shirt and breeches. No wig, his shaved head gleamed with sweat, his eyebrows a stain of black ink above blue eyes. I took two steps back to save myself.

"Sir, she treats me as a servant. And the Devil is in attendance. Look what lies in the corner," said young Robert, pointing to Jackson who must have understood because he shrank into the wall and covered his eyes.

"Yes, look what stands in the middle of my kitchen," said Robert, pointing as his laces bounced in emphasis. "A spoiled, unlicked cub, a—a whelp." He raised his other hand and in it was his riding crop. "Do you know the esteemed philosopher, Plato?"

"No, sir," the boy said, his face dawning with awareness.

"He said, 'The cause of all sin lies in a person's excessive love of self.'"

Young Robert began to strip. Jacket and waistcoat hit the brick floor as he tried to pull his yellowed linen shirt from his grubby breeches. His father yanked him by his hair, whipping him across his buttocks with the force of a branch torn about in a thunderstorm. I ran from the room right into Yearie who held up fresh clothes.

"He is regally drunk," I said. "Poor Jeremiah has to watch."

"Oh, Sary, no," she whispered. "Look, the tailor gave us an old suit of Jeremiah's."

Young Robert screamed, "Stop, my lord. I beg you!" Yearie and I scuttled along the hallway, our aprons ready to polish the crystal.

We worked silently and hearing the boy's wails turn to whimpers, I looked up when Robert appeared in the hallway, staring at us. His face was black, his lips frozen in a snarl.

"I warn you, Mrs. Wise, if my dinner is ruined by your constant deference to my slaves, be it Jackson or Yearie, you will face the consequences. I cannot have this disobedience in my house from anyone. Do I make myself clear?"

"Yes, Master," I said, folding my hands at my waist and bowing my head. "All will be well, sir." He was too drunk to remind him that Yearie was my bonded woman, not his. A small but valid point that barely quieted my beating heart.

CHAPTER 6

*H*olding up a decanter of tawny Madeira, Robert expounded on its properties; the casks, its excellent taste. The casks traveled in the steamy holds of Cunliffe's slave ships that made the longest journeys, bringing the wine to maturity. Wine, slaves and tobacco, a tangled commerce.

As he poured over everyone's shoulder into the sparkling goblets, the Tilghman's eyes grew wide. Gildart guzzled and held his glass for more. Robert winked at Yearie, who filled his with a watered burgundy. The captain never knew.

Subdued, young Robert barely raised his eyes to me. Captain Matthews had sent word that he would join us after dinner for song. Before we sat, Robert whispered to me, "A shame! Matthews' manners balance Gildart's crudeness." It was up to me to soften the captain's conversation.

The boy stole sidelong glances at my carriage. A gown of indigo taffeta, lightweight yet lustrous, was set off by an amethyst resting in the hollow of my throat that Robert brought from a strange land he called Salvador da Bahia. It never failed to impress. Yearie had piled my hair high, a lone ringlet upon my collar bone. I could have curtsied before the Dauphine at Versailles but settled for Mrs. Tilghman asking to purchase Robert's warehouse cloth.

My lord basked in the beauty of his table and talk of banned continental trade. Tilghman thanked Reverend Bacon for supporting the Tobacco Act and said he would make it worth his while. Mrs. Tilghman's cheeks grew rosy as Captain Gildart wove tales of the high seas. It was all for Robert. All for his future. And I with him.

Yearie set Hestia's tureen of oyster stew next to Captain Gildart. Fluid as melting butter on a hot roll she filled his bowl, never interrupting his conversation with Robert. I jumped when Gildart slammed his hand on the table.

"Oyster stew? Even Indians know not to farm them from the Chesapeake in this heat. Are you trying to kill me, wench?"

I spoke up in defense of my kitchen. "Good captain, I assure you our oysters were brought from the banks today and are safe, thoroughly cooked. If it's not to your liking, Yearie, please take his away."

She reached just as his hand flew wide, spilling the stew across the floor and his sleeve. She apologized, curtseyed and dabbed at his jacket. Gildart cursed her saying he had better service from his cabin boy. I started to rise when Robert calmed the ill-mannered salt with a promise of winter brocade for a new jacket. Yearie removed the offending stew, her face smooth, unmoved. My insides churned. We raised a glass to toast Gildart's ocean crossing.

Now the object of everyone's attention, the seaman put another damper on the conversation. "Morris, did you hear a merchant ship was taken in fourteen fathoms outside the Virginie Capes."

All merriment ceased. Robert set his wine on the table. "The mouth of the Chesapeake. Did you encounter cannon on your journey?"

"Lucky, we were. There were sightings." Gildart snapped his fingers. "Our trade is threatened. Spaniards in the Delaware Bay. French warships in the English Channel stopped those bound here.

"We requested a man o' war. The *Cunliffe* was attacked, Captain Pritchard killed," said Robert, his voice ponderous. "We have no luck with the king. Preoccupied. His land war with the French and Spanish."

"The colony will have to bring their own defense," said Gildart. "I can barely afford the cost of maritime insurance, my man. Do you have a solution as I depart these waters?"

"Tomorrow, meet me in the warehouse. I have twenty carriage guns," answered Robert. "You're loading cargo worth well over £20,000."

"I warn you these privateers are agile. Bermuda sloops and nimble frigates with guns that turn on a sixpence."

Robert frowned. Impatient that the conversation was ruined, I interrupted again. "Captain, what news of London's theatre do you have?"

Gildart set back in his chair and regarded me with a pompous smile. "M'lady missed the shutting of the Haymarket?" he asked. "Only a rehearsal of *Romeo and Juliet*. We are in short supply of drama."

"Then we must make our own here in the colony for you to brag of at home. Tonight, you will enjoy some excellent music."

Robert clapped his hand to the table. "Mrs. Wise calls us to order!"

A feast ensued and the men ate like hogs. Young Robert never picked up his fork. Instead, like a chawbacon, he held his spoon against the meat and sawed with his knife, spearing it to his mouth. Finally, dessert came. In the haze of sugar from a mountain of sweets, the conversation relaxed, and all was going well.

Anne Tilghman was exhausted. Encased in heavy brocade, a thin film of perspiration covered her breast. I played the lively hostess, ignoring my hunger to keep my stays from pinching. But Mr. Tilghman was having none of my geniality.

"What say you, Robert, of the Catholic redemptioners brought today?" he asked. "Motley crew. That one rogue put you to task."

Reverend Bacon wiped his lips. "God's children, sir. The Lord has directed us to have compassion for our brethren, for they must earn their freedom. We shall be good masters and bring them to the Anglican Church."

Mrs. Tilghman pressed her hand over her husband's. Only Gildart continued to chew, oblivious to the tenor of the room. This discussion would lead to political tempers and religious zeal, things Robert forbade at his table.

"Why, James," he said, "let us not belabor our evening. The Reverend is right, all is good in Oxford. Drink up, my friend."

Yearie appeared at Master Tilghman's elbow holding a decanter, but he dismissed her.

"I heard there was a murder in your warehouse," Tilghman said, laying an elbow upon my table. "Your yeoman was found floating in the grasses. If word gets out, rebellion could spread amongst the indentured and blacks. We are outnumbered, sir. Mark my words."

I felt a panic wondering if they had caught the Scot, if I would be discovered.

Robert raised his glass. "We have Goldsboro's militia. Oxford will not have an uprising like Virginia. We'll discuss after the ladies withdraw, sir. Time to make merry." He turned and nodded to me. Dinner was done.

"Merry MakeFun Morris," laughed Reverend Bacon. "The name follows you from Annapolis."

Robert ignored his hint of their Tuesday Club. Those antics were not appropriate for Mrs. Tilghman's ears. Polite but firm, Robert prevents harsh words.

I took my cue. "Mistress Anne, I'm sure you must be tired after crossing the Bay. We'll rejoin the men later and *Sing a Song of Sixpence* for Tench."

"Excellent, Mrs. Wise," said Robert rising. "Reverend and I will regale our company with original music. We are quite accomplished around these parts. Sarah, you must play the harpsichord," he said, nodding to me.

"Sir?" I asked, pouting. "I may not sing with you?"

"To cover me, my dear. I sound like a wounded donkey."

An old joke, it nevertheless got a laugh. Reverend Bacon brought his viola. Not to be outdone, Gildart boasted, "I'll play a sheng I bought from a Chinese sailor. A reed instrument with a melodic sound. My sailors badger me to blow a tune, but they would only steal it."

"To the parlor," said Robert to all this competition. He rose to take Mistress Anne's hand and escorted her from the table. Buckled heels made him taller, rounded his calves, looking the coxcomb amongst yard roosters. I waited, looking about. Captain Gildart gobbled cake, and young Rob picked his teeth with his fork, finally finding a use for it, while the reverend engaged in horse whispers with Master Tilghman about the slaves.

"Some slave owners are generous and thoughtful, Reverend. I understand you think slaves have a soul, but you won't get anywhere with that in Talbot. Food and clothing. They do not need religion."

"Surely you believe baptism will allow their entry into Heaven after a life of good servitude. What's the harm in that?" asked Bacon. I folded my napkin, waiting.

"They are animals better suited to picking tobacco in the fields."

I drummed my fingers on the table, a habit Mama always scolded. A lady always disguises her annoyance.

They must have felt my eyes upon them for the reverend pushed his chair back and bunched his napkin, saying, "Forgive me, Mrs. Wise. I find myself lacking. Come," he said.

I rose a bit unsteady. With a sunny smile, I took sips of air. "Lovely," I said, then confidentially, "Reverend, Mrs. Vanderkoop? She is destined for the almshouse."

"Money is short in the collection. But she's no strumpet. Robert booked her passage on a ship to the Swedes. We cannot have a mother and innocent children housed with epileptics and idiots."

"Ah, Thomas. You remain concerned for the least among us. I would not wish to be her." We passed into the front hallway and paused over the harpsichord. I ran my fingers across the inlaid cover. Opening it, I struck a key.

"You will never have to worry about such a fall from grace again, Sarah. Robert promised that he would take care of you. He did not want you to marry Goldsboro."

I felt heat rising to my face. They had discussed my choices, and this was their solution—housekeeper? Staring at the reverend, I said,

44

"Pay me no mind, Thomas. Only, can you tell me why Mrs. Vanderkoop found aid, but I did not? Why I was evicted?"

"I...I'm not at liberty to say, my dear. Do not spend time hashing out events of long ago. You have your security now."

He delivered me to the sofa with Mrs. Tilghman, who was downing a blackberry cordial, her toddler, Tench, in her lap. Yearie stood nearby perfectly composed, but I knew she was upset.

"Yearie, you may clear the table now and retire to the kitchen. We have no need of further service." She bobbed, barely creating a swish on her way out, unnoticed by Robert's dog sleeping under his chair.

Mrs. Tilghman said in astonishment, "You release your woman before you retire? Never allow them such kindness, my dear. Do you count your silver?" Her face was full of importance. She leaned over confidentially, "Mrs. Wise, don't dither between treating them humanely or punishing them like dogs. I have mine chained at night in Annapolis."

Tray rose and padded to the hallway, growling. I studied her countenance for a hint of kindness and said, "Why thank you, Mistress Anne, for your advice." I wasn't in her league, but it wasn't her place to criticize me. She knew I prevaricated, for her smile tightened.

Tray yapped in earnest at a pounding on the door. Yearie nodded to me from the hall, hurrying to answer it. I poured Mistress Anne more cordial. I wanted to hear her gossip of the capital. The front door creaked open.

"Take me to Morris," commanded the sheriff in his waspish voice.

Goldsboro glanced at us as he stalked by giving us nary a mind. His spurs clattered across the wood floors and I winced thinking of the damage they would do to the back-parlor settee. He never removed them in house as did all other gentlemen, for his were screwed to the heel of his jackboots. Yearie's low voice welcomed someone inside. Probably Tiberius. Sure enough the murmurs of sweet nothings reached my ears.

"That's the sheriff?" asked Mistress Anne.

I nodded.

"I suppose he is here over the redemptioner."

"I suppose. Let us not worry," I said. "Rather unsavory matter." I needed to dispense of her. Yearie could eavesdrop on the men if she would just stop flirting.

Mrs. Tilghman gulped her liqueur as Tench began fussing. They were both overtired. She shook his tiny shoulders and he wailed. An expected response. She was so incapable.

I took the screaming child from her arms. "Anne, you must be exhausted from your travels. Please, find your way above stairs. The second door on the right. Sleep as long as you wish come morn. If you allow it, I'll care for Tench, rise with him and keep him in the kitchen with goodies."

She gasped at my offer, placed both hands on the sofa, and pushed herself up like an old woman although we were both in our second decade only by a few years. By late evening, our bodies screamed for release. And I was sure she was used to handing her children off to servants.

I held the toddler across my breast and patted his back. His sweaty little body melted into me as if he were my own. Walking Mistress Anne to the foot of the staircase, I glanced over to the door. Yearie and Tiberius had slipped outside, unnoticed. Anne leaned over to kiss my cheek. An act of such familiarity surprised me.

"Bless you, my sweet. I am grateful for your generosity."

"Beg pardon if I wake you later. I must get my morning dress from the clothespress outside your room."

"A fire couldn't wake me tonight," she responded.

I watched as she lugged herself and her skirts up the stairs, and when she turned the corner out of sight, I hurried down the hall to the kitchen. She would strip to her shift and lie abed in the nighttime breeze. The sheriff's talk of the dead yeoman awaited.

CHAPTER 7

I ignored the booming of liquored men. Trudging the stairs, my skirts in hand, I passed the bedchamber door ajar, a lump of sheets in the middle of the guest bed. Mrs. Tilghman. My thoughts cleared.

I stumbled to the foot of the garret stair, slipped out of my bodice, skirt and pannier and laid them on a shelf in the hall clothes press. In my shift and stays, I took my gingham dress from a peg and turned to go up to bed. But lo, a shimmer emanated from under Robert's door. Surely he hadn't left his guests in the parlor? 'Twas not like him.

I pushed the door a mite, expecting to see him searching for something to impress his guests, perhaps his new Chinese shaving bowl, the one with blue fishes swimming round its rim. I blew out my candle to hide behind the door and let him pass, unseen.

A man bent over his desk, his face illuminated by a single flame. He held the distinctive papers of indenture. He wore the red coat of the Maryland Militia. Still in its scabbard, his sword lay a foot from him propped on the cushion of the wingback chair. A bit dizzy, I leaned, and the door creaked. His head whipped round, and dropping the documents he yanked the sword from its sheath, and stood, its point aimed at me. The MacIntosh in the flesh, covered in mud from his thighs to the toes of Mr. Vanderkoop's boots.

Not more. I was completely spent. "What say you, sir?" I hissed. "Why have you returned where you will surely be caught?"

"Are ye accompanied?"

"No. But you hear the rumblings of angry men? You risk your life. I only need to shout."

"But ye won't." He placed the sword in its scabbard and laid it across Robert's desk.

He was right. I moved into the room and shut the door behind me. Walking to the bed, I threw my gingham across it and wrapped one arm around the poster. I stared at him. Muck clung to him, clouding the air with its stink. "How far did you go?"

"Only across the river. Did occur to me that yer husband has me papers. I want receipt of them, me lady."

"He is not my husband. Perhaps will never be."

The MacIntosh took a step toward me, surprise writ large across his grizzled face. A day traversing the wetlands had done nothing to make him more palatable. He reached into Robert's leather satchel and pulled more documents from it, waving them before me. "Is this what I want?"

"Your indenture would be in that bundle," I said, nodding.

Brazenly, he sat in Robert's chair and plucking the first one from the stack held it behind the candle flame to read. I approached his side and read the name aloud. "Alexander Buchanan."

He read, "Archi McAnnis. Seventy if he's a day. 'Twill not live long."

"Charles Davidson," I said and the MacIntosh grabbed it from me, stuffing it in his sack.

"John Suter," he said, picking up another. "They carried him off in chains, I know not where."

"They carried you off in chains. And you escaped."

His eyes met mine, steel gray, rimmed in black lashes. "I have resources that my collaborators no longer can muster. Anger threatens to swallow me whole."

"Well, it better hurry because I wish there to be no evidence of your presence tonight."

"Madam, wi yer help, ahl be gone."

A document folded in thirds slipped from the pile. I knew this to be Robert's reminder to himself of unfinished work. I held it to the light. The name was clear, "McIntosh." "Take it and go before I have a change of heart," I said.

He stood and threw his arm around my waist, pressing me to him. He stunk like an open sewer, but his breath smelled of licorice. I pushed him back, and broke his clutch sickened by another man who thought me his possession.

"Do not take liberties, sir. Get out!"

He stepped back, "My apologies, m'lady. I read ye wrong. A consequence of being at sea for two months and in gaol the year afore." He bowed, a ridiculous action for an unwashed commoner and criminal. "Ye won't be lost to me memory. Not ever. Ahl take me leave." Stuffing the clutch of indentures in his shirt he backed away, sword in hand.

I crumpled my shift in my fist, pulling it up to my neck in embarrassment. I could not look in his eyes. He turned and climbed out the open window. I hurried to watch as he swung lightly to a storage box, jumping to the ground. His darkened figure raced for the ferry wharf where a dugout was tied. Dogs barked, but his path was relentless. He had garnered another method for escape, and I hoped his disappearance was for good.

I grabbed my clothes from Robert's bed, grateful the day was over, and sleep was at hand.

CHAPTER 8

A cloud of tobacco smoke curled into my path. Drawn up short, I stopped outside the parlor, rubbing the child's back as he slept, the dead weight of a four year old on my shoulder. The men were engaged in terrible debate.

"—your job, Goldsboro, don't make it my problem. I have fifteen slaves working the harbor. The redemptioner is not worth my time," said Robert.

"You have a responsibility, Morris," shouted Goldsboro. "What gentleman shirks his duty to his employee?"

"The man who secures Oxford's trade," answered Robert in utter calm. "You are welcome to stay for a cup, Sheriff, but I warn you. We are in merry spirits and you will have to fit in."

"Tilghman, do you not support me in this?" asked Goldsboro.

"Do not get me involved," said he. "The town does not want another gibbeted runaway."

"Then I will bring this negligence to the provincial court."

"Of course you will," replied Tilghman, "since your cousins own the lower house. Waste of everyone's time. Whence they convene in September, the Scot will be a distant memory, and Morris will have put more money in your pocket than you can make as sheriff. Do not fall on your own sword, Goldsboro."

I looked over the child's shoulder toward the kitchen quarter. Yearie was nowhere to be found. Having a moment with her prince. They saw each other so rarely, but even I could see the spark between them. The dishes were stacked on the hall service table and needed washing.

The talk of these men distressed me. I would not light candles for their argument and then play the harpsichord for their pleasure. Goldsboro said close by, "I earn my share of our arrangement, gentlemen," and he thumped his boot. "At great effort."

He stalked by me and under his breath sneered, "Ah, Morris' madwoman. Better his than mine."

I drew a quick breath and pressed into the wall, his proximity fixing me with unnatural fear. His yellow-rimmed eyes raked over my being and I buried my face in Tench's softness. The sheriff stopped at the door where Robert's spaniel lay alert. His hand on the knob, he paused, stepped on Tray's tail and ground his spur into his fur. Tray howled, clawed from under his boot, and ran to the safety of the front parlor. Goldsboro tittered at my horror-struck face and stepped into the night.

My head was dizzy, my legs weak, but I swung my attention to the fray in the back parlor and caught Gildart slurring his words, "Catch the ruffian and give em to me. I'll trade him to the English for a right honorable American sailor. I kin wait to sail while ya search for the Scot. Cunliffe's slaving is a long passage."

"...not up to us to decide what business Cunliffe engages," said Robert in a clipped voice. "The journey exists to please our employer. There's little profit in this Scottish detritus compared to the caliginous cargoes you've dropped on our shores."

"I don't care bout neither," retorted Gildart. "I bring em, you bloody colonists decide what to do with em. You'll get your share from Cunliffe, but he won't pay me until he sees the profits on the Scots."

"Captain, the king pays five pounds sterling on a Scotsman.

Cunliffe had no part in the king's demand for transport. *I* contracted for the *Johnson*," answered Robert.

I hid behind the doorframe watching with one eye. Robert tapped his pipe into a bowl. "Know me, Gildart," he said. "I took payment in tobacco receipts for them, lo the middling farmers have no silver. Some will never pay. Out of £520, I'll see as little as 200 in tobacco notes and Spanish reales. The rest is debt. Take half for your trouble."

"There you have it, proving my point. The Scots ain't profitable and the king be damned," slurred Gildart. "Stick to the black trade. Worth more. Oxford might have to brand them, but they don't escape like indentures."

"It's profit and loss, man. If you could guarantee the lives of more than half our black cargo instead of throwing the dead into the seas, we would all be as wealthy as the king," said Robert.

"One might consider our Savior's words about gaining the whole, but losing our souls," said Reverend Bacon.

Gildart guffawed. "Pish on your Savior, Reverend. I haul the healthy ones. Black as night. The printers up and down the colonies publish rewards when they escape. A man can't tell a white indenture from a colonist, but you can see a black plain as a hunchback. Faith and begorrah, that murderous Scot, what's his name? McIntosh — Goldsboro will never find him."

"I have no interest in a malcontent," said Robert. "My dead yeoman had no relatives, and no one's the worse for his loss but me. A dolt, he couldn't read and had no numbers. Five years of indenture would take me that long to train him. Then he's gone to the frontier with some village lass. The Scot's no different, just gifted with a mongrel's tongue."

"Your decision," managed Gildart, fully in his sots.

"Morris, you should consider bringing a shipment to Annapolis. Not field hands," said Tilghman. "No public auction bloc, but the tavern keepers at Middleton and Reynolds would be beholden. Business is brisk. The legislators require house servants, the more intelligent and compliant the better."

I shifted to my other foot and leaned against the table laden with dirty linens. The conversation held me in its grasp like I held the sleeping child. He weighed a ship's ton.

"Interesting," answered Robert. "I am of a mind to bring Mrs. Wise along. To evaluate the requirements of these homes. She is a most excellent housekeeper."

Tench raised his sweaty cheek from my neck and turned his face away. I pushed his curls down and moved closer to miss nothing. My thoughts drifted to Annapolis. In the years I had been in his service, Robert had never taken me anywhere. Dare I feel a tremor of excitement?

"Bring whomever you want," said Tilghman. "Call her by her dead husband's name. She may be more than a blue-eyed kitchen wench, but your son should have access to a proper tutor rather than the woman you call housekeeper.'"

"Provides a service, does she?" snickered Gildart.

There was a pause and the entire room bellowed as one, save Robert. I rolled my hair against the hills and valleys of the doorway's molding and pressed my eyes shut...mocking me, they were, with one word, laden with disdain. Might as well have said, "whore." The kitchen called me forthright, but I was chained to the wall.

"Mrs. Wise is an honorable woman, Gildart. Too honorable for my taste at times," said Robert with a laugh.

"Mores the Morris," cried Gildart, splitting his gut. "Five base-born of Lizzy Murphey in Liverpool and now the youngest follows you here."

"You're no priest, Gildart," snapped Robert. "The boy's mother is dead, God rest her soul. He was raised by his grandmother and she's too aged to persevere."

Five baseborn? My head pounded from too much wine and not enough air. Grappling with the picture of young Robert through the crack in the doorjamb, sprawled on a chair and barely awake, I calculated. His father had arrived in Oxford twelve years hence, so the boy, at thirteen, had been left with his grandmother still in pilchers. Now, he sat listening with one eye open as Gildart insulted me. And Robert had fathered a *family* and never told me.

I sank to the floor. Tench burrowed in my lap dead asleep.

Glasses clinked and I peered round the corner to see them puffing pipes and posing feet. In the candlelight, with swirls of smoke falling round them, they looked like gods holding court in the clouds.

I caught Reverend Thomas' voice over the laughter. "Good Captain, do not take liberty to critique our host in front of his guests. It is not up to us to judge our fellow man."

"I take no offense, Thomas," said Robert. "Anyone who has traveled to Liverpool knows my past. Cunliffe's success on this shore is my success. But heed me. Men have been destroyed by the gossip of the fairer sex, so I am obliged if you don't discuss my former life in the tavern."

They all guffawed, not just drunken Gildart.

"Tilghman," Robert continued, "about the court cases. The reverend has brought the county death rolls. Cunliffe will pay you for representing us in Probate Court. We can attach their property to collect on their slave debt."

I peeked again and could only see the back of his gray silk coat, his arms sweeping as he spoke, laces dancing at his wrist. M'lord, Merry MakeFun, capitalizing on other's pain.

"I am on it, Morris," said Tilghman. "Goldsboro relishes an eviction. I enjoy a day in court, and we split the profits. Cunliffe will never know how much we keep.

"I do not have your education, James, or your gift of sermon, Thomas, but one day I will equal the province's gentry," said Robert. "I'll be painted in oils and hung on the wall like Henry VIII." He chortled. "If not a king, I'll buy myself a knighthood."

His hand spanned the spines of his beloved books, more than 200 on his shelves, the tea caddy and silver cups, porcelain vases and jade boxes, his calligraphy tapestry and carpet from Far East trade. "This is all mine. I may not own the house in which we sit, but these small tracts spread in the backwoods of Talbot to the swamps. With an army of slaves, I can turn it into farmland."

The child nestled in the crook of my elbow, tucked under my breast. I was staggered by his resemblance to Phebe when she was a baby, his blonde curls, painted poppet skin and grey lids that rippled with dreams. I whispered nothings in his ear. Alone together, he felt like mine. The day had been so long and a sharp ringing in my ears left me swimming on the floor.

"Mistress."

I heard the word repeated, then, "Sarah Sahara, come with me."

A woman stood above me in the darkness. Mama? How long had she been watching me? She reached down as if to take the child, but I held the baby tightly. "No, no," I said. "She has just fallen asleep. We must not wake her."

"Sarah, my love. Your skirts swallow you like a great purple cabbage. Your gown will be ruined," she chided. "Come to the kitchen and we'll put her in the cradle. I saved you some lemon cake."

Mama pulled me to my feet and with her arm round my waist, I rested my head against her shoulder as I carried Phebe to the kitchen. "Mama, you are in a state of undress for our company. You should have worn your finery and joined us at dinner." A candle glowed on the worn chopping block, the brick floor had been swept clean and the fire banked for morning, which was her habit of every evening, of every season. A window stood open and a warm breeze carried the smell of salt spray, refreshing my soul. Home.

She set me on the trestle bench, my back against the coolness of the log wall and took Phebe from my arms. The weight was lifted and although I savored my baby's sweetness, I knew Mama's hands were safe. "Tuck her in tight," I said. "so no one can steal her in the night."

"Now, now. Stop this nonsense. The child be fine," said Mama as she laid her in the cradle.

I gazed at Phebe and marveled at her length. Her tiny feet were propped on the rail edge. She had grown so, filling it to my surprise.

"We must ask Edward to make a rope bed for her. She barely fits of the cradle now, so robust she is of a sudden."

Mama handed me a plate of lemon cake glazed with crystal sugar, and I wolfed it leaning to one side on the cushion. Licking my fingers, I caught her watching me with a critical eye. "Please don't scold," I said. "I know I'm not behaving like a lady, but I am so tired." Sitting up slightly, I patted the bench. "Come, Mama. You must be, too." She set next to me, and again I nestled in her goodness. She was lemon and bayberry, tallow and yeast bread, and wood from the fire all rolled in one.

"Sarah, you forget how old Phebe was. I be here to watch this child tonight." A hand patted mine. "Drink this weak tea and go to sleep. I be makin your excuse to the men. They only want to smoke in the back parlor and jaw on their perfection."

The details of our lives escaped me at night when my thoughts were so crowded. Besides, sometimes Mama spoke in puzzles. The day had been full of demands. Edward would come to me later, wake me from my sleep and hold me in his arms.

"What about Phebe? Will you sleep here instead of your bedroom?"

"Sary, you know where I sleep. You know who I be."

The tone of Mama's voice lay heavy on me. I hated to displease her. Gazing in her eyes I saw they were no longer blue but dark brown. Fear gripped my chest, my mind a blank and I didn't want to know more. I struggled to my feet and murmured good night, kissing her cheek.

"I be helpin you undress?" she asked.

"No, no," I said, feeling confused. "Stay with Phebe. I'll sleep but awhile and will come down for her. My love abides in yours."

She quickly loosened the laces of my stomacher and it fell away, held only by a pin under my arm. As I turned to go, she deftly loosened my bodice and stays. Freedom. Breathing deeply, I grabbed a wet kitchen linen and wiped the powder from my heated bosom. A brown hand reached for it and I looked into Yearie's smiling eyes. Mama had gone. I nodded to her. "Oh. My Yearie," I said and walked to the hallway taking a sputtering candle from the table.

CHAPTER 9

riday, 15 September, 1747

A month later, I had made my way to the sheep collective and watched as a nuthatch tore headfirst down a dead pine determined to hide a large seed in the bark. As big as his beak, the kernel was a prince's trove, and the little fellow defied flight in stashing his secret. Food. Worth more than a Maryland four-dollar bill. I nodded thinking of my chamber loot.

I had eaten buttered cornbread at dawn and brought with me a leather flask of cider. I wished for a day of rest to think of light and air and…security. I realized I would never love Robert, nor he me. It was the state of many unions, and… I wanted more.

A breeze ruffled my milkmaid's cap, the lace lifting off the damp hollow of my neck. Tying Ol Bets' reins to the split rail under the shade of the nuthatch's tree, I gazed at the sheep scattered across the field. Rolls of tan wool in pea green grass. There was not a shepherdess in sight.

There is little interest in keeping sheep since the sotweed takes everyone's energy. A shame. Mama warned never ignore the smallest possession, for once gone its real worth is mourned. Phebe's taking was an ever-present ache of guilt as I had made the decision to beg for food as she lay sleeping. Essentials evaporate, steam from a pot. Cloth, children, a mother's love. Before I was born the Crown's tax on wool made our sheep valuable. Now, I had all the clothing a woman could want.

Mama admonished when I left our cottage for the pasture, "Sarah, do not allow a thieving stranger to shear any of our sheep. You could lose your hand to the henchman's ax."

The thought of being one-handed was meant to terrify, though it was no longer true. I took my task of sheep tending seriously. So many tasks, but few I loved as much as carrying a distaff and drop spindle in the field, whirling yarn for my mother to weave. Times have changed. Robert laughs at me when I leave for the meadow saying he can send for as much finished Irish wool as the colony needs. It doesn't matter that he says we needn't spin as we have in the near past. Not everyone can afford what he trades.

So, a few years ago, I gathered a group of plain Quaker women who kept the memory of our warp and weft on their looms. Strong linen thread stretched in place, back and forth from edge to edge of the large wooden frame, forms the warp. Using the soft natural wool spun from our sheep, the women shuttle the weft over and under the linen producing a good amount of linsey woolsey. Rough and given to slubs of uneven thickness unlike Irish wool, no plantation wife deigns to wear it.

Good for the rest of us. The Quaker ladies keep to their weaving houses summer and winter. They work their looms for bed clothes, plain jackets and skirts, and children's dresses. Or for my purposes — as winter clothes for slaves. The rest of the village doesn't need to know. If some is given to the slaves on the large plantations, it is my secret to keep. In like kind, it's the secret Reverend Bacon keeps as the minister of all manner of men. The warp and weft of our village.

I walked the tall grasses and the sheep barely moved, lazy in the heat. Close to the rail, I found a newborn bleating for its mother. Her fly-covered carcass lay close, the victim of a recent wolf attack. I picked up the lamb, stowing it under my arm. It would have to be fed by hand to keep it alive, and I had no time to nurse it. I bowed my head in a quick prayer for the little tyke.

I heard a shout from the road and recognized Reverend Thomas.

"Mrs. Sarah, good day to you! You have a new charge, I see."

He reined in his pony trap that was filled with cloth from the good Quaker women. Covered baskets sat upon the floor. My heart sank as I wondered what he would require of me.

"Robert and his son are still in Annapolis?" he asked, doffing his cockhat.

I stepped near to take a closer look, lifting the covers. Scraps of linen and soap, broken buttons, thimbles and combs, and rusted iron pots filled his cart. Things that our villagers threw in kitchen middens.

"Thomas, we are friends, but you must not ask me to go with you," I said full of sorrow. "Robert would not be happy."

"Good Sarah, I must have a gentlewoman to accompany me in order to approach Mistress Handy. She's not friendly to men of the cloth as Reverend Maynadier was oft to remind me."

My hand came up between us. The little lamb wiggled to break free, and in its struggle wrapped its front legs around my neck, hiding under my cap.

"God rest his soul. We all remember his feud with Findley, but Robert would never countenance my interference on the Handy plantation. You have God behind you. I don't."

"Would that I could call the hand of God, my dear. Their slaves are tortured in Findley's care. I needn't tell you. Yearie spoke to me of Jackson's whipping after you retired the night of your dinner party."

"She didn't! Yearie would never overstep!"

"It was my fault. I could not avoid seeing Jackson groaning with fever in the kitchen, and when he turned from me, I saw the putrid flesh of his back. I demanded to know whose hand. I knew it couldn't be Robert's. He has no great love for any slave, but neither would he beat them within an inch of their life."

I leaned across the seat to set the little lamb by Thomas' side. It snuggled nearer and curled in a ball. "There!" I said. "You have to take this orphan to Mistress Handy and plead for its life. One of their slaves will find an ewe to nurse it." I grabbed the lamb's chin and looked into its golden eye. An unfocused ovum stared, docile, and the lamb nuzzled my palm. "Better you than me, little lamb," I whispered.

Thomas laughed and slapped his hat across his knee, startling the poor creature. "Mistress Sarah, you are a conniving wench. I implore you to accompany me and put the lamb in Mistress Handy's care yourself."

I pretended affront. I am rarely surprised at any man's choice of words. "You call me wench? I have an education, and I'm not your servant."

"No, no, of course. You know everyone in the village and beyond, better than your grand tradesman and certainly better than I, their vicar. I am beholden to you for your guidance."

He was chastened. He and Robert were friends but of a different cloth. They shared their love of music, wine, and the writings of the Greeks. They despised the Papists of the colony and fostered their persecution under the penal laws. From that point on, their opinions diverged. Robert believed in money and his right to make it. Thomas believed in his king and God, in that order.

And that had brought me to this juncture with a lamb, a cart full of lynsey woolsey, and carefully curated rubbish. Thomas knew I felt obligated to care for the desperate, the abandoned, and even the slaves on the Handy plantation, for no one else would. I put my hand up and he pulled me into the cart.

"I know I will regret this," I said as I whistled at Bets, leaving her grazing contentedly under the tree. Thomas cracked the whip and touched my hand in reassurance. The nuthatch had disappeared, probably in search of more seed in his upside down, flightless world.

The road out of Oxford was not well grubbed after summer rains. Connecting the provincial courts in East Town and Thomas' church at White Marsh with the ferry in Oxford, the road was vital to law and religion, if not commerce. Barely wide enough for two carriages to pass if one pulled over on the embankment, the road needed the constant attention of the sheriff's men.

The Handy plantation lay above the harbor on the Tred Avon more than hour by cart, less by fast horse, and even less by sail on a windy day. Coming by canoe to the harbor, Findley had made the tavern a favored haunt. But for the reverend and me, plying the river when all manner of craft were a' sail would risk gossip. I resigned myself to the bumpy ride and attempted conversation to lighten our journey.

"I hear Mr. Quinn is gathering a contingent of like-minded players to show *The Beggar's Opera* at the tavern," I said. "It will be a great success, you know."

"I am against it," said Thomas. "We do not need the town commoners rollicking in their cups against the king while they watch thieves and whores singing meaningless ditties."

"Why, Reverend, one would think you did not enjoy a tankard!"

"You mistake my meaning, Sarah. It is your singular characteristic, toying with men."

"Never, Thomas." I opened my fan and stuffed it in my bodice for I was bobbing about as two jellied fish in the bay. "I never toy with a man, especially a married one, because your sex is not known for its constraint," I said sternly. "I think the opera would be great fun."

"Because Quinn wants you to sing the part of Polly? You find the affair between innocent Polly Peachum and that lout MacHeath titillating. But you are naive if you think it won't add to village talk that you helped the Scotsman escape. They call him Mac the knife."

"Thomas, that is beneath you! Quinn is the root of all gossip in Oxford. He libels me to cover his true intentions."

"What, pray, madame, would they be?"

"He collects names of villagers who are secret patriots."

"Well," he said emphatically, "I agree with his intent, but he inflates his importance if he thinks he could catch the king's ear."

"Honestly, Thomas, you really are obtuse at times. It's not the king he seeks to inform."

"Who then?"

"Our sheriff," I said.

"Goldsboro? He holds entirely too much power." Thomas whipped the pony through a muddy pond in the road. "Subjugates everyone in his path."

"My sentiments exactly." So, Thomas had the interests of

Oxford's residents at heart no matter what their allegiances. Most had struggled for decades, hacking their lives out of the tobacco trade to put clothes on their backs and God in their hearts.

"Robert and I have influence," he said. "Goldsboro wants to tax those who seek independence. It will only get backsides up."

"He goes beyond unfair taxes. The man's a beast who values no one's life but his own."

"Oxford has its lazy element. Leash him and he will take it out on the populace."

"I suppose that's how he saw me after Mama died. Lazy element."

"He saw you as a prospect, my dear. A defenseless lamb to steal."

Thomas grew quiet and I held the lamb in my lap for comfort. Disagreeable words. I was anxious and hungry as we turned the corner into Handy Lane. The manor house was not visible from the road which was raked in perfect furrows of pea stone. On either side, naked blacks toiled in the fields, their bodies glistening with sweat as they hoed long ribbons of green leaves that ran as far as the eye could see. Beside them, women and children plucked fat hornworms that ate the sweet sot. Their work would not be done by sunset. It would never be done. I shut my eyes against the flashing sunbeams.

CHAPTER 10

*T*he tree-lined lane opened to a great clapboard edifice. Two and a half stories grew from arched brick windows at the foundation that revealed an underworld for workers. Centered in a massive black door was a square brass lock guarded by a liveried Negro who ran down the carved stone steps to grab the pony's bridle. Another spoke to Thomas and raced up the steps to knock. He turned to his side and announced us to the butler as if Thomas were King's Groom of the Stool.

I giggled as Thomas handed me down from the cart and whispered, "Watch out, my good reverend, or you will be emptying the privy before we leave."

He laughed. "Would that Handy trusted me as a privy council, if he had one."

"Oh, he does. That would be Robert."

The door swept wide revealing Mistress Handy in rose silk regalia. He muttered an "A-hem," bowing at the foot of the steps. Standing behind him, I was self-conscious of my attire, a shepherdess fresh from the field. I stepped to his side, smoothed my blue linen skirts and curtsied, my head down. As I raised my eyes to hers,

I saw the same smirk of derision I had met that day on the wharf. I clutched the lamb tighter.

"I am honored the village organizers have come for a visit," she said. "You are welcome, but do not request handouts for your poor. We do enough to support your licentious populace."

Thomas lumbered up the staircase and stretched his hand to kiss hers. "M' lady. Mistress Wise and I come bearing gifts, not to ask your help."

She removed her hand from his grasp. "Reverend Bacon," she said, fingers fluttering across her breast as if she were a girl presented with a suitor, "gifts for me?"

"'Tis true, Mistress Handy," I said from the drive. "We have brought supplies for your slaves, but the reverend is incorrect. We do ask one small favor. Would your shepherd take this poor lamb and succor it to one of your ewes, for its mother is dead."

"Supplies for the slaves?" Her face wrinkled like a prune. "We will have to see. I have no problem with the lamb. Follow Cyrano to the field, girl, and give it to the old slave at the gate." She stepped aside and waved a hand into the cool darkness. "Reverend Bacon, you are welcome to come in for a cup of tea. Cook is busy with baking today. Do you have a sweet tooth?"

Demeaning fussock not to offer me a cake or tea. My stomach growled. I shook my head and pushed the lamb into Cyrano's arms although his livery coat was probably cleaner than my apron. As we passed the workers' well, I scooped a drink from the bucket, and Cyrano watched over the lamb's fuzzy ears with sympathy.

My thirst slaked, I followed him down a dirt lane canopied by large oaks. Shortly, we came to the field. White-wooled and black-faced, the sheep's pristine beauty was a marvel. Each was branded on its neck with an H.

"Old Cyclops, mistress has orders," shouted Cyrano.

Out of a lean-to came a wizened dark creature propped up by a tall staff and clothed in a shift of sacking that matched his skin. Like all the slaves his feet were bare, whitened, and crusted with callouses. Tight white curls ringed a brown skull roped with muscle.

He bowed before me and, upon his rising, I saw that one eye was an empty socket.

"Good day, kind sir," I said. "Your mistress has offered your skills in fostering this lamb."

He grunted and swung the gate wide. Cyrano dropped the lamb at Cyclops' feet and ran from us, no doubt concerned that he not abandon his post as footman. I scooted the lamb in front of me as the gate swung in place.

With surprise in his voice, Cyclops said, "Young mistress stay?"

"I have nowhere else to go. I was accompanied by the Reverend Bacon who has been invited inside. The lamb has been in my charge since we left the village. I found its mother dead this morn."

"Ya come all dis way from Oxford jus?" he asked, his one brown eye locked on mine.

"Near two hours ago. Our pony is slow. We come carrying items to improve your life."

"I no need items, my lady."

"Surely you will need warmer clothes before winter?"

Silent, he led me, pointing at sheep droppings on our way to a cluster of white humps that sheltered under a large oak tree. As we drew closer, he gathered a small, supple hide of white wool from a stump and corralled my brown lamb with his staff. The baby had grown attached and bleated for me. I ran to it.

"No, lady. Not to touch again."

He tied the hide over my lamb's back and from a gourd shook a yellow liquid into his cupped palm. Rubbing this over the head and chest of my little lamb, I realized he was covering my scent with the urine of another sheep. He jerked his chin toward an ewe that easily topped my weight by four stone.

"She lost newborn two day ago," he said. "We be quick for her to take your lamb afore her milk dry up."

Better than my hand feeding a lamb. But then, Mama and I rarely had more than four at a time. They were as much our pets as our future clothing.

He kicked the lamb toward the ewe, and we watched as she sniffed. She pushed it away, doubting, but my lamb nosed in search of a teat. She must have been about to burst and after a sideways step, she stood still, her ears to the wind and let the lamb suckle. Fooled! I squealed in amazement, clapping my hands.

Old Cyclops tottered over to sit under a neighboring tree. He unwrapped a rag and held out a piece of moldy cheese and a hunk of stale brown bread. "Hungry, mistress? I share. Dis my food."

His boney legs were folded, the skin like desiccated brown silk. I couldn't take his food away.

"Kind Cyclops, eat your dinner. You need to gain some weight before the cold sets in," I said with great confidence. "Our presents of wools will keep you warmer this fall."

His one eye smiled and his lips spread wide in a toothless grin. "Slave not eat to store, we eat to live nother day. Whatever mistress bring go to young who work field. I not be here by winter."

"Oh, are you going to live with your family?" In his aged state, I was sure Master Handy would retire this devoted slave to those who cared for him.

I was met with silence and his outstretched hand of crusted bread.

"No, no. I can't. We are here to provide."

"Mistress, my family be at Rich Neck, Master Tilghman plantation."

"Then that's where you should go."

"I have dis crocus dress to wear and I sleep with de sheep, so I not get cold." His one eye contemplated me. "He sell me here, Master Tilghman. Be so old, I not able to work his terbaccer so Handy buy me for his sheep. Give me work. I be grateful."

I was confused. Tilghman had just bragged that as a good master he provided for his slaves. He said food, clothing. Was old and infirm not part of his bargain?

Incensed, I said, "If Mistress Handy has no plan for you this winter, I will discuss it with her."

His eye bulged and he reared back against the tree trunk. Bread-crumbs spilled from his gums and his gnarled fingers fluttered at me.

"Please, young mistress not remind my master of me. I die in peace." He pointed to his sheep. "Dar wool clean, mistress. I pick dem each day."

I was upsetting this old man. My intention was to bring him comfort and security and all I did was bring him another lamb to tend, a lamb who found a family. He believed he would die soon and probably with more certainty than I had in marrying Robert. I bent my head and asked God to bring him safely to everlasting life with all the saints.

Cyclops wept and stumbled over words of thanks, saying no one had ever uttered a prayer for him. With as much composure as I could muster, I told him Reverend Bacon would know of his passing when the oak leaves fell. We would attend service with his people and bid his soul Godspeed. It was a lie, of course, because Handy would never broadcast his death and the slaves on his plantation had no voice. I left him sitting in his field looking into the sun as if for deliverance. Shaking my skirts free of grass, I walked to the gate and down the path, hoping that Thomas had finished his tea and cake.

CHAPTER 11

*A*t the carriage way, I found the pony cart gone and Thomas descending the front steps. Mistress Handy waved her goodbyes, but upon seeing me she stepped from view and the front door swung slowly shut.

"Success, dear Sarah!" said Thomas.

"Do tell. I need a happy word!"

I fell in by his side as he strode toward the stable. Hungry, I skipped to keep up and looked to see if he had brought food. His hands waved about as they did from the pulpit but his deep pocket bulged. Was it goodies for me?

"She will allow us to bring household items for their use twice a year, but claims she must inspect it before her people unload the cart. She was particularly happy about the wool since she has more Negro women weaving for the main house bedding, but they aren't quick enough. In return, she will gift them the family's old bedding. A good trade."

"Oh, yes…maybe eight family beds for sixty slaves?" My sarcasm was not lost on him. I asked, "And what about food, Thomas? Did you ask what she feeds them?"

"They take the butchering seconds, get some dairy and have their

68

own kitchen gardens, which I gather are quite extensive. From her account, they are not wanting for victuals."

"Her account," I said, vexed. "Why that old man who tends the sheep was eating moldy cheese and it was his ration for the day."

"Now, Sarah," he answered, his hand on my wrist in warning. "You need to avoid her as it will not be good for our mission. She called you an interfering busybody. Do not take offense. We need to be discreet to get what we want."

My feet slowed as my mind wrapped around his words.

Thomas kept walking and when he realized I wasn't by his side, he turned and said, "Your place is to gather the goods to bring to the plantations. We will make the visits together, but I will do all the speaking. It's not your place to negotiate with your betters."

"Thomas, only three hours ago this was my point as we spoke in the village field—that you have God behind you, and I don't. Then you bring me here to see this misery and now I must stand silent?"

"Good woman, that is not my intention. Come, let's get the cart. I have some treats for you to eat on our way home."

I looked back at the manor house and gazed at the blank windows. I thought I saw a figure behind the glass. The slightest movement and the curtain dropped. Thomas followed my eyes.

"Did you see that brass lock in the front door?" he said. "Only Mistress Handy carries the key and she watches the butler lock when a guest arrives or leaves. The door is keyed from the inside."

"They are afraid?" I asked.

"Undoubtedly."

The stable was down a shaded lane lined with water troughs and hitching posts on either side. Bay doors were open for each stall to let in a breeze and many fine racehorses neighed at our presence. A slave boy beckoned us inside where our pony was idly munching on hay. The blacksmith stood over a forge turning pokers in the white-hot coals and darts of live ash flew in the darkness. My eyes adjusted to the orange glow of the fire and I saw Findley, the Handy overseer, watching from a shadowed corner, whispering to someone who stood behind a post.

I heard a groan. A shard of light from a window revealed a man, dark as coal, and a lighter-skinned woman, sitting in the dirt, clutching each other. Their eyes were drawn to another bent over near our pony, his hands tied behind his back. Stripped to the waist his skin glowed pearly white, his thin chest heaved, the look of a wild animal was caught in his eyes.

As Thomas and I watched open-mouthed, Findley seized a rope and threw it over a roof beam. He tied the other end to the man's wrists bound behind his back. He said, "See if you do it again," and pulled on the rope, dragging the man upward, his arms distended behind him ready to pop out of his shoulders. One long scream curdled my blood.

It was then the figure emerged from behind the post and in the darkness of the stable, I recognized Goldsboro, his hounds loping behind. Tiberius remained in the shadows.

"Careful of his arms. We want the ship's carpenter kept whole," said the sheriff.

The muscles and veins of the man's neck bulged and lengthened. His visage purpled and he spluttered trying to command his pain. His legs stilled and he faced the dirt floor like an animal ready for slaughter. Findley secured the rope around a post and stood under him, looking up.

"Master Handy grows weary of your escape, John Suter. I'm not accustomed to branding my brethren, but you have earned it like no other."

Findley grabbed an iron and jabbed it on the man's neck. Skin sizzled and smoked. The man screamed again and went limp. Mercifully, the overseer unwound the rope and John Suter, the redemptioner, fell in a ball to the dirt. The smell of burnt flesh permeated the dank air.

"Sarah, you must leave this minute," said Thomas. "I will speak to Findley." He took my arm and spun me toward the open doors.

I yanked my arm from his grasp and held my fists to my breast. "No, Thomas, better to have two witness this."

Goldsboro clucked. "The good woman and her vicar desire a show. Give it to them."

The smithy strode to the black man, grabbed him by his chains and pulled him to his feet. Shackled, he wobbled and the smithy spit in the black man's eye. Findley hollered, "Hold him still!" and plunged the poker on the slave's cheek, letting it burn long before he pulled it away. The slave moaned. A raw "R" covered him from cheek to jawbone. The blacksmith threw him against John Suter and turned for the woman.

It was then I saw the babe in arms. She had suckled to keep it quiet, but as the smithy tore it from her, throwing it on the cool dirt, it wailed and crawled to its mother. I could not contain myself and ran to pick the babe up. Findley advanced toward me, but I reached it first and shielded it from him.

"Mistress Wise! You, who can't discipline your own slaves," he shouted. "Have you come for a lesson? I can oblige."

The freshly branded young slave writhed upon the ground, his eyes flashing as he said, "I won't *never* run way no more."

I was struck dumb, looking from one to the other, holding the baby to my breast with my shoulder to Findley who bobbled his head over me and the child, taunting.

Thomas shouted over the din, "Master Findley, Sheriff Goldsboro, no one challenges your territory. Please, we will take our leave. Sarah, put the child down and let's make haste!"

"I will not!"

Findley turned from me and grabbed a hot iron from the fire. I feared that he would burn me, but instead he headed to the blacksmith who held the woman by her elbows.

"Yes!" shouted Goldsboro. "Do it." He drew a handkerchief from his sleeve and dabbed at his face, "Hurry, these sparks hurt my eyes."

Looking over his shoulder at me, Findley shouted, "Here you Papist whore. Look and learn!"

The blacksmith pulled the scarf from her head and buried his hand in her thick hair, holding her cheek to the poker. Her eyes widened following the orange brand. Findley toyed, drawing it near and far, then said, "Bathsheba, every night you will sit in shackles in the master's cellar so he can have his fill of you. You will birth his children. And when the master is done, you'll have mine." He plunged the hot brand to her cheek. She stumbled, a small wail burst forth, but she never fell.

I ran past Findley, holding the baby tight. In a blur, his arm came out, clenched my shoulder and he pulled me to him, the baby between us. Bloodshot eyes, heated breath. From behind him I heard the faceless wail of its mother, "Mistress, take my baby. Run!"

Findley grinned, those yellow teeth so close, a tiny hole through which the tip of his tongue flicked. His grip loosened, an opening to escape. I hesitated as he pushed me toward the reverend, letting me go. The baby's weight, his whimper in my ear, his slick blackness was too...onerous. I was merely a servant.

"Sarah," came Thomas' voice. "Come. Now!"

Findley felt me waver and my chance was gone. "What would Morris say about your black baby?" He drew me close. "Watch, missy," he said and shoved me to the ground, grabbing the baby by its ankle and held it upside down as his victory. Its wrap fell—a boy, a fine boy. The mother screamed. Findley jammed the brand against its thigh. The baby shrieked, losing his wits.

I crawled across the dirt, sobbing, "No, Findley, no! You will burn in hell. I will tell Master Morris what you have done today."

The sheriff exploded in laughter, watching the whole from a distance, then thought better and took steps in my direction, his spurs clicking, his dogs faces wavering near. He stepped on my skirt. "The preposterous Mrs. Wise. How naive." His hand came under my arm and pulling me up, he slowly ran the back of his other hand down my neck to my bosom as he drew me to him. Yellow-rimmed, his pale eyes roved into my cleavage and I felt the twist of his fingers on my nipple. "When I come for you, housekeeper, you will pay again," he said.

I turned my head and watched out the corner of my eye as Findley dropped the child into the grit. Against the dirt his wound gleamed red. "Sheriff's only sorry he ain't do it himself," he said.

I tore my dress from Goldsboro's heel and stumbled to Thomas. Stepping backward, yet drawn by the tragedy before us, we watched as Bathsheba struggled free of the smithy. She scooped up her bellowing baby and leaned against a post. Taking in her situation, she weakened and slid to the hard ground where she rocked, moaning and jiggling the inconsolable child. Looking up, her eye caught an iron dibble stick hanging from a nail and her eyes focused with intent. She glared at Findley's back the most hateful look and cast one sorrowful gaze on me, full of recrimination. Taking the sharp implement, she drove its point into her baby's chest. The child beheld its mother's love, surprise written on its fat cheeks, its lips rounded in an O. Blood grew like a flower that opens to the moon at night.

"Sarah, come with me, *now*!" yelled Thomas, dragging me along.

In blinding sunlight, Cyrano held our pony's rein. In a studied voice and unflinching eye, he took my dirty hand to lift me in, and whispered, "Mistress, you just another do-gooder. Get gone."

I sobbed.

Behind me, Findley shouted, "Throw that pickaninny in the dung heap." Thomas cracked his whip. Wild-eyed, the pony sensed our fear and tore down the drive to the Oxford road.

CHAPTER 12

Gulping air, I said, "Thomas, we must do something! We must stop them!"

"Who? Findley? Don't be foolish. He's protected by Samuel Handy. And forget Goldsboro. His wealth and family give him license, never mind he's our sheriff."

"Branding like they are common animals! Slaves have souls, Thomas, even our law says so—that they aren't chattel. For God's sake, Thomas. We are Christians!" I heard my voice, strident, cracking. "That baby is dead. The slave who tends the sheep…he's planning his death to save himself from a cold winter of want."

"Handy can do whatever he likes with his slaves." Thomas' eyes fluttered, "I object to unruly redemptioners being treated the same as runaway slaves. Handy can add years on an indenture for every attempt at escape."

"A child died today before your eyes. Have you no sympathy for that mother and her babe?"

"I do. Not as much as I do for your loss of Phebe. That slave murdered her own child. You turned your head at the wrong time."

He had changed the subject. I grew confused and his words struck me silent, lessening my guilt. Was it equal? A baby killed by its own mother and a five-year-old stolen from her bed by Indians? He knew what a pitiable subject it was, how it clouded my reasoning.

I took a deep breath. "Why did the church council not give me an allowance? If I hadn't been reduced to begging for food, I might have been at home when she was taken."

"It is the greatest sorrow of my life, Sarah."

He would not look at me and I studied his profile, waiting. Feeling my stare, he cracked his whip in the air.

"Goldsboro was angry that you did not accept his proposal. He was determined to force your hand and forbade me from providing you with assistance. I should have stood up to him, but I was new to the parish and didn't want to disrupt the ruling order."

"The ruling order? What kind of monsters do you think the patriarchy is? Most are good men on the church council, not like Handy. Why did you not ask them?"

"I did. That's how Robert discovered your predicament. That's why he made his offer and promised to care for you. You are the one who wasted time, not accepting it right away. When Goldsboro discovered he was competing with Robert, he was livid."

"But, but...Phebe's taking had nothing to do with Goldsboro. He said it was an Indian raiding party."

"Sarah. Why did no one else see this raiding party in town that night? Do you think the town is not on alert?"

I fell silent. "Taking Phebe wouldn't force my hand in promise. It only made me lost." I could not remember exactly. I would ask Yearie, though on this, she muttered prayers and was silent.

"Well, you wouldn't have been lost if Goldsboro suddenly made her appear again. You would have been grateful to him."

"He knew where she was? Where, Thomas? I must know. Perhaps she's still alive!"

"I only speculate. I shouldn't give you false hope. She's gone, Sarah. Probably sold to a northern tribe," he said. "Let us leave this unhappiness."

His face grayed in the bright sunlight. Thomas was incapable of understanding his contribution to my misery, and I was offended by his bemused arrogance, that I could just put the loss of my child aside. He was new to our town, new to ministering. Like the rest of Oxford, I hungered for a direct message from God— that Phebe's loss had some meaning. Thomas wasn't providing it. Yet, an earthly anger shook me that Goldsboro lied. The sheriff set out alone to search for her and returned quickly, empty-handed.

Thomas was droning on. We hit a bumpy patch in the road and the slave baby's wails echoed in my ears, his pink mouth open wide.

"—your purity in the eyes of others. I did not arrange for Robert to bring you into his home for a stalemate between you two."

"What mean you? There's no stalemate. He proposed and I accepted. He will post banns in November at the end of shipping season."

"Two more months for you to live in sin."

I blustered. Why was my future such a topic for discussion? "Thomas," I said, "I am a widow of little consequence, and my "purity" a thing of the past. You do not know of what you speak. Robert values me for my household talents, not some ephemeral virginity. We do not share a bed."

"You split hairs. Men value beauty, Sarah," he said shaking his head. "You live in his home and are always a challenge."

He paused, took a sidelong look at me and in his vicar voice said, "It's my duty to counsel you as a gentlewoman of some standing in Oxford. You risk your future by playing with the bastardy laws. You could spend months in gaol if you are with child without benefit of Robert's hand. Goldsboro arrests on rumors. Robert must publish banns immediately or marry you now."

We had reached the juncture of town creek, the river and beyond, the broader Bay. I stared off at the Chesapeake, its waters flat and gray. A dark ridge of western shore looked like an unknown future, one that would never be mine. Nearby, the shipyard bustled with broad shouldered men, both black and white, hammering planks on a schooner's ribs. Ships dotted the river, their graceful lines and white sails moving seamlessly across the water carrying the stuff that made some men wealthy, including my Morris. Very little of it benefitted the townspeople who paid inordinate sums for those raw goods.

I couldn't look at Thomas without seeing Bathsheba's eyes in quiet recrimination. My heart seemed to skip beats, heavy and awful. Tears leaked down my cheeks. I was insignificant next to the industry of these men. Tobacco and authority and laws counted. I kept their system in good stead as did so many women, for if we gave up, if we all escaped to the frontier, we would only die an early death.

Thomas had never spoken so plainly of my standing and risk. His moralizing rang true.

"You are my friend, good sir," I answered, "Please, speak with m'lord about the banns and do not give in to gossip. I am not with child. Robert's mind is with his business, not me."

Thomas patted my hand in comfort. My sensibilities were ravaged, all pretension of reason gone. When I looked in Thomas' eyes to see if he felt the same, I saw deep worry. "Thomas," I said. "you must tell Robert what transpired today."

"Findley's soul will burn in hell, Sarah, but he is spurred by the sheriff. My dilemma is that all slaves work for the glory of God. As their Christian masters, they must obey us." He laid the whip on the pony and said with a certain pomposity, "I am preparing a sermon on this subject."

Exasperated, I pleaded, "Not a sermon. You must intervene. They have feelings for family just as we. They are sinew, and bone, and red blood like us. Do you not feel responsible?"

"That goes too far, Sarah. You interfere. Robert is a good man. He has provided me funds to open a school for the boys of Oxford, including the Negro boys. They must all learn to read and write. Now, marry Robert and be a dutiful wife."

Anger seared me. As the sun beat down, my head began to ache from hunger. I swayed on the seat. Thomas spoke sharply and handed me a skin filled with cider. Straightening my back, I said, "I am dutiful. You could marry us this week in the parlor, but he is too busy. Only recently has he begun to allow me to help him with his accounting."

"He wavers because of the perception Oxford has of you. Honestly, you could be more demure."

Thomas was walking high in the instep critiquing my behavior, lumping me with his doctrine that every slave received eternal salvation for a life of obedience. Now he was going to educate them so they could read it in the Bible. He believed my own salvation was in question when he added one more layer of guilt. "Your master wants schooling for young Rob, more than you can provide. You can help me. I believe we can fund the school and you can teach the children of Oxford."

I ignored his plea for help. "Young Robert doesn't suffer from a lack of rules. He suffers from lack of a father. He runs off the minute I call him to lessons."

"Exactly. Like the rest of our village ruffians. Young bucks who defy their parents' authority. Who knows if they are behind the thievery in town?"

"Rob has no reason to steal. His father provides him with everything he could possibly want," I said. "Except time and fondness."

We paused at the field of village sheep and I tied my Bets to the back of the cart, saving me a lonely ride home. I had eaten nothing since the cornbread at dawn, but I was no longer hungry. I wanted to be at my kitchen fire with Yearie carding wool. Reaching our courtyard, Thomas reined in and as I stepped down, I saw exhaustion on his face. The day had taken its toll on him. He bid me goodbye complaining about the long ride home. I reached and patted his hand. He smiled weakly, and I thought his eyes watered. The weight of it all was so great.

CHAPTER 13

*E*vening was nigh, the western sky aflame, beckoning arms of light to the frontier. I was glad to see the large oak casting its protective shade and hear the quiet voices of Yearie and Hestia through the kitchen window. I wanted to share the day with them, but Robert's bellow interrupted. He had returned from Annapolis with his son, and I could tell he was three sheets to the wind.

Wearily, I tied Bets in her stall. Jackson appeared, bleary-eyed from a nap in the hay. He filled her water trough and began to curry her without me asking.

"Jackson, how be your wounds?"

"They heal, mistress." He bobbed in deference and I waved my hand.

"No need for that between us," I said.

Robert's spaniel bounded in and jumped all over me. My apron was filthy, so I removed it and my milkmaid's cap. Though my skirt hem was blackened as if I had trudged through the wetlands, I would say nothing of my day to Robert, only that I would organize the village girls to watch the sheep. He would roll his eyes in disbelief, the great merchant of fine cloth.

I sighed and smoothed my skirts. The summer sun perched like an orange ball over the water, cushioned above a line of black trees. A reminder of the smithy's forge. The cicadas' song swelled and died as the kitchen door groaned open. At the sight of me, Yearie squinted at my face and dress, then gave an imperceptible jerk of her head as she bid me good evening. She took the crumpled apron from my hand. Hestia was busy over the fire and Robert leaned against the kitchen cupboard.

His wig was windblown from the trip across the Chesapeake and his forehead smitten with the sun's blush. I grabbed a wedge of corn-bread from the table and walked to him, leaned against his chest and nuzzled his lips to give him a bite and then one for me. Gone for some days, predictably he would be affectionate, and it was my choice one more time if I would finally respond. I weakened, wanting a loving man's arms. My caring slipped away, defiant of Bacon's words. It was only two months' wait.

"My love," he said. "Where've you been? I expected you here when I arrived home."

"On a mission of mercy with the good reverend." Oh, the exhaustion in my voice.

His shirt smelled of salt and bay winds and seeing me open, he began his tired litany of reasons why he cared for me. I was his comfort in the storm, a diamond of the first water, no better beauty for his French couture. His eyes gleamed with the win of his trade deals and he claimed that our lives would be as rich as the greatest nobles of Europe. He said the rank and file would come to us pleading for sustenance.

"But, Robert, surely as you spread wealth in the colony there will be no rank and file left. Won't we all be like the ancient Phoenicians, rich and worldly?"

"Of course we will, my love. And the slaves will all be liveried in our colors. I will commission a family painting of us, you in your finery and me with my books and a globe." He clasped my shoulders and stood me in front of him like a child. "What is wrong? Something has happened in my absence."

"It was horrible, horrible," I said, my voice breaking, all my determination gone. "A killing at the Handy plantation."

"What?" he exclaimed. "Who has been murdered? We will report it to the sheriff at once!"

"Oh, Goldsboro was behind it. A slave child, Robert. A mother stabbed her own babe to save it from Findley's torture."

His hands fell from my shoulders and he turned away, his eyes on his goblet of wine. "Sarah, Sarah," he said, shaking his head. "You must not expose yourself to these savages. The Handy plantation is full of newly arrived Africans, unwashed and barbaric. The sheriff was protecting you from them." His nose came close to touching mine. "Besides, the mother is the murderer."

"How can you say that?" I said, pulling back, Yearie and Hestia's eyes on me. "You weren't there. Findley is cruel to their slaves."

"I won't hear another word," he said. "Slaves are like dogs. Some are built for labor like Jackson, some for running animals, and the more intelligent, like Yearie are house workers. Your problem is that you're too fond of her."

"I do not have a 'problem', Robert. You patronize. For all of Tilghman's moralizing, he sold a defenseless old slave away from his family because he wasn't useful anymore. His last days will be spent with sheep."

He laughed, his head rolling back, but I had played with his anger, tamped though it was. "This is business, my dear," he said reasonably. "After our dinner party, Bacon scolded me in front of Tilghman over the hog roller's whipping. If you must doctor my slaves, do it in their quarters, not in my house. And as much as you dote on Yearie, she ruined the evening spilling soup on Gildart." He leaned to my ear and whispered, "If your unnatural love of her continues, I will sell her."

Raising his head, he exclaimed as he waved his glass for Yearie to fill, "We should be gay and celebrate my return. Come, play the harpsichord and sing a round for me. Be happy. I have brought a portrait and gifts." He strode down the hallway. My eyes met Yearie's.

"You all right?"

"I'm fine. Fine," I said. She pushed me after him, her face stone.

At the foot of the wide stairs, wooden crates were strewn about and a slave boy of about fifteen busied himself emptying them. He was clothed in blue satin and a peruke that rivaled any in Robert's store. The boy bowed deeply.

"Good evening, mistress." He held one hand out, his face to the floor, one toe pointed before him like a courtier.

"Good evening. And who might you be?" I asked.

He glanced sidelong at Robert to see if he should answer. Robert wiggled his fingers in annoyance, never turning from opening a large crate at the front door.

"Master Morris has brought me from Annapolis, late of Philadelphia, madame. I am Voltaire, at your service."

"I'm happy to make your acquaintance." I gave him my hand. He touched with his glove, rose, and looked at some point over my head, uncomfortable with my familiarity.

Young Rob appeared in the parlor's doorway and I gave him greeting. Laconic, windswept like his father, his eyes narrowed hearing our interchange. "Miss," he nodded and glanced at my skirts, whispering something to his father so faintly. His father flicked him off.

"Look, m'love," said Robert. "A silver server, two crystal goblets and a humidor. And the pièce de résistance," he said, pointing behind him. "A freshly painted portrait of your greatest admirer only just completed by John Hesselius, the great portraitist of Philadelphia."

He tore the cover and batting from a frame that revealed a black garbed man, his face a glowing white orb supported by a dribble of lace. Cow-eyed, double chinned and diminutive, it captured none of Robert's vibrancy. He had paid dearly, for the portrait included a hand on his pocket watch, the other pointing downward like the Pope, only there was no holy book, nor a map or a globe. My lord's world stopped at his fingertips.

He was so delighted, he fairly danced in his hallway. "We will hang this in the great hall of our manor home. Then one of you in silver brocade to rival Goldsboro's mother's portrait in Annapolis."

"Oh, Robert. I cannot compare. I have heard she is inestimable in her beauty."

"Nonsense. Sit, my darling. Play a round. My son, join us." He propped the portrait above the harpsichord and pulled the bench out for me. Taking his violin from its stand he laid it on his shoulder, the bow raised in anticipation.

My hands hovered over the keys as I studied the would-be nobleman who blocked my sheets of music. Plunging my fingers into the chords, I played his favorite from the streets of Liverpool, *Bobbin Joe,* and wished the house were filled with guests dancing a cotillion. As I played, Voltaire unpacked the goods for Yearie.

I felt a prisoner in my own home as I struck the harpsichord's keys. I was beaten and hollowed. Once Robert had consumed a bottle of Madeira, he released me from the bench. I walked up the stairs, my skirts in one hand, a candle in the other.

"Sarah, you are wavering," called my master, looking up. "Let me help you."

He overtook me on the landing, standing one step above me and gazed into my eyes. Gently taking the candle, he put his arm around my waist and said, "Here, lean against me. I'll take you, my dear. I can see our music has not dispelled your mood."

I sighed deeply, grateful for his support. Two more flights seemed endless and gauging my weakness he paused. I wondered if he meant to guide me to my third-floor chamber. If he really meant to sell Yearie. If I gave him what he wanted...

We stepped together, me with him. Laying a hand on the brass knob of his chamber door, he whispered in my hair, "You are indeed a wise woman and one of great heart. Allow me to comfort you in your sadness."

I couldn't look into his eyes. Giving in, I allowed Robert to bed me.

CHAPTER 14

Saturday, 16 September, 1747

There were no consequences, it seemed at first. I returned to my chamber and spent a sleepless night, tossing and turning. The next morning was cool, songbirds twittered harkening fall's beginnings. Yearie had gone to market and Robert to the warehouse leaving me to inventory our household spices in the understair closet.

It was a relief being alone. My thoughts were jumbled, and I kept ordering events to no avail. The orphaned lamb, Bacon scolding my virtue, Findley's hand releasing me. In my ears, the cicadas' song rose and fell in a maddening chorus. I tried to excuse myself saying the reverend should have taken the child. That the Handys should fire Findley. But, in the end, it was me, my lack of fiber that left me miserable. I spilled the precious cardamom when I heard Yearie's voice in the kitchen. I brightened, anticipating a conversation about Sunday's dinner. Locking the sugar chest, I walked down the hall. A basket of peaches at her feet, Yearie looked up, her face hard. Hestia snorted and went back to work.

"I ordered a smoked pork from Handy's butcher. He goin deliver it later with hog brains since Master like 'em fried. You might take a bite if Hestia fry em in butter."

I hated hog brains and she knew it. "Robert will be happy."

She walked to me, a bee in her bonnet. Pinning me between the wall and the edge of the service table, her chin up, eyes stern, she asked, "The ropes loose on your bed, Sary? You lookin a fright this mornin."

I frowned. "I—I'm fine. Whatever do you mean?"

"Nothin you want to tell me bout yesterday?"

My head sank. She knew. House slaves congregated at the farmers' wagons on Saturdays. "I—I. You heard what I told Robert. There wasn't time to think."

"Not what I heard. Findley offer that baby to you."

I looked up. "Think of it, Yearie. Robert would put us out. You saw how dismissive he was last night."

"That be your excuse? Your mama be ashamed."

"Don't bring Mama into this."

"Want Phebe back, do you? God knows what you done, ain't no nevermine for your sainted mother. You can't take care of a dog, much less your own child. Look what you done to a black one!"

Words spit in disgust. I slid to my bum. She wasn't finished.

"You slobber over Tilghman's boy, then give him to me for the night." She slapped her hand back and forth on the table, "Here, Yearie, do this, Yearie, Yearie can you? I got visions, Yearie. Phebe, Phebe, Phebe. You a good Christian woman, but the Devil takin space in your heart, Sary. You got to make this right."

I blubbered on the floor and looking at my drool I was shocked. What a mess I'd made. *I must clean this before Robert gets home.* I wiped it with my sleeve when I felt her fingers round my chin, snapping my head up.

"Did you hear what I said? You got to give that baby a Christian burial or its spirit walk the earth forever lookin for its body."

I yanked my chin away and pressed against the wall thinking I had been in this very spot before, burdened with baby Tench. My stays too tight, trying to impress, I had forgotten my roots. Findley's words echoed in my head. *Dung heap.* "How?" I asked.

85

"Ride Bets over there tonight and bury him."

"The slaves will have buried him."

"Findley order them stable boys to cover him up with dung so nobody disturb it. That what you want on your conscience?"

"Disturbed? What did he mean? By wild animals, or—or slaves?"

"Do it matter?"

"Poor Bathsheba." Then, "I could. After dinner. What about Robert?"

"He goin to Callister's tonight. Big meetin over stolen goods in the warehouse."

"I-I don't know. I should wait till he leaves for Annapolis again."

With a tenacious grip, she dragged me to my feet. "Till wild hogs root through an there ain't nothin to bury?"

I tried to hug her, but she was rigid, cold, and it left me bleak. "I see. Of course, I'll go. If he notices, please—"

"I'll lie for you."

"I'm sorry, Yearie."

"Not me you got to say sorry to. Act like the woman your mama raised. I don't want no talk of visions, you hear? Master come in today, you be a sheep."

Robert returned after noon and handed me a list, items hard to come by on the Peninsula, the basics needed for building —iron works like locks and chains, hammers and nails. Finished buckles, bolts of cloth and ship's canvas. Tarring and rope were taken in the middle of the night. At first, I didn't know what I was looking at and then at the bottom I saw every parasol that Robert ordered was gone. Chicken skin rose on my arms.

He said with a grimace, "It's not just Oxford. These thieves have ransacked Cambridge and Dover Towne on the Choptank." He tore the list from my hands and exclaimed, "God's blood!"

"Will you tell Goldsboro?"

"And risk him demanding more for protection?"

Goldsboro kept Robert's secret that he skimmed Cunliffe goods and sold them for his own profit. He took his share as payment.

"I'll arm my redemptioners and post them day and night."

I found myself muttering and pleaded an excuse to get away — the strawberries, weeding, you know. He frowned. I left to hide in the stable.

Five stalls, two horses, a storage area where another set of doors led to the Oxford road. Empty, cool, quiet. I stumbled to the storage and looked for Phebe's cradle.

It was gone. The dining boards were there, the old gathering room benches. No cradle. Sitting in the straw, I rocked, prayer escaping me. Remembering her little garments stored in the hall clothes press, I raced inside and took the stairs two at a time. Flinging open the cupboard, I reached deep on the lower shelf and drew out her last shift and skirt. I buried my face, smelling her faint scent. A great weight settled on my shoulders as I climbed the stair to my chamber. I paced from window to landing, and, hearing Robert below dressing for dinner, I made no sound but crawled into bed. Rocking, rocking, I fell into a deep sleep, chained to restless dreams.

"Sary, get up. Master left."

I shot up, bewildered by a vision of Phebe, her heart floating in her hand, fading. The western sky was lit brilliant, the sun dropping out of sight. Yearie.

"Bets be saddled," she said.

At the stable door, she threw my cloak around my neck and handed me Mama's Bible. By the light of her lantern, she looped the red-handled garden trowel through the saddle string and said, "If'n that baby buried too deep, get a shovel. Jackson say the cemetery be down the stable road afore you get to the slave cabins."

"I'm ready, Yearie."

"I ain't givin' you no conjure bag. This be Jesus' work."

It was pitch black by the time I reached the Handy gate, the sky had clouded leaving it starless, the promise of rain ahead. Dread-filled, I lay across Ol Bets' shoulder and clucked her into the tobacco field, finding the slave path. Lanterns were tiered around the house and down the lane to the stable. Dinner hour. No doubt they supped with company. At a short distance, I saw the slaves moving about outside their cabins, working their gardens and cook fires, commiserating by torch light. Reaching the back corner of the stable I looked for any trace of Findley or the smithy.

I whispered, "Phebe, if you're there, help me find my way."

"Mistress, why ya be here?"

I nearly fell off Ol Bets. Under the dark shadow of the stable roof, I saw a ring of white hair emerge. His one eye glinted.

"Cyclops! Oh, can you help? A baby died here in the stable."

"Yes'm. Little Jonas, Bathsheba boy. He in the stable muck."

"We must bury him, Cyclops. With prayers for his soul."

"No'em. Nobody goin bury that boy. Findley say he lash us all till we say who done it."

"I'll do it, then. And I'll tell Findley. I'll tell all of Oxford. I just need help finding him."

Cyclops grumbled and swayed.

"Where is Findley at this hour, good man? And the smithy?"

"Fillin they bellies at the overseer's. Saturday night full o grog. Mistress, I jus want to die in peace."

"Nevermind," I said, stricken. I gave Bets a nudge. "I won't lead you in harm's way."

He shuffled into the darkness. Behind the stable a drainage ditch carried muck into the creek. The closer I came, the greater the stench. The dung heap. I slid from Bets, the trowel in hand.

My eyes roved over the mound, attempting to find the baby. One morning of shoveled dung had passed, but there were many horses, many stalls. I circled the stink and knew I needed a lantern. My purpose began to fade, and I blubbered, "Phebe, where are you?" How could my hands and feet be so cold, my mind shuttered? *I know you're here, my love.* I stumbled and fell, my knees sinking into the crusted edge, my hands thrust into the soft hillside. The trowel flew away from me, landing within reach.

Grunting, I crawled to it and a dry clump fell away. Baby toes. I sat back on my haunches.

Jonas. His burial. I dug, freeing him. Carefully, I put my fingers around his rigid body and drew him out. Death had frozen him in its savagery—the dibble stick, his mother's last mark. Someone had clothed him in a hemp shift hardened with blood. His fat arms reached out then abruptly folded across his chest. I stumbled to my feet holding him. His eyes blessedly closed, I stroked his burry cap of hair with my apron. When his skin loosened under my touch his head fell back and I sobbed. In the sparse light, his blackness turned to charcoal, his lips gray. He was Bathsheba's boy, forever unfinished. I walked down the path with Ol Bets behind.

Stopping under a tree's canopy I laid Jonas in the fallen leaves by the creek. I took Phebe's shift and washed him, his fat cheeks soft as if in sleep, tenderly cleaning around the wound. On my knees, I wrapped him in her brocade.

The slaves had moved inside their cabins, their shared campfires burning low. Now was the time to move out in the open. I worried that the ground would be too hard, that I wouldn't be able to dig a grave.

"What're ye doing here? A white woman in the slave compound. Are ye mad?"

I peered into the darkness to see the outline of a man's legs and a small lantern held low. He wore buckskin breeches and leather boots, a broken chain around one ankle. I heard his disembodied voice from above, "What do ye have in your arms?"

"Shhh! Who are you?"

"Yer Sarah, the reverend's friend. From the stable. The one who didn't run when ye shoulda." He stepped closer and raised the lantern. I could see the raw wound on his neck. "Yer singing to the dead babe?"

Was I? "John Suter," I said with conviction. "You're going to leave again, aren't you?"

"Crafty, I am, me dear," he said and held out a file in one palm. "The smithy were not careful with his tools."

His linen shirt was filthy, his blond hair long and stringy. He held the lantern over the baby. Kind blue eyes lined in dirt assessed me. "You must help," I said. "He deserves a proper burial. Help me dig. Please." I waved my hand toward the cabins.

"Aye," he said, lifting me up. "I see this be your penance. Ahl not be takin the time to dig for ye. I got to skedaddle."

I grabbed Bets' reins and pulled her from the shadows. "I'll help you. We can ride my horse. But only if you help me."

"We'll see, me lady."

He took her lead and I trailed after, Jonas in my arms. As we approached the cemetery a flea-bitten cur snarled and yapped. A single moonbeam lit rustic crosses that bore no names. In the doorway of his cabin a slave called out, "Be ye friend or foe, man or spirit, we gots no quarrel wit ya. Be gone!" We walked as Yearie said, all the way to the last line of wooden markers at the edge of the woods. The baby grew heavy, slowing my pace, but I swore to God I would make this right. Suter set the lantern on the ground.

"This as good a spot as any," he said.

It was tufted in thick grasses. I knelt, plunged the trowel into the dirt, barely making a dent. He said, "Lookie here, lady. Go see if there be a shovel in that garden. If you raise a ruckus, I'll be gone with your nag."

I picked my way through the graves to the cabin's vegetable garden. Rooting around, I was desperate and began to whimper. I skirted the corn rows and came up with a start, confronted by a delegation. Their faces contorted, wary. Frightened, my breath grew short.

"What you be doin in my garden, missus? Out to steal?"

The little band pushed toward me and I fell against the corn stalks. I tried to be confident, saying, "Good sirs, I do not seek food. Only a shovel to bury baby Jonas. Pray with me."

In a gruff voice an old slave dashed his stick in my face and said, "You from Morris house. Jackson say you comin. We don't need your kind of Christian. Not gettin whipped for some white woman."

"Please, for Bathsheba then. I have help. This is my doing."

They mingled about in heated conference and one broke free,

producing a shovel. He was young, barely out of his teens. "Go, mistress. These old men afraid."

He carried the shovel and as we treaded around grave markers, others joined us. Humming, they circled the baby and the lantern. One man sang, *"Sometimes I feel like a motherless child,"* and the others responded, *"Comin for to carry me home."* I moved to hush them, but Suter put the baby in my arms and said, "Singing their practice on Saturday night. Leave them be." He kicked the shovel into the dirt and flung it over his shoulder. I knelt near and opened Mama's Bible to the gospel of John. "'Let not your hearts be troubled. In my Father's house are many rooms. If it were not so, would I have told you that I go to prepare a place for you?'"

They took over, praying for that baby's resurrection and if my silent words earned a spot in God's heart for Phebe too, then I made it so. I stood, lifting his stiff body in my arms, uncomfortable in my skin. I was an interloper. Jon Suter must have felt the same for he dropped the shovel on the ground. I made the sign of the cross with my thumb on Jonas' forehead and lips, kissed his cold cheek. Bundling him in the brocade, I gave him to the young man who laid him in his grave. His attendants grabbed fistfuls of dirt and threw them into the hole, a hollow splat with each.

"I were leaving, missus," whispered John Suter. "You offered yer horse."

"I did." I curtsied to the slaves, but they paid me no mind, raising their voices in song as more fanned out from the cabins. Suter was in the saddle, hissing at me, repeating his threat to steal Ol Bets. Mama's Bible tucked in my bodice, I gave him my hand and he pulled me up behind him. Leaning to his ear, I asked, "Where are you headed, Scotsman?"

"Into the swamp. Where else is me life me own?"

He kicked and Bets took off as if a ghost was after her. The slaves' song dwindled as the wind picked up in my ears. I wrapped my arms round his waist and protested, "A few hours to give you a head start. I have to be back before dawn. I have work."

"Yer work'll have to wait, lady. We're headed to the Nanticoke."

The swamp maroons. Criminals and heathens. I had promised

Suter help but not this. Yearie would think me dead. Perhaps that was best, she was so angry with me.

He made haste to the Nanticoke River east of Oxford. Along the wide shoreline path, we passed a spray of white ibis pecking at minnows in the shallows. The water rolled gently, reflecting the moon which had grown great and round in the now cloudless sky. Willows covered the reeded banks and hoot owls called to each other in a lonely song that crept into my blood. In silence we passed plantation piers where hogsheads of tobacco sat upright ready for the trip downriver. Up terraced lawns, windows winked from stately homes.

Exhausted, I buried my hands in his rope belt for balance. The moon's light filtered through towering trees as the plantations disappeared. We circled a deep cove where three canoes painted in symbols rested in the shallows. As dew wetted my face, I wanted to wipe it and struggled to free my hands. Panic grew inside me; this place was so foreign. The farthest I had been from Oxford was Reverend Bacon's church, not even to East Town. My world was bounded by naked slaves picking tobacco, and rivers. I had no idea where I was, much less where to find the Indian reservation.

The thought that Phebe survived in their midst nigh on four years was not alien to me. Could I find her? The river narrowed, its bank steeper. Soon, the path became trail, wide enough for one person. Suter stopped, swung his leg over the pommel and slid off.

"Ahl walk now. Duck yer head or ye'll be thrown off."

I cleared my throat, endeavoring to be rational. "How much longer, Mr. Suter?"

"I wouldna know, mistress. I never reached the camp before the sheriff had me in his clutches."

And he could come for us. Or Suter could abandon me. Or Indians in the disputed territory could kill us. Black Foot, Nanticoke, Assateague, the dying tribes of the Atlantic forests had much reason for retribution.

The tree canopy reached low, slapping me. "I'll get down and follow behind," I called. He ignored me and kept walking.

My dodgy steps followed Bets' boney hindquarters. I slid in a hole and decided to keep my eyes on the ground, holding her tail.

The footpath was lined with oily ponds that hopped with insects. Trees closed in coffin-like, and, other than the squish of mud, the only sounds were those of insects buzzing and forest animals scurrying away. An occasional scream of a heron felt like the dead calling me. Our watery reflections on either side of the path were mirrors of the underworld.

"Yer making do back there?" he shouted.

"I am equal to your trek." I hummed for comfort.

Briefly, a nascent green glow played hide and seek through the tree trunks. Suter stopped, rifling a heap of dead cypress fronds. Our journey had taken many hours. I would not make it home before Robert left for Sunday morning service. Yearie would lie for me.

"Ah, them boys were thoughtful," he said, tossing a package in the saddlebag. I lost sight of him around a bend where black gum trees, still thick with leaves, blocked out all light. A red-tailed hawk screeched, drowning the buzz of insects. Standing in our way was a primeval forest of shaggy barked conifers.

I paused. Suter whistled, studying me from a distance. I could barely see his figure through a blur of mosquitoes that began to eat me alive. He came to me in ten great strides and flourishing a net, covered my head and torso. Disconcerted, I protested.

"Please, sir. I am not able to see well with this system."

"I lead, ma'am. You follow. Take the end of this rope and do not drop it." He tied the other end round his waist. He had a long knife in his belt, a hat on his head and a pack across his chest. He reached in it and handed me a hardtack biscuit. "Break off a bite with yer teeth and suck on it till it softens. It'll fill yer belly if not satisfy yer hunger."

The smell of evergreen filled my nostrils, the earthiness of nature clearing my mind. I walked determinedly for half an hour when the ground seemed to soften, and musty pools shaded by cottonwoods bubbled with amber water on either side. We were on a raised path, manmade, sometimes bridged in wooden planks over muck and mire. Undisturbed swamp.

The water deepened. Testing my footing, I was aware of being watched. The eyes of a predator gleamed nearby causing my heart to race. Drawn to its mystery, I slid into loose mud. Down into cold water, my foot snagged a cluster of roots. I reached for a sapling on the bank to pull, desperate to right myself, shouting out. With the sweep of his arms, Suter had me by the elbows, yanking me from its pull. He threw me over his shoulder, my skirts dragging, wet and stained. I did not protest.

From my vantage point as a sack of potatoes I could see knobs of gray wood rising from the watery depths and thought these were the cypress knees that I had heard about. Green algae floated atop the pools and fireflies sparkled above them. I pushed one hand against his back to raise myself so to see the massive trees, their trunks as big around as a made ship's mast, their strips of bark covered in luminescent mold. Enormous white egrets stalked in water, hunting. A muggy cool chilled my body and I shivered. I fell against Suter's back, resigned to my humiliation.

CHAPTER 15

*A*s I bobbed up and down with each step he took, I saw the ground was rising, and we appeared to be on an island of sorts. Terra firma. Shards of weak daylight hit switchgrass growing in patches. Dogs barked and I wiggled to be set down. Suter let me go and after I took a breath, pulled down my stays and smoothed my skirts, I followed him, searching for a sign of children.

Smaller trees had been cleared and dawn broke through the cedars, leaving circles of pink morn spread upon a path thick with pine needles. Moths and bees circled about, the latter feeding on swamp flowers. Oddly, in the clearings I saw a mishmash of beans and gourds that climbed corn stalks in a shared mess of vegetable planting. Nothing grew separately, all seemed dependent on the other for life.

We came to a cluster of bark huts and wooden shacks where my nose was filled with smoke although no fires burned. Nearby, worm rail fences penned three horses, a few cows and a hog. Mongrel dogs milled about sniffing us. Beyond, strips of meat were laced upon racks drying above white coals. A gutted deer hung from a low branch, its skin removed, its delicate pink muscle and white tendon exposed like the conch pearl ship captains brought me from the French Antilles. There was no sign of Phebe.

Africans wearing breeches, some with shiny white branding scars ridged against their dark skin, bent over felled trees. Their women stripped long sheaths of bark. Shipwrights had built a sloop that was near finished, no more than sixty feet or so. I wondered how they would move a finished boat to the river.

Such a practical thought was left unanswered as a passel of children, some black as a warm summer night, others the color of Dutch cocoa came to greet us, clothed in nothing but breechclouts and leggings. Whitened bones bounced on their bronzed necks. Even in the half-light I could see that some had blue-black hair tied with large feathers. They ran toward Suter and he picked the smallest up. Surrounding the Scot, their small hands pleaded upward. From his pocket, he divvied up spinners that I suspicioned he had made at the Handy plantation. I had nothing to give them.

The two braves I had seen in Oxford were silent as we passed, their red militia coats open revealing painted chests. They watched me coldly, but one old woman with flattened breasts and knobby fingers shuffled to me, her palms raised. She stopped, blocking my path looking for something — I knew not what.

"*Waappayu acquahique naam,*" she said and took Ol Bets' rein.

I hurried after the Suter, who was headed toward a humped lodge made of tree saplings and bark sheathing. I whispered, "What did she say? Do you know?"

Behind us a voice boomed, "Me brother made it! A sight for sore eyes!" The MacIntosh in all his forcefulness. Why hadn't I expected to see him?

"Aye-ye! It were a long ride and began with a hiccup. I bring a friend."

"And who might this be?" he asked.

I drew the netting off my head and flipped my hair out of my eyes. "What, sir? You do not recognize me? You said you would never forget." Filthy as a beggar woman, I stank to boot. He squinted. "The great Mrs. Wise? Ye've had a fall in yer circumstances, madam."

"So it might seem. Momentarily challenged. I intend to leave immediately but have one request."

Suter put his arm around his compatriot. "She were a brave woman this night. The old nag were hers. I woulda never made it here so swiftly."

"Ye make a practice of assisting we Scots," said the MacIntosh. "I am twice in yer debt."

"How kind of you to think of my needs. Then, a quick question to even the score and I'll be on my way, sir." Smiles and sweetness hid my determination. I waited to see his response.

"Anything, missus. How can I be of service?"

"Is there a white girl here? About ten years. My child, Phebe, was taken by the Indians four years ago. She has blue eyes and blonde hair."

The MacIntosh stepped back, his face blank. Seeing that I saw his astonishment, he composed himself.

"She *is* here, isn't she? Where, sir? Tell me."

"There's a child," he said with the utmost reluctance. "She be the sachem's daughter. I doona know her story but I warn ye, she speaks the English of a small child. Dutch and Nanticoke as well."

I grew impatient. I snapped, "Why do you need to know a story?"

"They be a family. Ye can't traipse in here to steal her without a how do ye do."

"Nonsense. This sachem is a leader? I'll explain. Indians are heathens and should never raise an English child. *I'm* her mother."

Seeing other Scotsmen from the prison ship, Suter wanted to drift away. Before he left us, he said, "She be bold, Mac. And devious. Might come in handy living where she does."

Fuming, I could not hear what they whispered, and once Suter departed for his friends, the MacIntosh and I were alone, nose to nose. "These people have been kind to me," he said. "I am in greater debt to them than you. They've suffered enough from white men, and especially yer Morris. I'll not be a part of creating more by stealing a child."

"I do not see how *my* Morris could cause their distress. They brought it on themselves by attempting to kill us all. But you wouldn't know about that. Despite their treachery, the governor awarded them land to hunt and farm. That, sir, is not suffering."

"Ye have jaded views, madam. I'll take ye to the sachem but I warn ye, do not make trouble." He strode off and again, I found myself following a redemptioner down a path. I couldn't believe his impudence. I ran to keep up.

We approached a bark hut, longer than our slave quarters, that belched smoke with no chimney to channel it. A fire trap.

"Ahl address the chief first. Bow after I point to ye," said the MacIntosh down his nose.

At the door, the old woman appeared repeating her gibberish.

"Wait, what did that she say?" I asked.

"White woman see," he responded, removing the sapling door.

Inside a group of older men with painted faces were seated cross-legged around a low fire. Smoke swirled through a hole in the roof. They seemed to be praying as they waved tendrils to their faces, breathing deeply, eyes closed. An aged woman dressed in a white buckskin dress sewn with purple beads sat at the edge of the circle. Behind her stood a young warrior, his head shaved except for a topknot that sported a large feather. He wore a linen blouse and as he stepped to the old woman's side, I saw a small yellow and black turtle shell hung from his neck. He was deferential to her and when she spoke the praying stopped. She grabbed his arm and he pulled her to her feet. I suspected she was a priestess, preparing for the sacrificial lamb.

The MacIntosh approached and bowed, addressing her with great respect. "I return, Sachem, to bring ye Sarah Wise, wife of trader Morris."

She raised weary eyes. Her face a wrinkled walnut, her hair grizzled as the cypress bark outside. "You come without warning, Scotsman," she said.

He bowed again. "I bring ye the object of yer discussion, Great Sachem."

I curtsied. I had heard these Indians had women rulers but never believed it. A barbaric people surely, but perhaps their leaders were gone, cowed after their foiled revolt. My breath was shallow, my head awhirl thinking I might have to bargain for my daughter. I sidled closer to the Scotsman and wondered why they would discuss me round their fire.

"I am honored to be in your presence," I said. It made no impression.

"This is Weocomocus, Mistress Wise. She is empress of all the chiefs of the Nanticoke. Her son, Robin, who negotiated the treaty with the governor," said the MacIntosh, pointing to the young warrior in linen. "Sarah Wise," he said extending an open palm to me.

I must have been quite the spectacle, the stink of dung in my bedraggled skirts. The five old men nodded, meeting my look with recognition, uninterested in my dress. Used to catering to the needs of men, going unnoticed except by their lecherous eyes, my position seemed stronger. I curtsied in return.

No sooner had I grown comfortable with this thought than a red-coated brave entered the long house. He spoke in his tongue and when I tapped the Scot in frustration, he translated, "He says you'll not help them. That you live with the Trader of Men but only make wampum beads for him."

I had never made a bead in my life. The MacIntosh bent to whisper, "He means you help Morris make his money."

A sidelong glance and I saw the brave's chin up like a bantam rooster, crowing his knowledge of the white man. I had been here before — at the Handy plantation and I was determined this encounter would end differently. Wampum beads? God give me strength.

"Great Sachem," I began, "I ask — "

"Ask?" she interrupted. "When white man ask, they mean 'want'. This is our last place. Go home and honor our treaty."

Her council of old men had bowed their heads. How was I to honor their treaty? These natives were famous for lying and stealing.

Determined or submissive? Which was it if I wanted Phebe back? I had seen a fur trader once when I was a child, the top of his head scalped close to the bone. Most didn't live through the experience.

"Great Weocomocus," spoke the MacIntosh, "the white woman will listen."

Quickly, I asked God's guidance, wondering if I must rely on the Scot for my life. He sensed this and shook his head in the slightest movement.

Out of the shadows stepped a small girl clothed in nature's leather— draped in the vertebrae of an animal, a small leather pouch round her neck, her eyes ringed in the charcoal of their fires. At the empress' side, she bowed and gave her a silver box the size of a brick. I peered through the smoke and started at seeing she was of white parentage. Pale skin and long hair flowed down her back. I studied her, feeling my throat constrict. Phebe? I couldn't tell. She was no slave to them. On the contrary, she looked quite content.

Unreceptive to my gaze, she listened closely to the sachem's words and translated in a pidgin English replete with the v's and z's of Mrs. Vanderkoop. The old woman spoke brusquely of the Great Turtle People—a people whose wandering hunts were corralled from tree to creek, from swamp to ocean waves. Metes and bounds on paper made a meandering fence on land. Peace with her people meant starvation, for at a fence the stag did not stop for the hunter. A hundred years of Nanticoke and Assateague kindnesses were betrayed with this one act.

I was tired. Her lesson was empty of their treachery. Listening to the girl, I hungered for signs. What might have been Phebe's fat cheeks were gone with her baby teeth. This child was the right skin color, but her hair was white not gold, her lashes and brows pale. I crept closer, looking for the tiny scar on Phebe's chin. Her jaw was slim and didn't end in the tail of a heart as Phebe's did. Light cheated further inspection.

She recounted the Indians' story with none of the wiggles and delight of my girl. Vaguely, I heard words of vengeance, of an army dead asleep from a poisoned drink. Fence rows, razed woodlands, slain wildlife. The child accused, saying the white man killed "by drink and disease." And now, she said, the Trader of Men had arrived in Oxford Town.

Sachem's brown hands rose between us. In his greed, Morris stole reservation land, useless land a white farmer abandoned to the pox. The Provincial Court agreed. And you, she ordered pointing at me, will tell your white man to honor the treaty.

Well, I thought, it's a vivid story, but — the sachem was only an ignorant Indian and, truthfully, like field slaves they were so limited they would confuse the terms of any agreement they made with us. They never knew a boundary and I was sure they accused Robert falsely. I wondered if the MacIntosh was behind this. He hated Robert. When the old woman paused, I spoke up.

"Great Sachem, I plead for your understanding. You dishonor Mr. Morris. He has been a friend to your tribe, trading finished goods with you for insignificant furs which he acquires from our trappers. If he has bought land from tobacco farmers, it is only to aid them in leaving their failing lives for the unknown frontier. I beg your pardon, but you know not of what you speak."

I watched as the smokey-eyed girl finished translating my last words. Sachem's eyes were stony pebbles. "We have no use for her," she said in English, her voice resigned. The chiefs stood and kicked dirt into the fire, leaving me choking. I waved the smoke away as the village braves came for me, but the MacIntosh stood between us.

"Ye've stepped over the line," he said, his face screwed in annoyance. "Canna listen and shut yer trap?"

He spoke to the braves and they hesitated. With a glare, he ordered me, "Stay."

The braves in front, the Indians traipsed outside. No simple conversation over my dining table, my expectation of a back and forth between reasonable people was gone along with any shred of respect they had shown me moments ago. I could only rely on instinct now. I felt someone behind me and turned for the girl child, who translated.

"How old are you, my dear?" I asked but she looked away. She was smaller than I thought Phebe would be and she had an odd, stunted walk. Serious beyond her years, I had to listen hard to

understand her heavy accent and wanted to interrupt, to ask if she
was Vanderkoop's daughter.

"Thou Morris spread zis pox to us. You vaste time talking to
Sachem aboot little cows and little calves vhilst ve suffer. You are
shtoopud idioot," she said with such conviction it took my breath
away. "Zis güd people do not vant to trade vis Morris. Zis swamp
vere safe from disease before him."

How were they safe? No one was safe. "You are confused, child,"
I said.

She grabbed my arm. "Master Morris came to Sachem at ze vhite
man's hüse to talk. He say ve can hunt in *hees* forest. Hees slave
packed güds from ze house and told us to take vhat he didn't vant.
Ze old blankets and floor cloth. He took livestock, and slaves zat *ve
had freed*. And now ve have pox." She gazed at me with bold eyes,
warrior eyes. "Thee who has butter on her head should stay out of ze
sun."

She made no sense. This wasn't Phebe. A far stretch it was to
blame Robert for their disease. The pox gave no favors and was most
likely in the colonist's abandoned home, their blankets contaminated.
Everyone's life is for the taking. Besides, Robert had given them
what they wanted—hunting rights on his land. As I turned to go, I
grunted in contempt.

The child said to my back, "Go outside and get a fresh nose."

An old woman pushed me hard and I stumbled sideways through
the narrow door. She pushed me again and I fell to the ground on my
hands and knees. Heathen women gathered, surrounding me. The
black women swayed in their calico, as if stopping to watch a street
show. The MacIntosh had disappeared. Panic overwhelmed me.

One Indian beat me with a stick and the more I protested, the
more who joined her. My head tucked in the dirt, the blows came
hard and fast across my back, my stays protecting my skin. I sobbed,
"No, please! You don't understand!" A sapling landed across my
hand, stinging and ripping the flesh. I tucked it under my chin,
sucked in my breath and fell silent. Squeezing my eyes shut, I waited
for the next blow, my nose dripping. I began to whimper when I felt
a strong hand beneath my arm, yanking me up.

"Mistress, ye've come to the wrong place if ye want to make change. These people have had enough of our change." Blinking, my vision cleared as the MacIntosh dragged me to safety.

"Good sir, help me!" I screamed. "You are recently arrived across the ocean. You know the pox plays fair game with all of England."

He hauled me, tripping from their clutches. The girl child came with us and I thought I would question her. Wiping tears with a patch of my skirt, I asked her name.

"Tayen," she answered.

"And your English name?"

"Dutch. Margriet."

Jacoba's girl. "Vanderkoop?" I whispered and she nodded. Kidnapped she'd been and now she worked for their sachem? "Your mother misses you terribly, Margriet. Why, Mr. Morris paid passage for her and your brothers to sail to Lewes."

A wincing regret flashed upon her bearing. "She vould not remember me," she said. "I vould not remember her."

"Where is your father, child? The story in Oxford is that you were taken together."

"He died. I meessed him at first, but Sachem saw my sadness and took me under the ving of her. She is mine moedder now."

"Child, you cannot abandon your family for these people. Look how you live." I was devastated at her betrayal.

"I am better here."

I leaned down. She had a scar on her chin like Phebe's but larger and crescent-shaped. She was slight and obviously not fed well. "How did you get that scar?" I asked.

"I vere clumsy."

Phebe wasn't clumsy. She was light on her feet. A little dancer. "Was there another child, a white girl about your age?"

Worry pinched her face. "Dere vas. She died years ago right after she came here. She lived in our hüt."

"Do you remember her name?"

"Papje called her Phebe when ve buried her. She vas sister of me."

A little cry escaped my lips. "She was blonde like you? Blue eyes?" That solemn nod. Not a more bitter existence. I wanted to ask how she died, if she suffered…if she ever mentioned me.

At a shout, Margriet gave me a grudging smile and joined a happy lot of children.

"Mistress, ye need to come with me," said the MacIntosh.

He led me to the edge of the swamp. Large white flowers bloomed along the way, dripping with dew in the rising sun, as if cultivated and treasured. Beautiful, but my senses were fouled by the smell of a dead animal that permeated the dank air. At a distance, three or four dugout canoes sat piled high with what looked like bones. We all ate well in the province, so why would these people save animal bones? Soon, I had my answer— human skulls, shining pearlescent, topsy turvy in their shared canoes.

My hands spread out. "Sir, colonists? They deserve a Christian burial! All round you is savagery. I beg you, do not encourage their ways!" Were they saving bones of those they had murdered for their sacrilegious dances? Were Phebe's in the pile?

"Ye have the blindness of privilege, mistress," he said his face closed off from me. "These be the bones of their families. Pushed beyond the limits of their ancestral lands, the living *choose* to carry these sacred remains, not leaving them for the militia to desecrate. Many of their people of mixed tribes are in these canoes."

My thoughts ran. We had not had any battles with the natives. They must have been a collection, decades old.

"Think, mistress. Ye see they are not yellow? These are their fathers, mothers, sisters and brothers. Some be small children, but all were living five years ago. Slain by yer Talbot men."

I turned and ran down the path right into Suter. "Have ye had enough?" he asked.

The MacIntosh passed me and stopped in front of his friend. "This be your big hero, Suter? The one who is key to our game? Another piece of frippery not given to sacrifice."

I wiped my sleeve across my eyes in anguish. Blood from my hand seeped across my bodice and I whimpered at my treatment. This man agreed with heathens laying responsibility at Robert's doorstep. My doorstep. I took a deep breath and launched into a rant.

"You insult me, sir, to *my* bones. My very soul is wounded by these scenes that you've foisted upon me. And to what use? I am a woman of no countenance, no power, no recognition in my community."

"Aye, would that it be so easy. Ye go from thinking too much o yerself and yer pretty things, to thinking like a sheep," he said. "Ye hold the power over the greatest men of the settlement and beyond in Annapolis who dine at yer table, like-minded mountebanks who make themselves rich with their schemes. Look here and ye'll know yer master's loyalty."

He led me to a pile of goods packed into a canoe ready for travel. "Some of these people depart for the great bay below the Dutch village where they hope to be left alone. Nothing but bad water and lowlands there."

My gaze passed over a jumbled collection of household goods and my eye was caught by an English cradle that lay overturned. I was drawn to it, reading upside down the four letters carved into the headboard—WISE. The cradle Edward had made for Phebe, the one that little Tench had slept in. Taken from our stable.

"They have stolen from my home? The most valuable memory I possess? Why? Why do they make a target of me?"

"It were not the Indians."

It didn't make any sense. If not the Indians rooting through our stable, then who? And how, when Jackson slept there most nights.

I felt discombobulated...all record of my brief motherhood lost, my daughter dead. Fear rose in my chest. I had not checked my store of stolen coins in weeks.

"Robert?" Had he discovered the coins I took? Then, he took the most valuable thing I own to give to these heathens? "He will put me out on the street," I said.

"Why do ye live with him, mistress?"

I looked at him in dismay. Could he possibly not know the difficulties of a gentlewoman of middling birth in the colony? Of not having parents, a dowry or two pence to rub together? Weren't the women of Scotland treated the same as me, as Mrs. Vanderkoop?

"You don't know for sure it was him. I want to go home."

The Vanderkoop child, always lurking, slipped into view at hearing my words. She asked me to take a present for her mother. Impatient, I answered yes, yes. Could I write that she was well and happy? Of course, I said. She held out the silver box the Sachem had given her. Opening it revealed a string beads. "For you," she said.

Their familiarity fired in me. I drew out the strand knowing it was what was left of Mama's rosary, missing the cross and the medal of the Holy Virgin, still in my possession. The filigree beads were gone as well. Or were they in my chamber's hidey hole? I couldn't remember and a dizzying whirl pitched me forward. My hand shook as I tucked it to my breast with a groan. I was sure Phebe had been here, that Margriet knew her.

I squatted to look her in the face. She believed the rosary was hers. Wiping the coal from her eyes with my thumb, I said, "These are your beads to remember your mother, Margriet. You should keep them and return with me."

The pain of it all sank me to the cold, hard ground. This mix of people busy in their own industry, who lived hand to mouth, not a slop basin or eyepiece among them, endeavoring to show a Gulliver the truth. A Dutch mother's love robbed, Indian families lost in an instant, their children dying, their future unknown, slaves and white men branded as runaways. All of that paled with the understanding that my Phebe had died alone among strangers with no mother to ease her pain, to whisper words of comfort in her ear.

She nodded and led me, grabbing my bleeding hand. Under a large cypress was a makeshift cross that read, Vanderkoop. Even Phebe's real name had not survived. Tears welled and the child tugged.

I held my arms out to her, but she was plainly of her own purpose.

"Mistress Vise, I haf ben gone of Oxford many years. Ze best I know is zat town is not vhat it seems." She held out Mama's Bible and a small square of worn linen tied with a reed bow. "You dropped your book. Be careful. I give you seeds from Sachem. Plant zem in shade and zey vill grow. It is called Jimson Veed. Ve use it to see the future. In a salad, you know, or boil for a cool draft is güd, but not too much as it vill slow your heart as if life's lost. Feed it to your enemies to destroy zem."

I thanked the little warrior and stood with much effort. I plodded down the path into the forest. The MacIntosh followed, lugging a package over his shoulder, leading Ol Bets. He shouted, "Remove all the bridges and bank the fires. We take the south road. If the dogs sound the alarm, lie low and be armed."

CHAPTER 16

*W*e trudged on, my eyes on every step, my head turned to pudding before I broke the silence. "Sir, I cannot enter the village in broad daylight looking like I do. There is every chance that Yearie raised a hue and cry. They will be looking for me."

"It will be late evening when we arrive, madam. Do not be concerned. A fine dress was had by the East Town Road. However, I may be missing ear drops for yer dinner tonight," he said, his brow arched.

Amazed, I turned to look him in the eye... They were green. "I considered you a rake, duplicitous. But I see you had purpose. To inform me and warn me." I cleared my throat. "I am...grateful."

Ridiculously, he took that singular bow, the tall cedars as witness, something Robert never did. "Ye are most welcome, m' lady."

"Fush," I said.

"Madam, we will proceed a different way, not by the river. *Je suis à votre service.*"Continental niceties. The path was shaded from the early morning sun. At least my skin wouldn't burn. I hoped my shoes would dry, but my stockings and dress were beyond saving. Scratches and cuts, grimy and ragged nails, not the picture of a lady.

Ahead was a lean-to under a grove of hemlock. An Indian boy whom I had seen lurking around Oxford waited under the eave holding the bridle of a magnificent black. The MacIntosh ducked inside and produced a saddle, similar to those Robert procured in the Pennsylvania province. He saddled the black, lifted me up on Bets and stuffed his package in her pack. He mounted the stallion.

"Tear it down, Wenetko. Spread the planks and cover em with the boughs. We'll collect the wood later." The boy saluted and the MacIntosh gave him a string of dried fish, saluting him in recognition. Here was not a mere Indian, but a swamp soldier.

Before long, we wound our way through the woods at a careful gait and broke free. Ahead, a green meadow twitched orange, undulating with the wings of tiger butterflies feeding on milkweed. We kicked our horses and flew to the edge of a dark forest. Our travel invigorated my blood, renewing my spirit and resurrecting a sense of adventure. The heaviness the Indians laid at my feet faded.

Entering a wood, I felt the temperature cooler and the insects that infested the swamp gone. Soft ferns covered the ground amidst mighty oaks. Beams of white light cut through the trees guiding our way to a clearing at the headwater of a creek. Itching, I asked how far we were from Oxford. I was filthy.

"We stop here, missus. Hop down." He dismounted, wrapping our reins on a bush at water's edge for the horses to drink. He pulled the bundle from the saddlebag. "Give me yer shoes and ahl clean em up." He pointed behind me. "If ye walk round the bush, ye can bathe. There be soap in the package and a dress."

I nodded and slipped out of my garden mucks. My stockings were torn, my toes poking through.

Hiking my skirts, I followed a well-trod animal trail around the bush and found a shielded spot along the stream to disrobe. Unwrapping the bundle, a sliver of bayberry soap lay atop a linen shift, stockings, a laced bib and tucker, blue bodice, and boned stays. I shook out skirts of calico blue. Someone in a shop had assembled a full day dress for a discerning girl of rising means. A small comb and chatelaine fell into my hand. They had forgot nothing.

Shiny pebbles sank under the weight of my foot and the cool

water quieted the bites and scratches of the swamp. I stepped gingerly to the depth of my waist, clothed in nothing but my dirty shift.

When I heard snorting on the shore, I turned, chilling at the sight of a great black bear and her cub, nosing my swamp clothes. Quiet, I thought, don't draw her attention. Where was the Scotsman? I tiptoed in the silt till its surface shifted. The bear raised its snout in my direction and sniffed. I slipped under, holding my breath, eyes wide open.

In the fractured green light, I could see a sleek black mass coming toward me and I fluttered my arms at it thinking some sea creature had come to eat me. But in the murkiness below, I saw the four hooves and relief bested my fears as the Scotsman's stirrup glittered, magnified by the waters. Not able to hold my breath any longer, air seeped from my lips and I floated, suspended in a watery world. I inhaled. Thick-lipped giant fish arose from the reeds, encircling me, pushing upward toward a yellow glimmer. I surfaced and coughed in a blinding white light. A shadow bent over me, scooping me underarm. Loose as a rag doll, I fell over a hard pommel, sucked in sweet air, and was seized with a coughing fit. Pushing my hair from my eyes, I peered through rivulets of water.

The beast pawed at my belongings and lowed, swaying side to side, squinting from the bank. It took all my strength to hold on, and, as I rolled at a kick beneath me, I slid, ready to fall into the water. A force gripped me tightly about the waist. I was weightless, cold inside, my skin cool as stone in winter. Sight blackening, I slipped from the pommel to a warm flat rock where I sat motionless, dripping. I heard a clatter of hooves and a voice distant and soft.

"Yer safe here," he said. "She won't leave her cub. We're not that interesting."

I leaned against him, thoroughly tired of alarm, my body giving out. There was warmth next to me, but I didn't know from whence it came. I decided he would have to solve this, for I had no strength. Colors swirled and my sight returned.

Across the stream the beast ambled away, her offspring in tow. He knelt, his arm supporting me and his rough hand came up in the most tender way to brush my face clear. I felt its warmth cupping my head. Dazed, I saw his eyes hovering over mine, intense and kind.

"My poor dulcinea," he whispered. "We've worn ye to a thread."

I didn't know what a dulcinea was, but thought it was endearment, in a tone not heard since Edward. I wasn't fooled and thought I should protest but had not the will. I closed my eyes at feeling the weight of his hand on my hip. A quivering shook me and I heard the chatter of my own teeth. I battled to speak. Morning doves grew louder, grounding me in their music. Opening my mouth, I was dismayed that I uttered a meandering, "Sir...make me warm."

Any hold I had on the situation was fleeting. Paralyzed, my hand fell on his chest. His skin beneath his linen was warm. He drew me to him. Breathing on my temple, I heard, "Yer shivering."

I nestled under his shoulder, overcome with the scent of smokey skin, pine needles and something else. My own earthiness. Taking a deep breath, I opened my eyes to a certain tremulousness, something wholly different but pleasant.

"I be thinking yer learning is not complete," he said, surprise in his voice.

Obsessed to know, I tugged his shirt over his head, laying him bare. He was covered in scars and bore one great slash across his chest. I touched it gingerly and could not bear to think of the great hollow of his suffering. He must have seen it in my eyes, for he pressed the small of my back, drawing me to him.

With his kiss came a wrap of tenderness that was unexpected, yet as normal as licking butter from my fingertips. Intensely hot of a sudden, still, goose bumps freckled my arms. Swollen with desire, my heart beat steadily harder. I grabbed his belt and yanked, barely aware of my sore knuckles. He unbuttoned his trousers. Not wanting to be denied or rushed, I lingered with his goodfellow in newfound awe. Pushing his chest away, I was undone. It was daytime with a man I barely knew who wasn't blindly hammering me as a fence post, drunk, or hurried to spend his shot. "Holy mother," I said.

His lips searched, kissing and sucking, ranging over my body. Panting, I rested my head in the pine needles. His eyes measured my delight as his studied hand played me in point and counterpoint like

111

a violinist glides over his strings, till the fiber of my being became so wrought and twisting that I no longer knew myself.

I groaned in agony at my sin but was helpless to its wave of desire. Here was a strange woman who had a power not known to me. I was no longer a chaste virgin nervous on her wedding night, or a middling servant dressed in silks and trussed in stays. As he took one last look in my eyes for acquittal, I gave it gladly and never was my body so electrified when the sum of that moment burst inside me.

He waited until my chin stretched to the heavens. When my back arched and I thought I could bear the ecstasy no longer, he sought me out with what was once was so familiar, yet so unknown. He was not Edward, dutiful and quick. Nor Robert, rough and drunk. No, he was euphoria spilling inside my very blood, he rolled me over on his chest.

Propped on my arm, I gazed down at someone who was—I could not think—and then it came to me. He was grateful…if not a little sheepish. Was he demon or lover, libertine or saint? I looked about and wondered where I was, and how it came to pass that I was in his arms. My memory eluded me. He pulled me to him.

Nuzzling, he whispered in my ear, "Ye are an artful woman."

I didn't think it was me who was so artful.

We lay, spent. Soon, I began to shiver again and he gathered me to him and stood, throwing his shirt over my shoulders. Leaning me against the pine tree, he mounted his horse that watched us with limpid eyes. His hand extended. My legs were weak.

"Give me yer hand, Sarah," and he pulled me up, sitting me in front of him.

He waded his horse into the creek and soon we were on the other side. The soap was half-eaten on the bank, but the bear was gone. We washed, scrubbing each other's grime away. I was so happy, I did not have a care. Barefoot and near naked, we roamed the shore playing hide and seek, surprising and capturing, laughing till the taunts and tickles ended once more on the creek's sandy bank. I felt the soft rush of warm wind against my wet skin and rose to slip into the clean shift. I lay next to him, my eyes lingering on the water that rippled over stones. I rolled on my stomach. He sat up, his profile against the white sun shielded my eyes.

"A magnificent hurdie, ye have," he said.

"Hurdie?" Such a strange language the Scottish have.

"Yer buttocks," he said laughing as his hand swept up the small of my back, pushing aside my shift. "What's this?" he grinned, curious. I looked over my shoulder and felt him thumb the Cunliffe "C" that branded my hide. He frowned.

"Master Morris, in a finer moment. To impress upon me that we are both servants to an English master."

He cursed. "A man trapped by his own infatuation."

I nodded but didn't answer. Soon the gnawing pangs of hunger forced us to forage. I found wild berries and the spiny hulls of chestnuts littering the ground. The Scot surprised me with dried deer meat from his pack and we refilled his waterskin upstream to slake our thirst. Sitting cross-legged in the warm sun, he placed the chestnuts on a rock and slammed each quite effectively with the cheek of his hatchet.

"Scotsman, I know not your name, yet you know me most intimately."

"Alex," he said. "Alexander Duncan MacIntosh, late of Inverness by way of Carlylse Castle and a British hulk."

"A hulk?"

"Aye. A crumbling prison ship anchored in the River Firth. Filled with dying comrades and vermin, it was. Disturbed the sensitive noses of the populace, so they moved us farther from shore."

"Oh," I said. My fingers traced a scar on his arm. His skin was mapped by the Jacobite War. Gunshot, dagger, sword had all left their mark. Robert boasted the king had wiped out the Scottish cannibals. Like the drivel he spouted about slaves, the French, and Catholics, too. He looked down his nose at all redemptioners, yet save Cunliffe's employ, he might have been an indenture as well.

I thought the Scot a man of great care, his touch so tender. I was curious. "And the castle? I take it you weren't an honored guest?" I asked.

"A gaol for the Bonnie Prince's followers."

"And did they have a priest for you Jacobites or are you a depraved Calvinist?"

"M'lady," he said as he kissed the inside of my wrist. "Ye probe."

"Not as well as you, sir," I said, pulling away with a laugh. "Did they force you to give an oath to the king and his church?"

"I be no Leviathan." He raised his eyes to the sky. "Nature is cruel, mistress. Men are brutes. I have no quarrel with government, or religion for its own sake." He looked at me and said with conviction, "Just not by chinless Brits."

"So, you believe in God's good order?" It seemed he rebelled against all forms of rule.

He plunged his hatchet in a fallen log. "I believe I'll live by the good order I create, not some idea of hated absolutism, be it king or pope."

"Well then, Alexander Duncan MacIntosh, I think you are doomed to suffer in these colonies for we are all subject to the King and his Anglican faith."

"Well then, Mistress Sarah Wise, I think ye are doomed to always be a servant of someone. An inhuman rule's afoot that will beat ye down if ye are not strong."

"Do not misread me, sir," I said, my hands folded in my lap. "I do not lend myself to embryonic thought. I have ways to survive."

"No doubt. But one must ask if yer methods be the wisest, Mrs. Wise?"

He squinted at me like the bear, only I thought him far more discerning. He knew so much about my household and I none about his. Impetuously I asked, "Did you steal my cradle?"

"Mistress, I may be shifty and given to nighttime forays in Morris' warehouses, but I canna enter yer home where there be so much activity." He slammed nuts with his hatchet and leaned over to me. "Morris gave it to the Indians at the farmer's house. I wouldna have known, but for Wise carved on the headboard." He spilled sweetmeats into my hand. "His son bragged of it in the tavern."

"Young Rob tells tales in the tavern?" I flung shells into the creek. Why would his father hurt me so? In trading the cradle, Phebe's story existed but in memory.

"There be no secrets at Quinn's," said he. "Just lies. Morris sells used goods to anyone who has Spanish coin interested in a dented copper pot or lousy mattress. What people don't know is he trades the reales to London for British guineas."

No one had British guineas. And sterling was rare as a colonial groat. "I sneak his Spanish reales," I confessed. "He never misses them."

"A dangerous habit."

"It's my insurance."

"Against?"

Could I say it? The words had never been heard aloud. "Losing my place in his home."

"Ye fear he will marry another."

It was a statement, not a question. Put like that I knew that it was inevitable in the Scotsman's mind—in everyone's mind.

Pretending nonchalance, I grabbed the stolen stays from the grass and put them on, lacing from the bottom. I would not let him see my failings. "And how do *you* escape his notice?" I asked, blustering with authority. "Or that of Goldsboro? Our sheriff, if you didn't know, is hellbent on punishing those who escape. He is cruel to all he captures." I tossed my hair and said, "It seems, sir, the pot calls the kettle black, for you have made a business of stealing from Robert's stores. *The* most dangerous affair."

"Madam, yer Robert has built an alliance against himself. Indentured employed in his warehouses, freed slaves and even Indians. We're spread far and wide, but we know what his warehouses contain." He reached to draw my hair from under the strap. "We never take from a small farmer or merchant. They are all slaves to their tallywags."

"Sir?"

"Their Whiggish lairds, patriarchs of civility when they aren't but English pricks charging inhuman amounts for their rent. So, while yer master steals from Cunliffe, we steal from him. See the dress ye so carelessly assemble across yer fine body? It were sent to the maroons by your Oxford tailor. A present for a Handy daughter that she never got."

"Do tell!" I said. "Our tailor is a remarkable man. Such a help to our household." Then it dawned there was a reason.

"I doona tell for ye canna know our plans. I wouldna want ye to slip in front of Morris."

Growing silent, I chewed on a nut. I drew my knees to my chin. "I think you didn't have me tour the swamp just to see the injustice of maroon life. You, the Negroes, the Indians— want more than trifling influence on the men at my table."

"Aye, but ye'll have to swear yer loyalty to us. Ye canna speak of what ye've seen today."

I sighed waving my hand in the air. "Alexander, you must think me a fool. I am lectured by an old Indian and a child. For their pox I am saddened, at their skeletons revolted, yet that wasn't enough. I suffer a beating, discover my child's cradle and grave, and am terrified wondering if God is punishing me for some evil I have done." Sternly, I said with finger pointed, "*You* made all that happen, and I should be affronted." I felt my shoulders slump and said, "Strangely, I am not."

He reached out and I shook my head. "No, I must say this. The tragedy of their lives far outweighs the sight of Phebe's cradle or my mother's rosary beads. I could ignore most of it in my own foolish superiority. It wasn't till Robert's betrayal came to me in such horrible truth that I understood." I took a deep breath and shook my head. "If Robert could be so personal in his cruelty to a woman who has taken care of his every need, then what of people who are of no consequence to him?" I turned my knees to the ground and raised one palm. "I offer my help."

The sun shone on his hair, a reddish-brown tangled mess that spilled across his massive shoulder. Softly, he kissed the hand that was now crusted from the Indians' beating.

"Ye're just a wee yin, mistress, and not capable of bigger things."

"I am finished with being scared. I can't live my life this way... And I do not know what a 'yin' might be."

"A child. Ye might have birthed a bairn, but ye be a novice in the ways of the world."

"I assure you, I was sheltered as a girl, but I've seen hunger and homelessness. I've lost my family and have only one true and loyal friend left."

"That would be?"

"Yearie. My bound servant. She's my sister since we were children. I protect her as she protects me. There are no secrets between us."

"I've heard tell of this woman."

"Really? Why would anyone know of Yearie all the way in the swamp?"

"She's a slave, not a servant, Sarah, and they all know each other in a world that ye apparently don't understand."

I felt my face heat. Of course, Yearie had friends. Other friends, besides me. I just didn't know them.

His eyes searched my face. "How did ye come to be educated living in such a backwater?"

I blinked, grateful for the change of topic. "My father. He tutored plantation children. Yearie and I tended the younger ones, and when they napped, their mistress taught me the harpsichord. Mother played a lute and father a viola. In our home, Papa had his own books brought from England, the Classics, philosophy, astronomy, science — he kept nothing from me."

He pursed his lips as he put the vestiges of our food in his saddlebag. "Ye'll find that some house slaves in town carry messages in secret. As mistress to the Morris household, yer privy to his parlor discussion," he said. "He stops at Quinn's of an afternoon but takes his plans to yer house for privacy and scolds his son for a loose tongue. The boy be tight-lipped now."

"Plans? His business, you mean?"

"He aims to purchase a knighthood. He brags in private that he will own a great colonial estate, marry well and seek favor from the king. But what he means is that all who deal with him will be so indebted they'll be little more than the slaves he trades."

I was skeptical. Robert was always scheming about the farmer's debts but something bigger? I had a vague memory of knighthood mentioned... "This is bragging at which he excels, but I do not think he is *that* organized," I said. "How do you come by this knowledge, sir?"

"We have an assistant in the court."

"Robert doesn't go to the provincial court or the county court. I would know as Yearie and I prepare his clothes for every trip."

"He daren't keep a secret from ye? The man have more courtly wigs than any cept the governor."

I laughed. "Oh, true. All are jealous of his dress, but that doesn't mean he is out to cheat the entire populace."

"Sarah, doona fool yerself," he said, his brow drawn in recrimination. "Think about his Tobacco Act. His pretense to compete with sweet Virginia weed. Even the governor pays his renters to burn their inferior crops. Not Morris." He pooled the last of the nuts in his hand. "Maryland chaw, as bad as some say, is desired in France and Morris' ships stop in Madeira for wine. He can ship inferior weed to France under a Portuguese flag."

"You imply that when his inspectors dump tobacco, he sells it to our enemy? That flies against the rules of British commerce, my man."

"Just one reason to inspect tobacco before he ships it out. The farmer makes no profit, can't pay for the slaves he has on loan from yer Morris, and the poor sot forfeits his land for the frontier." He threw his head back and popped the nuts in his mouth.

I remembered Robert returning from his Annapolis trip with his newly painted portrait. The night Voltaire appeared, all the packages in the front hall. "And I get their leavings for my house?"

"Aye, and he the slaves they can't feed, and their wine goblets. And yer Robert buys title to their useless land."

"But it does him no good to hold land that lies fallow."

"Of course not. Morris proceeds to charge rack rent to the next back country indenture who's earned his freedom with hope in his eye and tobacco smoke in his head."

I stood and crawled into my skirts, tying them around my waist.

"Reverend Bacon gives the death rolls to Robert," I said. "Someone will always profit on their misfortune. If not Robert, then another."

I pulled up the ribbon of my shift, gathering a modest neck when he moved to help. Twirling me around, he ran the comb through my tangled hair and began to plait it. I caught his gaze over my shoulder. He was lost in thought.

"Aye. The court records say it's always Cunliffe or Master Morris involved in the suit," he said. "If we're destined to beat the English system built on the penury of others, then we must begin a new world order." He flipped one finished plait across my breast, then the other. "We need information from ye, positioned as ye are at the center of commerce." He spun me around.

"How do you come to know so much about a woman's needs, Alexander MacIntosh?"

"Ah, want to know, do ye? It's not a story to tell."

"Everyone in Oxford has a story to tell. I think I should know yours after today."

He grunted. Softly, he said, "I lost me wife and our babe. We had but two years together."

"I am so sorry." We were two of a kind, of a sort. His hand rested on my shoulder and I kissed him, holding his face between my hands. His eyes filled, making them green. "We go on."

"Aye, lass. There's nothing else for it."

He cinched the laces of my bodice as I crossed the tucker around my neck. Handing me a perfect straw bonnet, decorated with blue ribbon, I felt complete with one exception. My hand. The marks were bloody purple and would require explanation.

He took it in his. "We'll stop in East Town. We can borrow some gloves."

"What if Goldsboro is looking for you—or me?"

"M'lady, after being at sea in the hold of a ship, a prison hulk before that, and a year at Carlysle—I'm sure me own dear mother wouldna recognize me now."

It was true. Besides the fact that his eyes changed color depending on the light, the Scotsman had meat on his bones, hair of a determined reddish hue, a clean-shaven, square chin and a self-possessed calm that was absent the day of his arrival on Oxford's dock. He was, as they say, a changed man. He had even lost some of his brogue to the maroons.

"Help me concoct a story. I left last night to bury a slave's baby. Robert knows of it."

"Well, better to tell a partial truth than get caught in a lie. Ye became lost in the wood on the way home. I found ye abandoned on the outskirts of East Town, a victim of a black'art who would take advantage of ye. I took ye to my friend's home to have his good wife provision ye, and we proceeded to Oxford from there."

"Describe the blackheart. Robert will send for Goldsboro."

His eyes alight, he simpered about with a high voice, imitating me, "'He was about yer height, sheriff, dark-eyed and dark-haired, wearing sailor's skirts.' And when Goldsboro says that would describe most of the men of the village, ye say, 'Yes, sheriff, sir, but it was dark out and the moon was clouded.' Then throw him a bone and tell him the swine sounded like a cockney sailor."

"And what was the reprobate's purpose in taking me?"

"Why, to cover up his evil deeds, stealing from yer employer."

"Oh, one of Cunliffe's own sailors stealing from the Morris warehouse! And you will make your escape once you deposit me at my home? I won't see you until Robert travels again?"

"The next time I enter your village, missus, everyone will recognize me. As I take my leave today, give me a wink in secret, my sweet."

CHAPTER 17

*W*e packed up my sodden clothes and mounted our horses. Before long we had followed the creek to its most narrow inception, galloping an Indian trail where it widened, ditch-dug on either side. A county road. Finger signs pointed left to East Town, right to Oxford and straight to the White Marsh Church. We trotted left and soon heard sounds of civilization, the hammering of nails, and the bustle of wagons.

By the look of the sun it was after high noon and the townspeople were busy with marketing. Quaker women in their black drab were followed by little ones in white collars. Painted houses lined the wide lane. Barristers' signs hung along the main street ending in the tax man's establishment.

I grew jealous and wondered what these townspeople had that we didn't. We approached the Talbot Courthouse with its racetrack on the greens. This was what Robert called the local seat, a place where arguments and deceptions were settled by a judge, where oft times protest became plaintiff, and in his words, the wealthy became wealthier. It was also the site of the province's largest annual horse race where bettors staked their life savings.

Trotting down a cottage-lined alley, the stench of dung hung in the September air. We passed under a sign that said, *Three Coaches and Horseshoes*. Behind a clapboard cottage was a cobblestoned yard. Horses neighed, raising their noses to sniff. Two *worn* buggies sat under the shed. Alexander dismounted and reached to swing me from the saddle. I stepped into the shade of a large maple, its leaves brilliant in color. At the Scotsman's shout, two men looked up from their forge and one set down his tools to come to us. He was fair and bearded, I suspected to protect his skin from the sparks. His arms were covered in soot.

"Ye come back quickly," he said, all a-smile. "Yer task is finished?"

"Aye, Timothy. Mistress Kate be inside? We have a request."

The farrier called to a young man covered in a huge oil skin apron, who promptly ran to the back door of the house. Soon, a healthy woman with babe in arms appeared. Laughing, her cheeks flushed and her hair curling from under a mob cap, she strolled to Alexander, one arm held wide.

"What trouble do ye bring today?" she asked.

Alex nodded to me. "Goodwife Kate, this is Mistress Sarah and she be desirous of a pair of gloves to hide a calamity."

The lady ignored me. "Well now, sir, ye can have anything Samuel and I have but it'll cost ye. And ye best stop calling me good-wife as we're not in Scotland anymore."

Alex laughed and gave her a hug, pulling the baby from her arms. "Where is Samuel? Filling his belly at yer table?"

"No, he were called by the sheriff to join a slave hunt this morning." She leaned her head toward me and said, "Seems a gentle woman of Oxford is missing along with her manservant in the middle of the night."

Alex smiled. "Aye, and being Samuel's the best tracker in the county, he'll be letting his dogs follow a scent south to Virginie."

"I canna say where it leads. Never back to us! Now, what be ye needing from me?"

He passed the child back to Kate and asked her for some biscuits and a pair of lady's gloves, promising to replace them. Another item from Robert's warehouse. Kate crooked her finger at me and, once inside, she pointed to the windowsill where the morning's baking cooled.

"Take a cloth and git whatever ye like." Then handing me the baby, she clomped up an enclosed stair to the second story, her step heavy above me. I selected some biscuits and cornbread and before I wrapped them, she returned, adding two raisin scones and a ham hock.

"Master Alex has himself an appetite," she said. She took my hands in hers and led me to the kitchen bench. With great sincerity, she said, "Now, ye canna be an innocent country lass. I know where ye and Alex have been, so ye best say to anyone who asks that these marks are from the lash of a horsewhip wielded by that escaped slave."

"Mistress Kate, I am indebted to you beyond words, but I have no reason to blame an innocent slave for my wounds. I cannot lie."

She roared with laughter. "So, being deceitful is not in your nature? But I bet ye can do it to save yer own hide. Mark me words, missy, if ye don't, the law will turn on ye."

"I...I can't imag—"

"No one is innocent, my lamb. We make our way under an oppressive rule." She got up and grabbing a linen towel, swept it across the table capturing the crumbs, then threw them in a bowl. She leaned both hands on its surface and said, "Samuel and I run a stable for hire, but the rack rent for this little slice of independence near a mortal wound each month. We make our money on the side and Goldsboro takes it from us not knowing it comes from his own pocket. In four years, this will be our piece of dirt." She stood tall. "If ye wish to be yer own woman, ye'll learn to parse the truth with the best of us."

I covered my ugly hand and nodded. Everywhere there was evidence of their machinations. Goldsboro, Robert, The Handys, Thomas Bacon, even the perfect Tilghmans. They weren't nobility, they weren't titled. As second sons, they would never win an inheritance. The best they had was their education.

But in Robert, that wasn't the case. He had the scars on his hands for anyone to see, and often complained to me of long days as a child standing at a slitter, cutting bars of iron for the blacksmith's forge. Iron wrought into rose-headed nails helped feed his grandmother. In polite company, he wears long laces at his cuffs to hide his marred youth and waves his hands like a Burgess of Annapolis.

"I can do whatever is asked of me," I said to the stable mistress.

"That's a girl," said Kate. "Did the Indians give you nothin? They only give a present to whites if they want something back."

"Seeds."

"Jimson, I bet. Ye canna grow the Witchesberry?"

"I will."

"Doona put it where children or dogs can git it. Plant in shade on drainable ground and forgit it. It be a weed but doona touch it without yer gloves. The provincials say, 'The skin will it die, blackness to the eye; armies dream of devils and hearts will be leveled.'"

She nodded and, now that I was in league with her, said with a wink, "It's best as a tea laced liberal with honey."

She enveloped me in her sugary scent, and we went outside. I tugged on the lace gloves and looked up to see a two-horse open chaise with a liveried boy standing behind. Bets was tied to the back. He stepped down and proffered his hand to me.

"M'lady."

Alexander appeared from the stable, nearly unrecognizable. He wore a yellow silk coat, brown vest and buff britches, white stockings, and an even whiter cravat. Under his tricorn appeared a wig with two curls on either side of his cheekbone.

"Alexander!"

"*Enchanté, Mademoiselle. Où est-ce que vous voudriez voyager?*"

"Alex?"

"Forgive me, my pet," he said as he bowed in his most servile way. "Allow me to introduce myself. Le Comte de Broussard, late of Saint Domingue."

"And what is your business, sir?" I asked, curtsying. "Besides delivering me to Oxford."

"Coffee, sugar and chocolate for the venerable agent of Oxford."

"From the French colony? You are mad. Robert will never bargain with a stranger to go against the king's act."

"I can bring him his madeira cheaper and an extra shipment of Belgian chocolate. Perhaps some pineapple."

"Oh, pineapple?" I said, dreaming of its sweetness in a cake.

"Ah, see how easy it be to lure you in?"

I lifted my skirts and stepped in the chaise. The boy grabbed the bar behind us.

"Walk on," Alex commanded, gingering up the horses.

On the East Town road there was much traffic, no one tarried. Once in the countryside, I took the reins so that he could eat. Growing sleepy soon after, he leaned back and dozed. I drove at a modest clip for, from the lay of the land, we had time. I glanced at his sleeping face wondering if I could escape my life for his. Even in sleep, he did not look innocent.

CHAPTER 18

I slowed to snail's pace on passing Oxford's tobacco fields. Poor farmers, lacking slaves to work their fields, leaned against fencerows and stared at leaves destroyed by the hornworm. We passed the rudimentary foundation of a drying barn that had been moved closer to a viable field. Down the road, a husband scolded his wife who labored upon a row in the hot sun, plucking pests into a sack. I grumbled and, waking, Alex drew his hand across his mouth and took the reins.

A bad case of sullied eyes caused me to see outlying Oxford in black and white. Weathered shacks and outbuildings built of bare wood, beaten by salt air stood ramshackle against each other. The best were whitewashed with the leftovers from ships, but none were painted in the warm colors of East Town. Some were slapped together from tobacco barns, their planks bowed inward like a starved stomach, their seams ribbed with mud. Whole families set about, hunched over, toiling in dirt, attempting to craft a way of life. Once, I had wandered homeless, begging a handout from these people. They had little but shared, unlike the masters of the great plantations.

As the road widened, a light breeze carried the salt air of the

126

Chesapeake. My mood brightened seeing the village, her windowsills dressed in flowers, their frames lined with cheery laces and lawns bordered by picket fences. This was my middle rung and I became anxious thinking I was one fall from crashing to the bottom. I wondered what I would face from Robert. Demands, of course. And work that defined my value but, ultimately, I faced his bed. I looked over the rooftops. The cloudless sky had turned to milk and was broken by the masts of six large ships, their sails furled. Robert would have heard their call.

My loyalties were suddenly divided. Caught by the bustle of Oxford's industry, the draw of my woodland dalliance waning, I stared away from Alexander. I felt his hand upon mine and weakly, I smiled at him.

This was my home. These people were my friends. I was a mere girl once a time ago, pledged to Edward, a young swain who idolized me. Our vows were celebrated with a round of invitations and toasts, for we were all related by our labors.

Sinner, was I. It mattered not my Catholic commandments, I had broken God's promise and would go to Hell for my fornications. I was shamed by the memory of my fleeting happiness, running half-naked through the woods, splashing the waters of the creek and tumbling to nature's gentle earth with a criminal, a thief. Was his goodness a facade?

A great chasm rose between me and the man at the reins. His country's fight was worthy. Carried across the seas, he had freed himself from bondage and aligned with others in their quest for freedom. The maroons—blacks, whites, Scots, Indians...*they were not my people*.

I would help, but I couldn't desert my village. The swamp was a cruel existence and the taste of homelessness still stuck in my craw. What seemed a simple calculation was the measure of the Scot's gentleness against my lord's sweeping presence. The Trader of Men.

I knew that Robert was at home. I felt it in my bones.

"Alexander, you mustn't do this," I said. "Think of the maroons. Do not jeopardize them. If it's true they are secreted in the courts and have befriended the authorities, you are one small cog in their wheel. Robert is not one to fool with. He is close to Goldsboro."

He searched my face for understanding. I looked down at my folded hands. "You have given me a brief happiness beyond all that I'm used to, that I will always cherish. But we cannot go down this path for it would be the ruin of us both."

He clasped my good hand. "M' lady, ye grow upset. Ahl not toy with him today of a trade in goods. Ahl deliver ye to him, from one gentleman to another, for the sake of yer reputation. Acting the foppish Frenchman will give him something to gossip about in the tavern."

The horse had stopped for lack of a whip or a cluck. I thought we best not dawdle in the open for even that would raise suspicion. "Go on then," I said. "I trust this will be brief. I have work." I sighed, committed to whatever might occur.

Wherever Robert was, drink was involved. There were two horses tied to the post in front of the house. The windows were wide open and when I set foot on the front stoop, I heard a scream out back by the slave quarters. Reaching for the brass knob, my hand fell to my side as the door opened before us. Yearie stood in its frame, a look of utter terror on her sweet face.

"What is it, my girl? What is happening?"

"Sary, he tortures Jackson."

"What? Who?" I asked.

"Findley. Goldsboro cornered him in the woods." Tears leaked from the corners of her eyes as she raised them to the heavens.

I pushed past her to hear that unmistakable badge of authority in men's voices. She stepped to one side and, seeing the Scotsman behind me, bowed her head and curtsied.

"Beg pardon, sir. I not see you behind my mistress." She grabbed my arm as I tore my bonnet off. I leaned to her.

"Trapped by his dogs, dragged behind a horse," she whispered. "Findley said he was on Handy's property, burying the baby."

A low moan was heard. "Why did Jackson go there?"

"Looking for you. I couldn't find you. But—but, you're here!" she said limply.

I turned and ran to the stable yard.

The back door was open to the kitchen garden and beyond to the square bounded by the barn, shed, and the lopsided shack Robert called his slave quarters. I heard a man's command, "Stop!" and I pulled up, my hand over my heart. Hanging from the oak tree by his wrists was Jackson, naked to his waist, the silver scars of many whippings curling across his back. My precious oak had never been used as a gallows. I dropped my bonnet.

In the last two months, Jackson had not worn a shirt for his sweat bonded with the scabs and pulled them off, seeping and raising the surface like a nest of baby snakes. Handy's slave debt wouldn't be repaid if he died.

The overseer stood in the long shadow of the tree, a braided bull-whip by his side. Robert and Goldsboro bent their heads in confer-ence, pipes in their teeth and pints in their hands as if strolling the bowling green. Everyone else waited their decision. The helmet dogs in the dirt, panting. Tiberius, ramrod straight at attention by the quarter door, eyes averted. Hestia and Voltaire on a stable bench, watching. Young Robert held a tray of grooming tools.

Yearie ran to Tiberius. At Robert's voice, Jackson's head fell back, his mouth open.

"You have disobeyed me for the last time. Steal my housekeeper for cover and abandon her to bury a slave's baby? Where did you leave her? Tell me, or Findley will curry you like the beast you are." He raised his pint. "Go ahead. I do not wish to watch."

Goldsboro took another swig and said, "I've spent an entire day pursuing this criminal. Just hamstring him and be done with it."

"'Tis true, sir," answered Findley, his eyes alight. "The leg atro-phies and you chain it to a neck ring, so the limb doesn't swing."

"Jackson's no field hand," answered Robert. "He's a harbor brute. I don't want my guests exposed to a hamstrung stable slave. Unsightly."

"Sarah, speak up," said Alexander in my ear, but I was filled with dread. Always afraid. Always debating. Always at a loss. Findley grimaced and pursed his thin lips. From young Rob's tray of rusted barn implements, he plucked a curry comb and laid it upon Jackson's back, pressing its teeth into the edges of his scars. Jackson groaned, and I thought *this will finally kill the poor man.*

I yelled, "Robert. Stop! I am here!"

He turned at my words, a startled face filling with relief. "Sarah!" He ran to me, smothering me in his arms. Bay water, gin, and tobacco blended in his vest and jolted me from my torpor. In his eyes was absolute joy and—confusion.

"M'love. I thought you dead or abandoned in the forest for the wolves." He held me at arm's length. "A beautiful sight and I know not how this comes to be!" He pulled me to him again. "A lovely new dress," he whispered in my ear. "You ordered it on your own."

I ignored him and said loudly, "I only went to bury the slave child, m'lord, for Findley had thrown it in a dung heap." Glaring at the overseer who had dropped the curry comb, I said, "That baby's end was inhuman."

"Are you besotted, Sarah?" asked Robert. "Yearie alerted me this morn. The good sheriff set out for you and found Jackson in the woods at Handy's. Where have you been, my dear?"

Had it only been one night, one day? A lifetime packed into the turn of one moon and one sun? I buried my face in his cravat, not wanting him to see the truth in my eyes.

"M'sieur Morris, allow me to elucidate."

"I beg your pardon. I am ze Comte de Broussard, à la Saint Domingue, a marchand de vin, ef you will. I discovered ze fair lady, Madame Wise, in need of my assistance zis morning on ze East Town Road." His hand waved as if he were beating back a swarm of bees. "She had been waylaid by a thief and was in great distress. A sniveling bastard wis a cockney accent held her against her will. Being unarmed, he took to ze woods on seeing me."

Alex tucked the edge of his long coat behind his gun and sword, resting his hand on its hilt. Its embossed silver flashed in the fading sunlight and Robert's eyes widened on seeing a hated Frenchman fully armed in his yard. Robert's flintlock would be locked in his desk drawer. A mask passed over his face, his eyes hooded.

"I am in your debt, Mr. Broussard. Have you saved good Mistress Wise from the evils of Man and Nature?"

I began to waver. I had consumed both Man and Nature. Robert smelled a lie.

"M'sieur, in ze nick of time! Mistress Wise knelt in the woods by ze side of ze road, her wrists bound and in prayer she asked for Our Holy Lord's protection. Ze thief demanded knowledge of ze next shipment of Madeira. She pleaded wis him, saying she knew nuhzing of your buziness."

Robert's lips tightened, his frown deepened. "The East Town Road is well travelled. In plain daylight, you say? Not a very astute highwayman."

"M'oui, m'sieur. Poor bastard. If not for ze coffee zis morning and rotgut wine last night, ze call of Nature might not have gripped me so strongly. I was in ze woods when I heard her cries."

Robert softened. "Ah, a good piss?" He gulped his pint and wrapped his arm around my shoulders. "M'lady saved by the watering can!" He looked at Findley who waited, ready to get back to his work. I hated the man with all my heart.

I hated them all at that moment. "Robert," I said, "you must let Jackson go. You have punished him enough."

Goldsboro laughed. "Your conscience speaks, Morris. Always soft on the dirty pickers." He tapped his pipe on the window ledge and spit. "You have no more need of me. I will leave the discipline of your property to you. It seems I have a certain highwayman on the loose. Broussard, can you describe him?"

Alex sniffed and raised a handkerchief to his nose, his sensibilities wounded. "M'sieur, we have not been introduced."

"Bloody right. This is not a salon, Frenchie. Answer me. I'm the sheriff."

I watched with alarm as Goldsboro's dogs rose to his side.

"Ah, of course. Zis would explain one's corpulence for I have never met a man of ze law who is not encased in ze armor of gluttony."

We all froze in shock for a bare second. Goldsboro charged at Alex, who sidestepped him with a squeal. Clumsy with drink, the sheriff stumbled to a knee, unable to draw his sword.

Robert laughed merrily while Findley flung the curry comb in the toolbox. Rolling my eyes, I put my hand out to the great Comte de Broussard and asked, "Your dagger, sir? I have need of it."

The Frenchman drew it from its scabbard and laid it in my gloved palm. I strode to Jackson and put the blade to the rope tied to a low branch. In a heap of ruin, Jackson dropped to the ground. I fell to my knees and took his hands in mine. "I am sorry, Jackson. It's my fault. Never will this happen again." My house, my yard, my stable. Our slaves. It had to cease for all time. His deep brown eyes were filled with doubt—and anger. No wonder. His body was not his own, always there for his betters to toy with, to test. He was not a Black Jesus.

Looking around the assembled men, I stood and ordered, "It is time for supper, and I suggest you find your way home. Count Broussard, I am grateful for your help, but I have no wish for Robert to entertain conversation about trade tonight. We are exhausted from the day's events." I put the dagger in his hand. "There is a tavern where you can get a meal and a room."

The sheriff stood, lurching to Tiberius who dusted his knee. Goldsboro pushed him aside.

"You must go, my lord Goldsboro. Return on the morrow for a description of the cockney thief. Young Rob, put the tools in the barn and help Voltaire get Jackson to bed. I will treat him, momentarily. I have tolerated you men far too long." I began to take off my gloves finger by finger. Concentrating on each word, I said, "Mr. Findley, you are not welcome here ever again. Make yourself scarce or I will be forced to explain to the courts in East Town your branding of a Scottish indenture on the Handy property."

Doubt narrowed his eyes and he threatened in the only way he knew, "Mr. Morris will not tolerate a woman like you running his business, much less his slaves."

"A woman like me, sir? You underestimate me."

Robert kicked the curry comb. "Whipped by a woman, Findley.

Do what she asks. The law says you may increase years of indenture, not brand. I will speak with Master Handy."He turned to me, both hands raised in welcome. "We shall eat now, my love!"

Goldsboro mounted his horse. "Morris, I will speak to you of your woman. Tiberius, now! Stop sniffing around that kitchen slave." He and his retinue departed. I was unafraid.

Always the magnanimous host, Robert looked the Frenchman up and down in a new light. "M'sieur Broussard," he said, "you will find the tavern a hotbed of gossip as Oxford is the crossroads of trade on the Eastern Shore. But I warn you not to trade in politics, for we are not kind toward Continental views of our king."

Alexander bowed. "My liege. I am grateful for ze advice. I pursue money and wine, sir, in that order and zat is all." He stole a sidelong glance at me and winked. Yearie curtsied and escorted him to the front door.

I was home.

Robert seemed imbued with a sense of joviality. Tossing his head, he fairly skipped through the kitchen door shouting behind him, "My son, take my bags to my room and fetch a bottle of wine from the cellar. I have much to celebrate!"

CHAPTER 19

*Y*oung Rob watched his father with a sullen face. It was not lost on me. Softly he asked what were slaves for if he had to do their work, but he shuffled over to the massive puddle of our stable slave. Hefting Jackson over his shoulder with Voltaire's help, he trudged to the slave cabin. Hestia followed them into the darkness. Soon, a candle burned near the one window and I watched as they dumped Jackson to the floor. Young Rob emerged, bossing Voltaire to carry his master's bags upstairs. As he passed me, he remarked, "Father makes connections for me, lady. My fortune is set but yours is cemented here."

I picked up my bonnet, giving him no mind. In the kitchen, Yearie laid a platter of scrapple and bowls of cold pottage upon the table. Robert went above stairs to wash. I thought he would eat, read in the parlor, and ask me to play the harpsichord. Then, I could talk to Yearie.

I lit candles and unhooked a frying pan over the fireplace. "We need something hot, Yearie. Maybe some johnny cakes," I said as I pulled an apron over my head. "Later," I whispered, "we should talk."

She looked behind her for Rob and said loudly, "I'll be steamin' oysters for the pottage then. Should I get Hestia, Sary?"

"No, no. She has her hands full with Jackson. Robert likes an egg fried in his cake. Would you get some from the larder? I'll make enough for everyone. As soon as it's done take some pottage to the cabin."

"Yes'm."

Stirring the coals to flames, I bent to place the rack when I caught a movement in the corner of my eye. Young Rob lurked behind me. I snapped to attention.

"Boy" I yelled. "Do you try to trip me?"

He leaned lackadaisically against the dry sink, holding a bottle of wine in the air. "No, missus. I wish to have you approve my selection since you spent the day with a tradesman of wine. Did you gain some knowledge?"

"I know nothing more than I did yesterday, Rob. Move away and take the bottle to the table for your father."

Yearie set a bowl of eggs on the hearth and deftly shucked oysters into warming cream. She set cider and napkins and reserved the remainder of the pot for the quarter. I scooped some bacon fat into the hot pan and poured seven cakes from the bowl of mix. The fat sizzled and rose in curlicues, browning the cornbread edges. Pushing a spoon to cup them, I cracked an egg in the middle of each. Rob was decidedly grumpy and in need of attention, so I laid a strip of bacon across his. Nestling the lid on the pan, I grabbed a dash of salt from the box hanging on the chimney and spilled it into a cellar for the table.

"Yearie, where did the boy go?" I asked.

"Outside."

Peeking through the window I could barely make out his figure in the gloaming light of sunset. I thought at first, he was playing a game with Voltaire, but soon realized that as he threw stones here and there, he commanded the slave boy to retrieve them one at a time and bring them to him, only to hurry and retrieve another. When he brought the wrong one, Rob laid a riding crop about his neck. Voltaire scurried about, his hands over his head, trying to please his young master. There was perhaps two years between them, and Voltaire was the elder and bigger.

Yearie had pulled the window down against the cool night air. I pushed it up and roared, "Rob, come here at once!"

He froze and looked over his shoulder at me, dropping the stones in the yard. Slump shouldered, he walked to the kitchen door where he waited, armored in insolence. I gazed at him, his hair wild, his clothing disheveled and a visage of molded impertinence. The boy's education was not served following his father's footsteps. He needed discipline and for lack of that...

"You will *not* treat Voltaire like a dog. He is your responsibility and you are his lord. You must gain his respect and loyalty. I swear you will attend Reverend Bacon's church on Sunday. Now sit at the table and act like a gentleman."

Yearie poured the creamy oyster stew into our pottage bowls. I returned to the fire and lifted the lid from the frying pan. Golden orbs looked back at me from the cornbread, sunny and cheerful. Scooping some hot fat across the yolks, I watched the yellow harden in their white rings. Hefting the pan, I walked to the table to serve ours.

"I don't want the egg," said young Rob.

I raised my eyebrows. He liked eggs just like his father.

"Yearie, would you call Master Morris to let him know his supper is ready?" I asked.

She nodded, a slight frown upon her face.

"I don't want it," he repeated. "It's yeoman food." His glare stunned me, so I clucked and returned his johnnycake to the hearth, giving the rest to Yearie for the quarter.

"It's God-given food," I said, wiping my hands on my apron. "It's here if you want it.

Bareheaded, Robert arrived rubbing his hands together as he looked at the table. His forehead had grown in size during my absence and I realized a barber had shaved more of his head. His temples were marred with matching sores from his wigs. Cured only three days ago, his vanity of wearing a wig into the wee hours had caught up with him again.

"Fresh oysters?"

"Yes," I said. "Yearie shucked them only now."

He scratched his temple and a small rivulet of blood trickled down his cheek. I dabbed it with my kitchen rag. "Do not fiddle. You make it worse," I scolded.

Robert took my wrist. "Whatever did you do to your hand, Sarah?"

"Oh, just a kitchen accident. It is nothing."

"I own the best cook in the county, and you persist in slaving in the kitchen. I will not have your hands scarred, madam. It is offensive to our guests at table."

I tucked my hand behind my skirt and put on a jolly face as I sat. I was sick of discord. Glancing at young Rob, I saw he still smoldered at his father's orders. Such a sour face I'd never encountered on the boy. "Youngster," I said to him gently, but he would not look my way.

Instead, he rose to his feet with fists clenched to accuse his father. "You left our family pounding nails to eat and you worry this housemaid has a welt?" he shouted. "My brother says our mother died with scars and burns that mangled her hands and you had no concern for *her*!" He leaned over the simple food we had fixed and fairly spit out the rest. "*Ironmongers*—all five of us, hungry and clothed in rags. Nana said you had no shame until the bastard court came after you!"

In a flash, Robert backhanded him, knocking him to the floor. I had only ever seen him treat a harbor slave with such quick savagery. He spit his words, "My cur of a dog gives me more respect than you! I give you food, clothes, a world above your birthright, and this is the thanks I get?"

The child matched him in heat. "Voltaire is worth more to you than me. I see it." He whirled and pointed at me, hurling blame. "And her escort was no Frenchman. I spent two months at sea with that bloody Scot."

I pressed my wounded hand to my heart, mocking him. "Rob," I said, "you should be ashamed to utter such slander. Your mind is warped by an ill humor. We love you. Do not bite the hand that feeds you."

"Cunt!"

His father shot around the table. Picking up the fire tongs, he struck the boy across his back. His son caved to the floor and scrambled away, turning in fear and revulsion, his arm raised in defense. Robert's face was beet red, his mouth curled. I thought another strike and he might kill his son. I rushed between them, my hands raised.

"Stop! Stop! Calm yourselves! You will bring shame on our house, never mind the law." I pushed Young Rob toward the hall, he walking backward, threatening his father with gestures over my shoulders. I turned to face m'lord who held the tongs above his head ready to rain down on mine. "Robert, please!"

Still waters welled in his eyes and he stepped back, the tongs clattering to the floor. Yearie stood behind him, her hand over her mouth. My lord coughed but could not speak.

"Child, you must go to your bed immediately and stay there until I say!" I shouted as I reached for the tongs.

We heard his step in the front hall, and his father fell into my arms, burying his face in my hair. "I cannot raise that boy in my household." He whispered in my ear. "He judges my every word and censures my every action with his looks." He raised his head from my neck and searched my face. "Why, in Annapolis we ate breakfast at Tilghman's, and what did he do? He stuffed his pockets with delicacies as if he would starve the rest of the day."

I couldn't help it. I laughed and Robert's face fell. "He is a boy, Robert. A hungry boy who isn't sure of his place in the world. Do you not see how desperation has scarred him?"

"He lies. I provided for them as I could. I sent money to Elizabeth's fishwife of a mother. She wasted it on gin." He sat abruptly on the bench, his head in his hands. "Desperation? We were all desperate and starving until I came here."

"How did you support them, Robert? There were five? Be they all yet alive?"

"Look at my hands, Sarah. An ironmonger, pounding nails for the colonial market until Cunliffe took me under his wing. He taught me record-keeping. I wanted to assist my betters, for, in the end, I understood it would benefit *me*. When he offered me agent at Oxford, I did not blink twice." He turned his hands up, pleading. "Rob was two when Liza died. I bear him no ill will, but I have never been a father to him and don't intend to become one now."

I had no great love for his son, but could not stand that his father had no compassion. "He is the youngest of five and grew up watching them struggle," I said. "It's why he thinks of himself before anyone else. He has a dream to be like you."

"I didn't send for him. His grandmother and my sisters sent him here, no doubt because they grow sick of mothering."

"Well, perhaps they are weary. Or dying," I said. I grew tired of his myopic defense. I knew if he didn't eat soon, he would pull on the cow teat of ill humor till its hoof kicked him in the gut. "Come, let's sup and be thankful."

He sat and I served, nodding to Yearie to disappear; I would handle him alone for the sake of peace. She took the johnny cakes and stew and left. I asked Robert about Tilghman's home. He brightened, telling me of the size of the mansion and terraced gardens. I poured him another cup of wine. He dropped names I didn't know—Lloyd and Chase, Peale and Tasker. I poured again.

He gobbled his food, spilling as he spoke with great enthusiasm of his introductions and how Tilghman advised he move to Annapolis and become Cunliffe's leading factor in the new capital. I poured some more. He spoke of purchasing prime land in Cunliffe's name and building a large warehouse with a great sign that would announce his benefactor's business. He would take his trade to Baltimore, for it was a nubile pimple ready to explode. I reached for a second bottle of claret, and, easing the cork, I poured the cup to its brim.

"A wonderful dream," I said, "and you will make it come true because you are Robert Morris." Digging some more, I asked. "My love, won't this take money?" I cut a heaping slice of orange cake and, topping it with two candied lemon slices, pushed it across the table. He bent his head and sniffed over his plate. His florid countenance grew wide in a smile, and he wiped the sweat from his forehead. Like a puppy sitting in its empty bowl with a full belly, his mirth spilled over. In the waning light, I lit another candle.

"Ah," he said, "Cunliffe will send me sterling when I tell him my plans. I make him a very wealthy man. I have no need of tobacco notes. God knows, after this rash of worms in the fields, farmers will plant wheat."

"I have little head for managing trade," I countered, "though I am good at numbers as you have seen." Needling him, I repeated the worry of which everyone spoke, "But even I know that we will never have enough sterling in the colonies to support trade. The Crown controls it well."

"Toady George and Parliament become irrelevant in this," he said, shocking me at the plainness of his words. I had thought his loyalty cut in stone. "The lord proprietor sets the value of Maryland land, although Calvert is a fool in speculation. The province land office will write me a note based on property I have taken near the Indian reservation."

"Oh, Robert, how wonderful. You are landed gentry!" He nodded rapidly. It was so easy to see his greed.

"I got it for a song. The old man died of the pox and couldn't pay his slave debt to Cunliffe. The fields are worn out. Lord Calvert disputes the province's boundary line with the Penn proprietor, so our land office wants those acres registered in the name of a trusted Maryland colonist."

"You don't worry that the Quaker governor will sway parliament on the boundary? If he wins, he'll claim it for the Penn colony. You'll have a deed of worthless paper."

"Nonsense! This is why women are not born to lead. Although it's a pretty head, yours is not fit for government."

I began clearing the table.

"Calvert has petitioned chancery court in London. We will win.

The court might not like his Papist loyalties, but they won't ignore the rule of law to favor that litter of Penn's. I've titled the land 'Rich Range' and it's my future in British coin." He beamed with self-importance.

It all came full circle—a twist of loans, debts, payoffs and hushed words. I poured him another glass and smiled. Robert saw the end game in his pursuit of money. He had enough collateral that he could buy his land in Annapolis and leave the backwoods of Oxford. I appeared joyful. I poured more wine, but my anxiety was complete. "I am proud of you."

He slid from his bench, pulling me down to mine. I leaned my head against him. Careful, I whispered. "If you move to Annapolis, you'll need a housekeeper for the mansion you will build."

He stroked my hair and kissed my cheek, my ear, my neck. "'Tis true. A woman of intellect and talent. A beauty to grace my halls. We will throw great parties. And then I will be invited to the most distinguished social events of town."

"And we will be married this November to prepare."

His hand froze over my check and slipped away. His eyes faltered and I knew at that moment that his ways in Oxford were no different than in Liverpool. The difference was he could afford to dream, where I could only afford to ride his coattails as his housekeeper—or his concubine.

I looked into his eyes. They were red-rimmed and clouded with wine. "My love," I said. "I will do what you require. Make your fortune."

"British sterling, Sarah. Cunliffe won't know how much the Annapolis agency costs, and I will keep the unspent balance or invest in more land. I will never live at Rich Range, but it will be the foundation of all other land patents in my name. I will be renowned as a great host of the capital."

He was drunk and a fool. Robert would never be accepted in polite society. He was a grubby merchant with a talent for making money for his betters. Long on avarice and short on title. But I would never be married, the poor farmers would be cheated of their land, and the Indians who lived on Rich Range would leave for the northern reaches. And a slave could only hope for a kind master. We were all full of wanton wishes, some dashed more than others. Alexander was right. Time for me to decide where my loyalties lay.

I looked over Robert's head and saw Yearie hovering outside the door. She beckoned me as if to say, "Come, you are wasting time."

I disentangled myself from Robert and stood. He blurted out, "You must come to my bed tonight. I have need of your charms."

"M' lord, you are in your cups. Make your way upstairs and get ready for bed. I will be up to remove your boots in a second."

He tottered in the hallway, his hand on the wall, blowing me kisses. I heard him lumber up the steps. At the kitchen door, I whispered to Yearie, "I'll return. He is a sodden mess. Wait for me."

The night was cool. Yearie had set a fire in Robert's chamber upstairs, but it had burned to charred wood. A cold room and too much drink had done the trick. Robert wavered in front of its glow, shirtless, still in his breeches and boots. I set the candle on his bedside table, gathering his clothes from the floor. Turning down the covers, I murmured, "Come, I'll pull them off."

Shoveling a heap of coals in the bedwarmer, I swept it over the linen. Done, I placed it on top of the bed and waited impatiently for his booted foot. He sat on the edge and lifted one and then the other. I stacked them at the door while he loosened the strings on his breeches and stepped out of them. There he was in all his glory, graying chest hair, a growing paunch, and a dangling flute he expected me to play.

The bed warmer lay precariously on the pile of blankets behind him. I reached for his nightshirt and threw it over his head, his naked arse buried in the mattress. His bald head poking through the neck of his shirt reminded me of sealing wax and the Cunliffe ring. Quietly, I nudged the warmer off the bedclothes, and said, "Oh m'lord, jump before it burns you!"

Too late, it seared his backside. Wallowing in the batting, he squealed like a stuck pig and, having mercy on him, I gave him my hand.

"Why didn't you care for the warmer, sir? It was right there for anyone to see," I admonished as I placed it on the hearth. I pulled his nightshirt down and patted his shoulder. Tucking him in, I whispered lovingly, "I am going down to the slave quarters, Robert, to speak with Yearie. I must help them, you know."

Drunk and whimpering, he pushed his head deep in the pillow, not hearing a word.

PART II
YEARIE

The most common way people give up their power is by thinking they didn't have any.
\- Alice Walker

CHAPTER 20

*S*leep and dreams in the over yonder were not mine on this night. But maybe Jackson could if I calm his spirit. I rock and sing—*Oh my Lord keep me from sinkin down*—and I sit on his pallet, curl next to his shiver and shake, knouted by Findley's leather whip and curry wire. I whisper in his ear to bear up, to overcome, that we be master of ourself. He blew air from his nostrils like some horse in a race, whipped to a frenzy by his white master.

"Reverend Bacon say it be our lot— that Heaven hold our glory," I say.

He snort and groan, "Best me, not you, Yearie. Angel Gabriel be a yelling in my mind, ready to call me home."

His forehead wrinkle with deep grooves and I pat it with a wet rag, bloody from sopping his backside. Takin in the total of his condition—bare legs all scratched and mangled from being dragged through the woods, wounds seep, and a worry his spirit be broke—I give advice. "Leave your mortal body and float to Heaven's door, but don't you pass through," I answer. "Our work not finished."

He moaned and cursed Master's existence, wishin them all Hell-fire an Damnation, then ask the Lord to forgive him. His eyes rise to the window an, lo, the cockerel's eye hang in a ring round the moon, its white lasso chained to the harbor. Bad weather tomorrow.

"Come for me now, Sweet Jesus. Master's soul belong to the Devil."

"They goin to Hell, Jackson, an we be sendin them," I say and stroke his long hair. "Do not leave me this night."

I crawl to my feet and look in the fat eyes of Cook, so dark there no pupils, like Morris' dog, dry and blank. There she be, I think— the silent slave. Got talent to hide what she know, who she be, and where she go. They can whip and demean the lot of us, and define us by our skin, but they can't take our Prophesy. There be too many of us now.

"You stayin?" Cook ask.

"Nay, you have a sorrel poultice?"

"Ah be a layin it on his rump and turn it in a bit. Get on with it," she say.

"Good Hestia, I be in your debt. See if he can eat. Time movin and I got to talk to Sary. Months of work come to fruition." She shake her head at me. In darkness, I slip across the stable yard, move in the shadows, hear an owl's hoot echo across the water. Oxford Town be close to sleep.

Listenin outside the kitchen door, I watch Master and Sary in the circle of candlelight, he extol, and she remark. I marvel at his barefaced words, honesty he not reveal to her before. They words I've heard whisper from many folk, but now I trust them as true. Come from the horse's mouth.

Master a shape shifter like the Ligaboo of my Ma's Trinidad. He leave his bed at night and walk the stable yard, sometime wicked and sometime charitable, but mostly my enemy. Just t'other fortnight past, I beat a rabbit with my holy water stick for it be a gnawin in the garden, listening to our plans for the rebellion. Not a minute later its dead body disappear whence I turn my back, and in its place stand Master laughin at me.

Now, he sit in his kitchen spinnin his tale of death and life, of buy and sell, of win and loss. All proud of his Rich Range. Most I know, for my Ma teach me afore she sold for White Man Greed. Sary's virgin ears ain't know this man for who he be. She be as much his chattel as I, just better dressed. But this be her test and she be provin true. She lit his ego and watch it flame.

I worried she would fail. Would she wipe her hands on his linen cloth and pick his nits afore his sleep? Dab her napkin on his dribble like he were her child, so long gone, haunt her still? She dance in his orb, sing in his glow, her fingers on his ivory keys while I scrub his kitchen floor.

This time, would she listen to *our* truth?

I surprised she command Master's whippin party to quit. The way she pull her finger from her glove and banish Findley. And then, the boy. Why, she near took him by his oysters and twist them till he confess he hate his father. And still, she play Master's concubine.

All I want was for her to bury that babe, make things right, and the story play out better'n I foresee, cept for Jackson. It were my fault for sending him to look for her. I ponder if she made it all the way to the swamp. This Frenchman be a friend, tho a dandy. Tonight, when he take off for the tavern, he tip two finger to his hat, a signal we have in common. I be glad he's gone, for I need to get word to the maroons after she lay bare her soul.

She wearin the calico of a landed woman, not trussed up high and mighty in court dress from Master's store. Like when we grow up in her mama's house. Long afore she be Morris' mistress, he ply her with satin and lace, baubles and perfume, makin her ridiculous. How is it that she be more a slave than me? And I know it be her greed.

If Findley'd had his way, I be a cryin over Jackson's cut hamstring, and he be hitchin bout on peg leg and a crutch, his ankle chained to his neck like a de-form scotch hopper. If she have one fault it be that she calculate consequence too long before she act. Sometime, you got to act on instinct, for pride goeth and shame come after. She been lost to Master goods, and now be the time to get her back.

Outside the kitchen door, wind from the harbor make my neck cold. They talk had grown soft and I leaned in tight. Master's son nowhere round. It be just the two of them, Sary and Morris, hallowed in the candlelight, him drunk as a lord, she hanging on his every word.

"Make your way to bed," she said and looked up at me over his shoulder. I beckoned to her.

It took only a flash to see it in her eyes. She be with me! But she didn't know what I been bout to ask. And I didn't know if she be in her right mind. She followed him to the stairs, out of sight. If she not come to me, I walk back to the slave cabin, words unspoke. Suddenly, she be there at the door.

"Quick, quick," she said. "I must go check on the boy and make sure he's fast asleep."

"Sary, you been off in the woods. I know the Frenchman's yarn be a lie cause you be different. A woman strong."

She swayed and bent close to my face. "Yearie, you know he is the Scotsman? Young Rob knows. Oh, I pray his father is fooled by drink and a short memory."

"The Scotsman who run to the swamp? That MacIntosh? Master in his sots. Why, if it weren't for the color of my skin, he think we one in the same."

"We have to lay evidence of a cockney thief," she said, her brow creased. "Swear to my secrecy." She shook my arms. "Say it, my girl. Tell me you will not whisper a hint of what I'm about to say, for it could be the death of you *and* me."

"You met the maroons," I say. "And now you know our plan, we people of all shades and accent bound together in common yield. You seen our defiance."

Sary threw her hands hither and yon. "How did you know?" she asked.

"I be part of the whole since before you and me be Oxford's vagabonds. Nigh on five years that I be workin in their assistance. You say I must swear to your secret, but since I know it already, I must swear you to mine."

Sary nod, her face a moonflower, heavy, innocent and pure. "I swear, Yearie. How come you to know all of it?"

"I be in their employ…inform them of Master's doings."

Her eyes rounded. "Robert's?"

"Not to hurt him. I only tell his conversations in the parlor."

"With his guests?"

"Of his business."

"Of how his evilness hurts the maroons?"

"To protect them." Then, to absolve him a mite in her mind, I say, "He not of Findley's cloth."

"No," she say, "Findley is the weed. Robert is the seed." She glanced into the kitchen, lookin for the boy whose ears waggle day and night. "I mustn't dally," she say. "Young Rob might wake, hungry." She took me by my elbow and walked me along the house wall, away from the door. "I laid with him in the woods," she whispered.

"Who? Not Master," I ask.

"No. The MacIntosh."

In the darkness, I peered into her face, but could only see her lips move with import. I raise my lantern to see her expression. No shame. Her eyes shine at me. What happened to the girl her mama raised? "God help you," I answered. "Your faith won't save you now."

"Faith be damned, Yearie. When has it ever helped you or me? Alexander was the most wondrous moment ever, except the times I held Phebe in my arms."

"You want that Scotsman for your own?" I say, my mind a windstorm. I never be settled till my mistress marry and release me. Once she be safe, I be safe…now, maybe all the rest of Morris' quarter go with us to the maroons.

"I *want* no man, only the *place* that he would offer us in marriage. Have you been to the maroon's swamp? Oh, of course you haven't. Do you know there is a child in the swamp who remembers Phebe? She had Mama's rosary and thought it was hers. Phebe died in that ugly place, living with Vanderkoop. And Robert took her cradle to give to those savages," she said, then in a whisper, "He strips me of my mind."

She just a child herself, my mistress. After all we've traveled, she don't understand that souls be made from memories. Bits of lace and buttons, tendrils of hair and thread, even a man's hammer or chisel make nothin but a dent in your mind. But when the master take it, and he always will, the learnin come hard. For it not be the mind on which we live—it be the soul.

I led her to the oak tree where, in the gold light of sunset Jackson been whipped and curried just before they sit down to eat. My gut be empty like my heart. She has to see if Master punish her, we be next, and what we get be that much worse.

The risen moon sit low and I shine the lantern on Jackson's trickled blood, dark against the white oyster shells. I put her hand on the gnarled trunk, its ridges and grooves feel like the marbled skin of his back. A cut swoll up on her knuckle. I said, "You be better than them that do this to our kind. It be your lot to help make us free."

She put her hands on my cheeks and kissed my eyes, one and then t'other. "I have been blind and probably still can't see. I will tell you everything I discover," she say. "His purchases, the ships' cargoes, his inventories in the warehouse and when the sterling comes from Cunliffe. I will make myself essential, like the stars to his ships' captains. He will rely on me. And we will escape our bondage."

We hear a clankin in the kitchen and I slip into the shadow of the tree. Sary grab Jackson's rope hanging from a branch and we both watch the light in the door. The boy stood, a candle in his hand, waving it back and forth in the night.

"Who's out there? Mistress Sarah, is it you? Who are you talking to?"

She whip round toward the house, holding the rope in front of her. "You waken from your slumber, young Rob? Here, my boy, put this in the basket in the kitchen so we can use it to tie the goat for morning milk. Are you hungry now?"

He stood straight, the candle between them and raised it to her face. "Do you have company, Mistress? I heard voices," said he.

"Just the slaves. They are restless after the day's events and fearful of spirits in the dark. I knelt with them in prayer to reassure them of their place."

He snickered and turn to go inside, but I hear him say, "Their place is at our feet. I will eat that yeoman food you made, lest you have something better."

"It is good enough for your father. So, it is good enough for you," says she as she looks out in the night, pulling the door shut behind her.

CHAPTER 21

Through sunrises and sunsets, Sarah become mortar to Master's pestle as two harvest moons go by. He travel to Annapolis more. She rise up in his stead and grind his accounts, separate what his and what is secretly ours. The ships in harbor keep a comin through a pesterin storm season and sometime the ones that make it, limp in with sails ragged or a mast broke, listing to one side. My mistress manage the house, the stable, our garden, the weaving, and now—the warehouse. And, poor woman, somethin else crop up —a gift from heaven, or a mark of the Devil as Reverend Bacon would say—only time would tell.

She usually up before dawn as the sun break later over village rooves, and we got to get an early start putting up food for winter. On Tuesday last, near seven week since the hullabaloo with Jackson, I not hear her salutations in the kitchen, so I come up the stair, all careful with her pitcher of fresh-scented water. The bed be empty, and I hear a noise by the window. There be Sary on the floor retchin into her basin, her braid dipping in it as her shoulders heave up and down. She look up at me with the most pitiable face, and I set the pitcher on the dresser to scoop her in my arms. There we sit on the floor wrapped together, a rockin in our sorrow.

"What am I to do, Yearie? I don't know whose it is, and it won't matter anyway. I'm not even betrothed."

"But you in your master's house and that's what you go with. He can't ignore his issue in his own home," say I.

"Oh, you're wrong," she say with great anger. "He's very good at that. I am such a fool to think his promise to marry was real. Young Rob is proof and four others in Liverpool."

I be near speechless at this revelation. "Well the bastard court here be more strict than that in England, and he a fool to not be afeared, just like every other man in Talbot."

"He wore me down, his constant pursuit." She shook free of my arms and sit up straight to say, "There must be a way to get rid of it. Surely, you know of some method from a witch doctor or a heathen?"

"No, Sary. I not be part of that scheme. Tansy oil or safin tea, it all like to kill you *and* the child. You be bound to tell Morris, but not till after you feel it quicken."

She nodded, her eyes full of blue. "If I lose it by God's Will, no harm is done."

And so, we kept her secret, and it be easy round young Robert as he think only of hisself. Morris travel and the Scotsman off in the swamp. I watch to see if Sary loosen her bodice. I give her ginger root and biscuit, and of the rare time when she not rise of a morn, I give excuses to Master's boy who had grown accustomed to her egg an johnnycake.

Planning for a baby, I be cleanin out for it. No accountin all the wares Master dump on us that pile up in the front meetin room. Rob sleep by the kitchen fire so his old corner be not but storage. If such junk be for entertainin, beddin, cookin, or clothin, we keep it. If it not, we hand it out.

And that be my first mistake. All them soft cover books that come on ships. Master read *London Gent*, Sary read *Lady Magazine*. Lately, she pressed about a soft book be called *Pamela* the reverend say he print in Dublin in his former life. Bout some white servant girl who make a world of trouble for her master. They all be dogeared and worthless, so I stack em up and take em to the stable for use in the

Jakes.

My dreams not found in no book. I believe Tiberius when he say he got near enough to buy his freedom. Then he work on gettin mine.

Lo and behold I hear a gruntin in Betsy's stall, and I make my second mistake. Jackson be leanin against Ol Bets, his head buried in her black mane, chafing at his stick like nobody be round to hear.

"You playin with the Lord's direction, Jackson," I say.

He look over at me all baleful-eyed, but his arm moving fierce. I look down.

"The Lord done give me one way to make pleasure, Yearie, and no woman goin take it away."

I dug my toe in the black earth. "Huh, well Reverend Bacon tell us it be a sin to spill your seed for no purpose."

He groan with disappointment, lacin up his breeches. "Well, you might give me a purpose if you not be so cold."

I pondered that for the time it took milk to curdle over a flame and said, "Well, I guess a man need somethin to do or he mess with a horse's backside. But if'n you not too far gone, I can give you a purpose bigger than both of us."

He laughed and slapped Ol Bets. "She a good ol girl but she not for me, Yearie. You keep your mouth shut bout what you see and don't tell Mistress. I don't need no more trouble from any of em."

"What you think of me, Jackson? I no tattler and neither is Cook lest you dumb enough to hurt us with your foolery. Reverend Bacon say we all need a purpose to get to Heaven."

"I not goin to their Heaven. There's a Heaven for us slaves and maybe them indentures. Why, if I made it to Saint Peter's pearly gates and Talbot men get there ahead of me, I just turn round and fly to Hell."

"The swamp not Heaven or Hell, just safe for us. That Mac need to know what be happenin here so they can keep themself secret and make our future."

"You talkin in riddles, woman. I kin steal from the warehouse and drop goods at the tailor's like I at work for Master, but I'm not takin no missives. That be proof of my crime." He roll his eyes at me.

Jackson smart but he a plain-spoken man who not waste time jawin bout things he can't see. Not like Tiberius who got a future.

"Well, you put them oysters to good use and take a trip to Kate's," I challenge. "Master be gone for weeks and Mistress Sary be your cover now."

Jackson's face all screwed up in disbelief. "You two gonna get me killed, Yearie. One of you enough, now I got to worry bout Mistress, too?" Then he nod and grin. "But the swamp be better than workin for Master or Findley."

"Exactly," I say and lay out the plan Sary and I brew up.

CHAPTER 22

The weather gettin colder but ships keep a comin. Master in the capital, visiting Province leaders. Of a bitter afternoon, I peer through driving rain from the Custom House window, disgusted as a Cunliffe ship off-load twenty-five West Indie slave boys, wet and dark as tar, miserable in their existence, the healthy ones bamboozled-eyed to see if life be hopeful in a new place. They hoppin cold, shiverin in their nakedness, and carted off to three plantations. Then from deep in the ship's hold, sailors bring us Cheshire salt and iron, wool cloth and china.

The rain pound through late afternoon, the ship sit tall in the water, mostly empty as Sary and I count. We take sailcloth from the ship log and leave it off the inventory, for Jackson takin it to the maroons. Sary got a system. Nobody look at both records cept us. It help that the cap'ns of Cunliffe ships respect her. They seen she can read and carry numbers just like Morris. She make herself a quiet trader in Oxford, scribin lists of slave names and plantation supplies. I see dark circles under her eyes and ask her one day if Master be a wealthy man.

"He is the poorest man I know. I cannot do it all, Yearie. I need more help," she say.

Then, like a stroke of good luck, the next day Master come home bringin Henry Callister from Cambridge warehouse to stay in town during rest of shipping season. I never trusted his pale self but maybe it a good thing, for Sary not a man stormin bout the dockyard commandin sailors and slaves. We whisper our worry that his presence interfere with pilferin from the warehouse. Now, Sary have to creep out with keys on a midnight walk unlocking after Callister do his rounds. He be young, got silky blonde whiskers of a boy half his age. He open like a cow birthing bout Master's affairs, so we not have to do much spy on parlor conversations. Still, Sary and I have trouble piecin the whole story of Master's future plan.

One day in early November Morris be gone and Cap'n Gildart come a knockin on the door. Voltaire set him in the front parlor by the fire. Sary at the warehouse with Callister, so I send for them and meantime bring Cap'n hot tea, blackberry jam and biscuits. I try hard not to show annoyance at his muddy boots caked all over my hearthstone. What for Jackson put in a boot scraper at the front door if he not goin to use it?

Gildart ask me for a spot of whisky and I think he should go to Quinn's if'n he want hard drink. Holdin no contest, I bring it from the lockchest and watch how much he pour. He sober on ship and a drunk on shore like the rest of them sailors. Sit by hisself, he pick his ear wax and flick it on my floors.

By the time Sary and Callister come, he drink half the teapot and all the whisky. His tongue loose and when he command Callister to sit, she and I retire to the hallway and put our ears to the door. It start off innocent, Gildart complain Master have nearly 1500 acre of small farms scattered across Talbot he lease to poor farmers. I thinkin, *what do he care how much Master own?* I look at Sary and see her frown.

"Can't squeeze the rent out of them," says Gildart.

"'Tis true but Morris is very tolerant. He holds their notes and they pay in installments."

"Foolish. I earn a headright for every slave I bring," bragged Gildart. "Coin in my pocket. Province don't give them indentured a land claim once their five years are worked. Get a bag a corn, a hoe and sailor petticoats." He guffaw. "Then they move west to Indian Territory. Slaving better."

"A viable business plan, Gildart. Some captains choose it, Morris doesn't. He prefers to be the head of mercantilism on both sides of the bay. Your Scottish redemptioners were the last indentured he unloaded," say Callister.

"Caribs are the money. Not indentured. He should have a mind. Sailing under the British flag ain't no protection these days."

I peek around the door and see him thumb his nose and wipe it on his breeches. He good and sauced.

"There weren't no naval protection. I have to avoid infernal French privateers roaming the West Indies, ready to take my cargo and ship. Firing more cannon these days than ever, threatening the Chesapeake. When I quit the high seas, I'll invest in land and become a country gentleman collecting rent like the lords around here."

"I suspect Master Morris will do the same, though I don't know the whole of it," say Callister. "So, you think George's war will be brought to our shores? Bold of the French Navy to sail past the shoals and Point Comfort guns. Hampton Roads is on alert?"

"Not the Navy, man. It's privateers under French marques disrupting our commerce. They're agile and have a new frigate called a corsair that runs with the wind. I'm surprised you ain't more informed here in Oxford."

"I'm sure Sheriff Goldsboro is, Captain. I concern myself with the warehouses, not the military. If you have no further questions, sir, will you take your leave?"

Sary wink at me that Callister trying to get rid of the skinflint. Henry annoyed.

"Morris off in Annapolis playing brother of the string with Bacon?" ask the cap'n.

"Yes, sir. They entertain at the Tuesday Club with the province leaders. Good business."

"Well, I expected Morris here to unload my ship, arseworm that he is. And leaving that well-rigged woman in his kitchen for any man to have — her bubbe declares my lips for a suckle!"

"Sir, if you speak of Mrs. Wise, you are greatly mistaken. She is an honorable lady of Oxford," answer Callister.

"No mind to me. I'll go to Quinn's and have me a beard splitter."

Sary grabbed my wrist and shook it, mad as a shrew. Callister coughed and say, "Sir, is there a reason for your visit other than to say your dissatisfaction with the day's doings?"

"You can tell Morris that a corporation is formed, and we want him to join us. Goldsboro, Tilghman and me. Morris has land that sits at the headwaters of Island and Goldsboro Creeks, west of the great cedar swamp. The British Isles are barren of wood so's I'll bring the black labor, Goldsboro and Tilghman supply the seed money and Morris savvy it for us. We'll cut the cedar and bring it by packet down the Pocomoke to Oxford then ship to London on my frigate."

Sary's eyes widen and she drag me down the hall to the kitchen quarter where we belong. We all bristly, our noggins together. "We have to get word to the maroons," she say. "Gildart's not the only one cutting wood, yet he'll be the first to find them."

"Tailor's too busy to let Jeremiah do a run to the maroons. Goldsboro be watchin travels on the East Town road, so that leave me out."

Sary press her lips together. "We'll get Jackson to pole the barge tonight."

He been a bringin the maroons supplies at Kate's in preparation for winter. Jackson love the thrill it bring him, but he wily enough to know the risk. Goldsboro still tramping through them woods lookin for a cockney sailor.

"Let Kate get them word," I say. "Look here, they not chop trees in the dead of winter. We have till spring."

"We need to be spry, Yearie. If they have to find a new camp, they should start moving the boats," she say, pursing her lower lip like to trip over it.

"If'n we not careful, Sary," I warn, "one day Jackson not come back."

I drag myself through the kitchen, grab some cornbread and cold pork and wrap it in cloth. Outside, I take a stroll of the muddy garden that lookin a mite forlorn. It be time to bank the plants for winter. Walking past the gourds and pumpkin, I notice a plant flowering, running like a weed across the ground—the Indian seed Sary bring home. I threw it out not thinkin nothin of it, and in the wet weather it done bloom a pretty pink and white ruffle on dark green leaves. I scratch my head pondering its name when it come to me— Jimsonweed. Sary think it be banewort, but she only know her kitchen garden. Indians make their enemy mindless smokin it.

Could be useful.

Jackson asleep in the hay under Bets' nose. Shakin him, I tells him of his new mission, that come dark in another hour, he should head to Kate's hire stable. I make him repeat the message twice as his brain fogged with dreams from being up all night a thievin and walkin. When he see the vittles I pack, he perk up.

I say again, "You gots to wait for cover of dark. You hear?"

"I ain't deaf, woman. Goldsboro and them helmet dogs walking round with the night watch till the moon be high. Maybe tonight he sleep."

Come dinner, Hestia, Sary and me, we eat in the kitchen. Rob is at Reverend Bacon's, helpin his wife with their children in his absence. Master think he learn in Reverend's shadow. I don't see it, as the boy not have a Christian bone in his body, just a keen desire for makin coin like his father.

As eventide draw to a close, we have our say, sit round our fire, pourin brandy for ourselves. We laugh bout Gildart and Sary say it not make a beggar's chance in a king's court how much land he have, no woman of Talbot be interested in the likes of him. Her legs spread, a pipe between her teeth, she play jester in his image. We laugh till our cheeks hurt.

Hestia groan with good times and take her leave for the quarters sayin she have bread to bake come morn and I yawn big, now the excitement of the day over.

"Yearie, I am lonely at night and sleepless with worry about this babe," say Sary, her hand on her belly. "Sleep with me. Keep me company and we'll pretend to be little girls again."

I reflect on the position this put me in, for at once I am her best companion and sister, but I can't scrub the black from my skin if Master discover us, for he make me the Devil's handmaid.

"I know what you're thinking— that if Robert comes home early, he will make trouble," she say. "But it's Tuesday night and he's playing his fiddle as we speak, so he won't return till morrow's eve." She lay her head on my shoulder.

"A warm bed on a cold night." Not as attractive as sharin a bed with Tiberius someday. A step in love that lack opportunity, but it be in my future. He a tall hunk of regal manhood, got a purpose beyond yes sir, and no sir. I tingle all over when he around. But on this night all's I want is to be tucked in warm.

So we busy ourselves cleanin up our mess and, hand in hand, we climb the stairs to her chamber, me carryin a coal bucket from the fire, she lightin the way with a candle talkin of a little girl memories —giggles and gossip, playing knucklebones, and a whisperin rhymes that got us a scold for open eyes. The safety of the cottage, the hurt of my mama sold, and the firelight of childhood vanished. We replace them with hardship and not knowin, with master's whims and cruelties...but mostly now, our separateness.

I turn down the bed while she shovel coal in the bedwarmer. She hand me a linen shift to wear, one I just wash and fold in her cupboard. We scrub our faces with fresh water from the pitcher and she scent my collar bone with jasmine perfume, and I hers. She oil my hair and I brush hers, leaving a wad of her curls on her dresser's lace. I steal a look at her shape outlined through the gauze of her shift by the candlelight. She small and round. It betray her and she see the look in my eye.

"Ah, what of the bastard court?" she say. "If it's Robert's, everyone will expect us to marry. If it has red hair, I'll get the lash."

"Well, you needn't get stuck on a worry. Master adore you. Lookie here, he can give money for a children's school and an almshouse, so's he got some heart. Come now, I shiver down to my feet," I say. We crawl in, greedy for sleep, snuggle like two girls not knowin our difference, only our likeness.

In the night, I dream I be taken from our bed and locked in a cold, stone room that float above Oxford like it hold no weight. I be wearing the homespun of a convict, and sit at table bereft of friends. I raised one of Master's big silver soup spoons that I use to feed the hungry. But there no children, no slaves, no sick to nourish.

My target to fatten with gruel be a half moon that hang on the wall, him an angry slice of pearly pie. He open scrawny lips and suck down my potion between a bloatin and braggin of his celestial wins. I be calm and unmoved as he spew out his night dung through a pipe in his tail. I see he on the wane getting smaller the more he eat. Determined and quick, I churn his manure on a crank, make it blow through the pipe and up through the ceiling into the night, spread a firmament of stars in God's perfect sky.

I woke with a start to see Sary layin beside me, her face a moon-flower, helpless and plain. I rise up and slip from the bed to find my conjure bag in the pocket of my skirt. Inside be the magic of three... cloves, a coffin nail, a needle. Dignity, the binder, the worry. I hang it round my neck, light a taper from the sputtering candle and burn the wad of her hair.

CHAPTER 23

*I*t weren't long till Desperate hit. Not like when we a wanderin the lanes of Oxford for a handout. And not like we be in need of a roof over our head. For although we in two different beds, we both have shelter and clothes on our backs, not hungry. A different kind of Desperate, this be the Devil incarnate.

Miserable Quinn overhear some gossip and he follow up in his sneaky way. Jeremiah, the tailor's son, hear from old Ruth at the tavern that the tavern keeper still wild-jealous of Morris since the day Master bring us in his door. Quinn can't find a woman to marry and cook, scrub and sing in his grog hole. So, that squealer want a way to get back at Master and Sary. And he found it.

He tell Sheriff there be too much activity at Morris house when-ever Master gone to Annapolis—that people be a comin and a goin beyond the normal commerce of factoring. What he don't know is since Master goin to Annapolis two Tuesday a month, playin his viola, gammonin, parading in the street, and call hisself Merry Make-fun, it be a perfect time for us to provision the maroons. A spell of dry weather make it easy for Jackson to pole a barge with finished ship's iron and ballast up the Choptank, past Dover Town to an abandoned dock.

Tiberius come to me afore dawn, a risk he never take. A whistle, a stone's clink and I wake to see him lurk outside the slave quarter. No straw hat, no silky coat, just him in homespun, lookin like a prince, those high cheekbones cutting a shadow against the moon. His voice be low, telling me Goldsboro lie in wait and catch Jackson polling in the shallows by starlight. Well, sheriff call him 'boy' and whip him till his back be flayed meat, but Jackson hold his tongue, sayin he deliver goods to the village upriver for the master. No amount of whip take the rebel spirit from that man no more. He got vision, just like me. We shake our haids, marvel at the change wrought in all of us.

Tiberius take me in his arms, "We cannot wait years. My master may hold me in some esteem for my service, but I'll not be indebted to him beyond that. He promises if I pay, he will write my manumission."

I hold him to me and whisper in his shirt, "My mama ask when I was born how long I be a slave. For all her years, they answer. That's why I be named Yearie. I'll wait for you to come back for me. Sary will let me go."

He brush his fingers across my eyes and say, "Ask her now. So we can plan our life."

A thrill go up my spine, and I turn my lips to his. We kiss with a hunger not known by any before us, desperation and sorrow, and dare I think—hope? Then, I think I'll not leave Jackson on this morn. "Go," I say, "afore you caught."

When the sheriff come a knockin on our door later, he storm inside with his helmet dogs in tow, they slobber for game all over my floors. Tiberius not with them. Sary sit in her mantua robe at master's desk in the parlor, Tray curled at her feet. She lookin peaked and shocked, her fingers stained with ink from an artful cookin of the warehouse account. Truth be told, sheriff never study the book, just figure that she too dumb to be a workin them numbers and make them entries. He ask her what she be about.

"Why, Sheriff," say Sary, her eye all aflutter, "Mr. Morris instructs to ready the ship logbooks for Mr. Callister. Two ships in harbor are Cunliffe's."

"Stealing their goods for assignment up the Choptank in the dead of night? Your slave gives you away. You have friends you're helping, Mrs. Wise. I have it on good authority."

She squared her shoulders up like a general. Her bosom heave and full as it be, Goldsboro a hummingbird drawn to nectar. Jackson not make it home, and I wonder if my faithful slave be dead. Fear strike my gut as I wish Master home to stop this now.

"Sir, you insult. I am loyal to Mr. Morris," she say.

"Loyal to your sniveling one horse farmers. The sun rose two hours ago, and you lay about in your dressing gown. Spoilt kitchen wench."

He click his tongue and them dogs stand at attention. A shout, and a blast of cold air hit me from the front door. Tiberius drag Jackson inside. Ragged, bloodied and cold, Jackson lean against the wall, wiping his nose on his sleeve, not looking at me. Tiberius stand at attention in the hallway. I move next to Sary, and she rise from her chair. A dance we perform, like the white man's reel.

"If Morris sent him on an errand, he'd have a pass, Mrs. Wise. But no, he was holed up in a cove running away in his master's absence."

Then I see Jackson got a fresh wound on his cheek. A R for runaway.

Sheriff move in and lean over Sary. "I could have branded you and your kitchen slave with a V for your vagabond ways, but Morris intervened," he say, all soft like. He point his sword hilt at her middle. "I have informants who tell me of the doings in this house and it will stop whence you are called to the provincial court."

Sary drag the chair between them. "You may leave now, Sheriff. When Robert arrives from Annapolis, I will have much to say to him about the license you take today."

His brow jump like he number words. Guess he expect her to lay down for him. "I take my leave," he say. "There will be a full investigation." His spurs click with every step nearer. "Morris will be interested to hear of the contents of this barge on the river, powered by his beggar slave and directed by his resident harlot."

That did it. Her face flood red and she pick up a brass candlestick and strike him across his jaw. His dogs leap at her, and she turn the chair legs to they snarl. Tray crawl under the desk. Terrified, I reach deep in my skirt pocket and drop my conjure bag on the floor near they noses, calling on Ma to make it good. Sure enough, them helmet dogs freeze in place, not liking the scent of clove. Sheriff hold his cheek, his yeller eyes gleam in hate, but Sary not be done with him.

"You are a venal brute. Leave, now!"

Time stand still and we all hold our breath, wonder if he grab her. He hold his position, weighing a move. Cursing, the sheriff turn and click his spurs across the floor, sayin, "I'm an officer of the court, Mrs. Wise. You face arrest and a stay in the town gaol for your attack. I am not beyond indicting you a witch. Prepare yourself."

"No one believes in witchery anymore," she shout after him.

I think to myself, some do.

Voltaire hold the door wide, all the while bowin to his highness' arse as the sheriff and his dogs make scarce. Tiberius and I trade a look of shock, he nod his head and leave. Voltaire shut it quiet, and we all stare at each other, cows stuck in a town square waiting for market. Sary blink.

"Be quick. He will return. We must hide the accounts." She shake sawdust over her numbers and blow it off the page in a cloud. I watch as she sit at the desk and write a note to go who knows where.

"Yearie, pack a bag of clean linen for changes and fresh stockings. I'll dress in brown drab, befitting the occasion. It will draw sympathy from those who are about. Voltaire, have Hestia fill a basket with victuals. I'll share with the riffraff and perhaps the gaoler will be lenient. Bring me a basket each day until I return home. Oxford will not stand for this."

Voltaire turn to run for the kitchen quarter when she put up her hand. "Wait! Give this to the ferryman." She turn the wax over the candle, drip a dollop of red on the paper edges and stamp it with the Cunliffe seal. "Tell him he must find a traveler to deliver it post haste. It's addressed to Dr. Hamilton, where Robert stays in Annapolis. Take this coin to make it worth his while."

She stand and I see her fear in one small tug of her wrapper. I follow my mistress up the grand staircase and dress her silently in plain cloth.

CHAPTER 24

"*H*estia, we got to bring her home," I say. "I gots a plan." It was nigh on twelve days she been locked up and Master nowhere in sight. We wonder if her message even find him at Hamilton's home.

"You hain't gonna get me do none of your conjuring, Yearie."

How be it that woman know what I up to just lookin at me? I say, "I do it alone and you best believe your hide not be saved when our mistress show up on the doorstep."

I had my hands on my hips standing near her cook pot. It be a steamin with bone soup and kale. The larder gettin bare. Hestia give me a one eye squint. She be comfortable in her kitchen. Take her out and she get a case of the nerves.

"Well, I guess I gotta count on my cooking to save my hide," she say. "You get Jackson go out wit you. Nobody seen me walking round Oxford and I not taking no chance on them knowing me now."

I nodded fast. Then I give her a hug. She get all flustered and push me away, but I know she with me. "Master Callister come by for the account book after he finish up in the warehouse," I say.

"Uh-huh. You planning your dumb magic, do it now, afore the

sun rise. And don't be lighting candles. Everbody know they not home and it just bring suspicion if our shadow be seen skulking round."

"That's fine. I do it out of hope, Hestia, cause so far Reverend's prayers not workin. If'n you hear a noise don't come a runnin. You stay right here cooking."

"I'm not hearing nothing come out your mouth, Yearie," say Cook, as she bent over her pot stirring like there be somethin good in it.

I bring a tin of fresh water to the hall, run fast up the stair and take the key from Sary's headboard in her room. Stop at the window to see if anybody move round. There be one ship mast tall over the rooftops, its topsail shine white in the moonbeam. Chimneys be a pumpin out smoke, and cats be darting round hunting field mice too stupid to go inside. It be colder than a dead seagull frozen in ice. I got to move fast. I run to Master's room and above his shave stand be his looking glass.

Tempted, I look in it, feared of what I might see. My face not fat like Cook's. My turban be wrapped tight and stick out geranium red in the moonbeam. My face look small neath it, my chin pointy, my shawl crossed thick under my neck. I blink and see eyes not clouded with doubt, just clear. I raise my chin and look round master's room. It feel so empty. His spirit not here and I know my conjure won't work. Then, it come to me. The picture of him hangin by the front door.

I gather four candlesticks from the upstairs rooms, nothin but nubs so nobody miss if they burnt a glimmer or two. Charging below stair, I place one in each corner on the hallway floor and light em. In the back hall, I unlock the cupboard, hear Hestia singin a hymn and think my timing be perfect. I pull the sugar box out with two teacups, scrape the spoon against the block and sprinkle sweet into a cup. Carry both to the parlor, I pour a dram o rum in t'other and grab Cunliffe's brass seal.

I lay it all on the floor under master's painting and Sary's harpsichord. Mama be proud I carry on her Trinidad way. The only thing missing is the mirror and my mistress. There not be a single likeness of her anywhere in the house, not even a watercolor painted in a flash by them wandering folk pretending to be artists.

Her hairbrush.

Upstairs, I dig my fingernail into the bristle and pull out a wad of that pale hair and tuck it in my bodice. In the master's room, I hike my skirts and kick my feet about to feel my nimble. I lift the glass, feeling the weight in my elbows, and tuck it under my arm, grip tight. I take the steps one at a time, hug the wall and set it over Sary's music book.

The spell work best when the people be present in the flesh, but as I talk in my head to the Obeah man, I know this be the next best thing. I whisper an incantation, "Sary spirit, your heart be your own, but with this spell, this man be your stone, caught in your shoe till you find someone new." I pluck her hair from my bosom, take a candle, and, before the glass, light it afire till it burn out gone. Then, so as not to dispel her memory in the glass, I lift the looking glass up to his likeness and move it in a circle to capture his visage. Setting it down, I take the brass seal and tap the glass hard. Tap it again and a small crack appear. Knock swift and the glass shatter all round the harpsichord.

Hestia stop her sing. There be silence for a moment and she start up again real loud. I stroll into the kitchen and take the broom down from its hook, not lookin at her. Outside in the stable yard, I pick up a shovel and return to open the front door. The road be quiet. Tidy-like, I sweep the glass to the stoop as the wind whip my skirts ever which way, tangle in my legs. I pull the door shut on myself, dig holes on either side o the slate step and sweep the pieces into the dirt. I tamp the earth to cover up the spirit trapped in glass memory. It be done, but I'm not safe.

I walk backward twelve steps to the road not looking over my shoulder, only at the door. With each step I take forward, I reach down t'gather my shadow and tuck it in my bodice so's the house have no memory of my doings. Almost done. Inside, I toss the sugar down my gullet, wash it with the rum and swallow a gulp of fresh water, tying my intentions deep inside. Now, I be safe from the sheriff if'n he come back to haunt us.

Better'n river baptism, or lightin votive candles to some old saint, I hope it work.

~

The afternoon be cold and damp, like to freeze the toes off a hen. I take my basket of victuals that Hestia give me, she huff and puff her what–fors? and God–knows? as she slam bout her hearth.

"You giving this straight to the mistress, no-how put it in the hands of that gaoler, you hear? Give him this pumpkin bread and maybe he leave the rest for them that needs it."

"I do my best, Hestia. Not a soul more worried than me bout this state of affairs," says I. Pulling my cape round me, I make my way to the strand and head uphill, past the Custom House to Hels Half Acre where the gaol and all manner of degenerate being held. The wind off the Chesapeake be bitter and a spray of saltwater freeze my cape stiff. So icy be it that even the seagulls disappeared.

I cluck along, thinkin. That gaoler provide a stick of firewood at night and no embers last till dawn. He let me in everday, rummage through the basket and steal Cook's confection, and then with a curse he leave for his apartment where it be warm. I take meat from my skirt pocket once I see Sary, and she secret it away in hers. She be the only woman in the room. The other three be asleep on the floor ever time I arrive. Time move slow for all.

It been a turn of three Saturdays thinkin Reverend come home for the Sabbath with Master in tow. He be hell-born once he see Sary. I be careful to inspect my mistress for signs of her apparitions. She been strong but this like to tax the faith of a saint.

Not a prisoner notice I stand in the door. The air be tight and stink so bad one ought wonder if the jakes ever been dug out. There's a new layer of stink though; somebody retching in a bowl that sit on the floor. Sary be nearby, her head propped up on the step to the jakes, her eyes open, but not seein. She mumble something I can't make out. I take stock and see the sailor gazing out the bars in the up-high window, the sleet spit him in the face, call him to the Chesa-peake. The rogue leaning against the wall, aflippin his cards between his thumb and forefinger. He glance at me and laugh. The pickpocket takin up all the space in front of the hearth, snoring away. I slip over to my mistress and quiet-like say, "Sary, it be Yearie here. I bring you some goodies."

Nothing. Like she deaf. I shakes her. Her eyes flicker but go out. Then she whisper, "I murdered her."

I thinkin who she a babblin bout now when the rogue say, "You best leave her alone. She's been mumbling about some Phebe ever since I came yesterday."

"That be her child she lost to the Indians."

"Says she killed her."

"Excuse me, sir," I say, "but did she say nothin else?"

"She asked me why I'm here. Cheated Goldsboro at cards. Didn't know he's the sheriff. Perhaps you have a master who can get us out of here?"

"No, em," I say, "but you can see what looks good in this here basket." The collection of them miscreants set on it like hungry wolves.

I turn to my mistress. I take her hand and press her mama's cross in it. Squeeze hard till she feel the points of that crucifix dig in her grasp. Her head turn in my direction. She squint at me.

"Sary," I say, "God be in your hand."

"Yearie? Is it time to pray? We must eat dinner first."

Yep. She full on skimble-skambled. I shakes her again. "You not at home anymore, mistress. You got to wake up."

She sit up and nod at me like a good toddler. I pull my packet of salvia sugar from my skirt and hold it out to her. Her eyes brighten and she peer at me closer.

"A treat? I love your herb for it charges me with purpose."

"And you'll remember what you got to do. We have work. Master Callister come this afternoon with Sheriff Goldsboro. You show em who got the upper hand." She all wide-eyed now, like she tryin to remember.

"I give you this Obeah bone, carved with the two-headed goddess. Put it in yer pocket and when you need it, blow on the bone so's the spirit bring you decision."

I think she understand, remember the spells of my mama, but then she fall back against the step like the life be drained out of her. I shakes her one last time, for I got to get to Master Callister and explain.

"Sary, listen. What you goin to do when Goldsboro come?"

She raise her head up and look at me, a right good stare. I see sorrow in her eyes. She pass a hand over her chattel and I whisper, "Has it quickened?"

"It has," she say. "When the sheriff comes, I will plead the belly and say it's Robert's. Come his return, my lord will rant and rave and lay the sheriff's reputation to waste."

I snort. Master will rant and rave, but who knows if he bethump Goldsboro or Sary? If'n he epileptic over another babe from his seed he might throw us both out. Then again, there no sense in a dawdlin over stuff I can't control, so I squeeze her hand that got the crucifix and the bone. She takin a chance confessing, but there's nothin else to do. "Put them in your pocket, and remember— one to pray for the future and the other to breathe on for the Spirit to guide you."

I left in a freezin rain wondering if any of this do me any good.

CHAPTER 25

I passed the tavern on the way home and bid mornin to Ruth, Quinn's house slave who sweepin a dust of snow off the front porch. She a be a good woman who see trouble in Oxford everday. Always givin bread to hungry children or dogs. She too old to market her honeypot with the rest of them harlots. Never known Ruth to conversate much so I be surprised when she ask if'n mistress still in the gaolhouse.

"Yes'm. Just brought her some vittles. It no place for a lady," I answered.

She grunted. "You too caught up with that white woman. Less you do now, the better it be for all of us."

I be dumbstruck and manage to say, "She be a sister to me."

She lean over the rail. "You a dumb cat, Yearie. Ain't no white woman ever your sister. She cain't save you."

Left me prickly worried, and I be thankful I find my kitchen warm. Cook's fire stoked high and mighty since Jackson split wood. He determined, nursing his wounds, but ready to go deliver to the maroons again. This time I make sure he carry a pass with Master's signature. Take me half a day to write it good. Goldsboro's men can't be everywhere but we takin no chances no more.

"Anythin, Hestia?"

"No word of Master," she say, grumbling under her breath and slam a pot on the hearth.

I told her what Ruth say, the words heavy in my mind, and Hestia tell me to make it no mind, "That ol woman just jealous of what we have. Master good. It Goldsboro we got to watch."

"Aye," I say. No, *we* in this. Jackson and me takin the risk. Cook's kitchen skill be too valuable for master to sell her off, but I decide to make sure she with us. "You say somethin to the man, an I swear I rain down spells till you speak in devil tongue."

She glare sidelong at me, those big eyes slitty and her eyetooth showing. "This house tame till you an your mistress come here," she say. "Master's business pour like ale down Oxford's throat and now it all complicated. He trying to climb that ladder. Always entertaining them hoity-toity, aiming to be royalty. His son and Goldsboro too friendly." She grab her kitchen cloth from the bench. "Then, Master gone and you and Jackson stirring my pot. I don't know what you up to, but this ain't end well for us. You not taking me down with you, Yearie."

"Don't bedevil yourself, Hestia. Nobody ask nuthin of you. You keep a stirrin your pot, keep your mouth shut, or you be grow horns at night and your eyes turn green, your pupils yeller. Then you see what the man do with you."

She look scared outta her skin and she splutter, waving her towel at me to stop. We be family of sorts, but I got to paint the way the world is cause she live in one small mouse hole.

I hear horses out back and Jackson's shout. I look at her stern-like and she nod, draw her fingertips across her lips to seal them. Pulling the kitchen door open, I look into the dim winter light of late afternoon and see a two-wheel wagon come a rattlin into the yard, driven by some stranger, a blanket coverin his haid. A child be wrapped up next to him on the bench.

Jackson point to the barn door and the stranger rein the cart and hop out, the blanket billow in the wind. Then, a frontiersman gallop at full tilt behind him and pull up short near the wagon. Jackson hold his bay while he alight. His tricorn and shearlin coat be dusted in snow like he been a fightin the outdoors. Flipping the canvas, I see the cart full of corn. He help a woman clamber from the back and slip into the barn. The frontiersman close the doors so I can't see who they hide. More on my plate. I take my wet cape from the peg and step into the yard.

"You got business on my master's property, sir?"

In four strides the tall man greet me. "Doona speak to Miss Yearie?"

"I am. And you be?"

"Alexander." And when I look confused, he say, "The Comte de Broussard, or MacIntosh, if you prefer. Yer lady is in the barn under the hay. I spect Goldsboro'll be around shortly, once he realizes his gaol is empty."

"Oh, sir," I say, "you let them all out? Gaoler be hoppin mad."

"And the lump on his head be his first concern," he say.

The driver and the child slip out the barn door and join us. Under the blanket wrap, I see she be a woman. She got a jolly face, red cheeks and blue eyes that smile at me, laugh like she have the time o' her life. I figure this be Kate. Jackson come over and stand between em.

Seeing the confusion on my face, he say, "It be a good plan, Yearie. Goldsboro racing through town on his horse looking for that gamin rogue who stole his winnings playing loo. Be awhile afore he get to us."

Quick, I step away from him, but he grab my arm. "No, it's no plan a'tall. How we keep Sary from being his prisoner again? We can't hide her in the barn forever, though it be better than that stinkin gaol."

"The gaol not be useful till they fix the hole in the back wall," say the Scotsman

I stare at him not believing he so dumb. "Sheriff just find someplace else to lock her up,"

He put his arm round my shoulders and bend down to whisper in my ear. "Yer master's docking in harbor as we speak. We gave him cause to cut his trip short, sent a message there was trouble at home."

My eyes like to bug outta my head. "I got to tell Cook. I got to light candles and set the fire in the parlor. Bring my mistress inside, for God's sake. What she doin under the hay in the barn, you fool? She got to be presentable!"

"Nay, and ye'll be handling this just fine, missy," he say. "Sarah's in one piece but talking out her mind. Let the Merchant of Oxford see what Goldsboro wrought. Tell him why yer hiding her in the barn, that he imprisoned her for no reason, and fear he'll come for her again. Yer master won't be happy."

"How you excuse a cart with all this corn in his yard?" I pronounce, my hands finding their spot on my hips. I losin control of my little piece of dirt and can't see these folk having a leg to stand on, come Master and Goldsboro.

Mistress Kate speak up and say, "I'll press him to buy my feed corn since Jackson says yer animals go hungry. And the child here will ask him for a handout. He's a soft touch on needy children, I hear."

I ignored the woman's scheming and grabbed the collar of the Scot's shearling, pulling his face to mine. "Sary be with child and that be Goldsboro's reason nuff to jail her again. Master not so fond of his own son. How you think he feel about yours passed off as his?"

I let go and the Scotsman stumble backward like a blow hit him in the chest. The woman and child grab him. I feel satisfied, but in my heart know I'm not cleaning up this pig sty.

"I'm goin to get her and don't stop me for your little playactin. She need washing afore the master see her. Time enough to tell the story after." I stomp off and Kate and her child hop after me like kids follow a nanny goat. The child drop the blanket and I see short white hair stickin up, oiled with bear grease like some heathen. He stunk. "What you want with me, child? Stay with your mother."

"I've no mother. Thou wooden shoe is breaking, slave. We maroons came to your aid."

I got no truck with children speak in verse. The barn door swing open at my push and in the dark I search for my mistress. Her face streaked with dirt, her dress covered in bits of hay.

"Sary, look here. It's Yearie."

Her eyes meet mine and I see hers be cloudy with dreams, like a sleepy child, unawares. I take her by the elbow to lift her up. She wrap her arms round her middle and look out the door, her eyes big.

"Robert arrives," she whisper.

The Scotsman grab her by the arm and shake her. "Canna come with me? I am yer heart, Sarah. Not him. We'll make a life with our baby."

His words make her dream fall away and with a clear voice she answer slow, staring back at him, "You, sir, are my imagination. I will not succumb to that again. Perhaps, in gentler times you will be able to prove yourself that man, but I do not know him as we speak."

Jackson slip his arm round my waist and squeeze. Sary stronger than anyone know.

The Scotsman hold her for a wink and a promise then say in a low voice that strangle with grief, "Aye, and I wilna part from ye, not in heart nor hand, no matter where ye are. Time will tell. Ahl return to ye."

He lead his bay to the back door of the stable that open to the back paddock. He mount, spur his horse and jump the fence. We be rid of him and I be glad for I want my family in order.

Purpose-like, Sary run her fingers through her hair and wipe her face with her cloak. Mistress Kate stand aside for her to greet the master. In the frame of the barn door, she lookin out at the bare oak. I walk round her to face the music.

Master holler as he ride into the yard, "Seventeen, Sarah! I have made this time advantageous. Prepare a feast. Seventeen warehouses up and down the Chesapeake."

He stop dead in his track, take a gander at Jackson hold his stocking hat, the obedient slave, his head low like to make me sick. The cart, the corn, the brown-haired woman and the white-haired child. His eyes rest on me. He dismount and say, "Who is this woman, Yearie?"

"She come to sell us feed corn, master. We near out."

"Well, where is Sarah? Certainly, she can handle it."

"Master, here," I say, pointing to the barn, to his good servant. And what a sight she be. From the top of her head to the tip of her

180

toe, she filthy as a stableboy, covered in hay, stick out like a white muskrat in black marsh.

The master lookin at us for a reason this lie stand before him. Finally, he run to her, swing bare of his greatcoat an wrappin it round her, he say, "You are wounded, my love. Who has done this to you? I will have his *head*."

Master's life so dependable as the sun in its rise and set, he not believe his eyes. Sary lean on his shoulder and they walk to the kitchen door as one. Hestia be a waitin, a spoon in her hand.

I ask Mistress Kate to take her heathen child and leave us in peace. They can make it to East Town afore dark. She order Jackson to shovel the corn from the back of her wagon, quick.

I gaze up in our tree, barren of leaf, its arms cracks in the gray sky. Like a map hangin in the parlor, its wiggly lines of creeks and rivers climb north and south of Oxford. Yes'm, master's reach seem far and wide and growing all the time. His baby, or the Scotsman's, will inherit it all.

And then I remember master's namesake, young Rob, who need be called home. I content to disremember him, but that be a mistake.

The reverend say all men confess and be saved. Only way to get to those pearly gates, say the preacher poor folk call Whitefield. Jackson think no room for us black folk gettin through them gates, but then I wonder be there any women in the Father, Son and Holy Ghost?

CHAPTER 26

A day or three pass, busy with all the work to be done now Master and Sary home. I be fetching all manner of goods from his warehouse and buying pretty thingamabobs in town for his Twelfth Night celebrations. Master like a dressed house. He in a generous mood, what with all the horse races and balls at the plantations.

One afternoon since Sary returned, Master hold a stack of invitations and talk to the Reverend and Henry Callister, not a worryin where his son be at. Just clean forget about him. I twiddle my fingers to see if'n he want me to pull off his boots and bring him his house shoes.

Lo and behold, outside on Front Street, Goldsboro drag a miserable figure to the stocks, them dogs nipping at his heels. It be the gammon prisoner, not so deft with his card no more. And who be among the crowd followin, hurling kitchen middens, but young Robert. Well, he done pick the wrong day to act like rabble since Reverend Bacon, Callister and Master lookin out the parlor window, their mouths agape.

Master toss his letters on the tea table, grab his riding crop, and run past me like a house a'fire. Bacon follow. Master quick and

Bacon be big as a sow, so they paint a comical picture pursuing the boy. The father pluck the son from the crowd and browbeat him with words all the way back to the house. Now, Master Morris got his reputation to uphold, so's I'm thinkin this ain't proper, but then who be I to judge? If'n he my son, he woulda got the whip. I move away from the window and Mr. Henry to tend the hearth, my back to the men.

"Ay-he, you bloodsucking, addle-pated, land rat," Master beller as they fall in the door, he a layin the whip about the boy's haid. "I'll have you respect your station if it kills me!" He yank his son by the collar and throw him into the parlor where the boy stand sulking. Reverend Bacon fill the doorway, smoothin his frock coat. He move into the room and I sidle out in the hall. Too much white man for me.

"Robert," the reverend say to Master, "perhaps you should take a seat and compose yourself."

"Wake up, Bacon," he say. "You think because you're a preacher you know what's what, but your boy John's just as much a knave as this one. Who was watching over them in our absence?"

Reverend swing his pointer in Rob's direction and ask, his face full of concern, "Son, where have you been the last five days? My home might seem a bore to you, but you were obligated to stay with my good wife until I returned."

Well, at this Master roar. "What? You left the Reverend's home? You disobey me? You did not have my permission to leave his hearth!"

"F-Father, I was in your employ the w-whole time. I only left to spy in the backwoods, you know — the Indian trail."

"What mean you?"

I feel someone at my back and Sary slip behind me. We in the hallway like guilty mongrels digging in the family garden. She put her finger to her lips and I nod.

"Action across the trails, sir, at night. Maybe Indians, but some-times they were dressed like us. I never came too close for fear they'd hear me. They carried goods on their shoulders and sometimes were on a horse or a mule."

Master and Reverend have their back to me, but we can see Mr.

Henry and young Rob's faces. I worry the boy on to my eavesdropping. I hang back and whisper to Sary, "You take over. I'll bring em tea." I head to the kitchen and who do I find a jawin with Hestia but Sheriff Goldsboro. I like to die. Tiberius stand by the kitchen door, his eyes full of warning.

"Just locked him in the stockade. A day in this cold will frostbite his sticky fingers. I'll have him confess who assisted his escape."

I keep my haid down and go bout setting lemon scones on a plate. The minute Goldsboro see the scones, don't his paw reach for one? He stretch his neck lookin at me.

"What's your name, woman? You're Mrs. Wise's slave, the one I see shopping at the tailor's all the time."

Aye, I think. The one you follow when we be homeless. "Yearie, sir," I say with a curtsey. "Mr. Morris send me to fetch their finished cloth." I keep my nose to the plate, not a chancin an eye to eye.

"Yearie. Yes, I've heard speak of you in the East Town courthouse. You carry Morris' warehouse goods to the craftsmen in town. I've seen you handle a rig. How does a woman like you have so much skill outside the kitchen?"

I curtsy again, my eyes stuck to the floor. "Thank you, sir. I learnt to drive a rig in Mistress' home."

He step back and I sneak a glimpse as his face fill up with knowing.

"That's right. You're the one that followed Mrs. Wise after her mother died. Knocking on doors, she was jabbering out of her mind. She should have come to me for assistance."

I couldn't take it no more and roll my eyes at Tiberius. He not even have the grace to remember. But he remember putting in a bid for her hand right after we put her Ma in the ground. I think, *what's he talkin about?* Nobody go to him for help. Go to Bacon and the church.

"Sir, the master wait for his tea." I set two more scones on a plate, hold it out, hope that make his mouth water.

"He's in the parlor?" and he stride right by me clattering spurs on my polished floors, leaving my plate in midair.

"What Sheriff say, Hestia?" I ask.

"How he find the gambler in the woods. He don't know who yank the prison grates from the window. His foul dogs try to come in my kitchen, but I tell him they got to stay outside. Probly giving poor Jackson trembles."

I put one more cup on the silver tray and Tiberius smile. "Let me carry it for you," he say. We file down the hall. When Goldsboro see Sary, he pause for a moment, whisper something in her ear and make his big entrance, slapping shoulders and glad-handin. It be a regular social occasion—they congratulate themselves on catching the gammon cheat, setting up more Chesapeake warehouses, and Master and Bacon playin fiddle for the Annapolis crowd.

Sary scared out of her wits and she try to run, but I block her way and say, "Now, this no time to be a cluckin in t'other direction. You defend yourself. Pour tea like nothin wrong."

"Yearie, he said I'm due for a public whipping."

Well, I take that tray from Tiberius and shove it in her hands and say, "Go!" Truth be told, I all prickled too, but Goldsboro on the wrong side of my conjure and prayers. Master love Sary in his own skinflint way. Asides, at least she not headed back to that stinkin gaol.

I follow her in and served the scones. She begin to pour, not sayin nothin.

"Goldsboro," say Master takin a seat, "do you know about action in the Indian swamp?"

"The card speculator was headed there, but, being a fop, he had no appetite for the cold. Begged me to take him to Oxford," said Goldsboro, braying like a donkey.

"I'm talking about illegal actions, man."

"The swamp is full of reprobates and Indians," he say. "Even if they live off one another in some fashion, they cannot survive long. It's too brutal an existence."

Master tap his pipe on the hearth, a sign he set up an argument. "My boy tells me they're stealing from my warehouses. On the other hand, Mrs. Wise has kept the accounts in my absence, and she tells me there is some pilfering but not more than usual."

"Whilst you were off to Annapolis having yourself a merry time, your man-slave was poling the Choptank. I brought him back in chains and Mrs. Wise told me he was taking goods to Dover Town, just blankets and such." Goldsboro glance at Sary. "There was more than a blanket on that barge."

With an eye on me, she nod, draw herself up and look at Master. "M'lord, Jackson took items from your warehouse to the good people of Dover Town. Their children are suffering from the pox and needed clean blankets. Their shipyard workers requested supplies for the upper Choptank." She fix a glare on the sheriff. "It's winter and everyone needs to renovate their barques much like we need to renovate our Christian spirit."

Reverend Bacon sit down between the two men warding off evil spirit brewin between them. I pass a cup of sweet, hot tea to Master. Mr. Henry stay out of the action, leaning on the hearth mantel.

"Goldsboro," Master say in that reasonable way that mean somethin else, "I hear you think Mrs. Wise is stealing from Cunliffe. You imprisoned her."

"Morris, don't be a fool! She steals from your enterprise. Cunliffe will know before long. Quinn has connections in London."

I not believe my ears. The man blame Quinn for his aggression. Be they in league...two spurned suitors?

"You usurp my position in my home, Sheriff," say Master. "Tamper with my livelihood, my servants, and my reputation. I am astounded that you would take such a thing upon yourself."

"She studied your accounts. An imbecilic servant trusted with our vital work? Are you mad, or will you believe any cock and bull?"

Master lean back in his chair and tap his heel in warning. Sary and I wink, thinkin it's all right, Master got the upper hand.

Goldsboro know'd he swat dust cause he blurt out, "Mrs. Wise pleaded the belly once she spent a few weeks in the gaol. I ordered the midwives to examine her in the presence of the other criminals. Your servant is with child," he say, swellheaded, tapping the top of his cane on the tea table. "Sir, you have been cuckolded in your own home, my merry making know-it-all."

"It's not true, Robert," say Sary.

She put her hand over her belly and smooth her skirt. It be a tiny gourd and she sink to the parlor bench just inside the door, her hair lay cross her shoulder. She a leaf ready to fall from its branch, and I want to tell her buck up, but the room too cramped with all them dick-livried men standing round lookin knowledgeable —Goldsboro puffed up, Master simmering, Mr. Henry wilting, and young Rob's face a quivering mouse, dart from one t'other.

The room fall quiet. Goldsboro insulted Master and accuse Sary in one fell swoop. She sit stock still, the teapot resting in her lap and all eyes upon her dress. We all know what this mean—a visit to the Bastard Court come spring. Five months afore they hear her case, and the baby be in arms by then, I hope without no red hair. I took the teapot from her.

Now, the authorities don't like a man not claim his progeny in Oxford. A sheriff don't like not finding the father, and the father don't like being caught. And worst of all, a lord whose servant be big in the belly better have a good excuse or she likely to get the lash. The hair on my arm stand straight up.

They forgot about the accounting book, and about Jackson poling the Choptank. We be one step away that it all be solved like nothing but a stolen finch egg.

"Sarah has told me she is with child." Master's eyes fill. I let out a sigh.

"A Morris child," say Sary.

The Reverend take his turn. "Gentlemen—Sarah," he begin in that preacher voice, "Shall we pray this new life is cherished and provided for? My good Robert, you must post banns immediately, and I will marry thee at St. Peter's over Christmas season." His hands spread palm up and his eyes raise up to the ceiling.

Goldsboro interrupt. "Reverend, what makes you sure the child is Morris'?"

The room so quiet we could'a heard God make a snowflake outside and drop it in the water. I chilled to the bone, and it not be due to my distance from the hearth. I see a flutter to my left and young Robert enter the circle of men. "Exactly, m'lord," he say to his daddy, "Mrs. Wise disappeared for a day before that Frenchman returned her."

"I have written testimony from the town midwives that she confessed to a dalliance in the woods," say the sheriff like he preparin his testimony for court. "Probably the Scotsman who murdered your yeoman or the runaway sailor. Well, it has come back to haunt you now, Morris."

I thinkin Sheriff a lyin son of a bitch. Sary not that dumb, even if she lost in dreams.

Master place his teacup on the tray real slow while he windin up his thoughts. The tap in his foot climb up his leg till his knee start a jigglin, and he push his hand down on it as he stand, the words rush from deep inside hisself, low and grizzly. "You mistake me, Goldsboro, for a man of humble means and little honor. You abuse my reputation in front of my friends and colleagues. You have tortured my handmaid in your gaol, embarrassing her and defiling her reputation in front of the village gossips as if she is one of them. Young Robert's opinion is of no consequence to me as he has continually proven disobedient."

Goldsboro tisk, tisk and start to speak, but Master pull his cutlass by its hilt and point it under the sheriff's nose. In a panic, all my calm vanish, I rush Sary to the door. I fear it gone too far, that I put too much loyal in the spell and Master goin to kill Sheriff. We hug each other, not able to pull our eyes away from the sword tip now tucked in the fold of Sheriff's chin.

Mr. Henry take three steps to Master's side. "Mr. Morris, you have been greatly offended," he say, "but this is no way to resolve this disagreement. Put your blade away. Goldsboro is a reasonable man who sees his error." Callister glance at the sheriff. "We are gentlemen of Oxford. Surely we can discuss this with reason."

Master think twice. He blink. The sword move a hair's breadth. Goldsboro exhale.

"Robert?" say the Reverend.

Master drop the sword to his side, slap his breeches with it, swing his haid away from the fight. He look at the floor and say with great authority, "I challenge you, Goldsboro, to a duel. Callister will be my second." He raise his eye to the sheriff. "I will not be insulted in my own home and have you live to gloat about it in the tavern. Your days of intimidating those you deem lesser than you are over."

Sary clutch my arm near to break it off. I drag her past Tiberius to the kitchen, she breathe hard, gulping air.

"Yearie, he can't. He'll lose. He asks his death."

Hestia be gone. I set Sary down on the bench. "Mr. Henry. Can he talk him out of it?"

"I will speak to him," she say, nodding. "Goldsboro must write an apology. The sheriff must think of his reputation. Robert is well liked in Annapolis. It won't go well when Goldsboro tells the world he killed him."

We grew quiet at the consequence of men. Sarah stirred the coals in the fire, banked the wood to sweep the hearth. I took a cleanin stone to the inside of the iron pot, like to wear away its stubborn black. Bye and bye, we both grunt with effort. She say, "There's not much else."

"I'm thinking, Sary. If all's lost, we go for the Scotsman in the swamp. If Master die, we have to leave. We won't have nobody protect us."

She prop the broom against the hearth and brush her dirty finger across her forehaid.

Spewing tight little words, she say, "Cunliffe will get another factor. Henry, no doubt. I'll be thrown on the streets or a planter will take me for a kitchen maid and indenture my baby for life. And you —Yearie, you'll be sold away from me."

She sigh in great globs of tears, rubbing her neck and a rockin. She mumble and I worry she goin to fall into visions as she pace the kitchen. Of a sudden, my nose in the air, I stand, for I hear Tiberius sayin, *plan our life*. Shouldn't we save ourselves the best we know how? I wonder if now be the time to ask for my freedom.

The harsh voices of men still argue from the parlor and we stand on the point of a needle.

"I have it," says I. "The sun. It be blinding at dawn. Tell Master Henry to demand pistols, not swords. Tell him to pick the entrance road to Plimhimmon. You say the Tilghmans ain't home."

She grab my arm. "They're in Annapolis or at Rich Neck. Plimhimmon's construction has stopped for the cold."

"If'n I remember, a grove of cedars be near the house, offering cover. We'll put the MacIntosh in the wood with his rifle. There'd be three shot — Master, Goldsboro and him."

Sary frown, concentrating. "Callister will count to ten and the Scotsman will take his shot the same time as Robert and Goldsboro."

"Yes'm. And Master will miss. All's we have to do is make sure Goldsboro do too." At dawn shots echo across the water, hunters shoot stags wild with the rut, ready to plough soft does with their seed. Blind to man's firepower just like Master. "Sary," I say, "think of the sound."

"What if Goldsboro doesn't miss?"

I scrunch up my face. "We'll distract him somehow. It'll come to me." I throw the obeah bone in Cook's pot. "I'll conjure, you pray," and she reach in her pocket to hold out the crucifix.

CHAPTER 27

S ary shake off her time in Goldsboro gaol and put her mind to the duel. Her face thinner, and her skin shine pink and white like the inside of an oyster shell. Blue veins show at her temple, but the one at her neck pulse a warning when we plot. Round-bellied and weak as a newborn pup climbing a hill, she hide it to the world in heavy clothes and songs of cheer. Sary an actor. Master Robert be gentle to her as she in the family way nigh on five month. He wondrous of her looking so frail and needy. Together, we got a heart of iron.

Coupled on either side of the fire in the front parlor the next night, they comment on the wind's whistle through the eaves. Master have a book of ancient learning in his lap and Tray at his feet. I bring them bohea tea steeped black and know this be a time to watch and listen. Sarah tong sugar in his cup. She workin a pile of mending, the master weave stories of playin MerryMakefun, prancing through the streets of Annapolis with the Reverend Bacon who call hisself Signorini Lardini, Esquire. They carried their fiddles and wore gilt badges on their old militia coats. Master not long in the tooth, but he no youth either. Come on forty years. I imagine they look like dumb bears drunk on honey.

She laugh and flatter him and he smile a tender moment and say, "I am sorry, Sarah, for leaving the accounts in your charge whilst I was gone. Goldsboro thinks himself a great judge of character."

She get up to kiss his cheek. He ask what happened in his absence. Sitting on the arm of his chair, Sary recount how Goldsboro hunt Jackson on the barge. The beating, the branding, dragging him through the woods, she said. She slid to the floor at his feet like he some ancient god, her face lit by a fire that lick and spit. She pulled a letter from her pocket and he read that Dover Town in awful need of new Scottish blankets for winter. Mrs. Harrisons say the town be riddled with pox. Sary tear up and point. "You see, Robert, Mrs. Harrison lost four children." It bring a tear to his eye, too.

Well, Master not realize halfway to old Dover Town be the maroons on the Choptank.

I throw more wood on the fire, pull the heavy curtains shut. What she didn't say was what be below the barge deck. Jackson and Voltaire loaded bolts of raven duck cloth, enough to sail a light ship, some ten grote and six penny nail, and ten gallon o tar. In shallow winter water Jackson pole that barque slow, and that be his mistake. Goldsboro seen him.

Sure and away, master will notice how much canvas gone from his warehouse. Sary hum a little tune, get up from the floor and sit in his lap, sayin she did the best she could with the numbers. With worries about feeding us pilin up, she may have missed a mite in the log afore Goldsboro drag her off to gaol.

While I busy in the front hall cleaning, Master put his arms round her waist and kiss her neck. His wayward hand reach in her bosom and he suck air at the fullness of it. Sary laugh and push him away, sayin he not fulfill his promise, and she still wait his betrothal. She never bring up the duel, just move back to her seat and pat her knees for that spaniel to jump up. Always in need of a stroke, he claw in her lap just like his master when of a sudden Mr. Morris pose a question.

"Sarah, my mirror is gone upstairs. I have none in the warehouse and will have to send to Liverpool. Do you know what happened to it?"

I not say a word to her about my conjuring, for she bound up in her saints. She think on her feet. This just the kind of thing that send him into a rage. "Why m' lord, while you were gone we cleaned your bedchamber and polished it some. That might have loosened the nail on which it hung. Yearie, do you know?"

I put flustered on my face which not hard to do, and say, "I beg your pardon, Master, for with the Mistress gone to the gaol I forgot to tell you it fell hard to the floor one morn and shattered in its frame. I threw the pieces in the kitchen midden the day afore you come home."

He look over his shoulder at me and say real calm, "I hope you saved the frame."

I jump from foot to foot thinking the net be cast around me. "I'll get it from the midden right this very minute, Master."

He look hard at me and turn away to sip his tea. "That's a very good idea. After your mistress retires for the night."

Sary glance at me and we both take a breath of relief. She put the dog on the floor and tell him she weary, the baby grow so fast. She ask me to come above stair with her, but he ask me to stay a moment. A ripple of fear grip my heart.

Sary bid her goodnight and head to the stair. He hear her tread above and pick up the teapot and move it off the tea table. I wonder what he up to as he take his kerchief and polish the surface of the silver tray. He wave me to him and, obedient, I come. I smile a little at his closeness thinkin he might reward me, this being the season of givin, but he grab my neck and push my cheek to the tray, squeeze the air from my throat. I roll my eyes over his face as he bend near me. He goin to kill me.

"Don't look at me, Yearie. Look at your reflection in the tray. You want to know what you look like? There, you see?" He press my face hard and squeeze even harder. I gurgle and drool on the tray.

"Oh, be careful," he warn. "You've spoiled your reflection and you can't see what an ugly island eel you are." The firelight start to wiggle and fade. I blink and try to breathe, but the air not go past his grip. He bend to my ear. "Be quiet, you black rodent. I'm going to get rid of you and your innocent singsong voice. Hestia dug up a piece of my glass after you buried it. You break my things and you'll pay when I visit with my branding iron." He snorted, and say, "You tell Jackson if he's found stealing, I'll sell him south."

He threw me to the floor with a thump and kick me for good measure. I yelped and he charge at me again, foolin a capper to his game, but it be enough to scare me stiff. I clap my fingers over my mouth when Sary call down the steps, "Did something fall?"

He put his stop hand between us. "It's nothing, my dear," he answer loud. "Yearie tripped over her own feet." His eyes cold, he say, "Bring this up to your mistress and I'll have your tongue clipped." I get to my feet and curtsey, my hands folded in prayer. I clean up the tea tray.

The next morn be a freezin. I milkin the cow afore the full light of dawn, tryin to strike the best pose so's my neck don't hurt. Bets chomp on feed while Jackson muck her stall. I commenced a coughing fit and stood up to hold a kerchief over my mouth. Jackson squint at me and throw down his rake. He walk over all sweet and say, "You be getting sick, Yearie? It's early in the season to have the ague come on."

Now he know I'm hale and hearty as a bull in spring. I have my linen tucker pull up round my throat to hide its swell, but Jackson's long fingers pull it away.

"That be master's work?" he ask.

I smooth the tucker up and say, "It none your business. You take care of the outside and I take care of the inside. You just be smart, never say no word to Hestia. Voltaire too dumb to know which end up, but she be takin note of everthin we do and say."

Jackson step back and lean against the stall. He wear an old wool coat of Master's that too short, the shoulder seams be split in back and he got a rope tied round his waist to hold it closed. But the collar be big and he can turn it up against the winter wind.

"When am I make my next trip?"

"We got to get word to the Scotsman about the duel, tell him where to meet us. Swamp in need of more tar." I pick up the bucket of milk. "I want to see what I risk my life for, so I'm goin with you next time."

"Now how you going to get away from Oxford without no suspicion?"

"You let me and Sary figure that out," I say, wondering why I speak with so much confidence.

"I'm not taking you, Yearie. No more'n I'd take mistress. Besides, you need to stay here and look after her." He throw the rake against the barn wall and walk away from me mumbling under his breath.

"What you sayin over there? You got somethin on your mind, out wit it."

He whirl on me, his fingers spread out. "You think you got some direct line the Lord gonna protect you? Well, let me tell you woman, there ain't no protection on the highways and byways of Oxford. You got to be smart enough to hear when trouble coming and get outta its way. And when it come for you, you gots to be ready to die. Takin you along ain't nothin but a fool's errand. I'll be damned if I hide you and me both."

"That so?" I asked. I not ever seen Jackson stick up for hisself to me like that. Maybe the man grow a spine after all.

"So be it," I say. "Master write a pass for you to take the barge to East Town tomorrow with two English wing backs and a settee for the courthouse. Sary make a fuss bout new curtains the East Town tailor goin to make, so's Master say to load them bolts of damask afore you leave. This afternoon I'll ask Jeremiah stop by Three Coaches, say we need the Mac to meet you at the dock." I grab his arm. "Now you listen careful, this your first time walking about them white folk in daylight, and they don't know you." I stuff the map Sary give me in his coat pocket. "Once you tell the Scotsman what we need, come back with an empty barge. If'n somebody stop you, you can say you done deliver to East Town for Morris. Only a half lie."

The only thing I didn't know was when and where the duel be scheduled.

"You gots to get me some better boots outta his warehouse if'n I goin to walk round that dock looking for him in this cold. These'n got holes and the toes be a flappin like Hestia's gums."

"Mistress got to ask Morris for that. He count his leather goods just this afternoon. Damnation. Make all these rules since he be home from Annapolis. Let's hope he so smitten with Sary, he bend to her will."

Afore lunch, I run to the tailor and ask him to send Jeremiah to Kate's stable with a message for the Mac. Only gone the time it take bread to rise on a cold day and the whole world change that quick. First inkling was passing the tavern and old Ruth look down at me as she wipe the windows of their grime. "Don't say I tole you so. Cain't trust no white folk, you fool, not even that mistress of yours." I fairly ran to the kitchen, but it be too late.

A tall, thin black man, his hair wrapped in a white cloth be stirring Hestia's cookpot while a slab of beef browning on a griddle. Pile of root vegetables all diced up sitting in a bowl, ready for a stew. He wearin a white apron.

"I be Yearie. Who you be?"

He pay me no mind. "I'm the cook. Paid. And a free man."

"Where Hestia?"

"Handy plantation. A trade, me for her."

Master like Hestia's cooking. "That make no sense," I say.

"When Talbot ever make sense? Handy can't afford me. I'm a better cook."

"So, you not living in the slave cabin with the rest of us?"

"Listen here, you little house slave. You ask too many questions. I'm a free man, Raphael Kent. What I do on my time isn't none of your business. I'll be here after the cock crows, and I'll leave once dinner is served. I don't clear table and I don't scrub dishes. That's what you're for."

I found Sary in the gathering room, tidying up more of Rob's mess. "Yearie," she say, "we'll have to load this in a trunk. His father's having a chimney and fireplace built here. Bookcases on either side. Won't that be lovely?"

She be on a different page in the book from me. "You talking sponge painting or dot, Sary? You do know Master sent Hestia to Handy?"

She held up a Quaker quilt and say, "Here, help me fold this. Yes, but there was nothing I could do. I explained Hestia is here to take care of our every need and this Raphael won't be. It puts more work on you and me just when the baby's due." She shakin her haid like Hestia nothing but a kitchen fire, burnin day and night.

"I talked him into new boots, stockings and wool trousers for Jackson. I said we shouldn't have him walking the streets of Oxford looking like he's a field hand, and do you know he returned with a new coat big enough for Jackson? It was meant for a yeoman on the harbor."

Seeing the look on my face, she say, "I'm sorry, Yearie. I told him any other home but Handy's and he said he couldn't. It was a trade that keeps Handy in debt to him."

What I see is that while she makin one black man happy, she helpless to save a woman she laugh and drink with, sharing a pipe on occasion.

That night, while Jackson wait in the stable for the nuts and bolts of the duel, I serve Raphael's beef stew to Master, Sary and Henry in the parlor. Callister say the sheriff won't apologize and, doom in his eye, he say, "We are committed to a duel."

Sary fall on her knees and tell Master he cannot die. She plead for mercy, that she need him to withdraw, but the man a stubborn stye in his own eye and can't see his way to make peace. He spout about honor and God, his reputation ruined at home and in the capital if he not defend his good name. Master throw down his soup spoon and head to the kitchen pretending to read by the fire.

It be a done deal. So Sary negotiate the particulars with Master Henry. Dueling pistols, Plimhimmon, dawn three days hence. Master Henry go to Morris and explain. I roll out the back door with the pots to clean, groaning, "Oh, Lord." With a shaky hand, Sary come to me with the particulars written like an invitation to a sunrise service for the MacIntosh. I give it to Jackson.

He set out in dawn's shadow, his breath smoke the air. So cold not even a dog bark as he scurry round Front Street, and the back of the warehouse where the barque be sittin in the water. He load the furniture. There be a strong wind and I help him set one sail against it. His barque take off like a shot of lightning. Then we wait.

CHAPTER 28

Sary and I card wool, polish silver, and dig up the last of the garden over the next day, not talking to each other. I still seethe bout Hestia, not trusting. Mr. Henry clean the dueling pistols and when he go lay them in the velvet case, Master grab one and take it to the stable yard where he commence walking ten paces from the oak and whip off a shot at a pie tin. His son watch him and shake his haid, so they take turns, Master shoot and young Morris throw a tomahawk. Master miss the tin every time, until finally he clip it, skittling across the shells. He hoot in delight until he think he probably be dead meat in Goldsboro's pistol sight.

At night, they sit by the fire, her needle and thread push in and out while he read to her from some Greek story about a horse filled with soldiers. She look at me sideways. We not ever get word of poor Jackson. Morris notice him missing bout dinnertime two days later and Sary say he laid up in the quarter with a terrible ague. Well, that be enough for him to avoid all us slaves.

By that time, Jackson be home all right, covered in stinking muck. We sneak about, draw water from the well for him, heat it on a low fire so's master not aware. Turns out the Mac never'd show on the harbor so's Jackson run into the swamp, gettin lost, nearly killed by wild animals, raisin suspicion from the maroons. By the mornin of the second day, he meet the Scotsman face to face and give him Sary's message. They gave him a horse and he say he rode free as the wind with a promise that the MacIntosh be happy to oblige.

That night, I steal a sapphire ink well from Master's parlor desk and smash its glass outside on the kitchen step. Scooping pieces into a conjure bag, I get my trowel and dig up a piece of Master's looking glass. Then I take a walk once they fast asleep. It be a restless night anyways and I want to get the lay of the land at the plantation road since I not seen it since the summer revival. Callister walked it and though he give instruction to Master, there got to be more to learn.

Plimhimmon sit right across the harbor on the Tred Avon. Betwixt the two on a parcel called Hels Half Acre, sit the ruined gaol and a makeshift cemetery of wooden markers filled with the bodies of middlin folk. Gentry buried at White Marsh Church, but this be the resting place for poor whites. We dark folk know Hels Half Acre be haunted with ghosts of pox-ridden sailors, children and blacks. I hope they quiet tonight.

The day been sunny so's the earth clutch its warmth and that keep my legs from freezing through my wool stockings. I trudge past the shipyard and the gibbet where Goldsboro's pile of slave bones swing in cages. At the end of ship's lane, *Skillington's* new sign be pretty white, a mark the old coot make British sterling. Smell of tar come at me. The sailors burn pitch to seal the seams of ship hulls during these rare warm days. It hang in the wet air and the night sky push its oily blackness down on me. I pass a farmer's pumpkin patch, them glisten with dew in the moonlight and I think, once this all over, we make a slew of pies for the Twelfth Night, eat till my belly full.

My step crunch-crunch on shells, stirring a gaggle of snoozing mallards. They quack and waddle out of my way when I hear rustle in the road thicket and a heron squawk in the wetland. It make me no mind. I pick up the pace, wrap my cloak tight and pull the hood over my face. Not good for a slave woman walking the main road at night. Goldsboro might be lying abed, but his deputies could roam, looking for runaways. I wish Tiberius and me could take a walk on a cold winter night, maybe in Philadelphie where I make coffee and peach cakes to sell. Thinkin our day be a comin, I hum a little tune. Won't be long afore I ask Sary to release me.

I pass the gates at Plimhimmon's brick entrance and walk the pea gravel lane. Up ahead a white clapboard mansion shimmer in what little moonlight travel out of the sky. The windows, black holes, watch me like Findley's eyes. A bad case of the dreads come on me and I scurry into the stand of cedars, lean against a hairy trunk, breathing hard. Maybe I not as brave as a think.

"Madam, I—"

I yelp, jump out of my skin, and whirl round to see a large shadow standing over me. At first, I think it be a highwayman and I make to run fast. A hand clap over my mouth.

"Ahl thank ye to be quiet. Sounds carry in the night air, m'lady."

No highwayman call me lady. I hiss and struggle and he let me go. My Ma speak in my ear and I throw the conjure bag with the sapphire glass at his feet. Get rid of fears, get rid of chains that hold me back. His hand slip.

"Who be you, hiding in the wood? I warn you I got a knife if you come at me."

"I beg pardon. I come at yer behest, Yearie."

I peer at him in the dark. I can't see nothin but the glint of an earring and the shape of his cockhat. My heart beat so fast that at first my mind don't work. Then I fancy my imagination run wild wit the suspicions of my mother. The MacIntosh stand afore me.

"You come to help, then?"

He turned and I made out the long rifle bound to his shoulder. He come on his own.

"They not be here for hours," says I. "Why you so early, Scotsman?"

"Best get the lay of the land, since I'm not making an appearance in this mess," he say.

Same reason as me, so's I guess we a matched pair, so to speak.

"I tell you the plan. You stay hidden in these trees. The house be empty."

He go down on one knee, bow his haid and listen whilst I lay it out. I tell him I hide by the house afore sunup. If'n he see me, I say, "Don't give no sign. The troupe may not be far."

"I'll shoot to kill the sheriff."

I plod to the smokehouse where I can set a pit fire no one could see. Finding a hank of ham on a hook, I shred it to see if'n it beset with maggots, but it not soured. I chewed a bit and my mouth fill with hickory that suck out all the spit. The smokehouse feel cozy and warm and I decide not to walk back through that graveyard, tempting fate. No, this spot was best to hear the animals stir at first light. I curled next to the fire and afore long I was asleep.

Too soon, I hear gulls step heavy on the roof and I rose, stretched, and push the heavy door open. A hundred gulls flying circles through a thick fog. Take a bright sun to burn this off. Wise men would schedule a different day to challenge death.

Outside, I squatted, raise my skirts and pee hard, a finger of cold wrap round my neck. A squirrel ran up a tree, field mice scurry bout, and I filled with doubt, wondering why I do this for two white men tied up butchering each other's precious prize pig. They so called honor a bad cut to start. Why I help make opinion on who be better? It weren't like me to worry with no white man's hide much less his stock with other white folk. Then I scold myself for being soft. Master might be better'n Goldsboro but that not saying much. I remember Sary and me. She my hope against becoming Hestia. Comtemplatin my future, I sprinkle the rest of the sapphire glass across the lane, muttering Ma's spells…protection for me.

Wasn't long afore the horse and carriage burst through the mist toward the house. I hide in unkempt boxwood at its corner, hope the MacIntosh stay hidden in the grove of cedars forty feet away, both of us facing a slow sunrise. It dark but not black, and I see Master and Mr. Henry disembark. Jackson yell, "Giddyup!" and drive the carriage to the house, horse hooves thundering loud. Sary's outline huddle next to him. Wishing we could be together I try to get her attention, but the night sky not lift enough for her to see me. We all separate in our places, not drawing strength from one another though we all of the same purpose.

Soon, we raise our haids at the sound of more hooves a comin down the lane. I can just make out Goldsboro and his second. Callister say he be his cousin fresh from university in Philadelphia. Sheriff bring a manservant, and my heart fall to my feet seeing it be Tiberius in a frock coat, riding his gray. Of course, he come with his master. Of course.

The four men make arrangements. Their long black coats swirl bout their boots, but they cockhats clouded in a rising pink mist. Mr. Henry and the cousin walk the lane, take a measure of the field. All scientific-like, the cousin lick his finger and hold it up testing the wind. So still, only the songbirds sing. Mr. Henry shuffle-foot, looking for ruts. The cousin peer into the fog for bystanders and I hide deeper in the bush. Master and Goldsboro stand about not speaking, for there be no words. The sheriff hand his coat to Tiberius. I see Goldsboro wear a sword and wonder if he think he going to pull that on Master to finish him off.

Then, the cousin open the dueling case. Bringing the pistols out of their velvet sleep, one of them twinkle in the growing light and I sigh my relief that sunrise come to the rescue. They load the guns, polish their silver, point them pretending to shoot and, satisfied, hand them to the principals. Them fools walk opposite ten paces and mark it with a stick. I want to get this over so's I draw the piece of Master's mirror from my pack.

I hear Mr. Henry, "Sheriff Goldsboro, this is the last time that I will demand an apology for Mr. Robert Morris of Oxford. Your words of insult against his servant, Mrs. Wise, against his home, and against his business cannot be tolerated. He requires that you profess your regret. If you will offer such as we stand here, we will be done with this ugly business and go home better men."

"Morris is my inferior," shout the sheriff. "I will not suffer his accusations because *I am the law* in this region. It's his life to lose. He can't shoot a scurvy dog licking his own boot!"

Just pile on the insult, that man. I wipe off the mirror and hold it up to the growing light that lift the mist above they haids. In the grove of trees, I see a long stick point down the lane, the MacIntosh in residence ready to shoot. To my left Sary clutch Jackson all suited up in his new wool coat and she pale as the moon. It be time.

Callister, the cousin, and Tiberius step to the side of the road. Master and Sheriff stand back to back and count they steps, Master toward us and Goldsboro down the road. They stop and turn. The sun glare in my eye and surely in Master's. Goldsboro stare at the house glowing white and I put my mirror up till the sun catch its rays. I flicker up and down, find the sheriff's face. I can see him squint in its shine. Mr. Henry drop the flag and cracks echo through the fog over the river. I can't tell if I hear two or three. I can't tell if my mirror catch Goldsboro's gun eye. I can't tell and all I want is to run down the lane and see for myself. My heart thumpin, I shrink small into the bushes.

Master droop, his pistol dangle. Callister run to him. Goldsboro spin, grab his side and drop to one knee.

Mr. Henry walk Master to the carriage where Sary cry, and Jackson wrap him up in their comfort. The cousin prop Goldsborough up on his knee and we all turn at his shout, "Morris, Providence smiles on you. A flesh wound I have."

Nobody say nothin. Sary urge Master into the carriage. Jackson start to climb up and take the reins when Goldsboro stand, leanin on the cousin. He call out all respectful in that milky voice, "Begging your pardon, Morris. Are you wounded?"

"Nay, Goldsboro. Whole and hearty. You missed me a stone's throw."

"May I follow your carriage to the barber if I offer my apology?" He take a few steps, his cousin on one side, Tiberius on the other. He clear his throat. "I will post my regrets for my words and actions against your house. You are a gentleman of fine cloth and honor. Oxford is proud to call you her own."

We all stand transfixed, wondering what come over the man. He shamed he missed.

"Goldsboro," Master say, "you are bound to honor your position as lawman of Oxford." He bow, "May I offer my services?"

The cousin try to lead the sheriff to Master's carriage, but Goldsboro pause and take his coat from Tiberius. Under its cloth, I see a flash of silver draw upward into the white light of morn. In the sweep of a bird's wing, Goldsboro draw its blade across my man's neck. Tiberius wobble upright for a moment and crumple to the road, blood pulsing from his wound. Sinking to my knees in the bush, a hand over my mouth, I not utter a cry, or a moan, not a plea for his life. Our life. I be crippled.

"Cousin!" yell his second. "What mean you to kill your servant?"

"Do not question me!" yell Goldsboro. "He distracted me as I shot. I will not have a traitor serving me."

My tongue be dry as I watched his life's blood stain the white shells. In a cloud, I see Robert Morris face the pig who bow for his forgiveness. Master not wounded. He set his shoulders and looking tall in his boots for a man of such misery, he say, "I am alive, sir. Unharmed, and secure in my position as the Merchant of Oxford. We shall call this quits. Please, tie your horses to my carriage and we'll drive you to the barber."

With that it be over. A spat between two Talbot men. Not a glance or a prayer. Not even the dignity of discussing a loyal servant left for the wolves. Leave, I yell in my haid. Leave us so I can come out of the shadows.

The carriage take off, Jackson whippin horse, Sary by his side on the hard bench searching for me in the boxwoods. Master and Callister loll in back facing Goldsborough and the cousin. A regular little church outing.

Every fiber of me shaking, I crawl from the shrub and totter to him, falling next to the holy body of a man I never experience. A splendid, proud man with dreams. Dreams of promise—our walk together, his a long stride, shoulders wide, chin to the wind. Down, down, he melting into earth, my prince cut. Blood run like water and I scoop it up, wiping it on my face and breasts where the obeah bone buried in my valley of love that have no lover. Angry, I hurl it in the dirt and run my red hand across his shocked eyes closing his look at a bitter world, pressing on the lips of his wound. "Stop, stop," command my words to his bloody essence. "I didn't mean for you to die. Please. It be my doin. Not you." I wailed, "Come back to me."

My hands not working and though I press harder his life gone. A sob escape me.

I untie my wooly tucker, wrap it round his neck. Slowly, I remove my cloak and spread it beside him covering his wound with my hood. I cry, but no tears wet my face. Layin beside him looking up in the pink mist, it take all my weak soul to ask God, "Why?" My eyes roam the clouds, the birds, and the glaring sun. On the wall, master's mirror reflect him whole, and in pieces, save Sary through a spell, but in my hand Obeah use it against us. He give me no answer, and I know in my mind that it be the cursed way of Oxford. I will not wait for any God, for He not protect the slave, just open His gates for our dead.

The MacIntosh appeared over my haid holding out his hand. "Yearie, I found a shovel. We must bury him."

I ignore his hand and raise to my knees next to Tiberius. "You dig. I'll pray." Under the cedars, he dug a grave. We drop him clumsy into the hole and seeing the indignity deep in my bones, the injustice, I scream at the sky, "You white man's God, why You make the world so cruel to the likes of us?" Raising my fist in the air, I spit out, "May the Devil sweep across this land, and curse these men and their harvest, their children forever after." I fell to my knees.

The Scotsman reach and hold me to him. "Revenge is a good supper, Yearie, but come tomorrow ye'll need a new hope."

Angry, I struggle free of his arms. "Why you not kill that bastard when you got the chance?"

Slowly, he draw his handkerchief and wipe the blood from my face. Tender as a father cleaning a child's mouth, he say, "A purple raven fluttered in the boughs and landed on my barrel just as I sighted. I had stood there so long, the bird thought my rifle part of the tree."

A raven. Death to come. I looked hard at the MacIntosh to see if he had caught the evil eye. "You be somebody's victim soon," I said.

"That's cow-slaver, good woman, but thank ye for your concern. We will help one another. Take care of your mistress," he say. "If ye be in need, I'm here."

"This world don't know the stuff of good men," I say.

"There be few good men in war, Yearie. Not even me," He nod and lead his horse from the cedars, mount, and touching the brim of his hat, he trot off in the yeller light. I take it slow down the lane and not see him again for a fortnight. By then I was eatin pie and pretendin to celebrate the season, while a nugget of mean grow inside me bigger than ever. I called it survival.

CHAPTER 29

Somebody decide we slaves need God. On the morn of Twelfth Night eve afore the sun rise, Raphael roast a suckling pig, stuff its mouth with apple, ring it with holly berries, and put it back in the spring house. Master throwin a big celebration for the baby Jesus. Captains of four ships in harbor, their seconds in command, and the usual Cunliffe folk invited. Master and Sary not invited to any plantation parties cause they not up to snuff to mix with the snobbery.

I bake cakes in the beehive oven, some with a toy Jesus inside.

"Going to burn, Yearie. Fire's too hot," Raphael say.

Bossiest man in a kitchen I ever seen. Instead of setting table, Sary and I ready a groaning board for food and drink. Master in a generous mood and nobody want to spoil it. He call us to the parlor, and I watch as Jackson mumble and rub his eyes when he get new linen cravats and two shirts. Raphael get a new apron and a strange white hat Master call a toque that sit high on his head. Voltaire get a new wig and he bow, disappointed, to hide his eyes. I know he wish for a checker game. My turn come and master smile and give me a pair of leather shoes and a blue gingham dress. I curtsey, say my thank you remembering his hand on my neck.

He turn his feet to the fire and lean back in his wing chair. Sary be seated in hers on the other side of the crackling flames, a cheery smile on her face, her hands resting on her belly. It were all too sweet and nice.

"Now, my good servants, let me pour you some tea," he say, setting out four crockery cups on the silver tray.

Darned if'n he not heat the water and steep the tea all by hisself. Making a big flourish he pour it and add two spoons of sugar to each and lift the tray all round for us to have our cup. I get a bad feeling of the Devil in the room.

"Yearie, Jackson and Voltaire, I have paid the smithy to install ankle chains by your pallets. We have a terrible undercurrent of crime in Oxford. My warehouse is thieved and slaves are kidnapped. Mrs. Wise was in danger four months back from some cockney sailor. I'm sure you remember the hue and cry when the Vanderkoops were taken by the Indians. Our family must be protected.

"The chains will clasp one of your ankles. It won't restrict sleep, just protect you from kidnapping in the night. There are general descriptions of slaves sneaking around Oxford at night. I know this wouldn't be any of you, but we must be careful lest you are accused, and end up suffering for the sins of another house. Of course, Raphael is a free man and doesn't need to worry about kidnapping."

I hear a low grunt come from Raphael. Master got to his feet and puff out his chest. "Enough of that. We will prove to Oxford that you are a loyal bunch on this holiday. I have an exciting outing for our family tomorrow. Raphael, you are invited to attend."

"Master," he say, "My wife and children will be attending our church tomorrow. Thank you for your generosity. If need be, I can come to the kitchen midday to prepare a simple repast."

I know Master figuring how much that cost him. "Not necessary. Take tomorrow off, Raphael and enjoy your family."

None of us get a promise of the next day to ourself. On Christmas and Twelfth Night even field slaves get a day of rest. Not us. Three wise men, my foot. Baby Jesus may been poor and dressed in rags, but I be one tired slave.

In the kitchen later, Raphael put on his new hat and say, "I'll not be kidnapped by a white man and sold south. You need to get out of these backwoods, Yearie." I want to ask him more, but, hearing a noise in the hall, he frown at me in warning.

Sary come in and pull me aside. "Alexander arrives tomorrow knowing we'll all be in church. I don't know what he's up to, but be ready."

That's all I do is be ready.

Instead, after slogging through a night of entertaining, we told in early morn we got to ride in the pony rig to the White Marsh Church for Reverend Bacon's sermon. Sary say she think we the only black folk invited and for us to take as much time as we need if we're asked a question. I tap my foot pondering what that mean as I stand in the freezing cold in my new dress waiting for Jackson to bring the horses. I take stock of my white folk as they come out the front door, for that be a measure of they magnificence.

Young Robert in a fine suit and matching wool coat. Sary be in a new red wool cloak line with beaver skin, and she ride with master in the new close carriage. She awkward with baby weight, so he hand her up and she glance over her shoulder at me, pressing her lips, winking. I don't smile back. Master climb in behind her. Oh, how impressive in his bearskin coat and beaver hat. Jackson black his boots for him till they shine dark as Carib skin fresh off the boat in summer. Then he carry foot stoves and charcoal to warm Sary's feet. Voltaire assigned to our pony cart, Jackson drive the carriage and two.

I grumble for I got religion. The kind that say do unto me. I made my peace with Jesus and the Trinity since Tiberius gone, but I know not ever let them see my conjure bags for that get me thirty lashes from these Anglicans. I got religion and it be the kind that tell me take care of my black hide. I got a tongue that do not speak, and eyes that do not see.

The sun a ghostly ball in a winter sky providing no heat, the air wet. Our ride be long and we arrive bone cold, huddled in the rig. I see White Marsh have no chimney and wonder why white folk sit in cold churches in the dead of winter, the windows fogged with the warmth of those inside.

Voltaire follow Master inside, carryin the foot stove. I can almost feel my hands and feet come alive if they only let us in. Instead, me and Jackson told to tie up everbody's horse out back afore the door open for us darkies. Now, I know I don't look like any stable boy. As we round the corner of the church, another carriage speed up the drive and stop. Out step the Handy family, all five of them in their winter finery. Up on the driving bench, two figures huddle, one wrapped in nothing but a blanket. It be a woman, a familiar shape, who climb down and the blanket slip off her haid. Hestia's face surprised at seeing me, like some fat cat thrown out from a fireside nap.

"Good Hestia, how you be? I not even get a chance to say good-bye," I say, looking her over. "They treat you well at Handy's?"

She quiet and I see her face be lined, her hair sprinkled gray. Not letting this stop me, I hug her like we sisters. Stiff as a board. We mill bout on the front stoop, waiting.

"They going to let us in, Yearie, or we just here to mind the horses?" ask Jackson.

I hop from one foot t'other. "They think we dumb animals, man," I say, disgusted and plotting, watching Hestia out the corner of my eye. "So, we live up to exspectations. You remember that ol cross-eyed Englishman, Reverend Whitefield, rile up the poor white folk round here last summer, preaching bout gettin saved? They's only one step above us, yet they rolling round on the ground like pigs in shit. Bet these Anglicans would let them inside on a cold day."

Hestia smile a little. She really hate two-faced white men. "I shoulda baked holly berries in my cakes," she whisper. "Give em the runs."

I nod thinkin how good Hestia's cakes be, far better than mine. As I raise my fist to knock, the door open and Reverend let us in. It all candles and white and smell like juniper inside. He point to a carpenter bench far from the box pews and their foot stoves. I rub my hands together hoping to heat the blue from my fingers. I look up from my feet and find the whole congregation lookin over they shoulder at us.

"Our guests. Please, rest," Reverend say loud to us four black hobgoblins ready to wreak havoc given the chance. Subtle is the way, so's they not see we make fools of them till they home in bed at night, wondering.

"The service will begin."

He walk up the aisle kicking his cassock pleat, throwing his arms out like he got wings. "Holy, holy, holy, Nations shall come to Your Light, and kings to the brightness of Your Rising. Isaiah, Chapter 60, Verse 3," he say. "And we shall open our hearts to those lesser than us, as God welcomes all to the Kingdom of Heaven."

This church gleam inside and the ceiling one arch after nother till it end in a wooden cross on the far wall. Ladies' hoods and gentlemen's perukes keep them warm. We huddle close. Popping my haid over this shoulder and that, I try to see the altar when all of a sudden, Reverend Bacon rise, climbin a stair in a circle till he get to a carved wood stand way up high where everbody can see his face. With a blood red cravat, he look like God's messenger for sure.

In his deep voice, he say, "We are gathered today on the Feast of the Epiphany."

Besides them wise men and that stable lore, I try to remember what that mean when Sary and I be little girls goin to a Mass in a secret house. Then it come to me. It were baptism day.

The Reverend do speechify more but my ears fade, for my flesh still frozen. I perk up when I fancy he talkin bout us.

"...indispensable duty of all masters to bring up their slaves in the knowledge and fear of God," say Bacon. "As His steward, I press you to work in His vineyard. All Negroes, being of the human species, have souls as well as we and are equally capable of salvation. Christian duty requires us to endeavor their conversion...bringing these children, your children to Baptism."

We look at each other, our jaws might well be dropped wondering when we get souls just like white master.

Reverend's voice rise above us. "Given the suffering our slaves experience in their daily trials, they only have death and everlasting life to look forward to."

Well, a rumble go up in the assembled and soon Master Handy pop up and say, "Bacon, stick to the Word of God. This is nothing but liberal lies, confusing our profitable village." Mistress Handy pull on his arm, tryin with no luck to sit hisself down. Next, a huge man —near six and a half foot, stand up on t'other side of the church. I recognize Master Adams, a sea captain who give up sailing for a little store in Oxford that sell farm implements and such. Folk say he roll in Spanish gold, but he not wearin his wealth like my master. Adams hold his cockhat over his chest and say in a humble voice, "I am not given to slave ownership, having traded in them for years, I've seen enough misery to last a lifetime. My fellow Oxfordians, you have as well."

Durn well perfect it, too, I think.

"Mr. Handy," Adams say, "there's no wrong in baptizing slaves and teaching them to love their fellow man. Gives them purpose and a belief that a better life is in store after death. Sit so we can hear what else Reverend Bacon has to say."

Bull crap. It must been his outsized presence or his reasonable tone, for Master Handy sit and Reverend Bacon proceed to bless the assembled and call on God to enlighten us to His Ways. Everbody bow they haid in prayer and I be cogitating on what to do next. I whisper to Hestia and Jackson, "They call you up to get yourself baptized and you be sure to see the Light of Christ, you hear?"

Hestia look straight ahead. Low and snide, she say, "Oh, I think I feeling it coming on my bones right now."

Fore long, that's what happen. She delivered by me and Jackson to the altar and the Reverend ask her name.

"This be Hestia, Reverend," I say looking dumbstruck. "You know her. She used to cook for you and Master at his home."

This produce a big laugh all round the church. They want simple, we give em simple.

"Hestia, do you renounce Satan and all his wicked forces?" ask Reverend.

"I do," say Hestia, trembling.

"Do you renounce the evil powers of the world that corrupt and destroy all God's creatures, including you?"

"I renounce them," say Hestia huffing and puffing.

"Do you renounce all sinful desires that draw you from the love of God?"

Well on this one, Hestia shake so bad that Jackson and me let her go. She bow her haid and quiver like a fat willow in high wind on the river bank. She moan and groan and her blanket fall away. Her dress be hangin on her.

The reverend look alarmed. He come to her side and ask, "Good Hestia, are your sins so great that they cannot be forgiven?"

Hestia glance at me and I shut my eyes tight. Next I know, she moaning, "Oh Lord, oh Lord, forgive me my sins for I want to see You happy that my evil black soul enter your pearly gates in Your Glory." Loud and quick, she add, "...with the rest of these good white folk." She heave side to side and fall on top of Reverend who give way under the weight, stumbling backward against his pulpit.

Jackson reach out to help Reverend and Master Handy yell, "Don't touch him. Get them out of our church before they defile the altar. Morris, you insisted I bring her here without the approval of the vestry."

Hestia still groaning on the floor, her eyes rolling round in her haid like we seen at Whitefield's revival. I flutter bout, sayin, "Oh my, oh my!" being some helpless child and enjoying every second of it. Only Jackson stand by, silent as a tree, knowing this end in a flogging for him.

Master stride up the aisle, his bearskins flapping. "Mr. Handy, the vestry approved," he say and take a post next to Bacon who sit on his backside. "You can see they want to accept Christ. But in deference to your needs, I propose that come spring Reverend Bacon hold a field service on your property and baptize your slaves with the village as witness."

Well, Handy stare mean at Master, but he caught between God's rock and Satan's hard place. He don't want to appear unchristian on the outside, while on the inside not let none of his slaves gain Heaven. Can't share, even in death.

Busybodies rush to help Reverend and one confront my master, but most just nod that we slaves need saved, just not in their holy church. Sin be personal, say one, and black sin a different mark on the soul, say another. I think on that for a blind second while I help Hestia get up, and wonder if God make our souls the color of our skin when, of a sudden, the front doors burst open and a cold blast hit the congregation.

There be that cunning Goldsboro, his cape all askew, his hand clutching his cockhat over his forehaid. He got three of his henchmen in tow on the stoop, holdin they horses as he stalk down the aisle, the power of his title chasing his heels. The congregation hold they breath.

"Here ye, here ye," he command, stretching the limits of his warble voice. "I have news for everyone's consumption, for our lives are at stake. A French corsair flies up the Chesapeake into the Tred Avon. An armed frigate, fleet of sail. The Virginia defenses at Hampton have failed." The sheriff climb the step to the altar as cries ring from the pews and take over the house. He raise his long rifle to the crowd. "A call to arms. Militia prepare!"

Mayhem strike. The men climb over the pews calling to they loved ones to return to town on they own, to barricade they homes. They shout and bare swords as if the enemy at the door. The women folk cry out and huddle till Sary take charge encouraging them to be strong for the men and pack food for the onslaught. We follow them into the cold and watch as they whip up to save Oxford.

I figure if this be the end, at least we got leftover cakes to eat afore we go. We hug Hestia, tellin her be strong and we come for her soon as the French attack.

"Where am I to go?" she say. "You just spread falsehood. If I die, I'll be sure to take some of their stingy asses with me." And with that, she climb up next to Handy's driver. As they carriage make haste, I wonder if there be a kingdom to gain like Bacon say.

Jackson rig Ol Bets to the close carriage and we get to ride inside with Sary. I be warm for the first time on this Epiphany day. Master and Young Robert take off on they horses and we pull the pony cart behind us. Make Volaire drive the carriage since no one want listen to his prattle.

The sight of all them pompous white folk rushing here and there, deciding who do what and where, make me laugh. I should be a'feared o the French enemy, but since they be the same color as this church-full, you can't tell one from t'other, as Captain Gildart once observe bout us as he suck down our whisky.

I prop my feet on the stove and say, "Sary, why Handy bring Hestia today?"

She hem and haw and say. "Robert asked him. He wanted to embarrass Handy in front of everyone for treating his slaves so badly."

I laughed big. "And using his good Hestia to do it? Guess he blind to how he treat slaves in his own backyard."

She not say nothin, but put her feet on the stove. I didn't give way, kept mine toasty and warm right where they were.

We arrive in town to chaos. Sary quiet but ask me to walk down the strand to look for the French frigate. The wind whip our skirts as we stop on the porch of Quinn's tavern to watch. Men kiss they wives like they goin off to war for years to come. Some dressed in red militia coats.

Quinn sidle out the door on seeing us. "Brings up memories of the Nova Scotia campaign against the French, don't it? Won that one but we ain't be successful this time if what they say is true."

Sary glance over her shoulder at him. "And what, pray sir are 'they' saying?"

"French be armed ready to pillage our ships in harbor."

"Two sit empty and two are partially unloaded," say Sary. "They aren't coming for cargo. They're coming to plant fear. You know that as well as I."

"They be comin for you, m'lady. Only you," he say with a laugh.

Sary look away and step off his porch, not interested in taking his dumb bait. "If that be the case, I'm sure I'll fit in on the Continent better than the likes of you."

"Aye, because you're a traitor at heart."

"Come, Yearie. Let's not soil the tavern door."

"It'll come to light. You and your island slave in league," he shouted after us.

We hurry to the shipyard. Hearing the boatswains blow they whistle calling sailors to ship, we try to find the master. "All hands, ahoy!" they yell as ships' bells ring on deck like a hurricane upon us. We glimpse Master atop his horse, watching the captains wave they arms. I think it all a mess, but soon the movement begin to make sense.

"Look, Sary," I say, pointing to the *Peggy*, Captain Ingram's ship. "They takin her out." Sure enough, sailors scramble up the mizzen mast and set sails one after a t'other to catch the wind. The mighty frigate that lean low on one side to load, roll up like a cow gettin to its feet in pasture.

"It just came back from Dover Town," say Sary. "Their cabin boys were all excited she's tarred and ready to go home."

"Poor boy. A tale to tell his mother."

"If he ever gets home."

We not seen sailors behave in such order, for they been a nuisance to most of Oxford. They clamber over ships, all in position like white folk dancin they formal reels. Officers call an order and sailors repeat. The *Peggy*'s men break out in chant, "Always ready, steady, boys steady" and the men on the *Marshall* sing back, "Fight and conquer, ready men, ready."

Sary and me wave and cheer and that's all it take for the rest of Oxford's women to collect, doing the same. I watch as the cannon appear below the quarter deck and I think for the first time, this be real. My skin prickle as I hear the captain order, "All hands, up anchor!" Sailors walk a circle on *Peggy*'s deck, pushing the millstone. The giant anchor rise slow from the depths and dangle at the prow o' the ship.

Behind us I hear Goldsboro's warble sing out, "To arms, men! The strand!"

Militia bumble about, not remembering how to march when Master take charge, riding his horse down their flank ordering them in line. Sary's mouth open at the sight of him still in his bearskin coat and I shake her arm till she shut it. The Oxford boys fall in and holdin all manner of huntin rifles to shoulder, they make their way to the strand. The harbor slaves grab pikes and follow and I wonder what use they be to fight a cannonball. Master call the warehouse men to fling the doors wide and four to each wheel, they roll out two cannon. Bent against the strain, they push to the edge of the water where slaves pile sandbags. The militia split up two deep on either side of the cannon and stand at attention, their eyes locked on the water, waiting.

And wait we did. In an hour, the *Peggy* and *Marshall* sat broadside blocking the entrance of Oxford harbor, their guns pointed at nothin. And nothin it stayed. Sary and I talk to our womenfolk till, too cold to talk no more, we all make off for home as sleet began to fall. It be the Twelfth Night dinner and they have children to feed. As we step into the kitchen, throwing off our cloaks and rubbing our arms, I thinkin my feet like ice more'n at White Marsh. I surprised to see Jackson be a throwin leftover food into packs.

"Miss Sary, I'm not hearing no cannon shot," he say.

"Goldsboro, his false alarm," Sary say, "He sent a rider to Onancock to see what they know. Where's Rob?"

Jackson look at us like we drunk. "The young master not with you?"

"No, I thought he was here."

I hang up Sary's cloak in the under-stair closet and come back. They stand round, speculating. "Maybe he be with the master," I say. "Stop actin like the milk spoilt. He be back. Roaming is all." Then patting the cold from my skirts, I say to Jackson, "You think we best package up the rest this food for the poor, or you takin that down the harbor?"

Jackson stop on his way out the door, "Master say bring as much as I can to the militia. I'll hand out some to the harbor men afore he sees me."

I get busy while Sary prop her swollen feet by the fire. Her belly be round as a pumpkin. That baby sit up high. Best if'n we get a boy for the master want more to carry on his name now that he take ownership. I figure Sary got another three month to go but she so big, I wonder if'n I got the time wrong.

A cold draft hit me in the back. Master come in, brushin snow off his hat.

"While you're warming up by the fire the militia is about frozen outside," he say. "The food?"

Sary nod and look him up and down. "Have you seen Rob?"

Master's eyes get big. "I thought he was with you."

"Dear Lord," she say, "must we have so much contrariness from that child all the time?"

Master hand me his beaver hat and tell me to get his stocking cap for he need warmth, not fashion. Throw his bearskin on the trestle and when I makes to pick it to store, he wave his hand. "I'm going right back. This wind is so fierce it would freeze the stones off a sheep."

"M'lord," she say, "we've not seen Rob since church."

"I'll send Jeremiah to look. Gads about in search of gossip when he could help." He light his pipe and puff in thought. "Probably at Quinn's though I told him to stay away from bawdy women. Bored with sailors, they'll give him an education."

He lay his pipe on the mantle. "I must be gone. Goldsboro needs me to coordinate the strand defense with the harbor. Twilight comes and if they are on the Chesapeake, surely we'll see their lantern." He put on his coat and hat. "Mrs. Wise, make sure they're shackled tonight." His High and Mighty glance over at me with a smile on his face afore he departed.

I'm thinking that be some stupid Frenchmen that light lanterns on a dark night if'n they make to attack, but what do a simple kitchen slave know? What do master know but buying and selling? Fore long, Jackson and Voltaire get they coats and fly like messenger pigeons taking food to the men.

We women sit round the fire and eat my Twelfth Night cakes. I sink my teeth into the sweet softness and hit hard. A baby Jesus roll out in my hand. Guess I got religion, spite Bacon never baptize me. Sary laugh hearty and it be good to see her so happy. I soften to her a little.

"Who be that French frigate, I wonder?" says I, knowin what she'll say.

Sary pull a missive from her skirt pocket and throw it into the fire that sparkle with delight. "Oh, I believe a certain Scotsman has returned to our shore."

Our shore. For the first time I feel like it be my shore. Hestia not dead, even though she at Handy's. Jackson burn with our mission, and Master in love as much as he capable. Pret soon, we'll have a baby to unify the house and with any luck, it be the spitting image of Robert Morris. Maybe it all work out for me. Ol Ruth just be an old crone scolding anyone who listen.

"Sary," I say, "remember when we be at the Hebron plantation as children and you learnin the harpsichord and I be a playin with children of the kitchen slaves?"

"I was so jealous of you getting to play while I practiced my chords," she said.

"I were so happy rolling stones with all them kids. Then I pitched mine in the outside oven and tell everbody I bet they couldn't find them."

Sary laughed. "And the mistress looked out the back window and saw those kids throwing theirs in the oven, and they all got in a world of trouble."

"And I got away with it."

"I wanted to be you," she said.

Sary go to bed early saying for us to wrap the leg chains round our ankles and Master won't know. Then like it be an afterthought, she tell me to take a stroll over to the tavern, see if Rob be hanging with the clientele. She know I get bedeviled by Quinn and them old lechers in they cups. I take umbrage in my haid for her to expect it of me.

So late, after the sky dry up, I wrap in my new cloak and stroll the kitchen garden toking my pipe afore bed, debating what to do. One them Jamaicans give me terbaccer at market in trade for Jackson's worn-out boots. Puffing on my pipe, it were a different terbaccer and soon I feel warm and happy. Walking icy dirt rows, I see beets and parsnip greens laced in frost and I think of a nice soup.

Above, shiny green leaves climb the picket fence carrying the Indian flower in creamy whorls, unaffected by the weather. Its pointed seed pods look scepter-like. Moths flutter on the fragrant flower, not knowing it winter. I move closer to inspect.

Out pop a red rabbit, point its chin up at me, ears layin flat and innocent. I take a step back. Pale eyes blink and its nose wiggle. It got a little white beard so's it must be old. I turn to run when it say in my haid, "Yearie, who be you now?"

I take offense a spirit be a talkin to me through a rabbit. Disgruntled, I wonder why it not a message from a lion, or a bear, or even a damn goat. Bending down, I spy my eyes close to the creature and it burrow into a rabbit hole.

I look up in the night sky that be a sea of bright stars on which a ship with tall masts sail proud. My mouth open and my pipe fall. I hear my ma say, "Ride a great ship and you'll never go hungry." I look down to see if the rabbit hear her too, but it gone. When I glance skyward, the ship sailed away. Dizzy, I shake the smoke from my haid.

Trudging to the tavern, memories of Ma being dragged by a stranger, her yelling to *be good*, that she *come find me*, run through my mind. I were too little to understand that she be worth a year of food for Sary's family because she be priceless to me. Muttering aloud bout young Rob, I wonder what his worth is to anybody.

As I get in sight of the tavern porch, don't I see poor Ruth slap an old codger's face. I think, old as she is, she'll be whipped afore morn. I turn back to the safety of my slave cabin. At the door, I be overcome at its dearth of comfort. Jackson be a mound snoring under poor Hestia's ratty quilts and Voltaire's leg hangin from the attic ledge that covered in hay. Coals glow on a hearthstone giving no heat to a room riddled with cracks, frigid night air seepin inside. This be my future in Sarah's care. I grumble and vow never again to sleep inside with her like we did as girls. I be nothin but her slave.

Her baby comin to steal her focus and be my work. A white woman's child ain't nothin but trouble to a slave like me. And if history be any prediction, this one won't have no father, neither, whether it be from the Scotsman's or Master's seed.

PART III
GRIET

Throw me to the wolves and I'll return leading the pack.
- Seneca

CHAPTER 30

*J*anuary 8th, 1748

The Maroons

The Mac vere my boss, my commodore and my skipper. He vere fond of saying, "Yer my jack screw, and jack tar, but nobody's jack pudding." He calls me his cabin boy and though I'm a girl, this makes me grin.

At noon of Twelfth Night Day, we sailed south past Oxford harbor one last time and turned up the river, reaching our camp near Dover Town in the middle of the night. The sleet had stopped in a big wind and sky was salted with stars Mac call the Milky Way. He point and say, "If ye look close, ye'll see the *Ship Argo* at full sail." I looked but ain't see it. The moon vere full and the river below us deep and clear. I ran to light the whale oil lamps fore and aft. The river tightened, the banks a tangle of downed trees. Tied to a rope, they swung me from the prow to look for snags. Weary though I be, I vere thrilled for being so important. We headed to a secret cove deep at the edge of the swamp where we could tar our new ship.

A barn swallow could wing across the ocean quicker than I'd go back to Oxford. I don't remember the soft shoulder of Mam. She be a misty-eyed ghost sometimes singing lullabies, sometimes whipping me with words. I don't remember leaving, just Papje rocking me when my sister died of pox. He vere a bitter man in camp, building the schooner, cursing, *fok* and *Jezus Christus*, and yelling *idjoot* at the maroons. Everywhere he walk, he storm.

I scorn the memory of them for sail. I ain't embroider the sampler that came with me from Oxford. It vere a tapestry to godly obedience and iron rule by the parents of me, but mostly a useless skill. All's gone with my surname, Vanderkoop. Papje expired, I know not why. After Weocomocus left with most of the tribe, I looked for the sampler needle and thread. Gone. I tink to myself, all that vere left are Mam's silver beads. I gave a few coral ones to the mud lady with blue eyes like me.

I like the freedom of breeches and a waistcoat, my hair chopped like a Michaelmas daisy. The gang laughed at the disguise of me. We are the best maroons that sailed on our swamp schooner to the Caribbean. Mac swore them tars to secrecy and being a small and loyal band, the true self of me never came to the light of strangers.

I give way for no man. I do not lower my gaze. I shout, "Aye, aye, sir!" and do what I'm told, cept when it's not to my liking, for only an ass is bound to the family that uses him.

I wasn't rolling over, nor shouting *Aye, Aye,* this morn. Prickles of me ran down my back seeing the tailor's son stealing my place in the network. Sitting on a fallen tree limb, listening to Mac, his voice a bullfrog's, his swagger roped, I could see his breath in the air, his hotness coming out.

"Jeremiah," he say, "yer a bonny boy. Tell yer father ta let us know if cannon are delivered in harbor. So far, Oxford be helpless in an attack."

Mac not ever call *me* a bonny boy.

"They have cannon, sir. Morris bring four from Virginie," he say.

Jon Suter, his second hand, blew his coffee like a sneeze. "Yer thinkin like a true patriot, Mac. We'll hang the baw-heid Goldsboro if he come a runin at us," he said, jabbing his thumb at his heart.

"We have no time to go after him," said Mac. "My game is bigger and yer know it."

Suter sobered up and dumped the grinds of his cup in the fire, angry. "Doona be a fool. That two-faced driveller, Callister spill the loss of sail canvas in his Dover warehouse to Morris. Afore *ye* know it, Goldsboro hunt the swamp for us. Aye, an we want to live to tell the tale." He pushed his neckerchief down and rubbed the scar on his neck.

I knew what stuck in his craw. I knew the story of his branding.

"One minute ye claim me a patriot and the next a fool," said Mac. "Can ye not rejoice in a plan well executed? Didna we make them show their weakness?" He leaned a shoulder against a cedar tree, his eyes near closed against the sun's glare. Tinking, he vere...quiet.

Like the hive of bees Mam kept for honey, the men moved slow against the cold. Suter's carpentry plan for the frigate's upgrade vere the next task. Drawings of great whale bones covered a table in Mac's tent—the guts of the frigate. Lumber stacked on the makeshift dock and two barrels of tar ready to be heated in a great iron pot sat by a roaring fire.

I glanced at Suter remembering a night he vere drunk, not a month back. All the men had packed up to bed and left me minding his sloppy self. He riddled me a yarn about the Mac and him, fierce boys growing up in a far land in what sound like Marc-innit, learning trades in the shipyard. Suter vere the carpenter apprentice, Mac, the engineer's.

"Doona know even back then, kid, he had to win ever battle there ever was—even the good luck coin on a new ship's keel. Put a half groat under the keel and pocketed the owner's gold crown for himself."

I laughed hard and spit like the sailor I wanted to be. "The Mac been stealing from the rich and giving to the poor a long time!"

Suter wagged his head and drooled. "He be advised to keep this poor man happy."

I dragged myself to my bedroll that night tinking Suter had a hard head that vere harder when he drink. On this morn, I sized him up as a loyal dog full of bark and no bite.

"Ye won this foray," he said to Mac, giving him a Scots penny for all his effort. They vere both skinflints to the end. Then, in tribute to the pennant I hoisted over Oxford, Suter gave a tight nod. "It were genius runnin up the French colors."

Jeremiah's horse tugged its tether and I vere reminded of this outsider standing by his nag. Nobody spects a mere boy to be such a boon and that vere *my* role in camp. He veren't going to steal it from me without a fight. He vere older than me, fifteen to what Wenetko say vere my eleven. They all say my scrawny self make me look younger. I don't know how old I am.

Jeremiah waited, holding a knit cap in his hands, his nose flaming red from cold. Mac stretched his cap down over his ears. I was green at this fatherly touch. Jeremiah had a father and vere not in need of another.

"So, how long did the militia sit on the shore, m'boy?"

"All night, sir. Freezing their balls and wishing for battle. By morn the ships made back to anchor and their captains were cursing the sheriff for all their efforts wasted on Twelfth Night."

"Stupendous! And we couldna done it without yer help and that of ye father. Tell him for me, we'll run the frigate by Oxford at dusk come a fortnight just to keep the arsehole on his cockles."

"Goldsboro? Yes, sir," he said with a crafty grin.

Mac helped him mount and grabbed the pommel to stay the horse. "Keep scouting at Quinn's tavern and send word if ye hear any scuttlebutt I be needin ta know."

"There is one thing, sir," he said, "Master Morris' son is missing."

"That be a loss for us," I said and they all looked round at me. I guessed they forgot I vere there. "He's a loose lip and fond of bad-mouthing his daddy."

Mac winked at me and clapped his hand across the horse's flank. Jeremiah rode for home. I stopped afore I wished a poxen on him for Weocomocus always said an enemy wasn't a foe until you saw his warpaint. With good time he'd make it through East Town to Kate's stable and down to Oxford by dinner.

Suter pushed on his knee and rose from a tree stump. He hitched toward the water's edge, calling sailors. We all needed bread and a draught of cider. But it vere time to get work done.

Mac looked me up and down. "On the morrow, we'll take the

shallop down the Choptank to Cambridge Town," he said. "Suter and me'll visit their tavern for another thousand bit of information." He dug his fingers in his pocket. "Griet, take this coin and visit the bakery. Go to the butcher and docks to see what you kin. Then come night, we'll raid his warehouse for a hogshead of Carolina tar." He laid the copper in my hand. "Trade it for no less than eight pence."

I studied it, a fat-faced Frenchman on one side and crossed lettering on t'other. Ain't never seen it before and thought I'd be cheated on its worth. Mac saw my thoughts.

"Take what ye can git as long as it buys information. Fool Mary-landers are stuck on their terbaccer notes. Now, go git some charcoal and paper so's I can make a list."

He went after Suter. The sailors had finished tying heavy rope to the frigate's masts. She sat close to the banks, riding high in the water. I ran, quick off the mark. The tars clambered off her gunnels onto the riverbank, ropes laid thick over their backs. They slopped through the shoreline muck in three lines. Scrabbling, they faced the woods in formation and when Suter called out, "Me boys. On the count of four," the gang sang out, "One and two, a man! Three and four, a man!" Digging their shoes in the near-frozen dirt, their backs and knees bent, they pulled together as Mac and Suter shouted, "Heave down!"

The ship dipped at first and began a slow roll toward us. Their faces fired red with the effort; the jack's cheeks puffed like spoon bread. They hauled till their knees vere buried and their chins sat in cold grass. Once she vere settled on her side, they wound the ropes round the trunks of the largest trees to set her hull open to the sky.

"Go eat yer porridge. Warm yerselves by the fire," called Mac. "She's a worthy frigate, but she needs Jon's good eye."

Suter and Mac jumped in a canoe. "Come on, jack tar," called the boss of me.

I waded into the freezing water, so clear I could see the buckles of my boots. I tink our ship wouldn't find the barnacle worm here.

"She need near a half-acre of sail cloth and upper spar," said Suter. "New rigging. More ribs below deck. Space em close together for strength."

Mac ran his hand across the hull, feeling for softness. "The French craft the fastest frigate on water, but they not be known to handle attack," he said. "We'll make a bonny Scottish ship of her. Dub her the *Fearnaught*."

Mac paddled back to shore, Suter adding to his list all the while. Once on dry land, they drank a dram of gin and chased it with cider, toasting our good fortune bringing the frigate home from the Caribbean. "To the *Fearnaught!*" they shouted and it vere taken up by the men who mingled round the fire, waiting for their grub.

I heated a pail of water and threw in licorice root. I tink males of any age congratulate themselves afore they've won anything, especially if sucking down brew. I sipped my sweet tea and hoped it would make me sleepy, still running as I was on mine righteous force of the night before.

"I put Jeremiah of a mind to dare the Morris boy," said Suter, handing me his cup. "Suggested Jeremiah tell him to sailor up for adventure he misses in his daddy's care." He winked at me and stuck out his tongue. "Lookin he took the dare last night."

"Always plotting, are ya?" I answered.

Then Mac addressed the confounding vexation that ate at Jon Suter from sunup to sundown. "I'm not forgettin Findley, me friend. We strike when the anvil's hot."

Slapping his mate's back, the two skirted the campfire where maroons—escaped slaves and indentures sat wolfing down porridge. They'd cleaned the ship's decks before careening and after a nap in their boots would scrape her sides for oakum and tar.

"We got time while we're here to line er inside with cypress planks. Double er girth, strengthen her hull. Keel's good. Last a century," said Suter, yawning.

"Canna find cannon, Jon," say boss. "Ought to outfit her with 24—12 on each gunnel.

Jon scratched his head. "Confounds me that Frenchie stripped her guns."

"Done with privateering he was. Sold em to Domingue's fort," said Mac.

Jon laughed. "Fool," he said. "Can always use cannon wherever a ship takes ye." He pulled his cap from his head and slapped his thigh with it. "I'm ready for sleep."

Like an old man, he stumbled to his tent. Mac opened the flap of his and jerked his head for me. On his camp table, he rolled up the ship's diagrams and beneath vere a collection of secret missives stacked under a stone. I set Suter's cup down. One letter slipped out and the script caught mine eye. Mrs. Wise.

It vere the job of me to collect the letters for Mac. After breakfast once a week, he talked and I listened. He plain liked mine tinking since I vere slippery and innocent roaming round our towns. We had the cooper, freed harbor slaves, a courthouse recorder, and nigh on every indentured Scot from the prison ship who spoke secrets to the tailor, who gave them to Jeremiah, who rode them to Kate, who sent them by Wenetko through the backwoods to our camp in the swamp. This parcel of mail vere a month old, traveled with me to St. Domingue in hopes Mac would find the time. Tied with ribbon, sealed in red wax, the hand of the one called out.

Pulling out a stool, he sat against the tent pole and closed his eyes. He looked unwilling for another task, maybe stuck on the events of last night. "Mac?" I said. "You got to read these."

"We take a lesson from the French, Griet. Disrupt Morris' commerce. Disable and board, take prisoners and cargo, and tow a captured ship to St. Domingue. You be too little to understand, but that's how we came by the *Fearnaught*."

"And lucky we are to get her," I said tinking not to take insult for being 'too little.' I sat tall. "All the harbors on the Chesapeake ain't never be home for maroons, boss. You plan a tow to a French port every time we capture?" I wondered what kind of life it would be running from ship to ship.

"Suter says capture bigger and better. Sell the old ship in any French port. Never considers the British Navy." He held out his cup for more cider. I filled it, honored he talked such serious plans with me.

"Keep yer mouth shut, Griet. Between you and me if it be a better ship, and we can take it, then so be it—if not, we burn it in a vacant creek." He leaned on his stool, his back against the tent pole.

229

The legs of him vere so long, he didn't wobble. "We never engage the full force of English cannon. A vengeful lot, cruelest next to Barbary pirates." The stool leaned forward and he with it. "And if we're taken, our men will be pressed into the king's service until they perish on the high seas."

"What would happen to you, Mac?" I asked, trying to lean back on mine but nearly fell.

"Hang me and Suter from the yardarm. Have us drawn and quartered."

"And me, sir? Would they let me go?"

"Why, ye'd become the Admiral's boy till they found out ye ain't a boy a'tall."

"And then?"

"Why, they'd marry ye off to a scurvy son of a bitch, and ye'd be stuck birthin babies, one after t'other."

Well, I kicked the table and the letters flew to the dirt. "Poxen on them," I shouted. Spouting some kind of harum-scarum, Mac was. He laughed hearty, but I didn't see no humor in his story. We've escaped all of us and are a wicked gang made of whole cloth from all corners of the Atlantic. I'll not be tied to British scum, sailors, *or* babies.

Mac got up and walked over to me. He put his hand under my chin, raising mine face to his. "Yer a tough one." He waggled my jaw and winked again running his fingers through mine hair. The cap of me fell to the dirt. "I'll look out for ye, Griet. I couldna found the *Fearnaught* without yer help."

I bent my head. The Mac was short on compliments, so I tinking he wanted something more. Diggin my shoe in the dirt under my cap I flipped it into my hand. I stared at him, waiting.

Three nights ago, we passed Virginie's Point Comfort and Mac proposed to sail by Oxford and challenge the sheriff. War whoops vere heard. Counting that the town had no cannon and the trading ships in harbor would be empty of sailors, we made two passes yesterday at morn. The folk were in church, and the sailors of a habit to drink their way through any holy day. Boss grinned ear to ear as he watched through his spyglass their call to arms.

It vere fun for a while but our crew wanted more, like a pack of starving wolves. I begin to tink Mac vere a prisoner of his hate. His swagger and cockiness would get me in deep digs. No longer just about adventure, thieving and spying would be looting and burning. He aimed to wipe out Oxford's system. Seemed the name of Morris were on his lips with every breath. It vere not enough for him to be happy with coats and disguises, his stores of stolen goods, or even his loyal followers.

"I'll create a new world order," said Mac. He shout to the yardarm that somebody called Will were "the only Englishmun worth a quote," and the Bard, "warn us to 'keep o' the windy side of the law.'"

Suter whisper, "He speaking of Shakespeare."

I ain't know no Shakespeare, nor if the new world order had a place for me, but I had grown up with this lot of ragtags and bobtails since before Papje died. After scaring Oxford town, we sailed into cover of shoreline mist and up the Choptank. I fell asleep in my blanket on deck.

CHAPTER 31

The tars vere satisfied, sleeping with full bellies and now in the cold light of a winter's morn alone with me in his tent, I could tell Mac vere mastering plans. I picked up the letters that tumbled to the floor. I needed to watch my temper round the boss for he vere not known for his patience.

"That be quite a pile of letters ye lay on me table," said he.

"Aye, boss," I said, plucking out the one with the red seal. "And 'tis one special."

He took it from me as if he hadn't seen it. Mac did tings in order, finishing one project afore beginning a t'other, except in matters of love apparently. She had that effect and it made me sorry. He broke the seal.

"She's in need of assistance, Griet."

"So?"

"Jeremiah will have to do it. Morris has their slaves chained at night."

Jeremiah, Jeremiah. Always picking him over me. The foot of me began to tap. "What's he going to do?" I asked.

"Carry her messages," he answered.

Stunned, mine head could not understand. I knew how to get

to Morris House. I knew Kate's stable. I vere not afeared of the night. I tinking of mine loyalty, of being tied to the mainsail scouting enemy ships. Tied to the prow, scouting fallen trees. Running the flag up the yardarm. Jeremiah couldn't do these tings. The innards of me vere in revolt. He vere blowing me off. I stormed about his tent yelling and cursing. Busting out the flap, I screamed at the top of my lungs. "You ignore the good use of me, you hear me, Mac?" I fell to mine knees, panting, tears of anger streaming. I could not see straight, trees and dirt, fire and sky flashed before me.

The gang took no mind, wallowing as I vere. In time, my tears dried up and I rocked on mine haunches.

"You done, jack tar?"

It vere Mac, standing behind me. There he vere with a simple smile on his face, concern in his eyes. They had turned dark and questioning. I hated him.

"Why you don't ask me to be your messenger, Mac?

"Because you'd have to go live in her house. It's too far away."

Well, I see his point. He knew I vere not able to live in a house with all them habits and customs.

"Ja. Can't ask that of me, boss. I see you ain't of a mind to take away my freedom. I don't want to wait on nobody again, sleep on the floor by a kitchen fire and take orders from do this and do that. What's worse, Mac, is they know who I am and they'd send to Lewes to my mam."

"Ye spent yer wad? Ye flippin from port to aft."

I got up and hung my head. "Yes, sir."

He dug some coals from the fire and put them in a bucket. Grabbing me by the hand, he said, "Yer coming with me before ye make another scene," and dragged me off down the shoreline and into the woods a bit. I thought I was in for a whipping at least, or coals on my feet at worst as papje always threatened. My chest felt stuffed with cabbage and the mind of me couldn't tink. I hopped along trying to keep up with his long stride and soon he came to a glen of soft pines and tumbled limbs. My nose filled with juniper and I needed to empty her. Swiping my sleeve across my face, I looked up. The sun beat down. If it hadn't been for the cold air, it could have been spring. He set me on a fallen trunk.

"Take yer boots off."

I screwed my face up. "Ah no, Mac. I vere not that bad."

"What're ye sayin? The cold air's gone completely to yer head."

"I promise, I'll be good. I'll do whatever you say. Just don't burn my feet."

"Yer feet are soaked and poisoning yer brain," he said, frowning. "When be the last time you dried em out?"

"Don't know," I said looking down. What was he asking? Caked mud, wet stockings, torn breeches. "Weeks, I tink. They hurt whence they thaw."

"Chilblains, Griet. Take em off and let's have a look."

He gathered some twigs and dry pine needles and I tinking he vere making a fire, but I couldn't move, so tired I was. He set the coals over the tinder, blew on them and they burst into flame as he added more. "Come on," He tugged at my boots and threw them over his shoulder one at a time. "I give you money to buy yerself things and what do yer do with it?"

I couldn't answer, but I tink it went to sweets.

"Go on," he said. "Stockings."

A terrible fear wrapped round my shoulders and I began to quiver like a dog facing a bath. The Mac grew impatient and grabbed me by the ankles, ripping my stockings off and with it a layer of skin. I stuck mine bare feet out to the warmth and stared at them tinking they belonged to someone else, maybe a strange bird. Sure enough, my toes vere swollen purple, the nails rounded like clam shells, my legs a mottled gray. They began to itch and smart and I remembered the feeling vere familiar. I had just ignored it for weeks.

The boss produced a tin from his pocket and opened it for me to see what looked like yeller cream. "Bear fat and yarrow. Put yer foot on my knee."

I did as I was told, and he rubbed it all over then laid my stockings and boots by the fire. "How's it that a youngster like you has such scars on her foot?" he asked.

"An accident. My moeder made me watch my baby broeder an he crawled near the hearth. Shtoopud." I wiped a tear away, quick-like. "He grabbed a log from the fire and when I picked him up, it dropped and caught my skirts aflame. I vere barefoot."

Mac rubbed my ankles and the smell of herbs and pine filled mine wet nose. His head tilted. "A sailor's spirit's in his feet," he said. "Next to the wind in yer hair there ain't nothing more alive. One gives ye balance and the other gives ye hope. A will to live." He wiped his hands on my old stockings. "When we git back to camp, I'll give ye clean stockings, a mite big for ye. I'll git some new and shoes at the Cambridge warehouse tomorrow."

I nodded and felt warmth travel up my legs. Mine eyes wetted and I dragged the sleeve of me across mine face making much ado about the river of mine nose. I looked into the woods.

"Griet, yer a good cabin boy and a promising sailor. Nobody can raise a flag quick as you or scramble the yardarm in a wink. But life on a ship ain't nothing for a girl."

"You just want to be rid of me."

"Naw. I never said that. I just be thinkin we're not equal to raising a girl on a ship. Nor be ye ready to run confidence for Mrs. Wise. Her master be suspicious of her slave woman. She's an able reader and writer. A smart woman at great risk whom Jeremiah helps working from the tailor's shop."

"What're you saying, Mac? I'm no use but for cooking and cleaning?"

"Sarah—Mrs. Wise is having a baby soon and—"

"That! I want no part of that. I'm not taking care of no more babes. You pawning me off on her."

"Will ye shut up long enough to grow a smile on yer puss?"

I stared him down but his eye vere stronger than mine and I blinked. I looked at my purple toes. "I'm listening," I said.

"If ye work as a house boy, ye can still dress in breeches and keep yer hair short. Only Mrs. Wise will know who ye are. Ye been gone from Oxford near six years and ye don't look like a little girl. Morris won't figure it out as if he's not at his warehouse or across the Bay, he's drunk."

Mac took off his cockhat and sat beside me on the log.

"What's the excuse to take a grubby orphan in her household? I got no skills save cooking over a campfire."

"Haven't told her of me plan. Don't even know if she'd want ye."

"Aw, piss!" Mine head rolled; its anchor gone. "I can't write to you, Mac. Don't make me leave ya."

"Holy god. Are ye listening? Mrs. Wise and her slave woman can write. Ye just have to git the letter to Jeremiah, or, in a pinch, Kate in East Town."

"Let me stay. I'll do better. I won't cry no more or make a scene."

"Morris robs his craftsmen of profit on the goods they sell," he said, his eyes looking green in the sun. His beak nose cut through its shine, and I put a hand up to concentrate on his words.

"He takes their land in the courts. They pack up and walk away. He takes their belongings, their slaves, their fields and their houses to pay their debt to Cunliffe." He laid a heavy hand on my shoulder. "Now if you had worked seven years in bondage to gentry and earned yerself fifty acres, would ye walk away without trying yer level best to sell first?"

My feet vere toasted. My eyes vere heavy. The licorice tea was acting on my constitution, or maybe it vere boss' voice mesmerizing me. I ain't hear a word he say.

"Are you with me, Griet? We think it's Goldsboro's driving them off their land and working with Morris and Tilghman to run it through the courts."

I was about to fall against his warm body in a dead heap, but he heard a noise in the woods and climbed to his feet. My head fell against the tree trunk and I jerked awake. Through the haze of sunlight, I saw the Mac studying the forest, a stag alerted in the meadow.

"I need you, Griet," he said, "I need you to work with Mrs. Wise and get messages to Jeremiah."

Near to dozing, I ain't believe I'd heard him right. Did he say he needed me? I tucked my legs under me to hop up when I heard a rushing in the wood, branches breaking and a great cry of attack. Mac bent low, putting his hand down to me in warning. A crack echoed through the timber and a musket ball whistled by mine ear. In front of me, Mac whirled on his feet, but recovered, and raising his long rifle he took an answering shot at what, I could not see. I scurried to shelter behind the tree trunk in time to see a figure, dark as Odin's raven carrying a hatchet over his head and charging Mac. The hatchet flew through the air and landed in the wood next to mine hand. I reached and yanked. I yanked again and putting two hands on the hilt, mine bare foot on the wood, I yanked with all the strength in my gut.

It fell to me. In a rage, I charged the raven, hatchet in hand and hurled. It bounced off his wing and he rolled his raven's eye at me in astonishment. With one blow to the beak from the stock of his rifle, Mac sent him to earth on his back, clawing the air. Breathing hard, we stood over him. A black cape flung out. A black cockhat tossed. A black hood covering his face. Mac bent and pulled it away. It vere a white boy.

"Morris' son," said Mac.

"Ain't," said I in disbelief.

"'Tis," said Mac.

Sailors come a running. Gathering him under his arms, they dragged the boy back to camp and threw him by the fire. Mac and Suter vere locked in discussion. I watched them, and seeing blood streaming down Mac's arm, I crept close to eavesdrop. Words like "liability," and "foolhardy," and "revenge."

I knew what the last two meant.

CHAPTER 32

hree days later, the boy was still tied to the tree like a dog. It vere my job to bring him porridge in the morning and stew in the afternoon. When I neared the first time, he pretended to be asleep. Then, like a cat, he sprang, his hands out like claws. I dropped the bowl and glared. He grinned. I kicked the gruel and walked away. The next time I brought a trencher and a long sword that banged against my leg almost tripping me. I laid his food on the ground and pushed it with the sword's point not daring to get in his circle. He laughed.

He was much bigger than me. Black mood. Black eyes. Black hair. Even wore a black suit. Like he vere headed to a funeral. I told Suter he wouldn't eat.

"He will when he gits hungry."

"How long we keepin him?"

"As long as it takes."

Takes to do what, I tink. A few days later, I went to see boss, passing the prisoner. His villain eyes followed me as I walked by the cook fire, sailors drinking coffee, and a line of shirts I'd washed the day before frozen stiff in the air. My hands vere chapped, but mine

238

feet were starting to look like they belonged to me and not some beast. I coughed loud afore Mac's tent.

"Enter," says he.

I pulled the flap and stepped inside to see his hairy, battle-scarred self. Sitting on his table vere a bowl and a dirty rag. He studied his shoulder wound, his gift from the Morris boy. It vere raw, the edges swollen and crusted in a plow line creasing the skin.

"Mac," I said soft. "Ya want me to help with that?"

He glanced at me and seeing the look on my face, said," Not to worry, Griet. It's just a flesh wound. Help me lay a clean cloth on it."

At an odd juncture, I had to wind linen round his chest, up over his shoulder to cover the wound. He smelled like smoke from the campfire, but I didn't smell mortification. I sat on his stool and watched as he finished dressing.

"We got some new letters from the doings at the courthouse," said I.

"Right."

"And Jeremiah sent a missive from Mrs. Wise."

"Ah, good. We'll have news of coming cargoes."

Her letter unfold like bird wings. Magic in words I couldn't command. Reading fast, he looked up, "Master Morris is angered with his son. Says if he doesn't stop disappearing, he will send him away."

I didn't want to talk of that bastard. "Mac," I pleaded. "I could ride to Kate's and meet Jeremiah. I could run that leg."

"Griet, shut yer trap." He pounded his fist, "Ye look like a beggar boy, ye got no subtlety, and ye pop off quicker than shit off a stick. Now, open up them letters while I eat."

He tore a dry crust of campfire bread. I could barely make out what he said, spitting crumbs. "Spect she wants to know when we're sending back the young master." He took a swig of ale. "Fookit, we needing some decent eats round here."

Being as I made the food, I bowed my head and said, "I'll get some porridge, fresh made this morn."

"Aye. Yer a good lass, Griet. I didna mean to hurt yer feelings."

I stacked the letters and tink to myself, why mine feelings

suddenly matter? And why did he tell his love in Oxford that we had the son? She would babble to his father and bring the sheriff on us.

"What're you going do with him, Mac? You can't send him back with Jeremiah slurping pottage in their kitchen and running secrets."

"We keep him till he swears loyalty, or we kill him."

I'm tinking about the son's cat moves. His sly looks and no words. "Ja, kill him cause there'll be no luck befriending him. He's been here a week and barely eats. Sits in his own mess like a dirty pig. Likely not going to call you friend."

"Gettin ready to change that. We'll know soon. Suter's talking to him as we speak." He drew the flap and to mine disbelieving eyes, Jon was leading the boy to his tent supporting him in his weakened state. Aww, and didn't it want to make me cry?

Suter called to me, "Gus, ye little shyte. Get this man some food. The stew ye made for me and Mac."

"Gus?" I asked and looked up at Mac.

"Yer new name," he said. "He's not heard ye called Griet. It be safer if he think yer a boy."

Jack tars called me every insult in the book, but never Griet.

Stew—I could kill the son of a bitch. The campfire pot vere hardened in globs of fat, beets, and gray squirrel. I'd thrown in old carrots as Weocomocus had taught me. Slopped in a trencher, it sat up like stiff pudding, so I passed it over the flames. Feeding a scoundrel stuck in my craw, and I sauntered over to a holly tree and plucked a handful of berries.

At Suter's tent, stenkend Morris wore a new pair of breeches and sheepskin coat—better'n anything I had that didn't still hide the smell of him. I threw the bowl on the floor ready to stalk off.

"Gus," said Suter. "Sit down and keep Robertson company while he eats."

Robertson, huh? Surprised, I sat with a mouthful of teeth and couldn't reply. There I vere cooped up with the Devil tied to the tent post. Mine jaw tightened. Eat the berries, I tink.

"How'd you come by that frigate, boy?" he asked. "Mighty fine ship for a bunch of tapewormed tars."

Not one to take an insult, I said, "Easier than poking a stick in yer eye."

"I meant no insult. I'm speculating you stole it."

"It's a sailor's yarn you don't deserve."

Suter laughed. "Making friends, are ye? Go on, Gus. Tell him. I'll be back."

Morris shrugged and laid into the stew. I took a breath. If Suter vere out to make this fripper one of us, I vere the hammer driving the nail. Then Mac would give me a job of mine stature. I brushed the quill of mine head back and forth.

Suter kicked the flap dragging in a sack, wooden boxes under his arm. "Finish boxing these pee-cans. Throw the moldly ones out afore we ship em to Boston."

"Pee-cans?" asked Morris.

"We brought a load back from Georgia," says I.

"I've never eaten a pecan."

I started to brag on the nut then sealed mine lips. A gift this was —a light shining on his weakness. I spilled them on the ground, looking for white spots on the shells. Tossing them over I said, "Suck on the shell and crack it. Inside is the pecan."

Fingering one, he popped it in his mouth. He leaned back on Suter's pallet a growing pile of moldy nuts in his lap.

"I found the frigate on our schooner's maiden voyage. The trade routes vere empty, the seas quiet heading due south. We sighted a British convoy guarded by two mighty ships of the line headed northeast to England."

"And they didn't storm you?" he asked, chewing. "Hard to believe."

"Shows what you know. They vere on a mission home, arsehole," I said. I vere talking fast watching to see if he would fall over soon. "After rough seas, we saw St. Domingue. A place of water so blue, mansions so white, and trees made of green feathers. We docked and Mac sent me off with his clothes to find a laundress."

"You be his cabin boy? Figures. About all you could handle," said Robertson, ready to die of mine poison, but he leaned into my words.

"Sew your mouth shut. I'm telling the tale," I said. "I heard another cabin boy yell for washerwomen to hurry with his captain's clothes. He answered mine questions. His cap'n vere going to retire to his land grant from the French king. In Lewziana. Had no need of a frigate on the Mississippi. I saw his cabin boy pay in a pure gold coin. I asked where we could find his cap'n and he said, *a tavern on Dumaine.*

"After a night of drinking, Mac made a clean trade—our schooner for the frigate. The Frenchman wished us Godspeed for she had a torn sail and would be slow in battle. I vere cabin boy *and* lookout. I made a blanket cloak, climbed Jacobs ladder, and reached the top platform. Tied a rope from the waist of me to the mast. Dozed on the deck high above, waves rocked, and the mast swayed back and forth. Then, one morning, I saw a sea monster on the horizon."

"Rubbish!" said Morris. His head fell back on the cot. "But you tell a good yarn."

"If you do what you're told, you'll get more than a yarn," says I, crawling to my feet.

He snorted. "Time in the Oxford gaol is what you'll get."

"Maybe. Maybe not."

Suter came in and spoke behind me, "We be smarter an that." Then he picked up the boxes of good nuts and said, "That's enough, men. Ye save the rest to sell."

Men, he called us. I didn't tell Robertson it vere high season of Christmas on our return and my comrades accused Mac of being a heathen pirate sailing the seas at Jesus' birth. Up on the spar, I vere feeling guilty and tried to sing a hymn, but mine head vere swimming from the waves. Being a dunderhead, I grew scared of climbing down in the wind forty yards below. So, I tied the rope to the futtock shroud, clambered under the platform, mine foot pawing the air looking for the ladder's rung. Suter beckoned me and the tars joined him, calling me in like a treed cat. Whence I hit the deck, I threw up and fainted.

"Suter," I said, "We got more good nuts than will fill the boxes. I'll ask boss if we can eat them."

"The big Scot? Don't bother," said Morris.

Suter looked at me and I looked at him. We raised our eyebrows, tucked in our chins and curled our lips, making fun of him. I rolled mine eyes. Suter shook his head and said, "Ye making it hard on yerself, boy. Ye'll be tied to the tree if you buck the Mac."

Robertson tink about this some. He had everything a boy could want and he wanted to kill the man who might as well be my papje.

"Ask him when I can go home. Ask him what's he going to do if I tell Goldsboro where he is."

That did it. Suter trussed him up, his hands behind his back and walked him out to the camp. Sailors stopped to watch. Suter stripped the shearling coat leaving him with nothing but his linen shirt in the cold. He took the rope tied to his hand and led him round the fire.

"You're all going to be rounded up and executed!" Robertson yelled.

He strained, swinging himself wide and fell by the smoking flames. Raising his eyes to the heavens, he screamed, "I don't care if I die. My father doesn't care one whit. But the sheriff does and he'll have your heads."

He breathed in gasps and wheezes and rolled onto his knees, his face near the dirt. His shoulders heaved and foam came from his lips. Soon, he fell over curled in a ball. Blue-faced, I saw his spirit fading right quick. I approached and knelt mine lips to his ear. "You're going to die."

"Prop me up," he choked out.

I gave him a little kick and looked round. Suter swooped in and jerked him upright. His head lolled to the side.

"We can't let him die if he's a friend of the sheriff," said Suter, "Not unless we drop him in the sea."

I saw what he meant, and a panic took me. A search party, the backwoods folk questioned. A ship sailing up the Choptank on Twelfth Night. Someone would have seen us.

"Hold him up," I ordered and ran to the fire. Pouring mine licorice tea in a cup, I had a vision of Mam throwing a wet towel over the ague-ridden head of me. Laying a rag on the firestone, I poured tea on it from the pot and brought both to Morris. He slobbered and sniveled but took the cup to his lips and I laid the steaming rag over his head and shoulders. Soon enough, his breathing came more even.

Sailors circled, studying him like a game of crock marbles. Don't know what we would've done if his pipes hadn't cleared, but soon enough he threw the wet cloth from his face and drank a draught of cold air, commencing a fit of coughing that produced a fresh slabbering. He appeared cured, and the men drifted away, the spectacle over.

"You take him, Griet. He be spent," said Suter. "Take him back to me tent and holler if ye need me. Tie him up. I got things to do."

"Aye, aye, sir. Gus got this wrapped up," I said.

Suter grumbled at his mistake, but Robertson took no notice involved as he was wiping the spittle from his chin. I yanked at his shirt. He stumbled to his feet and followed me to Suter's cot where he lay, his hand thrown over his face. It vere mine duty to stand watch. Glancing around, I see'd the stew, cold and congealed sitting in the bowl. Hungry, I was. Finding a spoon, I gobbled some down, pushing the berries aside.

"That was supposed to be for me, you tart."

The spoon clattered into the trencher and I looked up. He vere sitting on the cot, staring me down.

"You're a girl, ain't you?" Morris demanded.

"Why, you're an arsehole for calling me that," says I. "I have a mind to cut your throat." I drew my dagger in one hand reluctant to give up the stew, but he made no mind.

"My grandmother knew that trick. A wet cloth over my head."

Carefully, I put down the bowl. Where was Mac when I needed him? "So did my grootmoeder. There's a lot of dust in a Dutch sawmill. The only way to spray it down is to draw your prick and piss on it."

He guffawed, coughed some more, and red eyed me. "What were you doing in a sawmill?

"Planting tulips," I said and thumbed my nose at him. "I worked it with my papje. He vere a shipbuilder."

"Mine was an ironmonger in Liverpool. Pounded nails as a boy in Cradley Heath, same as me."

"Master Morris worked in a foundry?" I asked amazed. "How'd he learn trading?"

"Pa sold nails to Cunliffe and Sons for their ships. Taught him everything once they pulled him out of the ships' foundry." He paused and considered the next before he asked, "Where're your parents?"

"Dead. Pap died in a shipyard and Mam succumbed birthing my broeder." I was layering up the lies like a Dutch spoekcake, sixteen deep.

"You're awful small to have worked in a shipyard. I don't believe it."

"Suit yourself," I said.

"Why'd Suter call you Griet?" he asked.

"Gustav is the name of me. He vere making fun of my size." I sounded firm and true, even to mine own ears.

"You got…what'd you call them—brudders?"

"Two, in Holland. Younger'n me. Hardly remember their names. You got kin?"

"At least four. Probably more. I was supposed to go live with my sister in Philadelphia after I made my father's acquaintance. Margaret. But she were just married to an old widower, busy taking care of his children, so they got no room. Nobody wants me."

"Ja. Old story, same everywhere, I guess," I said.

"Just as well. I don't want to be trapped caring for a passel of sniveling turds."

"Akkoord. Not wiping no more kinder butt."

He snorted. His nose vere dribbling like a rill. "I guess," he said, surprised. "How old are you really?" he asked looking at the stew.

"Eleven." It was one truth in a pack of lies that didn't matter. I could've said eight and he would've believed it. I looked at the trencher. "You want it? I'll give it to you, but you can't go home tattling bout us. We're hardworking folk who ain't fond of your sheriff, for he's been nothing but the bane of our existence."

"The sheriff's no friend to anybody in Oxford. He's the authority. Two different things."

"Is that right?" I asked pursing my lips. "You haven't been properly introduced to the Mac. He's my boss *and* my friend. Won't find a single man in camp who don't feel the same."

"That so?" he asked and slurped up the cold stew. It veren't long afore he laid back on the cot. I brought the shearling and threw it over him. His eyes fluttered and before he dropped off, I heard him utter a simple, "Thanks, Gus."

CHAPTER 33

$\mathcal{R}$obertson couldn't go far with so many around, but Mac wanted me to keep him tied in Suter's tent. It veren't a challenge. He let me. At night, he sat round the campfire. He listened as British sailors told stories of Levante A-rabs in long robes, their hair and beards down to their waists, riding camels across the desert. They showed him their backsides scarred from whippings by the captain's mate for thieving a swill of grog. The escaped indentures told him of working on Oxford plantations from sunup to sundown in the same shirt and breeches they brought from England, never earning a penny.

The slaves ate at their own campfire, afeared of the son of Oxford's slave trader. One night, Suter's wool scarf fell from his neck and Rob saw the Handy brand. He vere quiet, I spect, tinking how that happened. He turned to me, catching me mid-laugh as one of the tars bent over, blowing wind and lighting it on fire with a taper.

"Findley did that, didn't he?" he asked.

I swallowed my laugh, seeing his face. "What?" I looked about. "Suter's neck?"

"Yes, yes," he said, impatient-like. "He claims he only brands criminals on their chests."

"Ah, you don't know the whole of it," I said, calling Tandy and Isaac to the campfire. Suspicious, the black fellers came to see what was amuck. I whispered, asking if they would mind. They loosened their belts and pulled out their shirts, and the gang grew quiet. Tandy and Isaac turned. The bubbled, silvery outline of a large H covered their black backs, two lines— shoulder to waist, one— side to side.

Rob stepped near and exclaimed, "It's made up of H brandings. Maybe twenty."

"Findley's work, Goldsboro's direction," I said. "Laid the brand on slow. One at a time while the rest of his slaves vere made to watch. Put a damper on escape."

Rob walked to the edge of the wood and stared into the darkness. Tandy and Isaac clapped my back, rumbling voices, shaking heads. They settled round the campfire to share some ale. In that moment, we be comrades no matter our birth. I felt lucky I had no brands, only a scarred foot.

"Gus," he said, appearing at mine side, "you're a bigger man than I thought. You're my brother now, better than those of my father's blood who came here before me."

I tink that mighty nice of him to say. Maybe Mac was right, it vere better to turn him to our way than throw him in the sea. He would never go home, that much was sure. I vere tickled to have me a broeder. To get me some respect.

Rob went to bed early that night, and I didn't tie him up tight. In mine little tent, I slept deep, secure for the first time since I vere in Weocomocus' loving care. Or with kind Mam before the harsh words of her. The next morning, I rubbed the sleep from mine eyes and set the campfire alight as the sun broke through the trees. Tars bumbled in morning chores. Suter been up awhile and vere nailing the carved wooden anchor to the prow of the *Fearnaught*. I tink, I'll get Rob, come help me make breakfast. I opened the flap of Suter's tent and looked round. Empty, not even the smell of a fart in the air, the rope I tied him with gone. I ran outside as a shout went up, "Yar boys, there be a thief! The brown gelding's gone."

Mine shoulders shook. Mine head exploded. Bamboozled I vere.

Tars ran here and there, hunting, tracking. I hung mine head and sat by the fire like nothing vere wrong. Porridge, strong coffee, and for extra, I sizzled the deer meat in a skillet.

It vere no use.

"Griet! Come to me right now!

Mac. He glared at me from Suter's tent, Jon at his side. I hippy hopped, making a spectacle of mine little limp, like the chilblains vere back.

"Yer a buffoon. Duplicitous, and a child. Shoulda never trusted ye," said Mac.

I felt his stare deep in mine brain. The eyes of me roamed the dirt and stopped with his boots. Clean, black, nearly as tall as mine waist, he vere proud of them, polished them, dug the mud from their heel every night before sleep. Mac vere like that with tings he owned, taking great care to make them last.

I would not be one of them on this day. "Mac, I—I vere sorry."

"Ye didn't tie him up, did ye?"

"I tought after last night—I tought he vere a friend of mine. I— he say he vere a broeder to me. He say I vere a man." I looked up in his eyes. "Better'n his blood, I—I vere big."

Mac backhanded mine cheek. Knocked me to the dirt. I lay there sniveling, him a tall cypress above me. Soon, he gave me the hand of him, and I stood as he knelt. His eyes pinched under the great crag of his brow. He said, "We have maybe three days, Griet, if he wanders in the wood. He'll set the alarm, tell his father where we be. A militia will come." He gripped mine shoulder. "We break camp today, sail down the Choptank and up the Pocomoke to the swamp. Leave the *Fearnaught* at Lewis' Wharf."

I nodded fast. Tried to take it all in. Help pack, carry for the tars. Bring them eats. Loyal. I vere loyal.

"Ye have a job, Griet. Ye must go to Oxford and warn Mrs. Wise. They be in danger, all of them now."

"Go, Mac? To the house of her? I can. I know how to get there. I can sneak to her in the night and tell her." And then I tink. "But how will I get back to you? I don't know my way to the swamp."

"Then you stay. You work your way into her house and tell that little bastard, Robertson, that we have spies who will kill him. He doesn't know his way home; it will take him longer to get there."

I vere bedeviled by the word, "stay." He vere going to abandon me to Oxford. His hand on the shoulder of me vere a vice squeezing tighter. "I don't know, Mac. Send a missive with me? Tell her she can trust me?"

"Jayzus, Griet. Ye want responsibility and when ye get it, when lives depend on it, ye become a simpleton. Just do it. Suter and I have work." He let go and I felt him gone, gone to his tars, to his ship, to the swamp. I watched him walk to the campfire with the sun behind him, making a burning man of him.

Jon Suter said, "Yer be Gus. She'll remember who ye be. Make haste down the river trail and when ye get to the plantations, stay in the woods. Come the wee hours of night, ye'll be in East Town if ye haven't fallen from yer nag. Warn Kate and switch horses. If yer smart, ye'll walk into Oxford at night and knock on her door. Be a beggar boy and ask for food."

He pushed me out, throwing a moth eaten blanket after me, and said, "The network be done and lives with it, Griet. Make it good."

CHAPTER 34

I dragged a goatsack from Kate filled with old stockings, a pair of broken-down boots, and hardtack. She took the news of Robertson hard and said Mac would never make such a mistake. I admitted it vere mine, not his. She slapped a frying pan on her table and said she would have the boy killed. Lure him away and set on him. Then seeing the face of me, she told me to try first, but her spies would watch and know if I failed. I left my horse, new stocking and shoes with her. She said a beggar child wouldn't have a horse to ride and she wouldn't abandon a good one in the Oxford wood with no way to get it back. A horse or a beggar child, I knew each one's worth.

I asked her to write a missive saying I could be trusted, but she wouldn't. Asked me, *what if I vere caught? What then?*

It vere a sweet-smelling afternoon– maybe from the sky blue of that flower growing along the forest path. Color of Mam's eyes. I tink of them following me in the good days when I vere small.

Three starts. I imagine the trip from Holland across the ocean when Papje said I vere just a baby. Stolen from Mam across wooded paths following the black boots of a big man with a seagull voice. And now, leaving Mac and the cypress swamp, the rest of mine gang behind me. I was firm that I could do what vere needed. Nobody said how long I was to be a prisoner in the house of Morris. I figured if it got too hard, I'd disappear.

It vere not hard to look a beggar child. Or sound like one, either. I practiced my introductions as I wound through the forest and soon I vere on the Oxford road nearing town. I passed over the lands of a large plantation house that looked empty, brick from some foreign place stacked by the frame of a new addition. Through a stand of cedar, I made my way by an old cemetery that seemed familiar. Weaving through markers, some standing, most fallen, I found a wooden cross laying on its side that vere carved with a "W". I tried to remember if this vere how to spell a Vanderkoop name, but I failed. My heart seemed to be stuck on this spot for in my tinking lots of people stood about crying and sniffing as a coffin lay in the dirt. I didn't have no prayers as those words had disappeared long ago, so I sat atop the grasses and sang,

> *The rooster's dead, the rooster's dead*
> *He can no longer say kukele-kuu,*
> *My rooster's dead, kukele kukele kuu!*

A tear fell and before another could travel down my cheek, I swiped it away along with a vision of Papje yelling at me in camp to grow up. A brisk wind caught mine cap sending it off. I chased it to a carved wooden marker of a little lamb, whitened and cracked with weather. Below the lamb vere a baby, laying in a manger. I tink maybe it vere the Christ Child. These vere the first signs to me of mine life changing.

I gathered my goat sack, sucking hard tack as I went. Images of baked bread spun in my mind. A fireplace for my feet, a window to prop my elbow, a candle to light my way. As I made town, passing cottages and barns, housewives swept doorsteps, dug in winter gardens and scuttled their children behind their skirts as they hollered for me to *keep walking* and *don't be begging at my door*. I began to worry. Would she remember me? Would she trust that I said the truth? That Robertson was a traitor? It is not possible to know everything. I scratched mine backside.

Kate said I would know Front Street as it vere by the Tred Avon where the ferry docked. On this corner sat Morris House, the only two-and-a-half story, painted clapboard anywhere in Oxford. And there she vere, crisp white with greenery stuffed window boxes. A house with glass in its windows. A glorious house of great wealth, much improved since mine memory of her nigh on six years hence.

I vere not going to wait for night to come. No sign of people at her door. No noise. I couldn't smell a fire. I drew air in mine pipes and knocked. Seem like nobody home, so I made a fist and banged. A slave boy covered in robin egg silks and waves of white lace at his neck answered the door. He bowed and I saw his hair vere braided in forest paths that wound to nowhere. Taking one look at me, he ran. I leaned against the door and waited.

In the darkness of the hallway, I could see a large cabinet, gleaming in the light from the open door. It had a line of teeth, some black and some white that sat above a matching bench. It had a purpose but I couldn't reckon it and reached up to scratch the side of mine head.

"You come to the back, boy." He had returned quick as a fox and disappeared again.

I threw the goat sack over mine shoulder and clumped around the house to a wide stable yard— slave quarters, a horse barn, and a big oak tree shading it all. Acorns, pebbles and oyster shells everywhere and I tink this vere a smart way to grub a yard from mud. The kitchen quarter door vere open a crack, the chimney pumping smoke. This where the people be.

I knocked on the door and pushed, peeking in mine nose. A slave woman in a red turban held up the end of a broom and pushed me back. "What you want, boy?" Then, "Another beggar, Raphael. Get a sack of vittles. Not much, he be small."

"Miss, you remember me?" I asked. "I vere here last fall when we busted the mistress out of the gaol."

She pushed me off the doorstep and I fell in the dirt. "Stay there," she said her face in a wrinkle. "Hush your mouth." She look every which way and spit. "What you doin back here?" she whisper.

"I have a message from the Mac. It vere important. I just come from Kate's."

Well, that did it. She slapped me with the broom and say loud, "Git to the stable. You stink a mile. I'll be bringing you food in the goat pen."

I made like a rabbit and on entering the dark stable, a huge black man raise up from the straw. He dusted the breeches of him and looked out the door behind me. He say, "You be that Dutch boy from Kate's come here in the corn wagon."

"Ja. Gus. I be Gus." I looked around as they vere doing. No one else. "You know the Mac. I come from him."

"Why are you here, young man?"

This came from a beautiful lady who stood outside the door. The blue eyes of her looked me over kindly. She vere dressed in a cloth that swirled like the leaves of fall trees, boughs of copper fell from her shoulders, and her hair a mound of gold curls, one loose ribbon dancing close to her swan neck. I sucked air again.

"Are you Gus?" she asked.

"Ja," I said, not tinking. Then remembering my introduction, said, "Yes, Gus is me. A beggar boy pleading for my gut which is empty as a dry well. I ask in God's Holy Name for a bite from yer hearth and I will work for ye day and night to make yer happy."

"Yer?

"Um, to make you happy, mistress."

She leaned down and whispered in my ear. "You must not sound like the Scot. It will give you away. Why have you come?"

I was doozled by the smell of lavender and nearly felled mine head in her bosom. I nodded. "I can speak, lady? I come to warn you. The Robertson—I mean Morris junior, will arrive soon and blabber of our workings. He has been our prisoner and Mac and the boys have only just left in the *Fearnaught* down the Choptank. There's a headwind and I'm sure they haven't made it far. They have to sail down the Chesapeake to the Pocomoke and up to the headwaters to the Lewis' Wharf and the sheriff will know and he will send a militia but only after he slays all of you."

Her arms vere crossed and she eyed me closely. "Stop!" she said. "Am I to understand that his father sent a search party south, and he has been east of here? In a camp with Mac? Why was I not informed?"

"Mistress, I am only the Mac's cabin boy and not privy to all he tink. He sent me to warn you. Robertson can't be trusted to keep his mouth shut. He escaped us."

"He will face his father's wrath upon arrival. He will want to lessen it with his loose tongue. I have to work faster on my plan to be rid of him. As soon as you have your food, you may go, Gus."

I looked from her to the black man and seeing the slave woman coming with a sack of food, I was feared of being set loose with no way to find the swamp. I would walk for days in the woods, be eaten by wolves, or starve. "Mistress, I have nowhere to go. I ain't up on the way to get to the swamp from here. Please, may I stay? I will work day and night to make you happy until Mac sends for me."

The slave woman utter a *Pish!* and throw the sack at mine feet.

I can't say it vere an easy decision. They argued the good points and the bad, but in the end, the mistress and the slave man won out, taking pity on me. Yearie, the slave woman, vere not won over. She stalked off before m'lady vere finished with her questions. Feeling lucky, I traipsed behind them to the kitchen quarter. Brick walks, herbs sending their fragrance to the nose of me, and a dog. Its sleepy face woke to mine and it wiggled over. It jumped up like it wanted to be in mine arms. Not knowing about house dogs, only that they were flea-bitten, in constant beggary, I pushed him down.

"That's Tray. He's the master's spaniel, but he loves us all and we share our tidbits with him," says the mistress.

My jaw drooped. "A dog, mistress? You mean the kitchen waste, surely?"

She rounded on me before the kitchen door. "No, Gus. We have more food than we can eat every day. Tray gets whatever we leave on our plates. Or when his desperate eyes stare you down, you'll be compelled to take a bite and give him the rest."

I vere tinking when pigs fly with their tails forward, but she entered the kitchen afore I could answer. I looked all around and see the skinny black woman operating a butter churn like to bust it open. One determined slave. But, I tink, *Oh, butter!*

"Yearie, Gus will stay. Underneath that layer of dirt, Gus is Griet, the Vanderkoop child I told you about. She knew Phebe. We will keep her secret. Safer for her to run errands as a boy." My lady wink at her and put the hand of her on the plunger, stopping the action. "I'll churn whilst you acquaint yourselves. Seems this is a good moment. Raphael just left for marketing. The kitchen is free from ears."

"Where be Voltaire, Sary?" she asked.

"I told him to trim the candlewicks all over the house. He won't be back for an hour."

The mistress took a ladle of water from the cask and give it to the maid. When the slave handed it back to her lady, she put her lips right in the same spot and drank before she threw the remainder on the hearthstone. Just like maroons sharing spit.

Yearie sit down on the kitchen bench and called me over. I listen to the swish and squish of the churn behind me and wonder what they up to? I step carefully.

"You be a sight and the master won't accept you no matter what," she say. "First things first. I clean you up. Master Morris be home from the dockyard later. In the meantime, you get some learnin on his household."

She take a kitchen rag, dip it in water, and grab me by the chin. Next I know, she scrubbing the face of me like to tear off the skin. Her fingers pick at mine hair looking for nits, and she scrub it with harsh soap that make me grumble. "Take off that rag of a shirt and let me see how bad this be," she say.

I obey, the eyes of me squinting from the soap sting. The eyes of her, what I can see of them, get all wide at my half-naked self. The rag scrub me in spots I never knew I had.

"You listen here, you little parasite. You be our little gardener. There be a clay pot outside the door holdin tools. You check it everday for a red handle trowel. If it not be in the pot, you stay home. If you see it, you wait in the old nag's stall for instructions. Sometimes you go to the tailor's, sometimes you go to Mistress Kate at Three Coaches in East Town. You have a good memory, can spit out details?"

"Yes'm."

She grabbed the head of me and pushed it down over a quarter barrel. A crash of ice-cold water hit mine neck and I rose up like a fish out of a crik, gulping for air. "You got to make it back here afore the night watch come out when the moon high in the sky, or Master'll catch you, and take you to the sheriff." She threw a dry rag over me. Shivering with cold, getting the job I wanted Mac to give me, I rubbed quick as I could. "I—I'm not sure of mine way in the dark."

The fine lady behind me on the churn, Mrs. Wise, spoke up. "You'll have to learn if you want to stay. I'm in the family way and can't bounce along on a horse." She glanced over her shoulder. "Yearie and Jackson can no longer go at night, for Goldsboro has them on watch. Make yourself useful."

She sounded just like Mac. I must've looked worried because the Yearie woman grabbed me by the shoulders and shook me. I looked her in the face. Dark-brown eyes, piercing. Her head wrap reminded me of the washerwomen in St. Domingue, yet she vere younger and pretty.

"I braid Voltaire's hair like a map," say she. "On his forehead is this house in a square. At the nape of his neck is East Town. If'n you can scribe lines, you can make a map. I can't be seen writin nothin for you and missus can't either, for Goldsboro will know it's not a child's hand. I'll be leaving paper and charcoal in the garden pot. Draw it from memory, not in front of Voltaire for he not to be trusted."

I couldn't do it having never written anything in my life. I held the cloth over my head like a A-rab. "Sure and enough, he'll see me studying him and report to your master."

The lady stopped churning behind me and laughed hearty. Yearie pushed my face away. "Voltaire the dumbest thing round here on two legs. Don't be followin in his tracks. And don't be blabbin to young

Robert when he get here. He's on his way out the door to Phildelphee."

"He's leaving?" I shouted. I wanted to tell him we would kill him. That he was a dead man.

Yearie clapped her hand across my mouth and Mrs. Wise looked alarmed and ran to the door. She turned and whispered, "You do not know young Rob. You're a beggar boy, here to muck the stable and tend the garden. After the last meal is done, you work as the kitchen scullion, but never touch the good silver and china, or we'll send you to your mother in Lewes on the next schooner."

At that, I fell over in a dead heap and wailed. My life vere over. One step away from Mam and her babes, from stays and a dress, from hearth fires and burning skirts. I rolled on the floor and wailed louder. I peeked open an eye to see what effect I had. The two women stood over top me, their hands on their hips, peering down like eagles inspecting their prey.

The slave woman kicked me softly and said, "You be good at playactin I see, but not better'n anybody else round here. Coulda taken a lesson from our former cook. Git up now and drop you drawers. You stink down there."

M'lady snickered and left, saying she'd return. Next I knew, I was buck naked, hopping on this foot and that trying to get loose of the slave woman and her soap. It smelled like vinegar and felt like it too. She scrubbed my backside, my insides and between my toes, muttering the whole time.

"Don't never seen a child as dirty as you."

"You just never had no swamp boy afore," says I. "We all look like this."

She pick me up and put me in the barrel. "You not no boy and guarantee no swamp girls this dirty. How'd you get that scar on your foot? Hearth fire?"

"It vere none your business."

With that she boxed mine ears, one and two. My head vere ringing like a church bell, but I heard her mean and hoarse say, "You tain't from no swamp when Master come. You walk here from the

Virginie woods after your parents died of the ague. You get that straight."

"Yes'm," I said.

"In two day, a ship comin to harbor. Once they take stock, you make a midnight trip to East Town with a message. Don't buck me, child. We know where your mama be." She took the wet rag and drilled down the ears of me. I struggled to get free and ran naked to the door, not tinking I might reveal the truth about my sex to anyone outside. Mistress come from nowhere and grab me as I go by, pulling me back. She threw a clean shirt over my head that came past my knees. I froze at the soft feel of it, remembering being little and warm, hiding in Mam's skirts.

The lady giggled seeing mine face. "It's Scotch cambric, child. Heaven's cloud."

Pulled me to her, she did, and burying mine head in folds of her dress, I began to cry real tears for the second time that day. Soon enough, I felt a rocking and losing my balance, I tumbled into her lap.

"You're so little. A bag of bones."

"Auntie Sarah," came a voice I knew from outside, "Yearie. Who is that boy? What are you two doing with him?"

Robertson vere at the door. Mine anger came to me, though mine nose in her bosom. I had to tink quick and decided to lay it out before the women folk shut me up. I rose from her breast and said, "You're a traitor." I reached to the butcher block and grabbed a knife, holding the point between us. "I'll kill you now." He stepped back but Jackson vere behind him. Robertson laughed at me in mine long cambric shirt.

"Whoa, whoa, Gus," say Yearie. "Not havin blood spilt in my kitchen. Sit down, both of you."

The lady stood and grabbed him by the elbow. "Jackson, come here," she yelled over the head of him. Jackson must have been outside listening to everything for he burst in the kitchen and took up most of the air. With two great hands, he pushed Robertson to the bench and me to the chair. I felt small and shtoopud in this strange gang of hospitable people. Like I didn't know the rules.

"Rob, you've been gone weeks and your father is livid. He has made plans. Do not ruin your future. You leave tomorrow for Philadelphia on the Baltimore schooner."

I took stock. He vere ready for combat.

"You cannot keep me quiet, mistress." His eyes squint, he rush her and Jackson sat him down. "My father should know what you do, what you are aligned with. It is a crime to steal."

He said these last words with great pride, as if he vere the first ever to know their true meaning. For us tars, it vere a way of life. I said, low, trying to get the whine from my voice, "You will die in your sleep, Robertson. If not by me, at the hand of our spies."

"It's not necessary to threaten, Gus," said the lady, so calm. "I know you're angry, but the groundwork is laid. Rob, in your absence, a trove of missing silver has been found in your belongings. You are a thief, a criminal, and your father is gravely disappointed in you. He has informed the sheriff, shy of informing the courts, but that can change. If you blame others, it will only make it look like you are trying to cover your guilt.

"Gus, you will stay with us to be another set of ears and eyes. You will bring me all mail, especially that from Philadelphia before it goes to Master Morris. You will watch for the appearance of messengers on any ship in harbor and question whence they came." She looked Robertson in the face of him and said, "We are in receipt of a certain letter this morning."

Yearie reached in her pocket and spilled pee-cans on the table. White spotted, rotten pee-cans. Rob nearly fainted. "From a Scotsman tellin of your plan to ruin your father's business," said she. "Be careful, young master, or it will find its way to him."

"Master coming from the docks," said Jackson looking out the window. "Who be you, Gus. Say it again."

"Aye," I replied. "I'm from Virginie and both mine parents are dead of the ague. I been walking a fearful time and am in need of bread." A recitation, another story. This vere not all up to me to solve. I should have known.

"You've come to the right place, boy," he say. "Get dressed and I'll introduce you."

"Ja. I mean, aye. I can muck stalls, milk a cow or a goat, tend the geese, scrub a pot and shoot a muskrat to cook in it. And I might spin a tall tale for his amusement." I ruffled mine wet hair and looked to the women folk for approval.

Yearie shushed me. "Put your foot in these here leggings quick as a frog hopper. Feet in these muckers. We got no proper stockins." She frowned. "It be on you to make an impression."

Rob sat on the bench behind the door ready for battle, and I smirked at his comeuppance. As I dressed, the lady spoke, then Yearie like they vere twins of a different color, stern and impatient, each giving an order. I tried hard to remember.

No tales of sailin them high seas.
Be seen and not heard, little Gus.
When the master speak, wear them mouse ears big.

And what come last, most important from the lady, *Never answer the sheriff or his men. Leave that to me.*

Full of Dutch blessings, I dressed in a hurry and toweled my hair into short grass.

The master come. He vere a compact man, not portly or thin, got round, brown eyes with a wrinkle between, and a wig of three rolls on each side. He rip off an oilskin apron while beneath, a yellow vest and buff breeches look clean as the deck of a ship after scrubbing. He wear boots to his knees just like the Mac and he walk with a purpose to the table, not seeing Rob sitting in shadow.

"Everyone's standing around? Get me some supper. I must be back at the docks to complete the inventory. Callister is a fool."

The slave woman hurry like me on the campfire. Mrs. Wise take his apron and pour him an ale. "My love," she said, pulling me to him, "this is a beggar boy who graced our doorstep this morning. I have tested his mettle by having him muck a stall and milk the cow. He says he can do more. We are in need of more hands for the animals and scullery especially since Hestia is gone." She plead with a merry smile, "May we keep him on as your babe is coming in little more than a month?"

"I am well aware of the condition of my house and everyone in it. Where is the cook I hired?"

"Gone to market, sir," say Mistress.

"A poor trade just to teach Handy a lesson about his slaves. Damned Bacon." He settled in an armchair and gave me a glance up and down. "Looks small and lightweight, but so was I growing up. How fast did he accomplish his tasks?"

"Seemed like the wink of an eye, m'lord. And he's eaten not a thing from the larder yet."

"Master, he handle the stable muck, sir," say Jackson from the door. "He answers to Gus."

Master grunt. "Jackson get out of here. I'll not have you lounging round my kitchen." He grabbed a curved pipe, the bowl a wondrous carved head of a man with beard and horns, something I'd never seen in all mine travels. The lady handed him a taper lit from the coals. Yearie set a silver plate before him filled with cold meat, cooked greens, cornbread and *butter*. When he spear his first bite with a strange knife that have two prongs, m'lady say like to a child, "U-uh, my love. You forget your napkin," and don't she tuck a fresh white linen embroidered in red with an 'M' under his chin?

It be a wonder they don't wipe his ass before he eats.

He chew and drink, swallow and speak, stuff in some cornbread and make a decision. "The boy can stay. Have him sleep in the stable. He can start the fire before Raphael opens the kitchen come morn." He wave the tankard in the air. "Maybe this one will earn his weight, since my son has been nothing but trouble."

As tall as he was, Rob sunk low. He spoke from behind the door. "Father, I have returned."

Well, Morris' head roll in his direction, a king at his serf, and he don't take his eye from his son, but neither does he speak. I tink his eyebrows never come back from under his wig. Robertson stood and bowed. "I beg your forgiveness, sir. I followed a woman from the tavern to her home. Her father found me in her bed and threw me out."

Morris roared with laughter. Then, as quick as he laughed, he stabbed the knife in the table and stood. "You have been gone three weeks and this is the explanation you have? Sarah, find my birch whip."

"Father, she never knew my real name."

"To wit, a bastard will be your responsibility, not mine."

We couldn't move. Rob for fear of the switch, and us for fear of his telling all.

The lady say, "M'love, he has only just arrived. He will leave tomorrow on the packet. This is your last day together. Would that we could spend it in some semblance of family unity?"

"Father, Auntie Sarah is right. I humbly ask your forgiveness."

The son stepped out, looking at his feet. For the first time, I saw he was not just dirty, but defeated as if his days in the woods vere a failure. I tried to see him as his father would, a disobedient son, a whoremonger, a thief. That vere the boy who stood before us, for he vere merely a boy.

Morris sat again, leaning back in his chair. His foot tapped, the lids of his eyes hid his thoughts. M'lady waited, all quiet expectancy.

"Mrs. Wise is right, as always," the father say. "You leave tomorrow for the home of Mr. Charles Greenway in Philadelphia. You will be tutored with his children and apprenticed in the shipping industry."

"Sir, this is a wonderful opportunity. I will make you proud."

"You can't make me any less than I am today. See that you change your ways."

"Yes, sir. I need a big city to explore."

"You need to explore the pages of a book."

"Yes, sir."

"Yearie, follow him to his belongings and see that he packs them." Then he bellowed, "And *do not* take anything that isn't yours!"

I vere sweeping the hearth, trying to stay out of the doings and sneaking looks all the while. Suddenly, the master belch and call me to him. "You boy, Gus. Come here."

I tink he rough me up, done with his son. He measure the girth of my upper arm between his finger and his thumb and stick his pointer in the mouth of me, pushing mine lips to inspect the teeth of me. Good and clean as the teeth of any slave boy, for I chew on sassafras twigs. He spoke no complaint. Good ting he not ask to look at mine feet.

"Where are your parents, Gus?" he ask.

"Dead of the ague down in Virginie, sir." I look sorrowful.

"How long have you been walking?"

This take me for a turn, but I recover fast and say, "I get lost in the woods, sir, eating berries and muskrat from the marsh."

"Muskrat, huh? Well, you may stay as long as you work hard and say your prayers. I won't tolerate stealing, swearing, or fisting your member in public. You must be obedient. You understand? How old are you?"

"Eleven, sir. I'll be no trouble. I'll be true as a river runs to the sea.

"Mrs. Wise, I've not seen an eleven-year-old so stunted. Feed him well. Maybe he'll grow."

It vere up to me to keep the secret. Gus, I be in his home, the Merchant of Oxford.

CHAPTER 35

*R*obertson spent the rest of the night packing in the front room. Late, after I finished scrubbing pots in the yard, Mrs. Wise whistle under shadow of the big oak. She blew out her lantern and clicked her tongue.

"Do not tell Rob the camp is moving," she declared in her flowery voice. "Mac has cleared the Choptank and is in the Chesapeake as we speak. He still fights a headwind."

Horror stricken, I said, "No, missus. I would never say. He's not one of the gang."

"You cannot trust him, Gus. Do not be duped by his compliments. He has not gone near his father, but we don't know who he spoke to on his travels home."

I considered this. I vere a fool in my want of a friend, but no more. "Why do you tell me what I already know? You tink he vere loyal to Goldsboro?"

"He is.

"And you want me to conversate with him?" I felt a pulse beating in mine head like the tap of a dead man's finger.

"I do."

"What should I know about Goldsboro besides he vere a cruel man and the sheriff?"

"He wields great power and wealth. Not enough to satisfy him, and that is the danger."

"You risk your own life in this house, m'lady. Will Rob say your connection to the Mac?"

"I don't believe so. He has become fond of me like a boy to his mother for some reason."

"I can make him tink I still shtoopud."

I turned to go inside, and the slave woman was standing behind me. She hiss at me and say, "Don't be playin with our lives you sloppy little beggar. I got no reason to trust you." She pinched mine cheek hard and I wriggled from her grip and ran to the kitchen house door.

Walking inside with the mistress, m'lady put her finger to mine lips and we parted. Down the great hallway, running the hand of me against the wall, I found Rob vere lying on the floor twirling a cockade of red, white and blue, an open trunk by his side. Wigs, combs, cravats, and a mirror that I slipped under my backside to steal a look once and again. Drawn to it, I was. Rob ordered me like I vere his servant, but mostly I vere entranced at my visage. "Fold my shirts," he said, and I lay the mirror beneath them so's my face appear under the package. Finally he grab it out and hold it up so I can take a long look.

"Well, what do you think?" he ask.

The tanned boy in the mirror have the face of a muskrat, but the eyes vere a pale shade of sky blue, not brown like a rodent. I touched the tufted straw on his head, his brows and lashes. I wipe his pointed nose and purse his lip above a short chin that vere marked by a scar. I tink everyone vere easy to fool, but I feel the sex of me deep in my haunches. Rob push the mirror close to my eyes.

"Take it," he said. "A gift."

Embarrassed, I took the wolf bone that hung on my chest and put it in his hand.

"A fair trade, Gus," he said. "I know you don't wish me ill."

I tink my necklace vere a Dutch treat not worthy of his gift, but he tied it round his neck.

"You are happy to go to Greenleaf?"

"Greenway. I'm a nuisance to father. He says I must earn my birthright. Says it can't be had in Oxford, and I must prove myself worthy."

"Of what?"

"Of my name, I guess."

"Robertson, we vere almost a team in camp," I said, playing his game, drawing him in.

"He thinks if he gets rid of me, his life will be simpler."

I busied mine self folding, tinking this talk vere beyond me.

"I told Goldsboro where to find the rebels. He knows these slaves are working together."

I vere alarmed, but kept mine head. "Ja, rebels. What kind of life is that? Surely m'lady lies that they have power."

"She's been tricked. But, I can't risk the courts. Ruin my future. Father would believe that Scotsman before he believed me." He slapped mine shoulder. "You're not part of that thieving cant, Gus. Just kidnapped against your will. Their's is a fool's enterprise."

"A run-down, backwoods gang."

"All they have is a broken ship and skeleton crew. They'll be dead by summer. Look here, Goldsboro appreciates me." He held a velvet sack and out fell a pistol in his hand, it's silver polished and engraved.

"A gift from the sheriff's family. More than I'd ever get from Father. Goldsboro said I was like a son to him. I'll never have to use it," he said, his eyes drooping.

I looked out the window, but it vere pitch black outside. All I could see vere the reflection of mine face. I smiled at me, for I didn't need his mirror with all these windows. I just had to wait for night and the moon. He didn't know of the rest of the network or the swamp.

"It's different in Philadelphia. Quakers, you know. Peaceable. Yet he wanted me to have this to remember him." He said with more confidence, "Greenway is a wealthy man. You could come work for him."

"Room and board, like here?" I asked.

"Servant pay," he answered.

"Should all the gang go? Maybe they would live happy there."

"For God's sake, Gus. No! Father says the misguided Quakers in Philadelphia want to free the slaves. Ridiculous."

"I'll not go to a city where some are not part of the whole."

Rob laughed and swore. "It's no different here. Suit yourself. You'll die on the ground, a sword in your heart."

"Will you come back?"

"Here? What for little man?"

Not me, I guess.

He left on the mail schooner the next morning. M'lady walked him to the ferry, I carrying his knapsack, Jackson lugging his trunk like the bull he be. Master Morris said his goodbye at breakfast, warning Rob not to be a burden on Master Greenway and not to be sent back. I shook his hand and wondered why his beginnings were so different from mine. His father had given him a name, schooling, clothes and a new city. I had a mirror and a slave woman who had it in for me.

I vere sad for a moment but remembered that blood does not buy loyalty, only family. An orphan I be for all my days. I let my eye water a bit on that, but tink it vere my freedom. When we get back to the kitchen, I spilled all of his words to Mrs. Wise. "I'll go to East Town with the news," says I.

CHAPTER 36

*A*t dawn four days later, Wenetko, the half-breed who vere a good soldier to Mac arrived in the stable yard with the news that the *Fearnaught* vere hidden on the Pocomoke and the gang had trekked East to the swamp camp. I was gathering firewood, for the new cook had not shown up to work. The sight of my camp friend warmed me. He bowed his feathered head at seeing Master leading his horse from the stable. Master vere already mad for having no breakfast ready to eat.

"A savage? Get rid of him, Gus," he said. "Thieving Indian on my property."

I jumped about, waving the arms of me like I vere fending off a mad cow when Wenetko raised a painted gourd that rattled. "I bring toy for baby that come. An offering from my peoples."

"I don't want it. Get out of here!" yelled Master.

Wenetko slumped off, winking at me as he left for Kate's saddlery. Master clatter away and I ran to Yearie with the good news. She frown and cuss, say to get out of her sight.

I breathed easy, knowing Mac vere safe. A busy place, Morris House, what with carpenters raising more slave quarters across the street, digging the well deeper for fresh water, and all the new horses for me and Jackson to tend, it vere a fairytale compared to St. Domingue adventures. Jackson vere lazier than a honeybee in summer after he work the wharf, so I had much to do.

I made a schedule for setting the cook's fire, milking the cow and the goat, and feeding the fowl. I set the table before anyone rise and steal dried apple from the larder. A comfort to me, my swamp habits vere like the scars on my foot—forever there. Mistress say it vere March on the calendar, but all I knew is it vere warming up, the frost on the windows fleeting. I missed tracing their spiky lace with mine finger in early morn that seemed a habit of long ago when I vere little, so I blew my breath on the glass in its place until Yearie yell at me to stop dirtying the view. As it turned out, living in a house with extra buildings afforded many a place to take a nap. By mid morn, I could lay down in the stable straw to dream.

I woke to a strange quiet one day and strolled under the big oak tree to see what was wrong. Sleep stuck in mine eyes and the belly of me grumble as I tink of cook's sourdough and butter. Seemed like the more I ate, the hungrier I got. That's when I see the red-handled trowel in the pot. I brightened, looking to find Yearie for my jaunt to East Town. I enjoyed a nighttime foray on the old speckled nag and especially Mistress Kate's baking. But, at the kitchen quarter I forgot all that. I straightened my new waistcoat and entered.

Master vere inside making a holy scene so bad I thought he full of Dutch ire, yelling and screaming like Papje. Up, he held a news-paper as Mistress cleared bowls beneath.

"Escaped slaves," he shouted, "boarded the *Lydia*! Rovers, armed with nothing but battle-axes and scythes." He slap the broadside on the table. "I pay a lord's share of insurance for these smugglers to rob me?"

M'lady turn to him as she stacked the dry sink. Still in her mantua robe, I see her belly vere big. "Robert, whatever do you mean? How could Captain Lewis not defend his ship?"

"Defend it? He and his sailors were in Virginie's Yorktown harbor drinking and carousing in the taverns. Left two jacks on board, one below deck and the other now lies with a split head in the sea. Took the simpleton tar a prisoner and threw him overboard when all was done. I will sue Lewis for my losses!"

"How is it possible?" she asked, fear in her eyes. "Is it a slave rebellion?"

Yearie vere sweeping the hearth behind her and tilted her head, listening. Mac always said the villages vere afraid of another town's slaves. I took the bowls to wash.

"A privateer. Cur-sed French hire black sailors. They laid in wait in the bay."

She put a hand to her breast and met my eye past his elbow. "Robert, it can't be accurate. There are no slaves on French ships."

"Are you not listening? Your intellect is soft as your belly. They were advance raiders sailing periaguers. To make it look like a rebellion."

"I'm sorry, sir. I did not hear you say that," she answered.

He had not said it. And yet, she gave him her sorry? Periaguers. I tink to picture it. Two dugout cypress canoes tied with a platform between. In the swamp, we put sails on them and called them perogues. I smile inside. This vere our boys at work.

"*Lydia* was anchored in the York River," he say. "They rowed up and boarded her in the night, pulled anchor and sailed into the Chesapeake where the privateer ransacked her. Lit her afire. The *Lydia*—burnt." He put his head in his hands.

"No ,Robert! What did they take?"

"Everything. £36,000 of tobacco, indigo and a cache of sterling bound for the Annapolis Court." His face vere stricken. "They even stole the cannon and the rigging."

"That is no small feat, sir. Stealing cannon in the well-traveled bay."

"On a black night. The idiot sailor said they rolled them across the gangplanks. They'll get their due," he said, jabbing the paper at her. "The privateer flies our red ensign but he's certainly not British."

She grabbed the paper from his hand and put herself to work, reading. "It says it was a frigate with French markings, a gold anchor carved on the prow and no guns on the upper deck."

"No doubt his purpose. The cannon. Short supply everywhere.

Cunliffe just outfitted *Lydia* with twenty-eight 12-pounders since the damned monarchy won't send us a warship." He snatched the paper from Mistress and threw it on the table so she would look at him. "He was followed south as far as the mouth of the Pocomoke and disappeared. He can't trade indigo and sterling on the Chesapeake without me knowing. He'll have to head to the French Caribbean. I'll trap him."

"M'lord, you are so busy. How on earth can you marshal a force?" She rested her fingers over her mound.

"Cunliffe. He must beseech the King," he said, spit flying. "In the meantime, I'll advertise for sailors and buy the cannon at Point Comfort. They sink in the sand and that damned Virginia governor does nothing to defend the Chesapeake. I'll arm Oxford's harbor *and* find that privateer."

"You must alert the sheriff," she said, "He'll have a bulwark built and organize the planters.

"For Christ's sake, you are slow. There's no time to build bulwarks. Goldsboro knows—he gave me the newspaper. Says the rovers are maroons defected from the swamp. He's wrong, of course. They're French Caribs. But it's time to clean out the swamp riffraff for good. He's amassing the militia on the East Town road as we speak."

"This is war, Robert. Lives will be lost. Oxford lives," say Mistress.

He nodded at her and fell silent. Then he made as if to go but stopped, saying, "I contacted Handy this morning. The freeman, Raphael, is gone. Left for Philadelphia with his family. Handy is sending Hestia back to us today. His kitchen is his problem now."

Yearie wiped the table, stuffing the gazette in her skirts and threw the rag over her shoulder to walk out the door. I followed, picking up the garden bucket. She walked that sway of hers toward the stable like she have all day, so I meander to the kitchen garden and wait for her to signal me. Soon enough, Jackson start hollering to come help him muck. Pancaking his job, he vere, layering on me. He vere worthless. I see Master and Mistress arguing, so I make myself scarce and run to the stable.

Soon as I enter the darkness, his hand come out and drag me to the far corner by Ol Bets. Yearie bent down, tearing the story from the gazette. She jut her little chin at me and say, "Gus, you gonna ride Sary's horse to East Town. Pick up Kate's stable boy and hustle to the swamp. Wait for Mac's answer." She held out the folded paper. "I wouldn't be sendin you all that way but we not have time if'n he need us to prepare." Folding it in my pocket, she say, "Tell him he don't got but a day an some fore the militia get to him. They loggers cuttin cedar by quarter acre a day and could join them militia. Make a regular army, it would."

"Getting slaves to kill escaped slaves." I pawed the stable earth. "Who's going to make mine excuse to the master?"

"You not that important he goin to miss you," she snapped, pulling off my waistcoat and throwing a buckskin and stocking cap over the head of me. "If need be, I can lie better'n anybody. Take this and put it round your neck. To keep you safe." It vere a conjure bag like the ones she always giving Mistress. "I'll be calling on the Marassa to spirit you quick."

She riddling a story, but I didn't care. Jackson tossed me over the saddle and tied a waterskin to the pommel.

"It going take you all day and most of the next to make for the maroons," he said. "Don't stop fer nothin. And don't talk to nobody, neither." He slid open the back door with one last warning. "You pass the militia keep yo head down and ride." He slapped Bets on the hindquarters and I jumped the fence, riding low, sneaking a look back as they waved.

It vere not the grit of Ol Bets but I rode her hard, kicking all the way to East Town, passing the militia assembling in Tilghman's field. A little before noon I come to the stable. I tinkin over master's conversation, the newspaper, the militia and loggers. Burbling the story to Mistress Kate, she gave me a fresh horse with no saddle and Wenetko to lead. He knew the way to the swamp.

Twice the size of me, he leap up, take the reins with I behind holding tight round his muscles as he kick. We flew, nearing the loggers who vere deep in the wood cutting pine and cedar. Slaves sawed in pairs, others stripped felled timbers and still others rolled them to the river. I catch a glimpse of their barge, stacked with fresh logs.

Their song drown out the voice of forest birds and one lone, deep and echoing, heard over all.

Master he be a hard, hard man.

A chorus rip up just like the tars on ship:

Hoe, Emma, hoe.

Sell my people away from me,

Hoe, Emma, hoe.

Lord, send my people into Egypt land,

Strike down Pharoah and break his hand,

Set my people free.

Hoe, Emma, hoe.

Hidden at the edge of the wood we slowed, drawn to their misery. Overseers whip those boys, working them to till they kneel, hands up to stop. Soon enough I can't watch no more so I squeezed Wenetko and he kick our racehorse. Hours passed; daytime waned on the paths of long-gone Nanticoke when I see distant torch light. Clutching my Indian, I lean in. Soon I recognize my way home.

CHAPTER 37

*D*ogs barking, I feel eyes upon us. I forget the muskeeters'
bite, drawing blood. I took a deep breath and air thick
with wings clogged the throat of me. Deep in the forest, I miss mine
old life, mine freedom. Swamp water closed in smelling like pine tar,
seeping reddish brown, a skim floating on top. I tink of sitting in the
jakes at Morris house, the stomach of me aflame from all that eating.
Now, it feels good to be hungry again.

Hours and hours of riding, night turned to day and to near night
again, jiggling the insides of me. The horse balked in a tangled mess
of vine and Wenetko slowed to a crawl. Pines changed to century
cypress and I hopped off to lead by the bridle. I know where I be. A
pile of ship's rope and oakum lay on some moss. The jacks be at
work on the stolen rigging. We heard a shout.

"Whoa, Wenetko. Who you bring?"

I turned my head to see Tandy come a running, carrying a long
rifle over his shoulder. Mac must've been teaching target practice for
we didn't have much armaments before.

"Tandy, it be Gus," I hollered. "I got news for Mac."

Wenetko swung his leg over the horse's head and popped to the
mud, taking the bridle from me. Running to keep up with Tandy, I

275

found the path to the camp had changed, the bridges connecting the hillocks of dirt pivoted like draws to a castle. The gray sky peeped out as the cypress thinned. It vere after suppertime in the camp. I smelt meat roasting. Tars came to greet me, poking and laughing. It vere good for mine soul to belong again. Suddenly, the boss stood afore me. Big as life.

"Why're ye back here, Griet?" he ask.

"Mac, you gotta listen."

"Come to me bench and we be having a sit," he say like all vere normal.

Well, I told him the whole and didn't leave nothing out. His face grow more concerned as I relay the whos and whats of Rob and Goldsboro, of the *Lydia* and the militia and soon he stood, rounding on me.

"Yer saying to strike camp? Pull it down? Can't be done. The *Fearnaught*'s guarded not a few miles from here full of cannon and swivel guns. We got sterling buried under the Indian bones. Plus, I can't pack up the women and children. Too many little ones, too many with child."

I frowned. "Camp has to stay light, you said. Women and babies, Mac, always a problem. You got to go, or they'll slaughter everyone and take you back to be drawn and quartered. You don't know how evil that sheriff of theirs be."

He laughed loud at that one, throwing his head back, his eyes gleaming. "Now that were what I need to hear. I'll unhorse that behemoth, scalp him and divest him of his innards."

"Mac," I yelled, "you got to take this serious."

His face turn to stone. "I am serious, Griet." He pace. He rub his forehead and walk off. Then he holler for Suter and they throw open the door of a shack so sloppy all it could do is keep out the rain.

"Pull the torches. Heat the pitch on the campfire," he say as he call the men to arms. "Jack tars, one and all! Isaac's men follow Suter and clear out yer belongings, the silver, and our trade goods. Don't leave em here. Take the women and children and meet us at the *Fearnaught*. Tandy, arm yer boys with shot and find yer position, spread out like we planned. The rest of ye, gather the torches. We light the swamp on fire tonight."

Oh, it did the blood of me good to be in the mix. The women folk packed — the candle rack, the soap pot, even meat drying on the line. A gang of vagabonds they be, following Suter down the baneswort path to the canoes where the silver vere stored under the bones. A struggle to make haste out the back of the camp, for it vere riddled with cold swamp water and few paths. But one creek flowed due south and fed the Pocomoke.

Afore long the camp look empty, all evidence packed in the long houses like the place be abandoned. Some determined swamp women armed with axes and blunderbusses, positioned themselves behind tent doors. Tandy and his tars take position at the entrance to the camp where they pull up the bridges, all cept one.

Suter return with a chest covered in dirt. The sterling. He pack it on a mule and with Isaac and them tars, ride the river trail, driving the cows and goats in the swamp. The rest of us wound cloth round torches and coat them in hot pitch. Mac led us across the last bridge. I looked back and considered in a second if I vere making a mistake.

"Griet, you and Wenetko catch up to Suter."

"No, Mac. I'll die with you or not live. You said yourself, they won't send me to gaol."

He grinned. "Not worth wasting the space on ye."

The woods vere gloomy at dusk, the black outlines of the tars hopping from path to hillock seem like some tribal dance, their torches smoking and glowing white hot above their heads. We swept through the stand of cedar to the river of cypress knees, carrying our pots of heated tar. In no time we lined the edge of stinking water between us and the loggers. We could hear their singing distant and sad, sound carrying through the woods on water.

Mac poured the tar into the swamp, swing his torch in a circle and tip it into the water. It ignite, sending a stream of flames running the surface. Maroons follow his example and soon a ring of fire vere blazing across the bank in a circle. The flame stop, sparks flew, a cypress knee caught while flames jumped to another spot on water. A cloud of smoke rose, shielding us from spying eyes. Soon, we heard the collective beat of forest animals on the move. It vere beautiful to me, and I couldn't help finding Mac and tugging his hand as we watched the orange glow slurping an oily black sea.

Standing next to him, I felt a thunder beneath mine feet like the ground trying to talk. I looked down and the knees of me quivered. "Mac," I said, "somebody coming."

He knelt to put his hand against the dirt, ear cocked. He whistled the signal and the boys gathered, running down the return path, lighting dead pools along the way. I forgot how fast the gang moved and mine pipes were like to blow up trying to meet their pace. They ran across the camp bridge, Mac standing guard. Last to make it, he yanked mine arm, and breathed into the face of me. His eyes were fierce with war.

"Find Wenetko, take his horse and ride the river trail out o ere. Ye head back to Oxford afore yer master finds ye missing."

"No, Mac!" I screamed, wiggling free. "I'm not leaving you."

"Ahl be fine, Griet. If the militia make it past the fire, we'll pick em off one at a time. The gang be good marksmen now. Once we make mincemeat of em, we'll head to the ship and down to the Caribbean."

"No, no, Mac. You can't. Morris going to have a ship o the line out there to catch you, to bring you to justice."

"Nonsense. There not be an English warship on this side of the Atlantic that can catch me frigate. Ahl not be arguing with ye. Get yer bones gone now afore I whip ye with me belt."

He shook mine shoulders until my teeth rattled in my head, and in a mound of frustration led me to Wenetko. "Take this here to Kate and keep it safe. Do not let me cabin boy slip from yer grasp. Understand?"

Wenetko nodded and threw me over the horse, pinning the leg of me under his hand. Hopping up behind nimble as a cat, he kicked and we plunged into cold swamp water. I pulled mine feet up and he grabbed me round the middle, I still crying to go back. The horse picked through the pools to the river trail and we headed away from home, from Mac. Riding a fast gait, I had to bury my fingers into the horse's mane so's not to fall off I vere so weary. I fell asleep like that, my noggin lolling about, and only woke when I hear hooves clattering on stone.

The moon was high, a fingernail, but the stars vere singing in the cold night air. Half dreaming, half awake, I tink I see smoke clouding the sky in the shape of two heads, one inside the other, fat-faced babes and I wonder if this be Yearie's Marassa. I felt a grip round my waist and someone dropped me into waiting arms. Carried inside to a smoldering fire, I vere laid on a straw bed by a hearth and though it give me a fleeting worry that my foot would burn, I gave it up. Listening to voices, I knew one of them vere Wenetko and the other Kate. Warm and secure, I fell into sleep of fires and swimming, of Mac bound and hollering, of me climbing the yardarm to hang a noose.

CHAPTER 38

$\mathcal{I}$ ride back to Morris House the next morning on Old Bets. On the Oxford Road, tinking about lies I could tell Master I get so confused I decided to just do normal. Kate had wiped the face of me clean, but I feared the rest of me smelled like smoke. I vere pestered.

The poor farms along the road vere quiet, just the womenfolk and children up to their chores, doing normal, too. I rode tall in the saddle, pretending a crown on the head of me like I vere coming home from battle. Across mine chest, I wore a packet of fresh perukes Kate had supplied in case I vere stopped. As I neared the bridge across the town creek I was stopped by a red-coated soldier older than a Spanish galleon with ears wagging in the breeze.

"Whereat you be a coming, young boy?" he asked.

I smiled and doffed my cap. "East Town, kind sir! On an errand for Morris to the wiggery. Why're you stationed here?"

"Yer Morris' new house boy!" he said with a toothless grin. "Goldsboro has me looking for escaped maroons. Slaves easy but them indentures be slippery."

"Aye. Should be one of his militia men defending our village here.

If you need assistance, I'll ask the mistress to come back and stand by your side."

The old man snorted, raising his rusted hunting rifle in the air. "Git on wit ye, chucklehead. The militia be in the swamp. I kin do me job."

"Good day then, sir. I must be getting back to my master."

"He be gone to Point Comfort," he shouted. "Goin petition the Virginie governor for his cannon and halp capturin that cur-sed privateer."

Eh, go catch a pox I tink. Kicking Ol Bets, I rode into a town so quiet a blizzard could have wrapped the houses though spring be at hand. Birds singing, grass greening, not even a hammering from the docks. Nobody amuck. Clattering into the yard, I slip off the saddle calling for Jackson. Then Voltaire. And Yearie. As I enter the kitchen quarter, I look around, see it empty but for Tray sleeping. I said, "Cook?"

My ears prick when I hear a low groan from above stair. I know that sound. Labor, like to signal a baby dying…or its mam. My heart heavy, I picked my way inside and see Jackson standing at the bottom of the grand stair ringing his hands.

He nod. "Gus."

"It be her time?"

"Yep."

"Who's upstairs?"

"Just Yearie. Nearly a night and full day now. Master left after you. They had a fight like to scare the bejesus out me."

"Over?"

"Him leaving."

"Anybody send for the midwife?"

"Voltaire. Got four in the village and not one show up yet."

"I'll go up."

"Can't, Gus. What if one of em come and catches you? I mean, you is a girl, but sure can't nobody tell."

"Don't matter. I seen more babies born in camp than you seen in a lifetime of slaving."

"You callin me useless, Gus? Cause I can roll a hog of terbaccer across a field faster than any slogger at Handy's."

"That's why they got rid of you, too. Findley rather see you tied to a tree than chasing you at night again. Now you're stuck mucking at master's beck and call."

"It better n scrubbing pots, you ignert house girl."

I shake my head as we hear another moan coming down the steps. Her pains not so close for a day and a half of laboring. "Guess neither one of us got much use," I said. "I got the message to the Mac."

"He prepare for battle?"

"Ja." I tinking with Mistress down and Master gone, why vere Jackson sticking round. So, I asked.

"Don't wanna live in no swamp," he answered. "Can't swim across the Bay. Asides, if'n I keep doin for Yearie, one day she gonna see me for who I be."

"What's that?" I asked. The man got so much care his face is heavy from wearing it. I hear another moan, louder, and head up the steps. On the landing vere a black woman I not ever seen afore. Sitting on a stool in the corner she sang, a far look in her eye. I see her hands resting on her knees. Burned with a H from wrists to knuckles. The skin be scabbed.

"My name's Gus. Are you Hestia?"

She looked from her hands to mine eyes and say, "Yes, child. A cook whose name begin with H."

"I'll cook with you, Hestia." I say, tinking if I can work the kitchen, no more pot scrubbing. I took the stairs two at a time.

She vere leaning against the bedrail, bent over in her bloody shift and hanging onto Yearie. If'n her legs give out, she fall in the pile of straw. She raised her face to me, streaked with tears and I see her disappointment, tinking me the midwife. I said little, except, "You need mine help."

"Pah," say Yearie. "You help. Find Voltaire." She left Mistress sink into the rushes. Raising her shift, she drip oil on mistress' tight belly, rubbing it in circles, muttering, "Faith, Hope and Charity — bring the baby in service of Thee."

"You shtoopud, Yearie. I'm one of us. When you going to let me fall into your house with a door?"

She glare at me. "Stop speaking in riddles, you two-faced Dutch monkey. I said go get Voltaire."

"Shut up your trap and listen to my point. I've helped deliver more babies in the maroons than you have working under Mistress."

Eyebrows disappear on that one. "Is this your first, mistress?" says me.

"No, no. Second," she say, breathing in short little bursts.

I didn't remember. Babies die like flowers in a cold snap... Sorrow. Mam crying. Papje digging a hole behind the cottage... I shake my head so to stop seeing the dirt fall in, pushing the blanket from the gray face of my broedder. I can't remember his name, now.

"Sit on the chair, Miss Yearie," I said, shoving it to her. "Mistress between your legs."

Yearie nod, grimacing. "A chair birth."

"Yes, ma'am. Lock your hands under her breast."

Mistress doubled over, howling before she take her place on Yearie's strong legs. Neither of them argue. I tink they too tied into each other to be sensible. I get more straw, mound it beneath her and throw a linen sheet across it.

"Mistress, can I see?" I ask, but she were not in a mood to conversate. So, I raise her shift to take a look, pushing her knees wide. Gleaming wet, stretched, her native skin were pushing out soft pink that might be a foot. I sit on mine haunches tinking. Coming like a foal.

"We better hope this baby vere not four-legged," I said, laughing, and Yearie reach to slap mine face, almost dropping Mistress. I sober up and feel ashamed for my joke. Mistress so healthy I not believing she could die. Or the baby, since this house vere blessed with much. Not like the swamp camp.

"You'll not be casting humor on my lady during her time," she say.

"It's upside down. I never turn one."

Mistress moaned and I wonder if I should keep my trap shut. Yearie lay her on the rushes and mistress prop herself on both elbows. Her hair vere dark with sweat, her face pale. Determination press her lips in a line. "Well, you're going to turn one now," she says. "I have to get this baby born before I lose God's strength."

It not good when womenfolk start calling on God, we so used to doing it on our own. I never known Him to come to the rescue of me, so I have no devotion that direction.

Yearie and I began to stroke her belly, she on one side, me on the other, like turning the anchor wheel up on the ship, steady and direct. The room be stifling with the smell of blood and sweat, not unlike tars working, minus their foul musk. It were more pleasing, and the work vere surely more tender.

Full of encouragement, in the long minutes we worked, it came to me that Mistress Sarah had no more idea whether she would live or die than an Indian delivering in the woods. We pushed and stroked as if she vere garden soil, to push a sprout out into the sun.

All of a sudden, I felt a hardness under my hand flip below her belly button, turning her a pear shape instead of an apple. Mistress erupt, shouting, "Aye-ah, oh my." She lay back and confess, "The pressure is different. Not on my back."

I jumped to mine feet and order, "This vere no time to relax. Back to the chair."

Yearie drag her from the linens to her lap, holding her tight so she don't slide to the floor. I sit before her, ready to catch the ball.

The pain come swift and hard. Miss Sarah recognize the end of the game, and she bear down. I smile up at her, waving my hands to bring it to me. With Yearie counting in her ear, she push and hold so's the head pop out. Small as an Indian peach, I reach, hold its sticky hotness in my hands and yell, "Again, Missus!"

A tiny shoulder come and with a half push the other. We all exclaim and praise as Miss Sarah fall against the chair leg and Yearie's foot. One tired little effort and the whole baby come, so tiny, like a ladle in a bucket. Yearie hop up and bring over the bowl of water, a knife and rags. I run to the fire, grab a taper and light it to run the flame on the blade as the maroons do in camp. Yearie cut and tie the cord. The baby lie on the bloody linen, silent. I reach to pull on its chicken foot. I stroke its chest and it gave a weak cry.

"What is it? Tell me," demand Missus.

We forgot to look. Yearie place it on her bosom and say, "It be a girl, Sary. A dark-haired girl. Look just like Master."

Mistress roll her into the tuck of her breast and we gaze on her perfectness. She have black fur all over her body, her twiggy arms vere limp, but her legs pumped. She opened her eyes and they vere dark, almond-shaped as his picture over the harpsichord look. Maybe the painter spoke to God and He made her flat-faced like him. She push her big tongue out of her little pink lips. I look closer.

Yearie give a shake of her head, warning me not to flap my gums. She was different. Not born with a witch's caul, or a birthmark, but different. Master not be pleased. A girl, eyes of a Chinaman, and a big tongue. Yet in such a house, this child will be loved.

I hear heavy steps on the stair, and Hestia appear in the doorway, holding the skirts of her up like she still climbing. Her chest heave, between breaths she say Voltaire not find a midwife, for even when one answered the door, she say, "'I won't come to Morris house and help that whore.' Said it's God's judgment on her sin."

Yearie roll her eyes and wrap the baby in a blanket. I get my shoulder under Mistress and help her to the bed piled with old linens. She fall into it, dizzy and white.

"I told that old harpy when mistress in the gaol," spout Hestia, "'You gonna die from your own evil, right soon.' She call me a dumb blackie, even if I can cook."

"No use arguing with mean," answer Yearie. "They can call Sary whore, but she not be unchristian like them. They inspect Sary at the gaol, lookin at her privates, pinchin her belly and titties, spittin on her and calling her names. Probly put a hex on her then."

Hestia lumber over to Yearie with a sly smile and say, "Don't you know what to do bout them witch doctor harpies?"

"I be saving my best spell for em. And the sheriff."

Hestia push the blanket from the baby's face and her smile fall into her bosom. "Uh. Uh. Look like Master. Ugly little bird."

I start singing to cover up the talk.

"Shh, shh," say Yearie, smacking her hand away.

One thing I know is true, every mam tink her baby perfect, but even I couldn't see how this one would fool Mistress Sarah.

I started, remembering from whence I'd been—the outside world of men and hate. "Eat the food, wear the cloth, open the window to breathe the air," I recite to get their attention. They look at me like a donkey vere sitting on my head. "Stand or fight. Which it going to be?" I ask.

Solemn, Yearie says, "The Scotsman bring the fight to Oxford, child. We been suffering the battle long afore him. Did you reach him?"

"Mac's headed into the Caribbean with the loot."

Yearie push the baby on Mistress. "Here, Sary. Suckle so your milk come in." She run to the door, yelling, "Jackson, you get your big self up here, now."

We all huddle on the landing, me with one ear cocked as Hestia sing to Mistress and her baby. I tell them that Mac order all to scatter to the wind. I told them that if any be left alive, Mac and some of the gang vere sailing to St. Domingue. "That's where he'll sell the wares of *Lydia*, but he got to get there first. He be out the pan and into the fire," I said, my voice cracking.

Mistress Sarah got ears like a dog. She tell Hestia to be quiet and shout to us. She vere trying to wrest her tired body from the bed. "Robert is on the *Johnson*, under Gildart's command going to Port Comfort for cannon. He wants a naval detail to go after the *Fearnaught*."

Yearie and Jackson follow me inside, listening, their faces all a worry.

With one bare foot on the floor, Mistress Sarah order us, "You have to sail down to the Pocomoke. You must warn him. Yearie, give them our coin."

Yearie turn to Jackson. "Take Gus on a tender boat and sail. Get word to the Scotsman."

"You a useful fool, Yearie. I'm no sailor, just a swamp mucker," he said, all stern. "I go and that make you an accomplice. Asides, when Callister come to lock us up tonight, he'll tell the sheriff I'm gone." He blew air. "That man got a hankering to slay me like Cain did Abel."

"All the more reason for you to get outta here afore Sheriff return. Gus can't sail by herself. We don't know if the maroons ever going to rise again after this swamp war, so we need to be ready to save our necks. Yours in particular."

CHAPTER 39

*N*ext morning before the sun broke, we had our packs, some cider and a note Yearie write for Mac. We bundled up since the wind vere strong. The sky vere gray, ready for dawn. I hopped on the tender skiff and set the sail. Jackson stepped on, rocking the boat till he plunk down safe, his head tucked between his knees. At the tiller, I set her to run against the wind and we vere off like a sailfish away from sleeping Oxford.

Like Yearie said, Jackson vere no help. He could haul terbaccer or a load of sailcloth across land, and pole a boat in river shallows, but he couldn't sail no boat on big water.

"Sure is quiet, Gus," he say looking up at the fading stars.

I snorted. "You live in a hellhole." After a few weeks in town, it felt good to be free.

A dog's bark rumble across to us, ferocious but distant. I light a small lantern and hold it to his face.

"How long this here boat take to get down Pocomoke way?" he asked.

I didn't know, but I tink it best not to say. Jackson vere itchy ever since I woke him, unlocked his ankle ring, and we run to the harbor. "The time it takes to sail," I say.

"How we gonna know his ship from the others?"

"Has a gold anchor carved on the prow. He flies a meteor."

"What that be?"

"The Union Jack on red."

"I know it. That don't set her apart. An besides, what if we come on her stern?"

"Mac fly thirteen red and white stripes from her foremast."

"That French?"

"You ask too many questions," I say and strike the lantern. "Mac not beholden to nobody, not even the French. Thirteen red and white —that vere his call for independence." I tink in the time it take a bullfrog to breathe, and say, "You just a nikker and wouldn't understand."

We sailed on, silent. The eastern horizon vere lit in purple sky so we see the outline of big ships anchored behind us, nothing but choppy Chesapeake waters in front and to the west. I make the decision to keep land in view. The wind vere steady, driving us through the tide, when Jackson open his mouth.

"Nikker, huh? I been called a lot o things," he say, squinting into the rising sun. "Seem strange a stupid Dutch girl who can't read, or scratch her name, call herself a boy when everyone know she a girl." Then he look me in the eye. "Least I know who I am even if Master try whipping it out of me."

I stared back at him. Now, I were itchy and getting madder. His eyes were on me, measuring and that made it worse. I tried to reason like mistress, calm and cool, but it vere beyond me. Mac never called the maroons names. Suter either, cept for shyte. The tars called me every name in the book.

"I know who I am," I said.

"Uh huh." Jackson chewed on a chicken leg from his pack. "Bout like a girl tryin to bugger another girl."

"What of it, you summa bitch!" I threw myself on him, wailing away with fists that bounced off his huge hands.

"Whoa, whoa!" He grabbed mine shoulders and sat me down, all in control. I spluttered and cried and it vere no act. I tink I vere a poor image of a good girl, playing high and mighty, lording it over poor Jackson the way I'd heard Rob, or the master do. But I didn't like either of them, and was disappointed in mineself, for I vere just some street monkey performing.

I dragged the sleeve of me across mine nose and hiccuped. "Sorry, Jac-Jackson. I don't know who I be without Mac. I don't know why I'm working in Morris house. And I don't like all them fancy clothes. I just want to be Mac's cabin boy."

Jackson pat me on the back a couple times nearly knocking me off the bench. He put a hand on the knee of me and say, "When you can roll a hogshead in the morning, tend animals in the afternoon, and run messages at night, you can harp on me for taking a nap. It no use hurting others cause you angry your life changed."

I patted his knee. He vere right, of course.

"Lookie here," he said. "I call you Gus when we around folk, but I call you Griet when we alone. That way you figure out which one sound best. Lord knows there be a pile of names I answer to and none of em nice as yours."

I gazed at the water. I only had two that I vere called and none insulting as what I called Jackson. "I couldn't have made it in Morris House if not for you. Life going to get better, Jackson. For you at least."

"Not on no ship, it won't." He pointed to the broader bay, the shipping lane and I quickly grabbed the tiller and steered her back to shore. Safer. Quiet. Known.

Mac said a hundred years ago Dutch settlers counted Oxford as the third haven going up the Chesapeake. Its river vere called Tredavon, a better name than a Dutchman calling it Turdhaven, though that vere true once the English came. The Virginie fort sat by a string of islands at land's end. Our little boat rock with each swell and I feel the power of mine sea legs coming back. Oxford's lamplight long gone. A new adventure, and I vere a new person.

There was only Jackson and the shadow of black shore against the sun and I was scared. I questioned myself, becoming diddlewitted, wondering if each cove was really a river. Then mine anger boil as I realize living in a house had made me soft.

In the parlor the night before Yearie pointed to the map. "If you miss the Pocomoke," she said, "you'll sail into shoals at Port Comfort, where the soldiers are." The *Johnson* vere there, too. I mutter to Mac, tinking he can hear me...*find me.*

"Gus, we getting awful far from shore."

"If we get any closer we'll hang up on a tree. I steer. You keep an eye out."

"I got me a blade to kill the river monsters come out o the deep," he laughed.

"Eh, you breaking my wooden shoe, here," I said. Truth be told, Jackson *was* brave and would make a grand maroon if only he could give up Yearie who I tink might never leave her mistress. But for him to be a sailor, I didn't know.

Hours later, the afternoon sun burned our faces, and tall ships plied the middle Bay. Jackson spin a yarn of his days on Handy plantation. I don't know much about terbaccer, just that men die over it. So, he say, all the farming soil nearest the river vere spent at Handy's, and the slaves moved the drying barns inland. One hogshead of terbaccer could weigh more than five wild boar, so one day the slaves decide to pack the bottom with poison oak, laying fresh weed on top. "I roll them to the river and when they get to Morris' inspector, they make Findley burn the whole of it in a bonfire. Well, he covered inside and out, his white ass get a rash like to itch him to hell."

I laughed for it vere good as any sailor's tale. Evening come on the water and the western sky get dusky as we pass between shore and a string of vacant islands. Jackson been sweating in the late sun so he stripped his shirt and poured a bucket of water over his head. His back rippled like a mess of live maggots stuck to his scarred skin. Sick to my stomach, I turned when I see a light deep in the forest. A cabin. Jackson laid his head on a coil of rope to sleep.

The better part of the day vere spent. The hand of me on the tiller, the other dug in mine pack for biscuits and cheese. I washed it down with cider as I watched the western sky, the sun sending streaks of yeller ever which way. There'd be no rain tonight. Mine eyes were bleary and mine stomach bloated. Desperate, I tied the tiller and shook Jackson awake. "I got to catch some winks. If you see shoals, ships or a light, wake me."

He take guard while I curl up on the prow to sleep. No sooner I dreaming than Jackson holler, "Griet, Griet. Look here!"

Sure enough, far in the trees we could see a cluster of light. Not candles in windows. A camp. I snapped up, took the tiller and steered us in. Swarmed by muskeeters, we slapped every inch of bare skin. The cove grew in size and light as we entered and I seen that there were shacks built around its edge, fishing boats anchored safe from the Chesapeake.

"Ahoy. Yer werk oat dem fish in de dark?"

"Sir?" The boat vere gliding right into the bank and I furl the sail quick, tinking maybe this bumpkin know bout the *Fearnaught*. I shout, "We searching for friend, not foe."

"I naught be gainst no man. Woonderin if yer naught fishin, what yer be dayin?"

"Oh, aye," I said, waving Jackson to lie low. "We look for a big frigate, sir. One that come to these waters down the Pocomoke recently."

"Dayn Pocomoke way, yer say?" He scratch his head under his cap.

As we get closer, I threw him a rope and I see he vere old, but he catch it handily to pull us in.

"Naught tellin no tales round here. Who be lookin?" he said.

"A friend, sir," I jump out and stand at attention, trying my best to look trustworthy.

"Whyn't yer come n take a mite er cider? We gits some kern puddin."

"Thank yer. That be mighty fine," I said sounding like him as I adjusted the knife beneath my tunic. I followed him up the shallow bank by a freshwater stream.

"Yer naught brangin dem feller?" he said pointing a gnarled finger at Jackson.

"Nay. He watching the boat for me."

A slow walk inland, we entered a shack, the opening of it vere covered in a sheet of oilcloth and I see a figure bent over a cook fire. Warm and cozy, it vere home to them. But the hearth be loose stone, the chimney full of holes. A fire trap. An old woman turn, her face a wrought of wrinkles and whiskers glowing in the firelight.

"Dis be my mam, Miz Crocket. Me name be George Crocket." He shuffled across the packed dirt floor and waved his arm in the direction of me. "Ye ain't tell me yers."

"Gus, sir. I'm Gus Koop of Oxford." I held my stocking cap in both hands and ducked my head up and down. "Miz Crocket, I thank ye for yer hospitality."

"Oxford, yer say?" she asked, squinting. "Dain't know newbody from up der. Big tradin toan, full o ships."

"Aye, ma'am," I say. "Bringing goods across the Atlantic to unload there."

The old man snort. "Stuff naught make it dayn ere."

I looked round and this were truer than a garden of headless tulips. One room, one window, ready to burn to the ground. Then I saw it. On the shelf vere a tureen that match the plates in Morris house. Two wooden trenchers sat next to it. They both followed my gaze.

"It be last of me dar sistar's crockery," say the old crone.

Sure, I tink. And she be the queen of England. "Aye," I said, "it vere hard for those of us raised in the backwood. I ain't never had much till I met a Scotsman tink we deserve more for our labor."

A glance pass between them. The old man pull out the chair and sit. The crone put a dab o corn pudding on a trencher and set it on the table in front of me. Did the same for her son. He stick his fingers in and scoop it all in his mouth. She give me the stirring spoon from the pot and grab my chin to look at me up close.

"Yar ain't no boy. Ye be travelin wit protection?" she asked.

It vere no use to lie. Country people got a sixth sense. "Yes'm. I got a man in the boat."

"Dain't know but one furcat round dese parts," says the old man, pudding dribbling down his beard.

"Furcat, sir? Oh, frigate, ye mean." I measure the risk and said, "Aye, it would have a big anchor carved on the prow and fly thirteen stripes, red and white." Mr. Crocket leaned back and I sat on the stool to slurp the pudding. If he vere a Loyalist and going to kill me, at least I'd go with a full belly.

"Naught sayin I knew bout it, but folk round ere not be real fond o de king," he say.

"Not saying I know either, but some folk fond of storing English goods for Americans who need them most," I answer.

He reached in his pocket and pulled out a pipe look just like Master's — Viking horns.

I meet his eyes over the bowl as he light it. "Some trade goods come all the way from Germany," I say.

He nod. "De *Fearnaught* come trew ere a day pas-sed. He been might good to us ere in Somer Cove, nigh on ten month. Life changin. Getting bettern. Yer lookin for de Scootsman?"

I licked my lips and nodded. "I need to get a message to him. They going after him in the Atlantic. Oxford sailors on the ship *Johnson* and the Virginie governor for naval support. I got to warn him.

"He be anchored on Smith Island, boy. On de east side off de marshes. How de Scoot goin to spot dat dar ship?"

"She be the prison ship that brung him here, sir. He'll know that ship like the devil it is. It vere armed now with cannon."

"So be he, boy. So be he."

Old Mr. Crocket walked me back to Jackson and tell me to go on home to Oxford where it be safe for a girl. "Ain't noboody but thieves an pirates round ere." He would sail his pirogue through the rough Tangier Sound and find Mac.

"Beggin your pardon, sir. But how'd I know you got the message to him?"

"Yar turst me, or ye give me yer man to tell him. Tha be all I kin do."

I saw the wisdom of this. He showed no surprise when he see the size of Jackson. I introduce them, wary that they sound like long lost Dutch uncles, not trusting either way.

It vere my lot to negotiate a treaty between them, saying Jackson a fugitive of the Morris house and Mr. Crocket receive the stolen goods of it. They form a compact. Jackson don't know how to steer a boat and Mr. Crocket so weak he not able to defend it. I sealed the deal by saying they owed it to Mac, for without him neither got a future. I watch as they sail off, dead reckoning at night, Jackson doubtful and grumbling about a life at sea.

I stood there in the moonlight, watching a bale of turtles still warmed on a fallen limb creekside, reminding me of swamp life and Weocomocus. Her stories of Mother Turtle, the land on which they lived, swirled like the eddies of leaves in dark water. Black with gold patches, the turtles vere painted as the Province flag in Oxford harbor. Talbot stoled everything from the Nanticoke, even their turtle land.

I vere hungry still and built a fire using the striker stored in the boat. Soon it was roaring and, pulling mine knife, I sneak behind the biggest turtle and grab its sleeping self. I stick the blade in its nostril and hold it upside down, letting the blood pour. I wait, listening to the shorebirds caw and smacking the skeeters that light when the wind blow the smoke away from me. Afore long, I turn the shell over and crack open the carapace. Whispering a prayer for its spirit self, I butcher it and roast the pieces over the fire to make a good meal. Satisfied, I kicked out the flames and climbed in the skiff for a nap, covering up under a fine Morris blanket.

Darkness was thick when I woke. I daren't shove off all by mine-self and was feeling quite lonesome, a new circumstance for the likes of me. I tink about Rob and Jackson and vere jealous of them, even though they going in opposite directions. They vere living life while I vere stuck at Morris house. I pondered whether to brave the rough waters to this Smith Island and the Mac, but I had to take the tender boat back to Oxford. Anyway, he'd be right mad at me if I showed mine face without waiting his permission.

Come morn, the sky vere red and orange, clouds like ship masts gathering over the trees in the west. My boat vere small and out in the broad Bay, it be no match for wind and waves. Certain death. I reckoned if I sailed the way I come, with luck I might be there in a day, the tide pushing at the back of me. The sun vere staying up longer, warming the earth. I tried to remember the month and year and all I heard is Mistress saying sweet April showers do spring May flowers, that her baby be christened in May. I tink this be a good happening and maybe I could carve some wooden shoes as a gift. A name day celebration, for her babe, Sally, but I have to get home first. I pause. Home—mine blessing or mine curse?

CHAPTER 40

*N*igh on a week later, I vere wearing my frock coat like a good houseboy, running errands for Morris House, covering up the true feelings of me. We not hear a ting from the *Fearnaught*, or the swamp, not that we expected to know so soon. I had recounted my adventure to Sarah and Yearie, who grinned knowing Jackson vere safe. It vere small consolation, for Master had not returned either. Then we worried they both vere dead as doornails.

At night around the kitchen embers, Sarah, Yearie and Hestia talked about which plantation was reputed to treat their servants and slaves well, tinking they might have to clear out. Hestia growl, saying she'd stick a knife in her neck afore she'd go back to Handy's. Yearie leaned down to tie her shoe and said Philadelphie'd be a good place to go. Hestia smiled and nodded. Sarah nursed her baby, a frown on her face. No talk of including their new houseboy.

The sky filled black with hundreds of passenger pigeons, raining their poop across the harbor. I ducked and thumbed the scrap of paper in mine pocket. Yearie had drawn my morning purchases, candles, soap, fresh fish, and witch hazel from the apothecary. I insisted I knew, it was only four, but she said look, and next to the drawings were words. I studied them and pointed to each, saying the names out loud. She had given me a farthing to buy some dates or lemon drops for me. I wondered if she vere softening up.

Standing on the doorstep of the candlemaker, I had a view of Oxford Road. Horses trotting and farm women calling, I spied the militia stringing along. Raising a shout, I ran home thundering into the kitchen where the women busied, cleaning the hearth.

"Sheriff's back!"

Sarah grabbed the baby from the cradle, and we rushed to the front windows in time to see the procession. Not many soldiers trailed past our door as most had dropped out to their farms along the way. It had been a hard battle. Their horses wheezed, nostrils gray and puffering, some with sword wounds across their shoulders and flanks that glistened in the sun. But it weren't the beasts who suffered most. The men were a band of chimney sweeps, gritty and bedraggled, slumped in their saddles. At the head, Goldsboro sat ramrod on his steed, holding his sword upright, fisted in its gold hilt. The feather on his tricorn drooped and beneath, his profile was stone. My heart was full only because I remembered the gang had made it to the *Fearnaught*. But what of those who didn't sail?

"He's headed to the harbor," say Sarah. "I have to hear his speech because you know he's going to regale us."

We joined Oxford's women and children, the aged and crippled who flocked outside Skillington's, welcoming the men of them home. We Morris women were apt listeners, starved for news of the maroons. I pushed through the crowd, weaving in and out of skirts till I stood at the toe of Goldsboro's booted foot, him looming over us from the deck of a dry-docked schooner.

"It is done," he announced, waving his bloodied sword in the air. "No longer will we feel the threat of these thieves who have stolen from us. We will no longer worry that the swamp scourge will defile our women and steal our children. You may sleep easy tonight, my Oxford, for they are decimated. See the evidence. I have the head of their leader!"

I pushed against the hull and arched mine back to see, dizzy with fear. Gulping air, I tried to scrabble in the arms of a tavern wench who pushed me away. He can't have killed Mac. He can't...

A Skillington yeoman climbed the yardarm, a sack over his shoulder. At the top, he pulled a blackened lump from it and hung it from the spar. I climbed on a carpenter's trestle, wobbling and throwing mine arms out for balance, mine chin raised, eyes under the spar. The head still dripped blood, the hair was light, the eyes hollowed caverns, but...it vere not Mac. It vere Suter.

I had seen much in the Indies, never anything so vile in the colonies. Oxford. It was supposed to be civilized under the king, under the Talbot men. I vere unmoored and fell to the dirt on all fours ready to vomit. I could not yowl though others did. I could not cry though many vere. I choked on the salt air. Not dunderheaded anymore, but clear-eyed looking at the detail of a clam shell under mine nose, the pink and purple ribs that fanned out from its heart, its joint. A shell's perfect defense was never opening up, never allowing anyone in. We had let mine enemy in. Rob. We had made our own undoing. I stood, gripping the shell in mine hand.

The heart of me vere wrenched and I tought this vere enough, *we've had enough* when someone shouted, "Take him down!" and another yelled, "It's a redemptioner!" And last I heard above me, "He's not even a slave, Goldsboro. You've killed one of us."

All the rest joined in, chanting over and over when suddenly a great roar was heard. A strumpet who worked Quinn's tavern tore through the crowd, landing next to me, pushing everyone aside. She stank of gin and sex and unwashed parts. I stepped back to give her the evil eye in case she wanted to touch me. The quiet spread, watching the shrew's act.

"What of Quinn's stable boy, Sheriff?" she growled. "He ain't in your rabble. Johnnie Layton's promised to me and he ain't ere."

Goldsboro's lip curled, but afore he could answer, there vere a tumble of demands from the honorable mothers, sisters, aunts and grandmothers.

"Aye, and Jimmy Dorsey. He were on a blue roan."

"My boy, Bayard Riggin. Did he make it? He wore a red coat from the campaign."

They moved forward, slamming me into the side of the schooner.

"Ephraim Wrangel, Sheriff. You'd know him by his bald head."

And when he did not respond, "Ye don't answer us," said another in frustration, banging her fist on the side of the boat. "We're not standing here to learn of the dead. Tell me if George Abbott lives. He were your first in command!"

I squeezed through the press, tears heavy on mine lashes, making it hard to see. Back with Mistress and Yearie who stood at the side holding the baby, I said, "I guess we can't ask him how the Mac's doing," I whispered.

"Why not?" said Sarah, her eyes bright. She took the baby to her shoulder and shouted big and loud, "Sheriff, Sheriff, what of the survivors?" She stepped on a tree stump and waved her hand, yelling big, "I'm just a poor servant with no master in my home, but I live in fear that the maroons will come in retribution."

The crowd grumbled. It dawned we were in the same straits—alone. Ja! A rusted rifle, a toothless grandfather, or that boy with a crippled leg stood between us and the swamp mob. The insides of me twisted in scorn.

"That's not their leader," shouted Sarah. "You bring no proof, living or dead. Only the head of a Scottish indenture."

A rumble went up in the crowd and all turned to the man on the schooner.

"Your proof is me and what I say!" boomed Goldsboro.

Mac said a man who lied wouldn't look you in the face and, sure enough, he stared over us and shouted, "Go to the swamp, if proof is what you desire, Sarah Wise. See the bodies. They are slave and Indian, none of ours. If your men have not arrived, I cannot account for their lazy ways. Perhaps they sit as we speak at Quinns, swilling ale and toasting their exploits." He pointed the sword tip at us. "You should go home and prepare them a good meal in celebration, for tonight the maroons are gone. We will have no more trouble from that quarter."

The camp—bodies bloodied, and shacks burnt. Vere there enough canoes to spirit away the women and children, Tandy, and those who didn't want a life at sea? Surely some had survived even if Suter hadn't. I couldn't bear the thought of Mac dead.

I made up the mind of me. I would go.

Goldsboro was done speechifying. He sheathed his sword and climbed down into a crowd of mutinous women. Looking up, Sarah smiled as he paused in front of her. With all the care of a baker icing all sides of a cake, he pulled his cat o' nine tails from his bandolier and laid it on her, one shoulder, then the other. Shielding the baby, it caught the side of her face and let a rivulet of blood.

"Teach you to question me in front of the populace. Get thee home, slut."

Being small, I pushed through the mob and dove between his legs, rolling on the ground. "I'm innocent, Sheriff. Do not strike me!" I screamed most piteously. He stumbled over me as the women pushed against him, his booted calves so near they filled mine eyes. Silver spurs caked with mud. Crescent moons on the shaft. I had seen them before, long ago. He roared and swung in a circle, holding the whip ready to punish more. The women surrounded him, and I hopped to the feet of me, squeezing through to Sarah. Yearie jiggled Sally, wailing at her mother's pain. Sarah reached for her baby and we ran. To my delight, Yearie swept Goldsboro's cockhat over her turban, its feather broken, dangling. "However did you get it?" I asked.

"When he fell," she said.

I sidled up to mistress, saying, "I admire your challenge."

She nodded and we heard words of support and rebellion whispered by the rabble as we passed. Mistress vere surprised and Yearie gave her arm a shake. I knew that action. A secret between them. I were snot on a Dutchman's mustache. I cursed, tinking I'd never win these women to the side of me so's they'd share their plans.

But I didn't know Sarah well enough and she surprised me. "Did I tell you that it be a new moon, Gus? Go sow the herbs— garlic and radishes in the kitchen garden. And take my nag to Kate on the morrow and deliver some iron for her blacksmith. I'll have Voltaire pack it for you."

I nodded and hopped back to Morris House. Just as I made for the kitchen door, Yearie smacked the ass of me and when I whirled on her, she put a clove of garlic and a small spring onion in mine palm. "Eat them. You'll hear a devil's story, and this'll make you strong."

I tink mostly they would make me putter mine way to East Town.

CHAPTER 41

I left halfway to noon. The iron in the saddlebags was an excuse of course, so she added a lady's saddle from the warehouse. Always making a lie. Tied to Ol Bets' haunches, I worried it might fall off. I rode easy. A breezy, sunny day, there vere no bugs, making it good for lallygagging. I'd grown accustomed to not having to scratch all the time. We clattered into Kate's stable yard after noon and I vere, as usual, hungry. I smelled the baking from the window. Kate's face poked out.

"Ye here, Gus?" Then louder, in case someone vere listening, "Ye bringing me goods to run me business, or ye just stopping to ate again?"

Wenetko smiled and took the nag as I scurried inside. In the shadow of the kitchen stair sat Tandy, his head in a bloody bandage, his clothes black and smelling of swamp, but he welcomed the sight of me. Kate shushed us with her hand.

"Aye, me Douglas gone, roundin up the rest and leading them north to the Indian river. He left outta ere back three days ago," she say, "but, we don't know who might come into me yard so keep it low."

Excited, I could barely hold down mine voice. "To Weocomo-cus? I should go. Wenetko can ride me. I want to see my old mother."

Tandy rose and say, his voice raspy thick from swamp fire, "She be daid, Griet. Long gone. We all knew, but Mac say not to tell ye. Her son Robin leadin that band, what's left of em."

Kate stepped to her door watching the yard, her back to me.

I grabbed a biscuit off the table and turned to hide a tear, stuffing the mouth of me. The last mother of me gone, I barely remembered her face now. Mumbling, crumbs falling, I asked, "What happened in the swamp, Tandy? Did they make it?"

A silence like waters stilled, then, "At first," he said, "we hide, smoke cover our positions. They rushed us across the water. They horses get caught on the roots, so's the first wave be easy. We thinkin we a winnin. But afore we knew what were happening, the rest of em slave boys, fresh from lumbering, tore across the bridge with axes and saws, tree limbs even. Anythin they could use. We so surprised the likes of our black skin be our enemy that at first, we didn't have our heart in it. Mac and the rest held fast a gunnin, but when they couldn't reload fast enough, we took to the sword."

I grunted and drew my sleeve across the table, clearing it of crumbs. Pulling a stool, I sat. "Did you kill them all, Tandy?" I asked.

"There be so many, Griet. They swarm the camp, so we surround em and struck as many from they horse as we could, stickin em in the chest. Some boys went mad and stabbed the same over and over, not thinkin to look behind for another ready to cut they throat. We held our line in front of the longhouses where our women an chil-dren hide but we forces be split in two."

His eyes filled with hunger, "You think that be good—we get them comin and going, but it weren't so, cause they outnumber us. Done torched the longhouses and the canoes, pushin the women an children in the water. They were after Suter. They hacked the rest to death as they ran."

Tandy began to cry like a bird warbling and I went over to wrap mine arms round him. His shoulders shook, this man strong after torture at the hand of Findley. He struggled to talk and when I said, "Hush," he waved at me and continued.

"Mac called us to retreat and carry anybody alive any way we could. I lost him along the way and hid in the swamp water for a day, freezing, waiting for Goldsboro and his men to leave. Some gave up the ghost and floated away, pretending death that took them later. I crawled under dead bodies as the sheriff came close, him dragging the water with a branch looking for those alive.

"Then, sure as it started, it were over. Goldsboro stood on a pile of dead men, a yellin that he be our master, that we bow to him. If'n he see the whites of our eyes, he goin to pursue us, drag us to the gallows and hang us to an inch of our life. Griet, he say he goin set us on fire to make a spectacle worth watchin." Tandy raised his hand as if he vere Goldsboro, "'Mark me,' he say, 'this be no idle threat for any man who makes his home in this swamp.'"

I squeezed his big shoulder and sat on the step, to tink. It best not to tell him of Suter. "Tandy," I said, "You can't stay here. Mac escaped down Pocomoke way on the *Fearnaught*. I have it reliable from a resident down there. The gang vere headed to St. Domingue last I heard, with a Virginie naval force on his tail. You want to join them? I can get you there."

His bloodshot eyes roamed me over and I knew he felt my position had changed, that I looked the enemy in my gentle dress, but he said, "You been a good swamp boy, Griet, and someday soon you ain't be able to hide your true self." He stood tall. "I cain't be what I'm not. I be a farmer, not a sailor. I'll head north and maybe make it to Philada. Them Quakers there, I hear they kind to free slaves."

Kate broke up our confab. "Lookie here, little Griet. Yer stay close to Sarah Wise. Nobody let that woman down."

"I don't know," I said, "she vere not given any help from the midwives. Yearie and me had to birth that baby." I tapped the arm of her. "Working folk of Oxford tink a French privateer threatens their existence, or so Goldsboro tells them. They not trusting anybody no more."

"Only weak-minded sheep believe the wolf at the gate every waking minute. Yer sheriff hold the midwives' feet to the fire so's they not help Sarah, and we hear the town think the worst of them for it. He got a terrible axe to grind over her."

"Mistress Kate, the heart and mind of Goldsboro a two-headed viper. He brought the skull of a maroon to us and dangled him from a yardarm yesterday. Fear vere a big talker."

"News travels fast, Griet. We heard last night. And the people of East Town be disgusted. I guarantee Oxford folk no different. Sheriff be no Christian."

"Take care of Tandy. He vere mine gang and now I'm with women. If Mac send a message either way, we share." I gave each a hug and passed Yearie's conjure bag on to Tandy for his trip north.

Outside, I plodded to the stable, the shoulders of me sinking. Seeing Wenetko holding Ol Bets, his bear-bone necklace around his neck, I vere reminded of how long I'd known him. Five years old when I came to the reservation, I had little memory of it now.

"Wenetko, we are long on six years I reckon of remembering together. Can you tink of the first day I came to Weocomocus with Papje?"

He look at me all but cross eyed. "Little girl not come with Papje. Came before Vanderkoop. You came to old reservation with Yellow Eyes, Oxford sheriff."

I nearly fell over, a lightning bolt struck. Half-moon spurs. "Yellow Eyes?"

Wenetko sat down on a low fence rail bringing his eyes level with mine. "He say you were orphan. Town not want you. He order us stop hunting land he call Rich Range. You were poor trade for our peoples."

I laughed. "Poor trade, eh? Is there a good trade for Indians and orphans?"

Solemn, Wenetko look down at his moccasins. "Yellow Eyes run us off reservation to swamp. Robin carry you. Maroons welcome our ways, so we teach them. They need help to make boat, so we raided shipyard and bring back Vanderkoop."

"And I became Papje's daughter," I said. Singing with another girl, running with sticks, trying to teach her to milk a cow, she vere blue-eyed and light-haired like me. A rhyme we diddled, me to her, *patta cake, patta cake.* "Who am I, Wenetko?"

He scratch his head searching, and say, "Tyan."

I plunked down next to him. "Do you know who my parents vere?"

He look at me surprised. "Weocomocus and Mac," he say.

CHAPTER 42

September 2, 1749
        Nobody hear about Mac and the gang. Like he disappeared. So, I worked the scullery, the garden, the laundry and the stalls, cursing Jackson the whole time and pushing back memories of a life before the swamp. I wanted to curse Mac. I wanted to curse Weocomocus. Mostly, I wanted to kill the sheriff. I worked like a bee darting from flower, to hive, to plant, and back again. The only consolation was Yearie watched me, and seeing I take the load off her some, she bring me into the fold. Though one night in particular, it vere not where I wanted to be.

Master had returned after a month at sea, angry and tight-mouthed. First thing, he packed up all the account books. On the way out the back door, he stumbled over a basket of peaches Hestia had left there and roared that he would be rid of her yet. I scurried to pick them all up and move the basket, bowing and scraping in an offer to help. He cursed me and said to get out of his way, a look to kill on his face. His meetings with Goldsboro were now held at the warehouse so's we couldn't listen. And, saddest of all, he avoided his baby like she had the plague. After one glance he not even ask her name. So Reverend Bacon christened her little Sarah...our Sally, and Yearie prayed over her through June a mix of Bible words and incantation.

Nursing day and night, Mistress carried her in a sling under her breast. Being haggard and tired, m'lady ask Morris if she can move upstairs to the garret with Sally, and he yelled, "Please, get out of my room!" Relieved, m'lady took me with her and my straw pallet in the kitchen vere settled on the garret landing. Sometimes the babe's thin cry wouldn't wake her mam and I would rise and bring her to suckle, then drop back to sleep at the open door.

Master drink heavy, worry over his accounts, but nothing stop his visits to Quinn's for gossip. Late one evening, Sarah take the babe in arms and bid us goodnight. Yearie and old Hestia finish the kitchen chores and close up the hearth. As they trudge to the slave cabin, I vere left with feeding the horses and I cursed Jackson one more time for leaving me.

The night vere warm so I took off my vest, shoes and stockings and walked barefoot across the smooth shells to the stable. They felt cool on my feet but the soft dirt of the stable vere mine carpet, like being in camp with the maroons. I threw an armful of hay in each stall and rubbed Ol Bets' soft nose. Her watery eye gleam in the light of mine lantern and I vere tempted to bed down with her to get a good night's sleep. She snortled. I kissed her. I thought, here I vere taking care of a baby that veren't mine family and living a life foreign to me.

The Indians had whispered about Yellow Eye in camp, but it never made me no mind as I understood now I vere only a child trying to figure a new place. Walking to the kitchen, I felt an unease as if mine life vere not mine own, but a lie crafted to aid people I didn't know. Not for fun like a sailor's yarn. All my distant memories and none jibed with the other.

Sunlight. A buzzing beehive, a pretty lady with light hair holding the comb dripping with honey. Singing a lullaby, playing patta cake, and kneeling by the fire mine hands pointed in prayer. Her voice distant but soft and full of love. And then, another hearth and another woman with a sharp voice, and little boys I vere left to watch. The boy who burned mine foot. The mother angry and a girl, her eyes big, saying she vere sorry, it vere her shtoopud broeder.

More than this I didn't know, but I knew this vere no time to tell mistress, for I vere naught ready to go to another strange house, especially if it meant wearing skirts and stays.

I caught a chill and shivered. The kitchen door was open, a candle lit inside and I thought Yearie must have returned for something. I skipped in mine hoppy way to the door. Master's horse vere tied to the post and Tray vere curled on the doorstep. He sat in the armchair, nursing an ale. Waving, he said, "Your mistress sleeps and suckles her babe. I didn't have the heart to wake her, so you will have to answer."

"Sir? Answer what?"

"There's rumor at Quinn's you helped the hog roller escape. That you and Jackson took the tender boat."

"Sir," I said, thinking fast and bowing my head afraid of his whip, "I took the tender a month back to pick up sailcloth at Cambridge. Jackson vere gone when I returned."

"Who wanted sailcloth? I should've had plenty here."

"A plantation, sir. Don't know which one as they came to get it next day by the Oxford Road. Nobody tells me, sir."

"That so... I'll check with Callister." Pinching mine cheeks in his hand, he leaned near. "Don't ever lie to me, boy. I'll turn you out in the woods."

I wrenched away, rubbing the face of me. "Yessir," I said burning inside. "Do that." Putting me out in the woods, says he and I answered him back. "Trees be a friend of me, sir. Better'n the house of you."

Startled, he slammed his tankard down. We stared at one another and, of a sudden, he laughed. "Right outspoken, boy. I like that."

I went above stairs and stripped to mine shirt, shaking in mine shoes. Sarah snored soft, Sally nestled in the crook of her body. I picked her up and laid her in the cradle tinking this vere not the best family I could pick, but at least I had them figured.

CHAPTER 43

*E*arly October, 1749

      Being closed up, wings clipped, knowing the square acres of Oxford and nothing more vere a terrible thing. Our work never ended and I vere amazed that one man could require so much. The cabinets and shelves on either side of a new fireplace in the gathering room vere still in the works. The dust from carpentering inside Morris House floated in streams of sunlight till it hit the wood floors, making footprints everywhere we walked. All three of us polished at night on our hands and knees while Hestia kept the kitchen.

In my days with Mac, I could garden, cook, wash and fetch for thirty tars and still have more time for the desires of me than I did in Morris House. But I never got no learning with the swamp gang. Now, it were constant. I carried scraps of paper in mine pockets and a pencil behind mine ear like the carpenters in the front room. I tink, if nothing else, I look the part.

More than a year had passed. The town folk whisper when Goldsboro walk by. He begun to charge everywhere he went. Master and him confabbed of capturing Mac and the gang. They pursued money and connections and Morris' merchanting blossomed without our thieving.

No word of the ghost ship. Every captain who docked in Oxford harbor was questioned at length. They would laugh and say there vere a sighting in Indian River or the Carolina Banks in Blackbeard's old haunt, but I knew none had traveled to St. Domingue. Gildart called his phantom enemy a *jimmy round* for he heard that's what the French tars say when their ships vere boarded. *Je me rend; I surrender*—words that never came out of Mac's mouth so I knew Gildart hadn't found him. When I made Master's deliveries to Quinn's, tales of looting and burning the Crown's ships on the high seas sauced the tables like spilt beer. The ears of me pricked for these stories. Sarah yearned to hear more. We dared never ask, but at night sitting at the kitchen fire when Master vere gone, I told tall tales of our swamp life, and Sarah corrected mine words like a professor.

So, our system of stealing from Morris vere done. Gone with Jackson, the maroons and Mac. Yearie took it the worst, never farting her real thoughts, now she vere silent *and* sad. The excitement still burned in our blood when one day, mopping mortar dust round Morris' desk, I stopped to count the number of letters. Piles of them vere stacked high next to a stick of red wax and a crested ring.

I picked up the ring—heavy, it rolled in mine palm.

"You best not touch that."

I turned and smiled at Sarah who stood at the door, a broom in her hand, little Sally clawing her skirt to nurse as her big tongue pushed out. "What be the letter engraved on it?" I asked.

"Are you twelve, Gus, and you don't know it? A strange print, it's a C for Cunliffe. Our master in Liverpool. The one who owns this merchant empire. Goods, ships, sailors, slaves. It's all his and his sons'."

"What? Morris is not the master?"

"No, dear. He is only one factor who makes it all work on this side of the ocean. Only here on the Chesapeake. In Oxford."

"The warehouses are not his?"

"Cunliffe's." She pointed to the stack. "Some of those missives are from London and Liverpool, some from Annapolis, and advance notices of our ships rounding the Virginia Cape. But that pile, there, are about the coming horse races in East Town and the balls that follow them."

"Balls?" I pictured horses dragging great leather balls in a race.

"You *are* an innocent. Grand dances where the wealthy dress in their finery to impress each other. See here, this is from Plimhimmon."

Across from the harbor, terraced lawns that overlooked the cemetery. "Will you go?"

"Me?" She laughed. "I'm a housekeeper, Gus. And, truly, the only reason why Robert is asked is because he finances the purchase of their slaves. They're all in debt to Cunliffe, especially Handy."

This talk was over the head of me a little. I whispered, "Do you read all of these, mistress?"

"Certainly. I am charged with keeping his affairs in order."

I grinned. "A housekeeper with guts in her brains. We'll figure out a way to get this to Mac."

She laughed and sat the baby on the carpet. Little Sally stuck her fist in her mouth and rolled over. Sarah laid her on her belly and scanned the view out the window looking for Master. "I have no time to engineer a network, Gus. Never mind we don't know where Mac is."

"He knows where we are." I dumped the ring on the letters. "I tink these missives remind me of his tent table. Difference is the town folk round here whisper but don't write for fear of the sheriff."

She blinked and pressed her lips. "Why do you say 'tink?' It makes you sound like a Dutch yokel. If you're going to speak about your thoughts then say, 'think...th, th. Understand? Say it."

"I *think* I vere thirteen, missus, and it vere time for us to create an adventure," says I.

"I *think* it *were*, Gus, *were* time for you to learn to read and write if it's adventure you want," says she. It weren't long before the lessons began.

"'For I know the plans I have for you,' de, de, dec..." read I, stammering.

Yearie peered over the shoulder of me at the open Bible. "Declares. Start over," she said.

"'For I know the plans I have for you, declares the Lord, plans to pro-sper…uh, prosper you and to not harm you, plans to give you hope and a fut…fu-ture, future.'" I finished and sighed.

"Rely on the Lord to give strength in time of trouble, Gus," say Yearie as she stirred the batter for a peach cake. "Just remember it be your head that git you out of it."

I slammed the Bible shut. Sarah appeared at the kitchen door. "The carpenters and mason are leaving today, Yearie. Robert brings home two more slaves to replace Jackson. William in the stable and George on the harbor will come here at night. Tell them to take the new slave quarter across the way with Voltaire and show them bedding in the attic."

"The chimney and bookcases finally be finished?" she asked, her face happy.

"Thank the Lord. We can stop mopping the dust. I'll help you move the dining boards in later and put the curtains back up. Gus, you watch Sally."

"But, missus," says I, "Master want me to run errands for him on this morn. Letters for the merchants in town he says to deliver."

"Well, they'll have to wait. We can't handle the post for everyone."

Sally whimper and Sarah swing the cradle with the tip of her toe. Her hands full of folded lace. She set it on the sideboard. "There are new missives on his desk?"

"U-huh," say Yearie. "We waitin till he drink himself to sleep or peek at them now? There be one from a rider down Virginie Cape."

"Announcing ships once a wind picks up. I wonder how many?" Mistress speculate, sly as a blue-eyed cat. "Three in harbor that need repairs. The Atlantic storms have been terrible."

"If one were Gildart's slave ship, that tie up accounts subtracting the dead," I answer.

A knock were heard at the door. I lean back in my chair and see Voltaire on the ladder, painting the entrance hall. He utter a *pish pish* and hop to the floor. I don't have to get up but train my eye on the visitor. Another rider I don't recognize.

"I bring material orders from merchants in East Town," he says.

Sarah, Yearie and I look from one t'other. Orders from East Town always go to the warehouse now, not to the house. How's it this rider didn't know?

"I'll take them, Voltaire," shout Sarah, rushing to the door. "Thank you, young sir. Do you need some drink? You are welcome in the kitchen."

"Thank ye," he say, "Ahl be on me way back to the coach house. Douglas and Kate ave more work on this day." He put two fingers to the side of his head, a sign I recognize from the tars. A French sailor telling an English to fook off. He grinned.

She walk brisk like and wave us come-come to the under-stair storage. "Yearie and Gus," she say for Voltaire to overhear, "Master will do some entertaining shortly. The silver is due to be polished."

Voltaire groaned for it fall to him mostly. Seeing us enlisted, he brush the paint more studiously. Never would he make a jack tar. In the closet, with Sarah blocking the door, she held the letters to the light from the hall.

"This is the one," she say.

I see the wax stamp of a ship and jump up and down whilst she read.

September 23, 1749

Dear Morris House,

May the Lord bestow his Grace on your Endeavors. We are ready to depart this City and wish to drop you a line. Since my last Visit with Sheriff Goldsboro, I have determined a propitious Visit to your Warehouse to 'purchase goods' is possible within a Month, during the Fall Social Season. I wish to meet with the sheriff again to discuss his Future with us. Your Advice is welcome. Providence has been bountiful, more than we could deserve. Thanks to the Good Goldsboro, many in town are determined to help us. We retain an unalterable Affection, unchanged by Time and Distance. Give our best to all in your House.

Your entire,
A. Tosh

"Tosh, it were now?" I said, giggling. "Do you have a list of ships, mistress? What bring they? When will they come?"

"Shh, Gus, calm down," she said, and I felt the hand of Yearie on my shoulder. "Fill Robert's glass heavy tonight. When he goes to bed, I'll say we must finish hanging the sheets in the yard. Then we'll hide between them with the lists and plan our action. I must get word to the tailor."

"See, Gus?" says Yearie. "The Lord say, make a plan for hope and future."

PART IV
IMMEASURABLE WORTH

It's a veritable Tower of Babylon, the way you people bubble on.
- Moliére, *Tartuffe*

CHAPTER 44: THE PLAN

Life is a jest, and All things show it; I thought so once, But now I know it.
- John Gay

SARAH

The next morn was clear of clouds, windless and warm with Indian summer when Robert left with his whip and George in tow. Griet went to muck the stable with William, a terrified Guinea slave from Handy's. From the look of their anatomy, he and George were so much flotsam, simple payment owed since Handy cannot make ends meet. Yearie, Hestia and I were absorbed in kitchen chores when I heard our master bellow from the yard. He wanted the letter announcing ships rounding the Cape I had forgotten to give him. A mistake I couldn't afford. We needed our morning time to plan.

I met him on the threshold as Griet came, buttoning her brown waistcoat, a pencil above her ear. She was fingering the lists in her pocket. One was of cargoes for Jeremiah to take to East Town, the other Griet's deliveries for Robert.

"Gus, you haven't left yet?" he called.

I waved my hand in warning. "Yes, Master. Coming," she said.

"Let me see your list. I want to add to it," he said.

I interrupted, but he silenced me. Could she draw the list of errands from her tight pocket? She grinned at his slick face. Beads of sweat dotted his forehead. His whip was tucked into his waistband.

She brushed her hand over the crop of her hair and looked down. Out came a list and as she handed it to him, I watched the other drop to the ground. I stepped over it.

He took the pencil from behind her ear and scribbled. "You have seven stops after the warehouse. Callister is waiting for you. I just added the smithy. You'll need to tow the cart for his new implements."

"Yessir."

"Well, get on with you."

"Yessir." He waited to see her run. I looked down. The list with their ship loads, their dates and an X to show if they had cannon. The list to A. Tosh. I picked it up.

"What is that, Sarah?" he asked.

"My list for Hestia is all. We're pickling cabbage today."

"You're reading Sarah's list now, boy?"

"Ja, mistress draw symbols for words I not learned yet."

I tossed my head for her to be off. He laughed heartily and clapped her back. "Let me hear you read your list," he said. "Sarah is a good teacher. Someday maybe you'll cipher enough to work in the warehouse, Gus." He turned to me and glanced back at Griet.

She bounced her head from side to side. "Oh, ja, ja. That'd be a great honor sir," she said as she ran.

He called her to come back, but she waved and shouted that she had to get busy or would never finish. I heard him say, "Admirable, Sarah, that Dutch boy. He grows bigger."

He mounted his horse and left to my relief. It had been more than a year since we'd run secret messages and I worried I was rusty. I would have to deliver to the tailor myself. I returned to the kitchen and with few words we chopped all the cabbage, prepared for lunch and dinner and I checked to see that Voltaire had emptied the chamber pots above stairs. Finally, I sat to nurse. Sally's big tongue did not get in the way and soon she was fast asleep. Yearie pulled at my apron strings and told me to be off. And so, it began.

Rounding the corner on Market Street I ran into Griet bent and lugging her full cart behind her across the rutted road. I grabbed one handle and soon we were at the smithy's door. Next the tailor.

"Look," she said, pointing to his window boxes planted with white chrysanthemums the color of Griet's hair. A perfect match. Jeremiah sat inside. He stood when we entered.

"M'lady. Gus, you getting tired of running errands?"

"Better'n cutting cloth," she said like they were old friends. "Morris keeps me busy delivering warehouse stuff outside and scrubbing mouse holes for turds inside. I don't never go anywhere."

"Gus," I said and slapped her shoulder. "It's not that bad."

"Nobody goes anywhere anymore," reeled Jeremiah. "Oxford be in the hands of Talbot men, for sure."

I drew the list from my pocket and put my finger to my lips. "Is your father here?"

Gus piled a bolt of silver damask good for a ball dress on the counter. The tailor stepped from behind a curtain. He saddled his nose with spectacles and said, "What have ye, yer butter-bug tar?"

"A Dutch sailor, ya say? More cloth," she replied.

"If we're alone, I have news." I said. He nodded and I opened the list. His eyes grew wide and a slow smile spread like apricot jelly on his face. "Are the dates accurate, mistress?"

"Not counting for storms on the Atlantic. October brings surprises."

"Aye. A busy month it is. We'll have to plan together, Mrs. Wise. Do you know his intentions?"

"To make it harder on my master?" To put an end to Gildart's ship?

"Aye, a good thing. Cunliffe and Morris squeeze us, mistress." He turned to his son. "Jeremiah, a ride to Kate's is in order. Mac sails in these parts."

My body tingled like an electric eel touched my little toe. Griet hopped about in excitement. We were off to the races.

GUS

*M*orris make William his jockey for the East Town race. Early one brisk morn, we had mucked the stalls and I were beset with tasks of William since he were not good at remembering. A shaft of light catch me bending over to pick up the waistcoat of me when I look up at a shadow.

"That not be the shape of no Gus," said Jeremiah.

Fast, I find the sleeves and push mine arms in. "What business were it of you?" I ask. "I carry the weight of me round here better'n this sapling slave boy, so you keep the mouth of you shut, Jeremiah."

He shrugged. "I can keep a secret." Then, "We have word of a plan that's brewing on the water."

I took him by the elbow and walked him to the back of a stall, the one where Jackson used to nap. "What kind of plan?"

"Once Gildart's ship is ready to unload, send us word. Mac plans a raid."

"But, we're not safe. The cannon," I said. "The militia."

"The East Town horse track runs the 25th. There will be pique-a-niques before the race and the ball at Plimhimmon. Everyone will be in attendance…the ship captains, Goldsboro and his militia."

"What do we do?"

"Talk to Quinn about making his theatre for the sailors. A dry run, readying for the play on Sunday after Saturday's ball for the gentle folk. Mistress Wise will lead us on stage. Papa lines up the players."

"Morris will want to be there and screw his fiddle."

"He'll be at Plimhimmon. We've seen to it that he'll have an invitation...without Mrs. Wise." Jeremiah strutted off, full of importance.

I didn't know about theatre and walked inside in search of enlightenment. Yearie, Hestia and Sarah were gathered in a circle around master's kitchen chair, looking down like they were ready to ring a ring o rosie. I peeked between their skirts and, lo, little Sally sat on her bum grabbing a leg to pull herself up. She were heavy and the chair shifted. Sarah cooed, put her hand on the rail and the child grunted. More than a year and a half had passed since her birth and, finally, she stood, pushing her tongue in and out, her fat hands gripping tight. You would have thought the sun popped out of the moon's tail. Lord, the clapping and squealing.

"Sarah... Sarah." No response. "Mistress!" I shouted over the din. "What's a theatre?"

"Uh-uh, what? A theatre? As in a play? It's a story that's acted out with talking in front of people. And the best is when there is music and song." She picked up her slow babe and tossed her in the air. "Why do you ask?"

"Jeremiah says to ask Quinn to put one on with you for the 25th."

"The day of the race? It's St. Crispin's Day. Why?"

"To keep the sailors busy while all of Talbot is at the ball."

She dove into me, throwing Sally on her hip, her face in mine. She were so smart. "A plan? It's going to happen?" She threw back her head and giggled. "It's too rich. The Battle of Agincourt relived in Oxford, only Talbot loses."

Sometimes when Sarah spoke, there were not a word I understood.

"Never mind, Gus. It's Shakespeare—the story of a king and his victory." She scuttled out but not afore throwing Sally in mine arms.

I sat so's not to drop her. I kept hearing of this man, Shakespeare, and wondered who he were. When she returned, she laid a little book in the lap of me and read the title, *"The Beggar's Opera.* Oxford will see its women wear honor greater than any king's." Her chin up, she curtseyed at Yearie and me.

"Do this be your Shakespeare?" I asked.

Her laugh were music and she say, "No, m'love. But he would approve."

The next day, I asked her if she would play Polly, who would play MacHeath?

"We won't get to the second act, dear Gus," she said.

YEARIE

*T*be the one to post opera broadsides. A day so free an hopeful, I spit out nails and hammer them notices onto ever post I see. Comin to the warehouse, I be thinkin Hestia bout ready for a new kitchen pot. The storage doors swung wide on the water, seagulls sitting atop the wharf posts, shriekin to they mateys. A cold afternoon, my breath puffed in clouds, marking a coming frost.

Mr. Callister be engaged with a group of town craftsmen and I strolled the aisles, remarking on the variety. The pier filled with wrapped goods for the fall dances an I fancied the warehouse need rearrangin to store it all. The workers be slaves like me, and, proud of they work, they gabbed like magpies. Callister and his group walk by.

"Sir, how many ships be in harbor come Friday?"

He squint his pale eye, annoyed at my asking. "Three bound our way. Two loading now."

Blocking his path down the aisle, I pointed to the harbor.

"Get out of my way, Yearie," he said. "You know the *Johnson* waits for timber from the swamp."

Six by Saturday's opera. A town full of sailors, three ships fresh from ocean crossins, and Gildart's tars a suckin gin at the tavern an carousin in the streets. All on leave for St. Crispin's holiday. I ran to tell Sary.

She be stirring a pot in the stable yard. "Time for the witch's berry?" I ask.

"I was just readying the pot. Master's gone to Cambridge."

I rubbed my hands afore the flames. A few steps to the garden, and I pull the plant, stalk, an flower from the fence where it be growin wild. We break it, twist it and roll it between our fingers and throw it in the pot. Alarmed at our foolishness, we look at each other and took off for the kitchen soap to wash our hands.

"Smell it," she say, on returning to the pot.

I put my nose over it and drew, creatin a fog in my head like to spin a top. "Jimsonweed sweet," I say." A guarantee of my freedom. With that, I beckon Tray from the kitchen. The poor dog bounced to us, hopeful of a morsel. Scooped a tin of tea from the pot and tossed in dried pork, settin it on the ground. Tray sniffed and lapped, his tail wagging. Finished, he sat on his backside and looked for more. I laughed. "I'll not be killin master's dog. Go on, Tray." I clapped my hands and he wandered toward the kitchen.

Not half a length he began to wobble. Draggin his paws like a gun dog wore out, he keeled over. We both ran.

Sary passed her hand over his snout. "He breathes, thank God."

"There be hell to pay if that dog bite the dust."

She grinned. "I guess we know the weed will work."

Gus come to the door and set Sally on the stoop. "Is Tray dead?"

"No," I say, "they not get me for killin it. I got plans." Plans I not be sharin.

Sarah hum a tune I remembered, then she sang,

> And if rich men, like us, were to swing,
> Twould thin the land, such numbers to string
>
> Upon Tyburn tree.

It's an air from the opera. How do I sound?" she asked.

"If one of us hang on Tyburn Tree, then all of us hang," says Gus. "On Oxford's harbor under Sheriff's order.

I turned away from them. "Not me. The two of you can swing without this house slave."

Sary wrapped her arms round Gus and swung her about. "Oh, we're naught but beggars three, are we?"

They having a thrill and I folded my arms and watched.

CHAPTER 45: THE PLAY

The Queens of Corinth and Their Subjects

SARAH

*C*arding wool with Yearie of an evening, I practiced my role as we cleaned the yarn. Gus choked with laughter on my song. Robert had eaten early and gone back to the Custom House.

"Murder is a fashionable crime," I sang with a wink. It was the perfect role of a soubrette, trilling and flirting with an audience. We giggled and Gus pulled her dagger on me, but Yearie seemed pressed, not ready to let herself enjoy. She was not herself. The next morn, I found her in the stable sitting cross-legged on the floor, praying to her mama. She glared and said, "Begone." I was wounded being cut out of her life and trudged to the kitchen.

Cold began to seep under the kitchen window by Thursday, and I pulled the oil cloth over it just as Robert came from the harbor with a pile of orders. He threw his great coat on the floor and told me to press his lace jabot. He looked freshly shaved, his nails cleaned and a beauty mark at the corner of his eye. Ready for the ball. Solicitous, I put the iron on the hearthstone and in the soothing voice I used for him, explained that if he wanted the part of Mr. Peachum in the play he would need to rehearse.

"I have no time, woman."

"Tomorrow, in the parlor after supper sir, we will run through

Peachum's lines, for he is critical to the play's success. He is the thieves' leader, the gang's king."

"And how will I know what to do on stage?"

"The rehearsal is Saturday at the start of Plimhimmon's ball. All the sailors in town are invited."

He stormed about shouting for me to change it. "I am attending the ball and can't do both, you fool. Why do I need to entertain a lot of drunken sailors?"

I frowned and sympathized, but said it was not my choice. "Quinn wants his tavern sluts to rehearse whilst the ball is in progress so they might work his beds later."

"Always after money, Quinn," said Robert, tossing his whip on the table. I glanced at Yearie, but dared not roll my eyes. As if he was not the king of profit and revenge. Yearie had warned me to hide my loathing, for it was too apparent.

In the parlor that night I plied him with wine, and soon he agreed to the rehearsal if he could leave for Plimhimmon after. I told him it were a good plan as he will be in a fine mood to remind all the gentry to come Sunday afternoon. I stroked the keys of his harpsichord and sang him a ditty, then, satisfied, took Sally above stairs to think.

Robert had little musical talent though the crowd at Quinn's wouldn't care as long as their pints were full. He could saw on his strings and sing the role of Peachum, his mirror image. If that little tidbit were not lost on me, it would not be lost on the sailors no matter how drunk they were. He took no note of our scheming, thought we had been rehearsing the troupe at Quinn's during the day. But we rehearsed far more than the opera, duping Quinn as well.

The sun rose on St. Crispin's Day with great fanfare, heralding a fiery scarlet glow over bare trees in town. Robert rode out midmorning on his stallion with William, his jockey, trailing on the racehorse. There would be much betting, and some would lose their fortunes. Yearie, Hestia and I made good order in the kitchen. Gus returned from the stable, her face shining.

"Gus, gather the sack of bodices for the tavern. The doxies will sing refrains as queens of Corinth," I said.

Swinging my indigo gown over my shoulder, torn and bedraggled as a proper harlot would wear, I had dared Robert to criticize me and seeing the look in my eyes, he let it go. We threw some chipped crystal and dented pewter, corn cob pipes and silk scarves into the pony cart to decorate the tavern. Quinn had been in salutary spirits since his first stage was built by Skillington carpenters. He said he had a vision it would become a center of high-born theatre. A pawn in our game.

I drove the pony cart to the tavern's back door where Quinn came to greet us. Yearie sat on the bench and Gus hopped around in back.

"M'lady. Your beauty graces my establishment tonight with all the glory of your renowned voice." He gave me a hand to step down.

"It's all honey or dung with you, Quinn," I said. Yearie hooted and clapped her mouth.

Gus snapped, "Why not ya give her horse a ladder to climb?"

He cursed at us and disappeared. We dragged the theatre property inside where the doxies descended on us, chattering away.

"M'ladies." I clapped. "We must practice. The sailors will arrive in three hours." They pushed and shoved, swearing for places, but sat eventually round a table where I passed out the lyrics hoping some could read what they didn't remember. It was a hopeless thought, wishing whores to be educated beggars. Still, they only had to remember words of old ballads.

Gus put a pipe in her mouth and pulled a chair into their midst, propping a foot upon it like a seasoned sailor. "Listen, you hopper-arsed tarts, we're not studying cards of the four kings tonight. No betting, no pickpocketing. Ya putting on a performance. Practice makes perfect." Stunned, they stared at the Morris houseboy who spoke like a tar. I waved Quinn over.

He lorded it over his women, saying, "Let me give the introduction." Looking at his house empty of all but tables, chairs and a wayward artist setting up his easel, he bowed and swept his hand across the missing audience, "I be Quinn, your host tonight at Oxford's first theatre. Drink hearty, mateys, but I caution ye not to judge an opera of highwaymen." Holding a script in the air, he said with great fanfare, "For this is a story of a band of thieves on the take for themselves against the gentry. All the while, they be at each others' throats in betrayal. That devil, Mr. Peachum, leader of the gang, is played by the illustrious Master Morris, his daughter, Polly, by the estimable Mrs. Wise." Then he bowed to me like a regular gentleman and turned to the painter, who held a brush between his teeth, "Paint me in front of these ladies so's I can hang it by the front door with me name above it."

I laughed. Quinn was paying to have a portrait done. I looked closely and saw a jar of water sat next to the artists elbow. Whatever came of his work, a pastel painting of swishes and swales would yellow quickly in a room of tobacco smoke.

"Aye, yer a blue stockinged woman can read yer letters," called Johnnie Layton's girl.

He had never returned from the swamp battle, and she was a hardened woman with spit in her eye and sour on her tongue. "Whyn't ye head to the ball with the rest of them ladies and gents?" she said.

"Because I naught be invited, madam," I said. "Mr. Morris is in receipt of an invitation and will take his leave for the lauded event after our play is finished."

"Aye, you ain't nothin but his concubine, no how," she replied and called to the artist, "Leave Quinn out o' the picture, man. Paint the lady in front, for she be Morris' watercolor wife.

The doxies chortled at the joke, clapping their hands and snorting. Though they couldn't read, they understood the opera. Tavern wenches balanced on a seesaw, they could hope if I had been homeless and made bed with a wealthy merchant, the future held promise for them.

"We should all be in the painting, then," I said. The artist waved his hands and gathered us to the edge of the stage so he could draw us in repose, chins up, leaning against each other, gazing at invisible stars.

He was done in a jiff and one of the doxies grabbed it before I could take a look. "Back to practice," I yelled. Near to having a fit after two hours of herding smelly slatterns on the stage, one called out, to my relief, "Mistress Wise, we never had so much fun as this. You be a fine woman to teach us." One of them slapped me on the back, knocking out my breath. Huzzahs went up.

I was stricken at the compliment. Looking from one haggard face to the other, a smile grew upon my mine. They had been nothing but strumpets and whores to us, just as the midwives and Goldsboro had called me. I picked up my lyrics from the stage floor and turned to eye the doxy who slapped me. With a laugh, I slapped her buttocks in return.

Then I clapped my hands and said, "Ladies, we are a part of Oxford's fabric and have suffered in our careers for lack of opportunity. I am grateful for your voices." I donned my cloak. "It will be a fine production. Now, I am off to nurse my baby, but will return quickly in case you think of more questions." Their applause followed me and Gus to the tap room which adjoined the dining area. Yearie looked up, suspicious. She wore Goldsboro's cockhat, a new feather installed.

"It's only us," I said.

"It be done, Sary. Quinn say the first tap—the ale be good. The second be a bit flat."

"And the gin?"

"Quinn got nothin but rag water," she said. "I doctored it with jimson to soften the tart."

"How will you serve it, Gus?" I asked.

"Free to him as wants it. Swizzle a tiff and pass it on to the next."

"Genius, beggars," I said. "It's time. Let's be off, handily."

GUS

The tavern were filled with smoke that hung near the ceiling. Evening sunlight couldn't break the dirty windows lit inside by ghostly candlelight. I gaped at so many salty faces in one place softened in the shadows. In back, I asked Yearie who the weasel man was leaning against a post with Quinn, leering at the women.

"That be Findley. Stay clear of him," she say, and I take her serious.

Our stage was set. Yearie filled the tankards, and I lugged them beside tumblers of gin to every table. Sailors hollered, toasting me at every turn. A lone violin screeched and we looked up. The tavern doxies stood in the wings, waiting.

Sweating in a threadbare greatcoat, Master put down his instrument, spread his arms wide and sang,

> *Whore and Rogue they call Husband and Wife:*
> *All Professions be-rogue one another:*
> *The Priest calls the Lawyer a Cheat,*
> *The Lawyer be-knaves the Divine:*
> *And the Statesman, because he's so great,*

Thinks his Trade as honest as mine.

On hearing the last, them tars roared, slamming their tankards for more. Soon enough, the laughter like to blow mine ears. They were ready for more and it came like a hard wind. Not able to find a woman with guts enough to play Mrs. Peachum, the madam to the tavern sluts, Mistress had asked the tailor. She pressed his flesh into stays, powdered his hairy bosom and drew cupid lips and tarted cheeks upon his face. A moth-eaten, red-haired wig sat upon his head like an abandoned bird's nest. In the strained pitch of a matron, he entered and sang his lament of Polly's doubtful virginity and how to turn it to guinea gold if she married.

The tailor winked and curtsied to Polly. The sailors groaned, for all knew how long Mistress had waited for Master's hand in marriage. Then, the tailor departed with Jeremiah who pickpocketed Master as he left, so's all could see. Oh, we had them in our clutches.

The beautiful Polly, wrapped in blue, sang of a plucked virgin's fair flower that, "fades, and shrinks, and grows past all enduring, rots, stinks…and dies!" Master were embarrassed, realizing he were taken for a yellow-belly bachelor. He eyed Sarah for setting him up and hollered, "If Polly marries, I will call her hussy and cut her throat."

That weren't in the play. I were horrified and poured his tainted ale, adding an extra draught of jimson. She gave him an evil eye, turned to them tars and seeing heads sinking on tables, she clapped and waved her hand for the master's tankard. I ran on stage and gave it to her like a church offering. She swung her hips to him and put the tankard to his mouth.

I swear his gulp was heard from feet away. His thirst slaked, he asked her smartly, "Do you love MacHeath, the highwayman?"

"*I do!*" she shouted.

His eyes raked her over and he muttered, "Slut!" under his breath.

Angry, I kicked a table, stirring the sailors awake and wondered if Master thought the Scotsman was her lover. Sarah were calm and sat on his knee, nursing his drink to his hungry lips as the doxies sang the refrain of Green Sleeves,

Since laws were made, for every degree
To curb vice in others, as well as me,
I wonder we hadn't better company
Upon Tyburn Tree.

Johnnie Layton's harridan threw a noose over a rafter ready for an execution. Master boasted, "McIntosh is worth money..." Sarah drew her hand round master's chin and said, "MacHeath, my love, not McIntosh," and bowed her head in dramatic sorrow.

He downed his tankard and sneered, "but I'm in doubt if he has two wives or three."

I jumped up and down with delight. The sailors leaned in on their elbows.

"I don't know what you mean, sir," she said, all innocent. She tilted his cup to see if he had emptied the draft. Turning, she sat on the edge of the table and crooked her finger at Master and pursed her lips, ready for a kiss.

"You wish to marry McIntosh to make yourself a rich widow!" he accused.

The tars rose up and booed Master. They wanted a love story, and it warmed the cockles of mine heart. And since no one were wedded to their lines, the play were now mincemeat. Standing up, Master faltered, steadying himself with a hand. Sarah pushed a dram of gin toward him and never at a loss, he tossed it down. She smiled merrily and in a stage voice said, "As I intend, m'lord. Your wealth is mine."

The doxies' voices rose in sweet refrain of the Tyburn gallows when off to the side, a scuffle with Quinn was heard in the shadows. He was helpless as the rest of the sailors, so drugged were he.

To mine grateful ears a familiar voice boomed. "Stand aside, you id-jit," and Mac shoved Quinn to the floor. He strode in on a ship's sail, windblown and rugged. His hair flowed to his shoulders, his eyes dark. Buckskins, salt air and a long rifle in his hand. He scanned the audience, looking for his own sailors in the riffraff. He raised his rifle, "At hand, me tars!"

"I-I know you," Master garbled, squinting and helpless. He put his hands up and reared back as a ghost stood before him. Mac took the stage in two steps to greet him, and, tying Master's hands behind his back, pushed him sprawling into a chair. Sailors giggled and drooled as they fell to the floor. The tavern women looked round and realizing their play had been hijacked, their song of Tyburn Tree dwindled. I dropped a fresh pitcher of ale, splashing it across the floor and boarded the stage.

"Mac!" I said. "Aw, you making mine eyes water."

Sarah stood back, her hands limp by her sides. Mac didn't even notice she was there.

"Me long-lost cabin boy!" he said, tossing me above his head. "Look at ye! A veritable gentleman's lackey ye are!"

Jackson jumped the stage, his hair long, held by a red sash, a knife in one hand. Always careful, Sarah stepped back from the fray. Fearing the heat of men, I took to her side. We heard a crash and turned to see Findley storming through the tables, screaming like an elk in rut. His face were purpled, snarled in spite. We froze as Jackson leaped down to meet him. It were a reckoning of God's making, a new play with the same audience, and the tars sensed blood sport. Waking, they hooted ready for game.

Mac followed his mate, holding the rabble back. Jackson brandished his long knife, Findley a sword. It were unequal in weapon, but not in power. They circled, one slow, the other light on his feet. Findley raised his weapon to swipe, but mine sailor-slave dipped away, slashing the overseer's shoulder. Findley glanced at his wound, but did not give up.

Yearie came from the tap room. Her hair were a black cloud round her shoulders under Goldsboro's cockhat. Her lips tight in concentration.

"Should we stop it?" Mistress asked. "An uneven match."

"And not see Findley die?" Yearie spit. "Do not be denying me this, Sary."

Yearie was right, and I saw for the first time that this night would not end without bloodshed. I preened, ready to plunge a knife in flesh. Pulling a kitchen blade from my breeches, I handed it to Mistress, and said, "You best be armed for your defense."

She raised her palms to look at them. "This is not what we planned, Gus. It was only ever a game to thieve, not to kill."

"Well you're in it now, Mistress. There's no going back."

Yearie produced the pistol from Master's desk. "I'll have my way tonight. Men be not the only ones to decide who lives and dies. Take the knife, Sary."

"What of Sally, girls?" she shouted. "Who will take care of her if I die?"

Yearie shoved her aside and say, "Then live, Sarah Wise. Be forever the dutiful servant."

The shouting grew big behind us and I longed to be with the men. I took one look at Mistress and said, "What do you want your daughter to know of you? That you can polish floors?"

Mistress blink, her mouth open. Her fingers wrapped round the knife.

"Aye, Findley. Your reign be over," yell Jackson, as his arm circled the overseer's neck. Pinned to the slave's body, Findley's eyes were full of terror.

The front doors flew open and a cold wind rushed us as the rest of the maroons, fresh from the *Fearnaught* took the tavern by storm.

Yearie called, "Take him to Handy's, to his slaves."

The doxies clapped and squealed. Findley's shoulders slumped and he began to whimper. Jackson's voice rose in triumph, echoing in the rafters, but there were so much noise, I couldn't figure what he said. He and Yearie led their garrison into the night. I got out of Mac's way as he scooped up Findley's sword and stormed the stage. His big hand cupped Master's chin.

"I told ye to call me yer enemy till the day I cut yer throat, Englishman." Letting Master's sleeping face drop, he finally went to Sarah and wrapped her in his arms. He were a shrewd man, but a little late in love.

"I didna see ye at first. How could I forget that dress? Yer a woman of me desires."

"Desire wanes, Scotsman," she said, but buried her face in his chest.

"When tonight be done, we'll be together, m'love." They kissed. I slipped behind the taproom door and watched. His fingers wrapped in her hair, his arm round her waist. Thinking they were alone, a tide swept only them; she tore at his mouth with her lips. and I wondered if she were angry. Curious if this were true love, I think I should know how it were done.

They heaved their pipes over necks and eyes, digging at clothes, dogs pawing the earth. Closed eyes, they did, even though they hadn't seen each other in so long. A flurry of clothes and arms, they grew frustrated and stopped, he resting his chin on her head. His hands held her ears. Ears, not nancies. This were not Master, grabbing her softness. His eyes fluttered open and he raised her face to his, kissing her long and dreamy. A frown deepened between his brows, his eyes shuttered. She opened hers and, looking at him, she sobered, her passion cooled. She broke from him, her hand on his chest.

Disappointed, I thought, *what's this?*

"Alex," she said. "You remember I said if we met in gentler times we would see. These are not gentler times. Let us not dally in heated display. There will be time later if we are successful."

Always thinking, my mistress. His eyes narrowed, but he smiled and grabbed her hand. "Ye be right, Mrs. Wise. Let's make havoc." They ran, leaving Master sprawled and snoring on the table. He looked near dead to me, so I followed.

Outside, farmers and townsfolk lined the street, looking for leadership. Some carried lanterns, others torches. They were not ready for war, just hopeful faces smiling at us, wondering what was in store. I kept pace, watching Mistress' indigo gown flap in the breeze, now her flag. The rabble surged to the edge of the dockyard, clamoring and raising their fists at the ships packed in like cows against a fence waiting to be milked. Hulking shadows on the water, they were lit by lanterns fore and aft. I looked for Findley and Jackson, but they were nowhere to be found. The tailor, dress dragging the ground, climbed up on a barrel with Jeremiah's help. He tore off his wig and tossed it in the air.

"Now is your chance, fair Oxford, to rise up against the Talbot men," he shouted. "Show them this town, this land, is ours for the taking."

The crowd surged in his direction. He jumped down, grabbed a torch and lit it from another. Gildart's ship *Johnson* stood at the end of Cunliffe's pier. I knew it carried a load of Jamaican blackstrap molasses bound for New England and their rum trade. Master's harbor slaves had yet to load the cypress logs from a river barge. Blocking the mouth of the harbor sat the *Fearnaught*, her cannon aimed broadside at the *Johnson*. I looked at Mac and Sarah.

"Do ye have the keys to the warehouse?" Mac shouted over the din. She shook her head.

"Robert has them."

"I'll return. Doona get caught in the crowd," he said and disappeared quick as he had come.

Our security gone, I pulled Sarah aside and glanced about. "Wait here," I said as townspeople flowed onto the flimsy walkway that ran harborside. The warehouse were above it, a windowless promise in the night. We were thwarted for the moment, and the crowd felt it. They climbed to the doors, pushing against them.

I caught sight of three figures beneath Goldsboro's gibbeted slave bones. Jackson moved with purpose. A shadow against a ship's dim light, he readied the tender boat for sail. Findley slumped against an overturned canoe, his hands tied. Yearie's arm outstretched, she pointed the pistol at him.

"Yearie," Sarah called, hurrying over with me at her heels. "What are you about?"

"Mistress," I said. "Come with me. We'll wait for Mac's return."

Not one of them paid me any mind. Yearie heard Mistress, though. Reaching in her pocket, she threw a conjure bag at our feet.

"Go away, Sary," she said, frog-voiced.

We were all in this together, she in more danger than us, and *she* needed her conjure bag. Within seconds, Jackson tossed Findley into the boat, climbed in and gave Yearie his hand. She turned to look at her longtime friend, her mistress. Behind her, no longer stupefied, Findley yelled for help. Jackson yanked the scarf from his head and stuffed it in the overseer's mouth.

"No, no. Please, you cannot!" yelled Mistress, her hand at her throat.

It were no use. Jackson shoved Findley low and mine understanding widened. Yearie's face was within inches of Sarah's. Her brow a V, hostile eyes bore into her face. She picked up the conjure bag and stuffed it in Sarah's bodice.

"Leave, Sary. You have no place with us."

"I do, Yearie. It's your life—and Jackson's that I protect."

"It's my life, not yours to live. Be gone afore I says what I regret."

Jackson set the sail. "Yearie, now! They's waiting for us at Handy's.

"Yearie, Jackson, you mustn't do this!" yell Mistress. "They will know. There are too many people who see." She shouldered Yearie away. "You will be tried for murder."

Yearie pushed her hard and Sarah landed on the ground with an *oof*. Shocked, I gave my hand to Mistress, but Yearie shoved me down and stood over us in warning.

"I be makin the decisions this night, Sary Wise. The world moves without you. Findley have no earthly right to live." She bent over, sprinkling dust on the faces of us. A soft wind kicked her hair, so it floated gauzy round her head. "Let your God decide what to do with him in death, and I'll decide what to do with me in life." A light glowed behind her and I leaned past to see who came.

Jackson. She turned and made for the boat. I watched her go, not knowing what to do when Yearie roared like a preacher her arms in the air, "Behold—a slave free!"

Like Mac, she were a demon of revenge. She wanted a terrible, awful death for Findley. I had no quarrel with it. But, if Goldsboro showed his face, that were mine choice.

YEARIE

*O*ur night not be about no thievin fun like Sary want, not even slicin ear nor stabbin foot like Gus want. It not be devoted to burnin a ship or settin some record straight. I don't own no store to be tricked out my profit by Talbot men. The thrill of carrying secret messages between them folk grown old since Tiberious killed. Now, it look to me like nobody profit from this scheme but white men, cause there be no plan to free us slaves. But tonight I'm free, either in body or in spirit. Probly not both.

Findley be curled at our feet, his eye wanderin from one t'other of us. Jackson not need to say nothin to me, nor I to him. We sail in quiet, the noise of the throng growin distant as we head up the Tred-Avon. He be different, not just a windblown tar, but he got sureness now. This what come of freedom and not lookin over his shoulder no more.

Suddenly, I laugh big and loud for darkness and open water let me.

"What so funny?" he ask.

"Middlin Oxford goin to suffer their gentry humiliation. By that time, we not around to witness. Just like the Lord to not give me satisfaction when it so close."

343

"Satisfaction nothin but ripe fruit. Goes quick. Rebellion be our milk and honey."

"You been killin men. I see it in your eyes."

"Nobody who not wish me dead first, Yearie. You got bloodlust for Findley?"

"Don't you, Jackson? He be your torturer."

"I've had enough blood. I'm thinking it be some others' turn tonight."

The sail be full, carryin us swift. Behind in harbor, I see a fire glow and think, *it's begun.*

Handy's dock empty. The broad lawn gleam wet in the moonlight, waves of grass welcoming us to the main house. Candlelight in the cellar windows, but all those above be dark reflections. Loyal English dancin elsewhere in memory of an old battle they call Agincourt.

"Follow me," Jackson say.

He unwrap a splittin maul that he carried to the boat. This man laid plans, not takin any instruction from me. Dragged Findley out the boat and stood him on his feet. "You coming with me, overseer. Keep up or I'll hack you to death right here."

I skipped behind, a cool wind in my face. Jackson walk to the dark side of the house and tie Findley to an oak tree. "Hold that pistol on him," he say and run low to the house. Soon I heard breakin glass. Findley be gettin his wits bout him now, the jimson wearing off. He wave his hand at me and I stepped back, liftin the gun to his face. "You stand still in them acorns afore I shoot."

Right quick, house slaves runnin quiet, they leg irons trailing broken chains that Jackson mauled. Lookin from one t'other, a mumblin low, one of them say, "The stable."

A tall woman push through the party carryin a candle, her face closed off. "Go to the smithy's house and bring him," she say with authority. She turn to Jackson and I see a brand on her cheek. "We'll make this our night."

Jackson untie Findley while she join me and we follow, he draggin the overseer who whine and plead. She eye me close, "You're Yearie? The one who lost your love on Plimhimmon road?"

That make my face scrunch up, remembering. "That weren't Findley's doin. Goldsboro's. Who you be?"

"Bathsheba."

"Yes," I said, "you lead." Soon, a horde of slaves come from they cabins to meet us at the stable door. They crowd inside, hanging cloth over the windows and light lanterns low. I see one stokin the smithy's forge. Jackson push Findley into their midst and they close up round him.

I touched his arm. "I got business in town. You stay if'n you want. I'll walk back."

"No. Not leaving you to walk the byways of Oxford on this night, Yearie. Besides, these folk got it sewn up. Just let me speak a minute."

I surprised seeing him raise his arm and whistle for they attention. "You all be prepared to run tonight," he say. "Split up. Best chances now be going north to Indian River and set in with the Nanticoke and Assateague, or go to Philadephie, then north. Take Handy's horses but git out o here fast. The gentry be worried about the harbor on this night, not about us. Godspeed."

They faces calm, serene like they all be baptized with the Lord. Some raise a torch and bid us goodbye. The forge burning bright hot and I see they not waitin for coals. The brands glowed orange.

We closed the door behind us and left.

CHAPTER 46: RETRIBUTION

Matching Buttons of Hope and Change

SARAH

I ran. The horde of merchants danced. Each friend confronted was a face of pure devilry. They pressed toward the *Johnson*, taking Gus and me with them. At the head of the throng was a cluster of tattered sailors from the *Fearnaught*. I fought my way free, leaving Gus behind. Some tars boarded jolly boats, their torches held high. I meant to find Mac. These were his men.

At whip's crack, they reached the *Johnson* and climbed the rope ladders that spanned her sides. Gildart's sailors stared down, and, knowing their deaths were at hand, tried to fend off the boarders with pikes. But the ship's deck swarmed with maroons yelling war cries as they tossed Gildart's men into the water. I panted, my hands on my knees, watching as they rolled barrels of molasses, turning them upright under the main mast. And then I realized the blackstrap was in the hold. It was gunpowder they rolled on deck.

"She'll make a pretty picture on such a dark night."

Mac had walked up behind me. I glanced over my shoulder, "Did you plan this?"

"Hardly. Doona give me credit, lass. They be men with a hankerin for retribution. I only want what be in Morris' warehouse."

"Looks like it's gone awry."

"Where's Griet?"

"In the crowd looking for you."

He held up the ring of keys. "You didn't need those," I said. "Just break the lock. No one can trace that to you."

"Better if it appears one of his own workers did it. Morris will think he canna trust anyone in his employ once we be done. I plan on dying some day, but wouldna cry if it were a date of me own pickin."

"Getting cautious in your old age?" I grabbed the keys from him and hung them over my shoulder. "Where's Robert? At the tavern?"

"Naw, I threw his self in a cart and left him in his stable yard. I'm not wantin his haid, but I do want his servant girl." He put an arm around my waist and pulled me to him

"I'm not available at the moment, sir. Was he conscious?"

"No, in a sleep the Sainted Peter couldn't wake. Give me a good laugh."

"This is not a humorous night," I said, pointing upriver. "Yearie and Jackson took Findley. I fear a slave revolt at Handy's."

"Their revenge?" He laughed hard and tight. "Findley'll naught be alive long." Pointing his dirk to a glimmer of lights on the terraced lawns of the closest plantation, he asked, "I'm takin to understand that be Plimhimmon and the buttocks' ball?"

I nodded. A walk of under an hour and if any in Oxford were ready to tattle, they would be on their way to break up the party. "We need to hurry," I said.

A splash in the harbor brought our heads round. Mac's sailors had heaved burning sailcloth below trying to drown those who would swim ashore. This was more than plain havoc. It was murder.

I pushed out of his arms. "You're their leader, Alex. You allow them to kill!"

"Allow them? It be their own free will, madam."

"No one has free will," I yelled. "We're all indebted. And I stop short of looting."

"Because ye've never lost what they've never gained."

I ignored him and marched uphill. "There are other things I want," I shouted. "God forgive me, I'll help you. And my townsfolk, but there must be no more bloodshed."

"I am not their liege lord, madam."

I was hopping mad. "Deathshead! There are no good choices," I screamed, throwing the keys at his chest. "Hurry. If they light that ship on fire, Goldsboro arrives."

He drew a bosun's whistle from his jacket and piped three blasts. His men broke from their watch of the ship taking flame and loped uphill to us. We waited at the warehouse door.

"Spread the sailcloth and fill it," he yelled. "Eight of you ready the tender boats. Once the enemy appears, we'll spend the ship's cannon."

He unlocked the doors and pushed them aside. Suddenly, Griet struggled out of the crowd, her face screwed up in worry. "Yearie and Jackson return from Handy's," she said. "They're tying up now."

"It's on them where they go tonight, Griet," I said, and we followed Mac as he slung his long rifle over his shoulder barking orders. It was pitch black, but the band of sailors were organized to a T, swinging their torches up and down the aisles inspecting Robert's goods. Scooping valuables from the shelves, the townsfolk followed. The cooper, apothecary, smithy, shoemaker, candlemaker—so many I stopped counting. They all owed Cunliffe more than their worth. Except for their grins, they proceeded as if they were taking Communion on a Sunday morning.

Jeremiah stumbled near. His torch wobbled and I caught it before it hit the ground.

Relieved of its weight he put a hand on the counter and bent his head, throwing up all over Griet's sleeve and vest. He slumped to the floor.

"You panty-waisted fool," she yelled. "What's the matter with you?"

"Sorry, Gus," he moaned. "I drank a dram of gin and it's got the better of me. There be four of you standing there." His finger came up as he counted her.

She kicked him and said, "You and your sorry arse shouldn't be drinking."

I wondered where the tailor was, for I hadn't seen him waltzing around in his dress. The boy was every shade of green. I vowed to take him home, but there was something I had to find first. I patted Griet's head and said, "Come."

We sidled into a crowded aisle where I knew I could find the osnaburg hemp sack. I hung the torch in a rack, the light casting low over the shelving. Stooping behind the counter I drew Griet near, stripped her vest and tossed a clean shift over her head. She smiled up at me and said, "I tinking I look more like the jack tar who come to your door a year ago, just a mite cleaner."

I hugged her. "You're tinking again?" I whispered. "Will you help?"

"And be your conveyancer? I can steal with the best of em, m'lady."

Out the corner of my eye through the open doors, I caught a glimpse of the *Johnson*, flames running up the main mast, jumping to its others. Mac's sailors leaped into the water and swam to waiting boats. I felt Griet's hand on mine. A thrumming noise sucked the air with such force it tickled my cheek. A ball of light grew large on the ship, lighting our faces as if it were midday. Thunder popped across the water thrice as barrels of gunpowder exploded one upon another. In a woosh of hot, wet air the *Johnson* torched and collapsed on itself, sinking into the harbor, its tall mast hitting the pier. I grabbed a candle, lit it from the torch, and we scurried to Robert's desk hidden behind the pier side door.

"What are we about, mistress?" Griet whispered.

"Blackmail."

She grinned like it was Christmas. We opened drawers finding slave accounts and land deeds. The rabble clamored behind us, arguing. Our fingers moved. From the last drawer I drew an old ledger of ship cargoes, wrapped in fancy ribbon. Feeling around the wood, I touched a mouse hole and a false bottom lifted. A leather-bound book wrapped in muslin. We flipped through the pages, peering in the candlelight to find rows of his profits siphoned from sales.

"Lawd, God. He's King Croesus!" yelled Griet.

"Shhh! They'll hear."

In the book's binding was a key, one I had never seen. Griet swept the candle across the desk drawers and sides. I pointed, and she crawled beneath, pushing against the warehouse boards. Squeezed under the desk, she whispered, "There's a shelf." She drew her legs in further and grunted. I peered around the warehouse door, but all were engaged.

"Here!"

A crash, a scrape and she crawled out, her face streaked with dirt. Reaching, she dragged a small strong box. The wood gleamed and the lock was oiled. Silently, the key turned. Just like Robert to take great care. Cold five-pound guineas glittered in my hands. I reached in further and found the amethyst he had taken from me. And more, there were folded parchment sheaves tucked in the side. I opened one, and, seeing it was an indenture paper, opened the others.

"Give them to Mac," I said. "I have one more thing to do. Meet me street side."

She gathered them to her budding chest and was off. I watched from the door, viewing the crowd. Their knapsacks filled, the sailors ran to the docks to watch the conflagration. Fiery shards blew on the ship anchored next to the *Johnson*. With the *Fearnaught* blocking the harbor, the other sailors drunk on jimson weed, and the captains at Plimhimmon, all the ships could go up in flames. I never wanted this for our town.

"Tis a beautiful sight," said Mac.

I jumped out of my skin as he wrapped his arms round me from behind. "Sir, why do you sneak up on me like that?"

"Keepin ye on yer toes. Are ye ready to leave with me?"

"It's the end of Oxford tonight," I said, hiding the strong box beneath my skirts.

"Nay, Morris' trade in flesh won't end on this shore. We only stick a sword in his foot."

The neck of his buckskin was stuffed with the indenture papers. The harbor fire reflected in his eyes a passion that was foreign to me. I didn't want to burn down everything and start over. "You ask too much, Scotsman."

"What? That we win? It's not just freedom I ask, it's a future without debt. Someday, we'll have our own Plimhimmon, a wife to honor me estate."

I blinked in disbelief. To honor his *land*? Like a prize racehorse? There were so many contradictions bound up in him, I wouldn't lay my future at his door and think it brought me freedom. I took his hands in mine. "M'lord, you should be off. The reckoning will come in less than an hour."

He nuzzled my ear and whispered, "Ye canna come with me?"

"And do what with my Sally? I won't leave her."

"Ahl be back for ye both. Doona fear. We belong together." His hand swept across my nipple and, despite myself, I felt a tingle. Down the short pier that had not caught fire yet, he hollered like a boy let out of his lessons. His men followed their liege into the tender boats and oared to the *Fearnaught*.

He could have stopped the killing of Gildart's sailors, I thought, *but he didn't want to.*

Quiet now, only the rustle of birds in the rafters. The fire raged outside, the warehouse looting had stopped and whether satiated or fearful, the townsfolk were gone to their homes. Behind me on the street side, I heard steps scrunch on shells. "Sarah, have you seen Jeremiah?" asked the tailor.

With his wig and stays gone, he seemed a used-up harlot ready for bed, wearing a nightshirt and breeches. He clumped beyond me into the warehouse.

"I've looked everywhere. I took some damask bolts and he wasn't at home."

I reached for his sleeve and drew him down the linen aisle. There lay Jeremiah under the sputtering torch, sound asleep. I said, "He had too much gin."

"Aye, the Devil be in him tonight. His mother will box his ears." The tailor bent over and shook his son's shoulder. I held the torch. The poor boy was mighty gray.

"Jeremiah, wake up now. The party be over and ya ain't sleeping here for the sheriff to find." A shock of hair fell over his sleeping eyes and his body slumped to the floor.

I knelt. "Jeremiah. Wake up. Your father wants you," I said, shaking his arm. "Jeremiah!"

The tailor fell to his knees, drew his son to him, and feeling for his breath he buried his face in the boy's coat. "My boy, my boy. What've ye done to yerself? Don't be leaving yer pa. Yer a good boy, ye hear. Yer a good boy." They rocked until the tailor fell against the cabinet, Jeremiah draped across his lap.

"Get up," I said, standing. "You can't stay. Look there. The fire burns out of control." He raised his eyes but they were sightless, sorrowful and black. "You must leave before Goldsboro and his men come."

He gazed at me and seemed to focus. "This be your fault, Sarah Wise. And that damnable Scot."

"Sir," came Griet behind me. "Goldsboro's docked at Skillington's. The others ride down the Oxford Road. Let me help you."

"I don't need your help," he sobbed. "I'll carry him myself."

With a keen wail, the tailor heaved his son over his shoulder and stumbled through the doors. His nightshirt tangled round his knees and, seeing the warehouse pony, he dumped the teen across its back. I swallowed a sob. Little Griet's arms wrapped round my hips and we gave in to silent tears. "Griet, I wanted to give him hope. I didn't mean for so much sacrifice. Not Jeremiah."

"Mistress, an Indian woman I knew said death pays all debts. Jeremiah is God's mistake, not yours. You want to erase the debts of the living? Our job were not done. Hurry."

She tried to lift the accounts and when I didn't move, her eyes pleaded with me. I lifted the ledgers and walked to dock's edge. My breasts were tight, ready for Sally's suckle, and as I dumped the books in the water, my shift and bodice soaked in a rush of milk. Griet shoved another over and we watched as they sank. I took a deep breath and lumbered to the warehouse and the gold guineas. A walking cart was propped by the doors. Griet rolled it inside.

I opened the strong box and scooped handfuls into both pocket purses. Banging against my thighs, I thought it better than any man's promise. Griet dug for the amethyst and tossed it to me. I nestled it between my sweaty breasts.

The matter of the ledger recording his crimes had me stumped. I couldn't carry it to Morris House. My eyes raked the shelving.

Griet pointed, "The foot warmer!" A little squirrel, she climbed and handed it down.

I tore pages from the ledger and folded them, laying them inside the metal stove. Griet yanked up a loose board and dumped the warmer beneath the floor. I laid the floorboard in place. Then, with one giant heave, we loaded the strong box in the cart.

"Wait, mistress. His current ledger! We need it to be believed!" shouted Griet. She dumped it beside the strongbox. Outside, the wind was brisk sending a shiver round my bare shoulders. My eyes burned from the heat of the flames, and in the shadow of the warehouse I felt suddenly blind, ridden with smoke.

A shadow loomed near, dragging Griet kicking and screaming. He grabbed me by the hair and slammed me against the wall with his free hand. "You traitor. This is how you repay my kindness? You gave them the keys."

"No, no, Robert. I wouldn't." His hand moved to my neck. I gagged as my fingers raked his grip.

"Stop it, you drunk bastard!" yelled Griet, kicking him. "They broke in. Mistress has your keys."

"Then you unlocked the doors! You will hang, you cunning bitch." His hand slid down my chest and he pressed me flat against the wall. I couldn't see his face but his spit flecked my cheeks.

"M-master." I coughed. "Your keys," I said and held them to his eyes. "The strongbox. They pilfered and Yearie and I swung a torch at them to drag it away. For you." I pointed.

His hand dropped to his side and he bent to the cart, opening the lid and running his hands through. He blubbered, "My hard-earned coin."

I grabbed Griet and we ran through the warehouse. I wanted to go, to be rid of Robert. Silhouetted against the fire on the *Johnson*, Mac stood at the end of the pier, his long rifle pointing at Goldsboro who sat atop of his great sorrel illuminated by the fire. He aimed his rifle at Mac.

Two shots, a puff of smoke. Mac dropped from sight and I hoped against all hope he was bound for his ship. Panicking, I thought he might be wounded. Griet dragged me to the bulkhead. There, black wings of multiple oars drew the tender boat across glowing water toward the *Fearnaught*. At the prow stood Mac, his long legs balancing, his rifle held high. Alive. At the rear was Jackson's colossal figure, his hair blowing about like a bush in a storm, his arm sheltering Yearie who wore Goldsboro's cockhat. I swear her face turned to me and she raised her hand, but I could have been wrong.

I understood, standing there with my orphan child clutching my side. My prison grew smaller. My sister, my only family from birth, had left me finally. Morris House was a scourge on our existence, hers more than mine. Just as it had been for Jackson. I never wanted to lose her for she was essential to me, but I was not to her. Her devotion had been long, her departure short and swift. I could have made it easier. I could have freed her. The price to pay was mine.

All discipline vanished and I slumped to my knees. Laying my cheek on the cold shells of the harbor I felt the whole cloth of Oxford wrap me, like a baby swaddled tight, suffocating.

"Get up, Sarah." Griet pulled on my arm.

"They'll try me for murder."

"You'll naught be going up no ladder to hang. Put on your innocence. Sally waits."

She was right, of course. I couldn't leave Oxford and sail with Yearie and Jackson without taking my baby. Robert would never care for her. And likely the provincial court would not find me guilty for the same reason. Sally, my adorable love, had become a useful oaf and my ticket to survival. I sniveled and dragged my torn sleeve across my eyes. Ashamed, I rose and shook out my skirts.

"I follow you, Griet."

The thundering of hoofs nearby raised our eyes to a phalanx of well-dressed men bound for the dockside cannons. Goldsboro rode at their head, his helmeted dogs racing in his wake. No sooner had we gained the strand, clearing the warehouse, than we heard the first round of cannon fire from the *Fearnaught* peal through the air toward the harbor. Shot rained down on the defenseless ships, igniting an inferno that spread quickly. Guttural shouts wafted in the wind as Goldsboro took position. He raised his sword high and commanded, "Fire!"

They missed, a round ploughing through the water short of the *Fearnaught*'s sides. Her sails furled and she turned slowly, making for the broad Chesapeake as more cannon were fired from the harbor. Griet covered her ears, her mouth open, horror across her face.

"Hurry, Mac," she whispered.

It was then I saw plumes of fire shoot off her stern and the whine of cannon balls one after another sailed through the air. They landed with precision on the roof of the warehouse, sending splinters flying. I grabbed Griet and we dove behind a row of hogshead. Successive explosions resounded, blowing fire and sparks into the night sky. All round us, hot orange shards fell, glancing blows burning only feet away as they hit the dirt. I looked at Griet's smudged face, her eyes black holes. "Did you see Robert?"

"No, Missus. He were so gin-faced, I only wanted to be free of him."

We huddled there listening to the answering cannon fire from the harbor, men cursing and yelling, Goldsboro's commands echoing in my ears. We had waited so long my breasts ached for Sally, but after what seemed hours, the booming stopped, and we looked. The warehouse was half gone. As we walked round, we saw the pier smoldering in the water, and the ships nearest the hulk of the *Johnson* aflame.

I looked for the cart with the strong box, but it was gone—burnt or stolen. We dragged ourselves down the strand to home. Hestia greeted me at the door, jiggling Sally in her arms. At a year and a half, she pitched herself headfirst, landing on my chest, searching for a breast. Breathless, she nursed, her eyes searching mine as if to ask, *where were you?* Hestia produced ale first, soap and water second. I stripped to my shift, Griet to her shirt and we sat eating cornbread slathered with butter.

"Is Findley dead?" she asked.

"I suspect. We'll hear soon enough. Yearie's gone with Jackson on the *Fearnaught*."

"Yearie."

She smiled and that was enough. I reached for her scarred hand. "Do you want to go, Hestia? I will forge Robert's signature on your manumission."

"Go where? To what?" she asked as if she had never entertained the idea.

"There will be changes. I'll make Robert. Your cabin rebuilt and pay for you, exactly what Raphael earned regardless of what Robert says. I have saved that man from destitution tonight. He will be grateful."

She leaned over the table and said very formally, "I would like to visit my sister and her children in Philadelphia. I don't know how to get there."

Patting her hand, the raised scar beneath mine, I said, "Then we will find out. We will go together so you have a fine visit, as long as you want. Robert can take care of himself."

GRIET

$\mathcal{W}$e did visit Philadelphia, right soon before the cold weather made the trek treacherous. But before we left, mistress dug a hole in her winter garden, put her coins and jewel in it and laid a stone overtop. I sprinkled the last of Yearie's conjure bag, a nail, cloves, and some blue glass. Master were forlorn at the thought of being surrounded by men and eating at the tavern, but he did not stop us. He gave us Mr. Greenway's address and told us to see if young Rob's letters were filled with truth or lies. We arranged for a wet nurse for Sally and he said, "I will take care of her."

Anxious to leave before Goldsboro bore down on us with his investigation, we sailed the on a bright November day up the Chesapeake and by coach to Wilmington—which the locals called Willing Town because I guessed they had a rule like slaves that everything have two names. We traveled west to the big city where narrow cobblestone streets were squeezed with wood houses by the river. Our guest house smelled of dung and rotting fish when the wind came from the south. I were not impressed with this city of so-called brotherly love until Sarah took me to go marketing. She stopped at a milliner to buy what the storekeeper called a 'silk chapeau' with a huge brim and bow. She bought me six silver buttons to sew on my

358

breeches and said, "If you decide to wear a dress someday, we will save them for a jacket." The milliner gave me a hard candy. At night, we strolled to a bloody bear baiting and nasty cockfight where a rowdy crowd laid bets, including the gentle ladies. I couldna understand use of animals in this manner. Relief of me came when we attended the Plumstead play of *Henry V*. Sarah said it were that guy Shakespeare again. The costumes and action were far better than our imagination in Quinn's tavern.

The day before our return home, Sarah finally had a note from young Rob. He said to meet him at the home of Charles Willing on the morrow. Hestia was at her sister's house, so we took a hire uphill to find ourselves dropped at the door of a right honorable town mansion. It were a fine place. The coachman warned us, "Act sharp, youse at the former mayor's home." Mine eyebrows raised in alarm under my stocking hat and I swept it into mine pocket out of respect. Up the steps, the doorman took one look at us and ordered us round back to the kitchen quarter. I tried to trip him, pointing my foot as he pointed a finger, but he was wise to mine action and bundled me off with a curse. We waited hearthside, ignored by a staff of busy white servants all dressed in black. I wondered why there were no slaves.

"Auntie Sarah. Gus!" Rob called, his cockhat under his arm. I shook the bastard's hand like we were family. The image of Suter's head burned in the mind of me.

"Young Rob," asked Sarah, "are you employed by the mayor?"

"Apprenticed to his shipping firm," he said, his nose in the air. "I cannot stay to talk. The price of flour rose overnight. And a British ship is docked in Cape May with a full load. I intend to buy up all the bakers' flour in town and have it trucked to our warehouse. If I can get to Cape May tomorrow, I will make a deal on the ship's cargo and seal the price in my master's favor. Mr. Willing says he will give me a quarter of the profit if I'm successful."

"Your father's son in the flesh," said Sarah. "You are settled then?"

His tossed his hat over his success catching it midair. "I am required to do what father does—earn of my own free will. I am needed here."

He hugged Sarah, nodded to me and rushed off. I watched the whole of him from his cockhat to his jackboots with the silver spurs. He looked every part the son of a wealthy merchant.

We sailed home with Hestia in tow, she pleased as punch to have seen her sister. I asked if she were going to live with them and she said, "No. There's no place for me here. I want my kitchen. Too old to live with so many wanting so much."

Family stink just like visitors who stay too long.

We unpack at Morris House and that evening master command Sarah to sit by the hearth. Little Sally follow me everywhere, but we all surprised when she toddle into the parlor and rest her hand on his chair. I rushed to get her, but he picked her up, jiggling her on his knee.

"Gus," he say, "get her rattle. I want to hear of your trip."

He sit up straighter, listening to Rob's adventure. Sarah pause, and her face pinched, I see she got the gumption to ask if anything come of that night in harbor. Master say Goldsboro's investigation hit a dead end at every turn. The stolen warehouse stock weren't found and there were no sightings of the *Fearnaught* on the Chesapeake. "Time to rebuild—the warehouse, the piers and harbor walk." And he say,"I will clear debris from the harbor come spring." He did not have time for finding criminals, only for making money. "Loss is part of the game and I'm prepared to take them."

That night, I put Sally down early and after a genial time by the fire, Sarah head up to bed. Master overtook her on the stair and grabbed her hand, a finger to his lips, whispering in her ear. I heard the door close to his chamber and listened for her tread above. Nothing. I went to sleep in the garret with Sally and woke to her prattle and no Sarah.

As soon as I finished my tasks, I ran to the warehouse, milled about the carpenters, and tapped old floorboards for one loose where the foot stove be. I drew it out and exclaimed, "Mistress got cold feet. That there floorboard need nailing, sirs!"

On my way down the strand, the tailor come upon me, silent and angry.

"How's business, tailor?" I asked, cheerful.

He softened and said he had more than he could do. "Handy sold his daughters' dresses to me second hand. The man's so in debt he's putting up tracts of his plantation for sale. Getting rid of terbaccer and going to wheat like everybody else. Said all his slaves run off."

"That so? Anything else?" I asked.

He lean to mine ear. "We are careful. Oxford merchants have traded Morris goods far from prying eyes. Those drunk sailors hallucinated for a week from that gin, tied to the jakes they were. Goldsboro accused Quinn, but the tavern keeper asked how when he was delirious, too." The tailor put his arm round mine shoulder and said Goldsboro accused Sarah of consorting with the Scotsman, but Master Morris denied it, for everyone know'd she saved his investments from looters.

Then he asked, "Gus, why would Morris not collect on our debt? Not anyone's. Said he's wiped them off the books."

"Don't know, Tailor," I said. "Maybe he lost his accounts that night."

He nodded solemn-like, aware. "I should see Mrs. Wise and apologize."

"She would like that. Seems most are fond of her."

I asked about his wife since Jeremiah's passing and he teared up. Said they were managing. "I miss me boy every day, Gus. You got to keep an eye on yer children."

We parted ways, me wondering who were keeping an eye on me.

CHAPTER 47: RECKONING

Tartuffe, Of Vice and Virtue

SARAH

$\mathcal{C}$ome April, there was a glint of spring with crocus blooming late. A hard winter had kept the townsfolk indoors and I was sure gossip was a boiling pot of old stew. I heard little as I rarely left the house, we were so busy. No wonder it had taken the mason and the carpenter long to finish the dining room. The bookcases and hearth were riddled with secret hiding places. Trusting me after saving his money, Robert revealed it was hidden behind the brick of the firebox.

"If anything ever happens to me, you'll know where to find it."

"Whatever do you mean, Robert?"

"Nothing. There are people, one particularly—who wants everything I have."

"Robert. Tell me? Who is this person? We must notify the sheriff." He looked at me with such disdain.

During the spring rains, I spun wool in the kitchen, funneling it in a figure eight upon Griet's outstretched hands. The thread from the spindle snapped and I cursed in frustration. Wetting the ends between my lips, I wound them together, one dark nub with one thin flax. Robert poked his wet head in the door, wiping his wet face. The new *London Merchant*, a well-armed Guineaman carrying dry goods and no slaves, arrived in harbor. The mood of our house hustled as it seemed my master had been brewing a plan for her arrival.

Robert invited Captain Matthews to dinner with Sheriff Goldsboro, Reverend Bacon and James Tilghman. He had ordered a lamb to slaughter a few days earlier. He purchased a country ham from Plimhimmon's store, and I made applesauce from old apples. Hestia made oyster stew, roasted potatoes and hollandaise for her early asparagus. We had no madeira, so Philadelphia whisky made do. I set the table in the small parlor by a roaring fire. Sheriff Goldsboro was seated nearest the front door, Reverend Bacon opposite, Tilghman with his back to the fire and Robert by the liquor stand. A repast about men, their station and their business. I was resigned to serve.

"Callister will finish the ship's inventory on the morrow, Samuel," said Robert.

Matthews grumbled, his mouth full of ham. "I must keep schedule. Once they load tobacco, we'll head to Boston for gin and return to Liverpool."

"Are you laying up then or will you return to us soon?" asked Tilghman.

"If you can bring us some Madeira and Caribs by July," said Robert, "I'll load you with cypress for a return to England."

I dabbed mint jelly on Reverend's plate and saw Goldsboro stiffen in his chair. "Morris," he said, "I believe we have an agreement with Gildart to carry the cypress."

Robert ignored him. Gazing across the table at Tilghman, he replied, "Gildart has been unable to acquire a new ship. His insurance on the *Johnson* did not pay."

"Surely you can make him a loan," said Goldsboro, looking around. "We are all friends here."

Robert chortled. Tilghman rested his knife and his fork on his plate. "Since you broach the subject, Gildart never took any insurance on our goods, or his ship, though it was a part of our agreement on the cypress deal. Robert and I refuse to carry the loss."

Goldsboro swallowed and cleared his throat. "That's impossible."

"Is it?" asked Robert. "Sheriff, forgive me, but you are either a genius or a fool. My private ledger shows that Tilghman and I paid the cost of insurance, yet no documents have been produced six months later." He tapped his plate with his fork. "A debt, sir, to be paid from profits which burned in harbor. You were paid in advance, but knew that rat trap would never make it to England."

Goldsboro rose and resting his hands on either side of his plate, he leaned toward Robert. "I knew no such thing. Gildart assured me he had insurance."

Robert leaned back in his chair. "Edward Lloyd has signed a letter saying there is no insurance. That the ship wasn't seaworthy. Furthermore, the letter states you pressed ahead with the plan, saying I didn't care." Robert's heel tapped. He nodded to the captain. "Matthews, as witness on this night, will you sign a statement that Robert Morris and James Tilghman, Esquire, of the Maryland Colony's Provincial Court, do accuse Sheriff Goldsboro of fraud on our investment?"

Matthews face dawned in recognition. If he wanted the cypress, he had to commit. He smiled broadly and said, "Of course, Robert. Unheard of not to insure the high seas."

"What?" yelled Goldsboro, knocking his whisky across the table. His face flushed rare as the lamb on his plate. "You lie! No one will believe you."

"On the contrary, sir," replied Tilghman, leaning back. "Everyone will believe it. You are aware how reviled you are in Oxford for collecting exorbitant rack rents and evicting hardworking residents. Your jealousy of Robert Morris is known as far as Annapolis. Did you think the governor would not inform me of your complaint that Morris, Bacon and I are stealing from *Cunliffe*?"

"Lies! We were in this together," blustered the sheriff, kicking his chair.

"We paid you in advance upon your demand, a mistake I will never make again with anyone. I have your signed receipt if you recall," said Robert.

"Do you think me a fool, Goldsboro? I have a reputation to preserve," said Tilghman.

"You have created false evidence, Morris," shouted Goldsboro.

"You have had it in for me ever since you stole that bitch from me!" His long arm extended, pointing at me.

Looking down, I curtsied but my heart was singing in heaven.

"My family will defend my honor. You will not get away with this farce!" he yelled.

"Sheriff, calm yourself," said Tilghman. "Only the assembled here know of your crime. You will continue in your position as Sheriff of Oxford and come the court's summer session, you will be called to Annapolis where you'll pay your debt to us. If you don't have it, I'm sure your illustrious parents will provide."

Silence fell and Reverend Bacon's sonorous voice cut through as his hands rose. "God for all eternity speaks what's right and just. Let us pray to bear Goldsboro's tribulation and upon his death let his spirit inherit everlasting life."

"God's breath!" yelled the sheriff. He turned on his heel and strode to the front door. "Damn you all to hell!" The door slammed in my ears, but we were free of him. Or so I thought.

Robert was kinder over the following months. Returned from ruin, he found generosity, not just with me, but funded the Reverend's initiative to start a school for town children and even young slave boys. He asked if I had news of Yearie and, cautious, I asked why. He said he wished her safe passage, that he wouldn't set slave-catchers on her. I was doubtful, but neither had I heard from her. He brought me trinkets and plied me with ribbons and laces for my sewing. I was unable to refuse him in all aspects of our relationship, though I never fully trusted him.

Seeing he was on hard times, I thought the townspeople felt some guilt after the bedlam they helped engineer. Griet spread the word of Goldsboro's deceit to the tavern doxies and it blossomed as a weed throughout town. The accusations against the sheriff and the death of Findley gave us all hope. Conversation in Oxford grew warmer as it was when I was a child. For the first time since I had entered Robert's home, I was included.

. . .

He traveled a great deal and the gossip mongers let slip he had found a favorite in Annapolis, one Eliza Burrows, a widow of some means with no children. They said she was quite beautiful, dark-haired and gray-eyed, graced with the voice of a songstress. I was instinctively jealous for all the time it took eggs to boil. I had what I needed in my garden and under the hearthstone. Blackmail in the form of Robert's accounts and my stash of Cunliffe's British currency.

Three months later, on July 6th, the ground shook beneath Morris House changing my world forever. Captain Matthews sailed, as promised, into Oxford with a load of madeira and Guinea slaves. Upon docking, the *London Merchant* heaved toward the pier, leaving her deck slanted. Robert complained that the *Johnson*'s debris had settled in the middle of the harbor from heavy spring tides, making it dangerous to unload ships. Coupled with a waning moon, shallows appeared leaving a smelly muck in the shore reeds as if every jakes in town needed digging out. Sailors believed death followed an ebb tide, and aware of their great superstitions, Robert said the harbor would have to be dredged. Lowly Oxford, dredged like a big city harbor. His vision amazed me.

I had worked my kitchen garden for Captain Matthew's welcome dinner and was putting on an apron when Sally screeched. She had fussed all night and now my heart sank seeing her tearful face as she tugged at her ear. I looked around and saw everyone hard at work. Robert burst through the kitchen door, stirring up flies that Griet swatted when she wasn't peeling peaches.

"I'm waiting for Callister to show," he said, unbuttoning his work vest. "I need a clean vest to board. I'll not have Matthews see me soiled."

"Well, the way to prevent that m'lord is to stop doing the work that soils you. How many times have I asked you to don an oilcloth?"

"You nag like a fishwife. There's a wardrobe above stairs. Go get one."

I brought a flowered waistcoat in greens and golds, a fresh linen shirt and gathered a green silk frock coat and fresh cravat. He changed in front of us without a care for bruising our eyes. At least he was gentleman enough to turn his back when he tucked in his shirt.

Sally wailed. I picked her up, but, ridden with fever, she didn't quiet. Robert glared at us.

Henry Callister stuck his head in the kitchen. "Sir, the sailors object. It's against custom to unload the cargo before we toast the captain's crossing."

"I don't care. If his ship is lightened, then she'll shift upright with the evening tide. He only has thirty-four Guineamen and the rest is madeira for my cellar."

"Hardly worth his passage across the Atlantic," said Henry.

"He picks up the blackstrap molasses the *Pearl* left last month. Taking up room in my warehouse."

Henry leaned an arm on the windowsill. "Ridiculous Captain Jefferd refused to take it to the gin distillers in Boston."

"Eh, Liverpool is swimming in gin. There wasn't enough profit in it for Jefferd. It's mine now, free and clear to send to Boston. We'll market our gin in the colonies," answered Robert.

Henry nodded. "I'll start processing the slaves. They'll travel by shallop upriver to the plantations tomorrow.."

"Feed them. I want them in good shape. This day has proved nothing but mischief so far." Robert turned to me and, seeing the care I had over Sally, he sighed and offered, "Do you want a replacement for Yearie?"

There was no replacement for Yearie. Warmed, though, by his offer I decided to be honest, "No, thank you, m'lord. I have contacted the cooper's wife. Her daughter, Abigail, can take over for Gus. Gus will do Yearie's work."

"And Voltaire in the stable? Poor animals. What's the cost to pay her? A slave is an asset, a servant is a liability."

I stared into his eyes.

He looked down in embarrassment. "I only meant one who is untrained, not you."

"We will feed Abigail. She can earn sixpence a month."

"Highway robbery! I pay the cooper handsomely. It's not my

fault his wife births nothing but split tails. Tell her we'll give the child a tuppence a month and be done with it."

"A bargain, is it, sir? Her worth is more to me. Once she's trained in three months, I'll raise her pay again." Robert eyebrows shot up at my boldness. Sally screamed in my ears. "Robert, will you stay to help me. Just rock her till she sleeps?" A long chalk tavern win, it was still worth asking.

A smiled twitched about his face. "You make my business every-one's gossip, my dear. Matthews awaits. Salud," he said and tossed back his ale. "Mrs. Wise, come to the dock in a few hours and board the *Merchant* with me,"

Griet looked up from her fly whapping. "Uh-nah, master. You know it's bad luck to have a woman aboard. You'd best be gone afore the mistress throws something at your noggin."

Robert laughed heartily, palming Griet's burr head. "Talking like your mistress I see, bossing me around." He was off to the *London Merchant* and the kitchen felt empty.

July's heat closed in as the day inched along. Guests were due at seven when the house had cooled down. Finding Sally's pilcher soaked again, I stripped it and dressed her only in wool and clout. She turned her head against Hestia's sourdough pap and we briefly entertained paying a slave wet nurse, but I was not landed gentry and would be criticized by the gossips of Oxford. I was reluctant to damage my new reputation. Desperate, I spooned sweetened goat's milk between her lips and, exhausted, she fell asleep as the sun reached its zenith.

Griet and I were setting the table when she looked up and said, "Mistress, I know what to do. Go down to the harbor and catch a breeze. Master never asks you to join him."

Hestia had watch of Sally. Voltaire had finished the stable and was sweeping the hall. I left. Down the strand was a hive of activity in harbor. Callister had locked the Guineamen in cages, their skin shiny with sweat. The tide was out, the putrid air like to gag me. Black flies swarmed everywhere, buzzing and dipping. I had missed my chance to join Robert. His wherry was tied to the side of the *London Merchant*, which tipped precariously toward it. Even the rope ladders to climb her deck angled out from her side. The sun cast the ship's shadow across the water, stopping short of where I stood. I shielded my eyes but could see the cluster of men onboard, drinking and toasting Matthew's crossing. Casks of madeira were lined up ready for the barge to move them ashore. Robert would be excited to open one for his dinner.

A tiny breeze ruffled the lace of my mob cap and I felt a prickle rise on the back of my neck. Rocking back and forth, my gut stirred low as if my womb were strangled. It passed quickly, but I knew the meaning. My breasts tingled and not from my milk drying up. I counted days and knew I had missed my monthly a second time. Another baby would slow me down, and Sally nowhere near potty-trained. It were a cause for joy that I would never again deny.

Shells crunched nearby. It was Henry, back from the slaves.

"Missus," he said, frowning. "Some of her tars say sharks followed them into harbor. It's a bad sign."

"Well, don't give in to their superstitions. They aren't known to be the most educated."

"True. Once we load the cypress and get her to sail, I'll be done with my worry."

"I'm sure, Henry." I put a hand on his arm. "You're doing a good job as Robert's under factor." I glanced at him. "Are you joining us for dinner tonight?"

He bowed. "I am delighted, m'lady. Looking forward to an evening at your fine table."

We heard a shout and Robert, Matthews, his first mate, and two oarsmen descended into the wherry. Robert clambered to the prow. Matthews stood in the back to signal for the cannon salute from his ship, recognition of Robert's welcome. The others took up the oars and swept them into the water. Hearing the grind of cannon on wood, my eyes were drawn upward as they slid in the gunnels. Not to waste a cannon ball, the tars loaded wadding. Captain Matthews bowed slightly and raised one gloved hand. I thought it too early for him to signal, for they were naught but twenty yards from the ship.

Above, a young sailor held a lit taper, glancing at his captain from deck. The flies drove Matthews mad and he stepped sideways in the wherry, waggling his hand across his face. The sailor, his face shadowed beneath his tricorn, nodded, and laid the match. In a matter of seconds, the shot rang out horizontally across the harbor, sailing by the wherry and the first mate's head with a splat and a slurp into the muck. Callister and I erupted in laughter at the noise. Wood ducks flapped in alarm and took to the air in droves, quacking in alarm. And then we glanced toward the ship to see if Matthews would berate his tars.

In the shallow water, the wherry rocked. One of Robert's harbor slaves had abandoned his oars and leaped to the prow, catching his master as he staggered, screaming in pain. Blood stained his frock coat and he curled into a ball. Henry and I ran the length of the pier and waited helplessly as they oared to us.

Laborers gathered, pushing me away as they carried him home, his cries garbled in his throat. At the kitchen door, he fainted in their arms. Griet, always alert, always calculating, swept everything from the table and they dumped him upon it. The captain ordered Henry to make haste to the surgeon.

"Tell him it's Morris and there'll be silver in his pocket."

"Gus, fresh linen," I said. "Hestia, a bowl of hot water and my herbals."

The laborer gripping Robert's arm cursed and pushed me away. "We'll wait for the surgeon, mistress."

"How dare you?" I said. "Get out of my way." Faced with intensity, he stepped back. I ripped the shoulder from Robert's jacket and yanked the sleeve down. His upper arm gnawed, flesh and muscle shredded, the white of his bone split in two. Inside his arm, dark-red blood pulsed, spilling onto the floor.

"Give me your garters," I said to the man, closing my hands around the wound.

"I'll not give you nothing, madam."

"Mistress, he could die afore that drunk gets here," Hestia said. Drawing a poker from the fire, she held it to the man's chest.

Captain Matthews ordered, "Do as she says."

Griet laid a stack of fresh linen by my side. I raised one bloody hand for a peek. Oakum roping, embedded deep. Plucked it out, tied a leather garter above the wound.

"Gus, press here."

Such fortitude in little hands. I wound the second garter. Cinched it. Griet layered linen. Immediately soaked. Interminable wait. Our doctor would *not* cut off this limb. His saw, a dim eye, a bellyful of gin.

The bleeding slowed. A collective sigh.

Hestia elbowed her considerable way into the circle, casting the tempest's eye, "You wanting the poultice, mistress?"

"The yarrow. Slather it on this linen." Greenish and thick from setting up in the dark, we folded the treated linen onto the wound and wrapped it tightly. Robert started to come round, his eyes fluttered open, then closed.

"All right," I said. "Take my master above stairs to his chamber. Get a dining board from the meeting room to set him on."

Once upstairs, Henry appeared with a man I didn't know. Dr. Walston introduced himself. Hat in hand, Henry asked the rest to leave and lurked at the door watching Robert.

"It's a broken bone, sir," I said, "and a bloodbath."

"Your master, Robert Morris, the merchant?"

"He cannot die. He's too vital to Oxford and too cranky."

Seeing the wisdom of this, he chortled and said, "Let me see what you've done."

With the wrapping removed, the wound gushed in surges. Walston put my hand over the compress, pulled a wooden tray from his bag and laid Robert's arm within it. Directing Henry to hold Robert's shoulder, in one swift move, he shoved the lower into the upper arm. Robert's scream reached the gulls on the roof, a chorus of squawks answering. Walston ran his fingertips inside the wound, over the break just above the elbow.

"Is he righthanded, mistress?"

"Yes, sir. Will he lose it?"

"Remains to be seen. If he has no will and testament, it must be written. I'll ligate the artery and use oil of rose and turpentine to prevent putrifaction. Then we wait. Change the dressing morning and night."

I had seen flesh mortify from cauterization and was thankful he wasn't given to searing it. A death sentence it was.

"Where were you trained, sir?" I asked. "I have not heard of you in these parts."

"On the battlefield, madam. Nova Scotia. Just visiting, trying to forget the war."

"Oh, Robert clothed the Maryland regiment." I bent my head thinking how vacuous that sounded. "Forgive me." I giggled once, uncomfortable in my embarrassment and looked away. "I will oversee his care."

"Prayers would be in order. If he's a Catholic send for a priest."

"Anglican here, sir." I paused. "Doctor, you must not breathe a word of your assessment. There are many who would walk over his dead body to gain his position."

I bid him goodbye and sat by Robert. It came to me in that moment that I might be free of him. Free of the shackles, the expectation, the constant demands. Free of the doubt that plagued me, that froze me into inaction at the worst possible moments. All the wealth and conviviality Robert had bestowed on the gentry did not equal the level of misery he dealt to those who had supported him during his twelve years in Oxford. Yet, he had changed, was more thoughtful as if his eyes were opened to the plight of those less than him.

Stirrings felt deep in my womb warned me and as I gazed over his slackened face, I was struck that he was empty of his ever-present vitality. He had penned a last will and testament upon young Rob's leave-taking. Papers probably hidden behind the firebrick downstairs. Was I named, or would I have to rely on my horde of cash buried in the garden? Would I have to leave Morris House? If he died, Henry would take over Cunliffe's business in the interim. But I had the ledger, the damning of Oxford's best. Tortured, I fell asleep, my head on the edge of the mattress. When I woke, I wiped the drool from my face and straightened my bodice, resolute.

Over the next day, Robert slept a tortured sleep. Griet and I fed him sips of whisky. At times he cursed us, at others he was weepy. Walston returned regularly and on the second evening said the wound had mortified. He applied more of the turpentine concoction, and, within hours, Robert was sitting up. I prattled on about the surgeon's skill, Henry's capability at the slave auction, and the *London Merchant* being loaded with cypress. A steady line of visitors blessed his beneficence and genius, claiming their dependence on his skill. They demanded a quick convalescence. Seeing the toll this took, I limited those who came. Only Tilghman, Bacon, and Henry. I eavesdropped on every conversation, wishing Yearie's ears along mine. Bold these men were in their station and confidence that nothing untoward could happen to them.

On the third morning, the smell of the wound made me gag and I vomited in a bowl. Disgusted, he yelled at me and said to send Gus. Angry, I told him he had left me with child again. "I am not one of your fawning sycophants, just a loyal servant to her master."

He looked away and said nothing. That afternoon, he told me to send for Mr. Kemp, the Register of Wills and search the fireplace for his papers. The red wax of the Cunliffe seal prevented me from opening its pages. As the old man ascended the stairs, Robert called from his bed for me to be gone and for Kemp to shut the door.

Four days after the accident, a summer storm nearly washed the town away, cooling the air and quieting the incessant whiz of insects. As a weak sun died on the horizon, I breathed. Walston left shaking his head and Robert fell into a deep sleep. I went to the kitchen and found Sally in Griet's arms, happy and well. Her fat arms wrapped round my neck. At almost two and a half, she finally uttered, "Mama, hungry." I bundled her to me, threw my arm around Griet and called to Hestia. We bowed our heads, held each other and prayed for hope and good.

I whispered, "Hestia, I will write your manumission tonight in Robert's hand. You have money to go to your sister. Griet, you can stay with me, or go to your mother in Lewes, whatever you want. We must be prepared for the worst and hope for the best as Yearie would say."

I laid the soiled bandages next to the wash bucket and leaned against the wall, a bundle of ache and confusion. My vision seemed to narrow, and I slipped onto the bench. "Is all good with the world outside?" I asked.

There was a knock at the front door. Repeated. Voltaire answered and came running.

"What is it? I have not time for your anxieties."

"We have visitors, Mistress. Master Tilghman, the reverend, and others. They said the doctor told them to come."

My house was not my own, even in Robert's last moments.

They stood in the hall, sweating, concerned. I went to each and thanked them for coming but said I would have to see if my master was awake. On hearing a loud moan followed by a scream, I took the stairs in twos, Tilghman and Bacon behind. It was dark, the light from one candle reflected on the hallway floor. Pushing the hair from my face, I found Robert braying like a wounded deer. He flailed across his bed. "Get him off of me! Shoot him!"

"There is no one here, Robert," I yelled. "Only your friends! Look."

His eyes darted about and came to rest on me with recognition. Out of breath, he could barely form his thoughts into words. "The hog roller, Sarah. He stood right where you are, his sweat dripping on me."

"Jackson? He's been gone months, Robert. A dream is all."

"He called on God to deliver justice. I have done nothing wrong. Nothing!"

"It's the fever, m'lord. You are safe with us."

"But he grabbed my arm, Sarah, with his dirty hands. See the wound?"

His head fell against the pillow. I held the candle high and, finding the arm perfectly wrapped in the wooden tray, leaned over and kissed his cheek.

GRIET

They were loafing in the hall, whispering as if Master were already dead. Callister, the tailor, the cooper, even a Dr. Hamilton all the way from Annapolis on the mail schooner. Others were coming. I bowed and asked if they would sit in the gathering room. I brought chairs from the parlor and soon it were a regular little confab, puffing up a storm on their pipes. Voltaire brought eats and I knew Hestia was mad when I saw her favorite orange cake wasted on their tray. Another knock and I went at once to find his despicable self, the sheriff in his new cockhat and plume. He laid it on the harpsichord and commanded me to take his dogs to the kitchen. I called them and he entered the meeting room, asking for Master's madeira.

I put the dogs outside the kitchen quarter with Tray who got up and left for the stable. Hestia took a bottle only just unloaded from the ship and twisted the cork. "You pour it. I can't stomach them hypocrites."

Voltaire gathered cups and we walked in together, a job I had never done except in the tavern. Seeing them all armored with drink and none spilt, I moved to leave when the sheriff ordered me to take his steed to the stable for water and feed. I didn't hop to, so he rose in a most threatening way. I left with his cockhat under mine arm as he exclaimed how things were changing at Morris House.

A new horse for him, she was big and light on her feet. I patted her nose telling her I was sorry for her lot in life. I fed her and Master's pretty black. I hung the vest of me on a rail and mucking a bit, I was glad to be outdoors away from the doings inside, mine linen shirt flowing free to catch a breeze on mine chest bindings. So hot they were, but I reasoned not as bad as stays, not squeezing mine air. I would keep my ruse as long as I could. Maybe Master wouldn't die.

Under the great oak, I stopped, reached in mine pants to scratch an itch and bemoaned a flea. One of mine new silver buttons popped and the pants of me dropped. *Jayzus*, I thought, grabbing the waist. Always something. Sarah would scold if I didn't find it, for matching buttons were hard to find. I bent in the dark and felt a brief delight as it rolled in mine fingers. Rising, I felt a presence behind me.

"Boy, you were at the fire. And in harbor when I returned from the swamp. What's your name?" asked Goldsboro.

"Gus, sir," I said standing at attention, Mistress' words, *do not speak to the sheriff*, rang in mine ears. His breeches were unbuttoned. Headed to the jakes, he were.

"That's it. Well now, things are going to be different, Gus. I'll be your new master. You and your mistress will work for me. She'll not refuse me again. I hear you are good with her halfwit."

He stepped closer, and holding mine pants up, I swayed a bit before him to see if his yellowed eyes could follow me. He weren't as drunk as a pitching sailor, just full of his own bloat. He gave me a lecherous grin.

"My ancestors are titled in England, you know. Don't listen to that folderol from Morris and Tilghman, fair boy. This little job as sheriff is not my true calling. I'll be a justice in the legislature soon. Tilghman will have his comeuppance. My father arrives tonight and will take charge of this mess." He leaned down and blinking fast, said in a heated voice, "You think you can trip me in front of Oxford and make me a laughingstock?" His hand lay heavy on mine shoulder. "You have an interesting look, boy. My tastes are quite varied."

He picked me up and threw me face down over the garden fence, the pants of me round mine ankles. I felt his member against mine ass and his hand on mine front. Feeling nothing and seeing I wore pantalettes, he laughed. "What do we have here?" Inching back with surprise, his hand gripped the fence rail for balance.

I sprang from it, kicking off mine breeches. "Sheriff," I said, "I tink your monkey come out of its sleeve." He reached for me, a mouthful of teeth coming at mine eyes, and I clawed his cheek, yelling like a dockworker. "Sarah, Sarah! Help me!"

He stumbled forward and I slid between his legs, trying to slip away from his clutches, mine fingers scrabbling in the dirt. His hand covered mine mouth and biting his pointer hard, I screamed, "Get off me! God, help me! Sarah!" This could not go unheard.

Soon, they all stood round us, me struggling free, and the tailor and cooper helping Lord Sheriff to his feet.

"Goldsboro, what means this display?" asked Mr. Tilghman.

"Why, the boy tripped me. He was angry and came at me."

I stood back, mine breeches tangled in cucumber vines. Bringing the hem of mine shirt to wipe the face of me, sniffling loud, Tilghman took license and lifted mine shirt further. Seeing the binding of mine chest above and pantalettes below, he said, "Gus, you're a girl!"

"Yes sir," I said, holding back sobs. Their eyes turned to the sheriff. He stood, his goods open to the air, his rod soft.

Reverend knelt before me and asked, "Is this true, Gus? Did you attack the sheriff?"

"N-no, Reverend. Why would I?" I gulped tears that were starting to roll. "He told me he would have me, sir. I-I don't know what that means, for I pretend to be a boy so a lord would leave mine girl parts alone, but he pulled the pants of me and—and I were scared." I held out mine button and crumpled in his arms, giving way to hellacious sobs.

"Hestia," called Tilghman. "Come take him, ah, her, to Mrs. Wise. The rest of you, take the sheriff to the parlor and tie him to a chair. I will return with an answer to this problem."

I wailed all the way inside. Leading me to the foot of the steps, Hestia hugged me and whispered, "What you up to, Griet? I know when you acting."

"I weren't acting none at all, Hestia. He said he would take Master's place with Sarah first, then me. He is so ugly, Hestia, like maggots in shit."

"Go above stairs and don't say nothing to Mistress till I call you."

I sat upstairs in my pantalettes, driven mad with hiccups as Sarah prayed over Master. I guess she think I were upset at his condition for she had not heard my screams. The room smelled like death and mine miserable self felt helpless. I toyed with the button of mine breeches as she fingered a cross, its strand of metal beads broken off above the crucifix. I reached over and pulled it from her, the eyes of me wide. Master were heaving his death throes, so I whispered, "Sarah, where did this cross come from?"

"My rosary. It was in my daughter's hand when she was stolen from her crib. Little Phebe, you remember? My heart still aches for her."

Little Phebe? I threw the cross on master and ran above stairs to mine bed. Beneath it were the leather pouch I brought with me from the swamp. A dear bone, milkweed knots, and filigree beads. I raced downstairs and draped the beads across Sarah's lap. Her hands rose, her gaze down. "Griet, these are the beads you presented me that day in the swamp. But they're different. They have silver beads like mine.

"Yes, mistress. I-I wanted to keep the silver ones. They were Phebe's, but Wenetko says I were not stolen by the Indians with papje. I were brought before by Yellow Eyes. By—by that heretic Goldsboro himself." I stopped and looked at her face to see if I made sense. "They—they match yours."

"The beads. They were Phebe's only memory of me."

"My only memory of you," I said.

Her pretty blue eyes roamed over me. She held mine chin, inspecting the scar, all thoughtful and distant like I were a bug under glass. "There are two," she said, tracing the pattern.

"One from before I can remember and one from falling on a rock in the camp."

"Why do you hop like a little frog, Griet? Phebe was burned at the Vanderkoop's hearth but she didn't hop."

"The scar on my foot grew tight as I grew, Mistress. Everything grew tight and misty. Bits and pieces come back to me—your beehive and the honey, the ribbons in your hair, praying like this by the fire before bed. It is Grandmama who is buried in the cemetary." I held my palms together, fingers pointed upward unlike the Anglicans who folded theirs.

Her arms circled me. "My treasure," she whispered, her voice breaking. "Oh, is it true? Pat a cake, pat a cake, my Phebe?" She held up her palms.

"'Bake me a cake as fast as you can,'" said I as I clapped hers. "See? I'm no Dutch girl."

I laid mine cheek on her chest wondering was this the change we had prayed for with Hestia? She rocked me in her arms and our silent tears fell, mingling on the master's bed cloth.

His breathing came shallow. Dr. Walston appeared in the chamber and said it would not be long, there was a crowd amassing below. They wanted Sarah. As she took me by the hand in my shirt and pantalettes, I reached for the button to mine breeches that had fallen to the floor. I would need it later. We walked below stairs to the gathering room where people stood shoulder to shoulder, faces full of contempt for he who sat tied to Master's dining chair.

In the hall, Henry Callister opened the great door to the night air and a slight breeze cooled their tempers if not their frowns. Outside, torches held by young boys in red and gold livery lit the walkway to the street. A rider on a huge black dismounted and I recognized Master Tilghman, stern-faced, determined. An open sedan chair drawn by a white horse swathed in satin to match the servants followed. I tugged on Sarah's hand for this must be a prince from St. Domingue.

I were so wrong. Master Tilghman reached and a woman sat up, her hair powdered white, mounded high atop her head, a fake bird nestled inside. She pointed one brocaded toe and waves of blue damask rolled out with her. Her breast was creamy white, her neck long and ringed in pearls. In the valley of her breasts nestled a large cross. Bold, she was to advertise her Papist faith amongst so many Anglicans. But a wealthy woman can do anything. A dog so tiny I hardly saw it at first was tucked in her arm, its long ears pointed in alarm. The boys drew the torches to their sides to make way.

"Who is it?" I asked Sarah.

"Shush, Griet. I don't know."

Master Tilghman offered his hand and the lady laid hers upon his. They walked across the slates, over the doorstep and I sucked air as people squeezed against the wall. She walked by us nodding to Sarah, giving me a most gentle smile and a wink. "Here, young maiden. Will you take Tartuffe for me?"

Maiden? I guessed it were my night for the dogs. I nodded and reached, holding it tight.

Master Tilghman bowed to the assembly. "Good evening one and all. Thank you for coming. I bring you the Lady Goldsboro from my home at Rich Neck. She arrived this afternoon from Annapolis by her schooner."

I had not ever seen anyone look so beautiful after a trip across the Bay. Tartuffe squirmed seeing his lady walk away. Sarah and I were left looking at her back. A train of blue flowed across the floor and I were glad I had polished it only this morn.

"This is a solemn time in the household of the great Robert Morris, so I will be brief," she said, her voice deep and proud. "My son, the sheriff of fair Oxford, sits before you a penitent. His father and I have been disturbed by the trouble he has caused you noble people. Therefore, it is time to bring him home to us. He will vacate his position immediately, leaving you and your good town in peace." She turned ready to speak to Sarah.

"But, Mother," cried Goldsboro, "I have opportunity here. These people listen to me."

She looked to her son and ever so slowly, said, "You are not a man of the cloth, my son. Nor are you an honorable man of justice.

The trickery is over. You have embarrassed your father and me for the last time." She grunted and said, "Get up."

Two Jackson sized slaves bundled him outside, he struggling and whining. They helped him mount a horse and his hands tied to the pommel, stood guard. Relieved, his mother paused before Sarah. "You are Mrs. Wise, the lady of this house?"

Sarah curtsied. "Yes, madam. May I be of service?"

"No, no, my dear. I have everything I need." She leaned over and said in a voice of conspiracy, "Do not expect him back. He will be very busy counting beans on my plantation." Then, louder, she said, "Mrs. Wise, I am grateful for your patience. I will pray for Mr. Morris, God rest his soul. Reverend Bacon, I expect a good eulogy."

Everyone had Master dead and buried before his last breath was taken.

Hestia lumbered from the kitchen, Sally asleep in her arms. She called, "Cane, Corso, begone with your master!"

Those helmet dogs raced through the hall skidding on the floor. I could not hold Tartuffe who leaped from my arms, snarling and yapping. He bit one on the neck and wouldn't let go. Swinging in the air, the little dog's ears twitched in pleasure. Lady Goldsboro cried, "Oh, save poor Tartuffe!"

Reverend Bacon rushed to dislodge his teeth, and a boy commanded the helmet dogs to his side. We were speechless. Here was the world of the sheriff where everyone took care of his mess.

"I've always hated those animals," the Lady said. "Can you put them to work in the harbor keeping the rats away?"

Henry Callister bowed and said, "Of course, m'lady. They will be very useful."

I doubted it. Liable to chase every slave about their business. Lady Goldsboro gathered Tartuffe to her bosom and he licked her chin like it were cream. She chortled. "I will be at Rich Neck Manor with Master Tilghman in the coming days, Mrs. Wise. Please call on me. You have performed a great service to Oxford, welcoming everyone to your table. Your reputation for hospitality has spread far and wide."

Sarah curtsied deep, her eyes resting on the cross. "I am your servant, m'lady," she said. "Perhaps we could talk about Robert's school. He dreamed of educating the village children and young slaves."

The mouth of me fell open. And I were her daughter. I let the button of mine breeches fall to the floor.

SARAH'S EPILOGUE

*G*riet delivered my third child, a boy we named Thomas Wise Morris who brought me great solace and hope. His cries filled the house and gave me confidence. A boy, a Morris son, would surely achieve greatness. I wrote Rob in Philadelphia of the news and, to our surprise, he promised never to abandon his half-brother.

In his will, Robert left me and the children a hoard of Maryland tobacco notes that were worth nothing outside the province. No matter, my stash of guineas was buried in the garden. We would not starve, yet I knew I had to be careful about using gold coins in Oxford. An unmarried woman with money.

Cunliffe made no promises allowing me to stay in Morris House. Henry continued to factor for them. He was a bookish man with a soft compass, not blessed with Robert's business instincts. Commerce declined. I was living on the borrowed good will of a distant employer.

Come winter, I was busy working Cunliffe accounts for Henry Callister when Mac showed up on my doorstep again with promises and misty eyes. I gave his words no import, bedded him upstairs in my old garret chamber, and told him to return when he saw me as a woman of consequence. As he dressed, I asked him of Yearie, hoping for some tidbit. He couldn't say, only that he dropped her in Wilmington's harbor with Jackson.

After he left, I drew her diary from my desk. Unfinished, inside her letters were perfectly arched in a hurried script. I had found it in a hidden nook near Robert's hidey hole in the meeting room fireplace. Covered in tanned cowhide, it held maps, messages and drawings of her secret workings before my time. It revealed a network of slaves and indentures looking for freedom. Interspersed were *her* aspirations—a hope of marriage vows and children, a home of her own. Flipping the pages, I couldn't find what she really thought of me, except some final stinging words, "I'll never be more than a slave in Sarah's house."

On market day in town more than a year passed, I saw a woman in a red head wrap and grew startled, wondering if it was Yearie. Obsessed, I trailed her through an alley only to be disappointed when a stranger turned to confront me, her eyes wide. I apologized. She climbed into the back of a Quaker's wagon, a woman enslaved by a man who believed we come to this earth in God's image, all the same. I watched as he gingered up his nag and rolled up the Oxford Road. I raised a hand to wave, and she raised hers in return. Griet caught up with me at that moment and searched my face. She needn't. She wanted Yearie, too.

AUTHOR'S NOTE

In 2012, I visited Oxford for the first time to soak up Chesapeake lore. A little jewel on the Tred Avon River, I wondered how I'd missed this charming Victorian village. Walking near the customhouse, I found a plaque remembering the ship *Johnson* that brought a cargo of Scottish Redemptioners for indenture in 1747. A later search of records found the MacIntosh listed. Both the customhouse and the ship were relics of a much earlier time that led to a distant past, and another story.

That night at the Robert Morris Inn, I was immediately aware upon entering the massive door that the grand staircase indicated signs of great wealth. Upstairs, two magnificent bedchambers spoke of a rich past. Here was where Robert Morris, Sr. took his last breath. Who was he? Was it his picture that hung over the door outside? Or his grown son, signer of all three founding documents of the United States?

It's easy to find histories of Robert Morris, Jr., Financier of the American Revolution. Unlike many of the revolutionary leaders who were shouldered with debt, he was one of the richest men in the colonies for a short time. He answered George Washington's call, paid for his army, his food, his armaments, and the fledgling navy.

387

Giving full credit to Washington's victory at Yorktown, the deciding battle of the Revolution, only Robert Morris, Jr. could be credited with funding it. He was America's first capitalist.

Histories begin with Junior's start in Philadelphia or a reference to a brief time in his father's home in Oxford. On visiting the Nabb Center at Salisbury University, a research archive of Eastern Shore history, I found the father's last will and testament. In it, Robert Morris, Sr. didn't name his son as his own, an act so unusual some would say unheard. The father named his "beloved" sisters and "cousins" but called his son, a "Youth now living with my Friend Robert Greenway in Philadelphia known there by the name of Robert Morris Junior," as if there was no relationship between them. He also misrepresented a key detail, saying young Robert traveled from Liverpool (sic) to Philadelphia, not Oxford. The father could not have realized at the time of his death in 1750 what the future held for his son. Robert Morris, Jr.'s brief stay of under two years with his father in Oxford might not have been a bonding experience. At the least, the father wanted his son to have an education or a trade.

Yet he left him almost everything, and nothing to his other four grown children living in the colonies. His will is astounding for its length, its detail, who was included and who was left out. It was in reading it that I found the basis of *A Wife in Watercolor*, in his endearing words recognizing a woman named Sarah Wise and his passing mention of two slaves: Yearie and Jackson.

The record of women in Western history is sparse. Through the sixteenth to eighteenth centuries very little is written by women, about women, and nearly nothing about women of the lower classes. For me, Sarah's story needed to be imagined.

With one child and another on the way, Robert left Sarah a considerable amount of money in tobacco notes but no home. I wondered what happened to her. I wondered who she was before she came to work in his home. Multiple searches at the Maryland Archives in Annapolis revealed only one mention of a Sarah Morris in land records. She was connected with the purchase of Rich Range after 1750 and I remain sure this was her. There is no mention of

Sarah in St. Peter's Church (White Marsh) birth and death records although there are plenty of women named Sarah. She disappeared.

There is no other information about Yearie and Jackson, except that Morris felt the urge to comment on Jackson's lack of worth. Perhaps, in doing so, he made Jackson unmarketable, leaving him in Sarah's possession. I would like to believe he had some compassion. His interest in starting a school for the young, free and enslaved boys of Oxford is documented in the writings of Reverend Thomas Bacon.

The diaspora of Black and Native American communities intersected on the Peninsula in the mid-eighteenth century, pushing them north and west. Maroon societies existed in the West Indies, and a large one is also documented in colonial Carolina. I could find only a brief reference to maroons in the Great Cypress Swamp. It's logical that it would become home to those on the fringe of rigid colonial society.

On belief systems, Yearie's conjuring should not be trivialized. She was a product of her time, combining threads of Christianity with her mother's Trinidad practices that were not an extension of Western magic. Principles of the Enlightenment and the Scientific Revolution would have reached Oxford, as had Reverend Whitehead's Great Awakening. Religion was a powerful force in everyone's life. Sarah was bound by her Catholicism in an Anglican world, but Griet was innocent of church doctrine. Yearie had every reason to protect a trusted white person in the only ways she knew how, hoping it would save she and Jackson in the immediate as Reverend Bacon's promise of Heaven for the dutiful slave after death was small consolation.

At the Maryland Archives I discovered a huge leatherbound volume of court records from the late 1740s. Imagine my surprise to find the very first page a lawsuit brought against a lowly Talbot resident demanding payment of their debt to Foster Cunliffe and Sons of Liverpool. Pages of Cunliffe lawsuits followed. The long arm of power reached across the ocean to play out in Maryland's provincial court with many competent county lawyers representing Cunliffe. Often, the defendant's land was sold, leaving them with no choice but to move west to the frontier. Cunliffe and Sons continued in mercantile and slave trade after the death of Robert Morris, Sr., until they were able to buy their way into England's nobility. They left trading in the late 1750s.

Oxford went into a slow but steady decline as war neared. English trade laws were onerous, profits from tobacco were irregular, and by turning to wheat, farmers and plantation owners no longer needed as many slaves to work their fields. Enslaved Blacks and Native Americans were marched south in coffles and sold to work the cotton crop. After the Revolution, Oxford's English shipping and trade industry was hampered and, it was said, some residents left their cows wandering the streets in their hurry to move to the western shore.

On language, Oxford was a melting pot of communication. People came from all corners of the world and many newly arrived Africans of varying West Coast tribes couldn't communicate with their masters, much less each other. Acquisition of the King's English would have been slow for anyone not educated in England or a major colonial university. The dialects presented are representative of working-class people from varied locations who influenced each other's speech. The people in Somers Cove more accurately represent the isolated language of Elizabethan times still present in pockets on the Peninsula, Smith and Tangier Islands. Word usage was checked through the Merriam Webster Dictionary online, the Oxford American Writers Thesaurus, Shakespearean vocabulary, and primary sources (written by men) too numerous to mention.

Robert Morris, Sr. died on July 12th, 1750 three months into his forty-ninth year. What follows are excerpts of his Last Will and Testament. The discrepancy of the date when it was first written doesn't account for the inclusion of Sarah's unborn child at the time of Robert's death. The commas are mostly mine to aid in understanding.

"In the name of God, Amen. I, Robert Morris of Talbot County and Province of Maryland, Merchant Son of Andrew Morris, Mariner, and Maudlin, his wife, both Deceased, late of the Town of Liverpoole in the County of Lancaster and Kingdom of Great Britain, being in good

and perfect Health and peace of mind, do this Seventeenth day of April One thousand Seven Hundred and forty nine make and Publish this, my last Will and Testament. Imprimis, I commend my Soul to Almighty God, the Author and giver of life, and my body to be decently Interred in the Earth in hopes and full Confidence of a Joyful Resurrection through the merits of Jesus Christ, the Son of God, my Redeemer and Saviour, and I dispose of that Worldly Estate with which it hath pleased the Almighty to bless me as follows...

"*Item*, I give to Sarah Wise of Talbot County in Maryland for the good will and affection I have for her, Two Hundred and Fifty Pounds Current Money of Maryland, and my two Silver pint Canns (sic), and Six Silver Table Spoons. *Item*, I give to Sarah, Daughter of the said Sarah Wise, One hundred Pounds Current Money of Maryland—*Item*, I give to the Child that Sarah Wise informed is now with Child of, One Hundred Pounds Current Money of the Province aforesaid, and it is my will that the last mentioned Items shall be paid unto the said Sarah Wise immediately after my Decease, for they are all of her said Children. I also give to the said Sarah Wise the *Item*, one mourning Ring, and the smallest of my two Silver Tankards, and all of my shirts and other wearing linnen that I shall dye slight of...

"*Item*, I give all my Lands and Tenements whatsoever whereof I shall die Leased in Possession. Reversion or remainder, to a Youth now living with my Friend, Robert Greenway in Philadelphia, known there by the name of Robert Morris Junior, who arrived in Philadelphia from Liverpoole, some time in the Year One Thousand Seven Hundred and Forty Eight, and to him, the said Robert Morris Junior now living with M. Robert Greenway, Merchant in Philadelphia, I Give and bequeath all the Land, Tenements I shall die possessed of forever."... "I likewise Give to the said Robert Morris Junior all the rest and Residue of my Good, Chattels, Merchandize, Apparel and Personal Estate whatsoever. ... The remaining part of my Estate to M. Robert Greenway of Philadelphia to be kept by him in Trust for Robert Morris Jun. till the said Robert Morris Junior shall ask and demand it..."

I am indebted to early readers from Rabbit's Gnaw, a critique group of the Delmarva Review, and the Coastal Writers of Rehoboth Beach Writers Guild. I am forever grateful to my editor, Arianne "Tex" Thompson, for her wisdom, wit and energy that helped me slog through the final stages. Her enthusiasm and literary locksmithing inspired a running conversation of dreams that sent my fingers to the keyboard. Sensitivity readers, Nicole Lewis, Kim Moore and Emily Gardner contributed to discussions of race, disability and historical context. I am thankful for their perspectives.

I'm eternally grateful to Chief Quiet Bear, Michael Morabito of the Assateague Tribe for his solemn descriptions of the Great Cypress Swamp and its strategic value in hiding what was left of his tribe. A generous and non-warlike people, the Assateague suffered greatly at the hands of Europeans, learning that survival depended on being "harder to find than to conquer." (Colonel Edward Scarburgh, www.easternshore.com.esguide>hist_assateague.html). Quiet Bear carries the weight of his peoples' history with such dignity and intelligence that audiences are reverent in his presence. I must also thank the staff of the Nanticoke Indian Museum in Millsboro, Delaware, particularly Sterling Street, whose early direction aided my understanding of the Nanticoke diaspora. Our discussions led to research of Weocomocus and her son, Robin, who negotiated protected land boundaries for the Nanticoke that quickly became broken treaties.

I am beholden to the modern town of Oxford, its residents and particularly Ian Fleming, owner of the iconic Robert Morris Inn for helping me imagine the town in 1750. Thanks are due to Coard Benson of the Benson Dulin Realty Group for his private tour of Plimhimmon. Although renovated, both the inn and the plantation remain steeped in the culture and history of early Talbot County.

A Wife in Watercolor brewed in my mind while I wrote two other contemporary novels until I could no longer ignore Sarah, Yearie, and Jackson. When I imagined the trauma of their lives, I realized that I needed an imaginary character not saddled with the sins of society, someone who reveled in her independence. And so, Griet was born. Still, I woke up at night thinking of them and what it must have been like to have no voice, no recognition, no place in history. Their stories are a product of my imagination for no one else would care enough to create such preposterous lies.

B.B.Shamp

BIBLIOGRAPHY

Berkin, Carol, *First Generations, Women in Colonial America*, Hill and Wang, a division of Farrar, Straus, and Giroux, 1966.

Callister, Henry, *Callister Papers I and II*, Maryland Diocesan Library, ca. 1716–ca. 1768.

Carr, Lois Green. et. Al., *Robert Cole's World, Agriculture & Society in Early Maryland*, University of North Carolina Press, 1991.

Dolin, Eric Jay, *Black Flags, Blue Waters, The Epic History of America's Most Notorious Pirates*, Liveright Publishing Corporation, 2018.

The Federal Writers' Project, *Maryland Slave Narratives, A folk History of Slavery in Maryland from Interviews with Former Slaves*, Applewood Books and the Library of Congress, 1936–1938.

The Encyclopedia of Colonial and Revolutionary America, edited by John Mack Faragher, DaCapo Press, 1996.

Fletcher, John, Vicar of Madeley, Salop, *A Vindication of the Rev. Wesley's "Calm Address to our American Colonies" in some Letters to Mr. Caleb Evans*, W. Whitestone, no. 33, Skinner-Row, 1776.

Gay, John, *The Beggar's Opera*, www.gutenberg.org/files, 1729, Project Gutenberg Ebook #25063, April 13, 2008.

Glover, Lorri and Smith, Daniel Blake, *The Shipwreck That Saved*

Jamestown, The Sea Adventure Castaways and the Fate of America, Henry Holt and Company, LLC, 2008.

Hamilton, Alexander, *Gentleman's Progress, The Itinerarium of Dr. Alexander Hamilton, 1744,* Alejandro's Libros, 2014.

Hawke, David Freeman, *Everyday Life in Early America,* edited by Richard Balkirn, Harper & Row, 1988.

Heite, Ned, *"The Winnesocum Disaster,"* www.nativemericansofdelwarestate.com/winnesocccum.htm, 2011.

Hildebrand, David K. & Schaaf, Elizabeth M., *Musical Maryland, A History of Song and Performance from the Colonial Period to the Age of Radio,* Johns Hopkins University Press, 2017.

Journal of Correspondence of the Committee of Safety, 1776 (Talbot), General Court, Eastern Shore Criminal Prosecutions, 1776–83, MHR, Maryland Archives.

Middleton, Arthur, *Tobacco Coast, A Maritime History of the Chesapeake Bay in Colonial America,* Johns Hopkins University Press and The Maryland State Archives, 1984.

Moitt, Bernard, *Women and Slavery, The French Antilles, 1635–1848,* Indiana University Press, 2001.

Moliere, (Jean Baptiste Poquelin), *Tartuffe,* edited by John Berseth, Dover Thrift Editions, unabridged, Dover Publications, Inc., 2000.

Morgan, Edmund S., *Virginians at Home, Family Life in the Eighteenth Century,* Colonial Williamsburg Foundation, 1983.

Preston, Dickson J., *Oxford, The First Three Centuries,* The Historical Society of Talbot County, 1984. *Talbot County, A History,* Tidewater Publishers, 1983.

Maroon Societies, Rebel Slave Communities in the Americas, edited by Richard Price, Johns Hopkins University Press, 1996.

Richardson, Samuel, *Pamela, or Virtue Rewarded,* Project Gutenberg, Ebook #6124, released April 23, 2009.

Scharf, J. Thomas, *History of Maryland, From the Earliest Period to the Present Day, Vol, II 1765–1812,* "Baltimore, Md: A.B. Piet, 1879"; Rpt in: Tradition Press, 1967.

Shakespeare, William, *Henry V, Entire Play,* www/shakespeare.mit.edu/henry/full.html.

Shomette, Donald G. *Pirates on the Chesapeake,* Tidewater Publishers, Division of Schiffer Publishing, Ltd., 2015. *Shipwrecks on the Chesapeake, Maritime Disasters on Chesapeake Bay and Its Tributaries 1608–1978,* Tidewater Publishers, 1982.

"Robert Morris, The Oxford Merchant, 1711–1750, The Worthies of Talbot," Talbot Free Library.

"The Chesapeake in the Seventeenth Century, Essays on Anglo-American Society, edited by Tate, Thad W. and Ammerman, David L., W.W. Norton & Company, 1979.

Taylor, Alan, *American Colonies,* edited by Eric Foner, Penguin Group 2001.

Taylor, Elizabeth Downing, *A Slave in the White House, Paul Jennings and the Madisons,* St. Martin's Press, 2012.

Truitt, Charles, *"Breadbasket of the Revolution: Delmarva's Eight Turbulent War Years,* Salisbury, MD: Historical Books, Inc. 1976.

"The Era of the Revolution, in Maryland: A History, 1632–1974," edited by Richard Walsh and William Fox, Maryland Historical Society, 1974.

Weeks, Christopher, et.al., *Where Land and Water Intertwine, An Architectural History of Talbot County, Maryland,* Johns Hopkins University Press, 1984.

Williams, William H., *Man and Nature in Delaware, An Environmental History of the First State, 1631–2000,* Delaware Heritage Press, 2008.

ABOUT THE AUTHOR

B.B. Shamp won the 2016 first place award from the National Federation of Press Women and the Delaware Press Association for her debut novel, *Third Haven*.

In 2017, *The Delmarva Review* recognized her short story, "The Sotweed Legacy," in their Chesapeake Voices Contest. Her second novel, *The Grist Mill Bone*, was a finalist in regional fiction for the Next Generation Indie Book Award and the *da Vinci Eye* from the Eric Hoffer Awards for cover art.

Residing on an inland bay, B.B. works on environmental issues, local scholarships, and channeling the beauty of the coastal plain in her writing. She is originally from the Washington, D.C. area.

See www.bbshamp.com.

Made in the USA
Middletown, DE
24 November 2021

53230904R00243